A *Globe and Mail* Top 100 Book (2012)

"*419* points in the direction of something entirely new: the Global Novel … Ferguson is a true travel writer, his eye attuned to the last horrible detail. He is also a master at dialogue and suspense. It is tempting to put *419* in some easy genre category, but that would only serve to deny its accomplishment and its genius."
—2012 Scotiabank Giller Prize jury citation

"*419* is more than a drugstore-rack police procedural: It's a deeply ironic, thoroughly engaged politico-philosophical thriller from a comic writer best known for winning a trio of Leacock Awards … You won't sleep until you finish, and then rest won't come easily. Riveting. Provocative."   —T.F. Rigelhof, *The Globe and Mail*

"Heart-wrenching, fascinating, and scary. A thriller with a raw nerve ending … Ferguson … dazzles us in *419* with an intricately woven, urgent story. It is an unflinching, ambitious work, flinging us back and forth across the Atlantic, and taking us into danger … It is a persuasive work of fiction based on a very original premise. Ferguson, who swings so deftly from humour to thriller, is a writer who can genuinely surprise."   —*Toronto Star*

"Ferguson's revenge novel will appeal to everyone … A sprawling but beautiful third novel. It is a mixture of intrigue, storytelling, parenthood, sorrow, vengeance, and fun. It reads a little bit like a Ludlum spy saga, a little bit like a Dickens character novel, a little bit like an Oscar-seeking movie … [Ferguson] designed [*419*] as a page-turner. He succeeds fully."   —*Winnipeg Free Press*

"*419* marks Will Ferguson's arrival as Canada's undisputable master of the page-turning suspense novel, easily the equal of any international master one might care to name."
—John Barber, *The Globe and Mail*

"This book shimmers. Tautly paced and vividly drawn, *419* captures the reader in a net of desire and deceit drawn tight by the interconnections of humanity in the twenty-first century."
—Vincent Lam, Giller Prize–winning author of
Bloodletting and Miraculous Cures

"*419* is an ambitious, fast-paced global thriller which I found impossible to put down."
—Camilla Gibb, author of *Sweetness in the Belly* and
The Beauty of Humanity Movement

"Will Ferguson's *419* unveils the brilliant layers of a Nigerian cyberspace sting that brings devastation to an entire family. Ferguson's characters live by their wits, employing techno-wizardry and the cold ingenuity of the old-fashioned con. Intrigue, coercion, shame, and torqued suspense unfold with harrowing speed and the illuminating elegance of a cyber click."
—Lisa Moore, author of *Alligator* and *February*

"Though there is a touch of humour in its pages, *419* is much more of a showcase for Ferguson's travel-writing talents ... A truly enjoyable book ... Ferguson is a keen observer of landscapes and cityscapes, and has a brilliant ear for dialogue and accent ... You will never see those creative 419 emails in your inbox in quite the same way."
—*The Gazette* (Montreal)

"A sweeping story with complex twists and turns that spans continents, breaks hearts, and ruins lives."
—*The Chronicle-Herald* (Halifax)

"A powerful read ... Ferguson is a heavyweight now."
—*NOW* magazine

"Ferguson's third novel, *419*, opens with a bang ... The blurbs on the back cover promise the reader a page-turner, and Ferguson delivers ... *419* is an ambitious and well-realized literary novel, a thriller with a conscience and a heart."—*Literary Review of Canada*

"Harrowing." —*Calgary Herald*

"Gripping ... Fascinating ... A multi-faceted look at globalization."
—*Fastforward*

"A richly textured thriller." —*More* magazine

Praise for *Spanish Fly*

"A work of impressive energy and grandeur ... Like Robertson Davies, Will Ferguson has the gift of linkage, of letting unlikely novelistic strands interleave and thicken into a significant braid."
—*The Globe and Mail*

"A remarkable novel that is sure to become a modern-day classic ... Ferguson combines fact and fiction to produce a compelling and surprisingly humorous coming-of-age tale that will appeal to all readers … An exhilarating and unpredictable conclusion that will have readers guessing until the final page."—*Winnipeg Free Press*

"Stunning … *Spanish Fly* will be in high demand because of Ferguson's name, but it should be in high demand because of his talent. Nuanced and enthralling, *Spanish Fly* is undoubtedly the best writing he has ever done."—*Quill & Quire*, Books of the Year

"Ferguson is a novelist to be reckoned with … If it were up to me, I would have put this book on the Giller list." —*Ottawa Citizen*

"A remarkable work, steeped in history and arcane knowledge but rooted in the intimate timelessness of the human heart and soul. There are a few laughs, but this is a serious and ultimately heart-rending story. *Spanish Fly* is the real thing." —*The Vancouver Sun*

"A solid read … Ferguson shows a flair for historical detail and pop culture." —*The Gazette* (Montreal)

"Some of the most fascinating and interesting reading I've seen in a long time. Ferguson's writing style flows smoothly … In terms of drama, humour, pacing, imagination, research, vocabulary, and the ability to express his ideas through his characters, Will Ferguson ranks up there with some of the best I've read."
—*The Leader-Post* (Regina)

"A wonderful ride." —*Calgary Herald*

"Ferguson's offbeat view of the world is on display in this charming novel about con men … Ferguson paints a vivid picture of the era, with its wild jazz clubs, pool hall sharks, failing banks, hapless farmers, and easy marks. It's funny, dark, and entertaining."

—*Toronto Sun*

"Ferguson fills his pages with fascinating historical detail and lovingly described cons. His lengthy descriptions of scams are enthralling, funny, and perhaps even educational."

—*The Guardian* (U.K.)

"This is a terrific book, lyrical and hilarious, bleak and funny, with a love of history balanced against a rippingly clever plot."

—*The Telegraph* (U.K.)

"A richly atmospheric novel that seduces you ... with its reckless hedonism, feats of incredible ingenuity, and fabulous costumes."

—*New Statesman* (U.K.)

"Ferguson's comic picaresque is a delight."—*Financial Times* (U.K.)

"A terrific novel—complex but fun, philosophical but sharp, perceptive but ambiguous. The dialogue is razor sharp and laced with dry wit, the endless cons are delivered with gusto, and even the deeper, more thoughtful moments zing along in page-turning fashion ... As Ferguson builds to a crackling multi-layered climax, the ideas of right and wrong, true and false are blurred, but you're just happy to be along for the ride." —*The Sunday Herald* (U.K.)

"Brilliantly entertaining."   —*The Times* (U.K.)

"*Spanish Fly* is a big, brawling romp of a novel. It will have you on the edge of your La-Z-Boy with suspense and action, while at the same time raising questions about the choices we make in life—and the consequences that follow." —*Driven: Men's Lifestyle Magazine*

"A delightful trove of con-man lore, as charming as a grifter working a mark." —*Fastforward*

"In *Spanish Fly*, the cons come as quickly and as often as dark clouds during the 1930s Dust Bowl, the setting for this satisfying, self-assured story … It's a pleasure to ride with our sort-of heroes in their 1939 Nash Ambassador." —*Telegraph-Journal* (Saint John)

"Ferguson's intriguing characters and rich descriptions of the depressed towns they inhabit draws you into the forlorn pre-war world of the Depression. I couldn't get enough of their cons and was seduced by the romantic notion of a grifter's exciting life. From the coffee tins full of cash to the getaway car to the hot jazz clubs, I wanted it all." —*Monday* magazine

Praise for *Happiness*™

"[An] uncompromising and brilliant satire."—*The Globe and Mail*

"The ultimate satire on self-help books." —*The Washington Post*

"A glorious romp through modern life." —*Literary Review*

"A must-read book!" —*Vogue*

"A clever, funny, and compulsive satire on the world of self-help ... There are just not enough books around like this."—*The Bookseller*

"*Happiness* ™ is a brilliant parody of the self-help cult, social mores, and fashions generally. It bears comparison with the works of North America's leading satirists. But where Joseph Heller is heavy, Tom Wolfe is dark, and Carl Hiaasen is strident, Ferguson is light, bright, and very funny."   —*The Mail on Sunday* (U.K.)

"It is refreshing to encounter an authorial tone that is so embittered. He allows his characters to fulminate on his behalf, seething about the reflected failings of the Baby Boom generation and Generation X, arrogance against impotence."   —*The Scotsman* (U.K.)

"Fun, well-paced, intelligent."   —*Edmonton Journal*

"Original wit, rich writing ... A pleasure to read."
                             —*Times Colonist* (Victoria)

"Gleefully nasty. If Mel Brooks set *The Producers* in the publishing industry, he'd come up with something like this."—*Kirkus Reviews*

"A laugh-till-you-choke send-up of contemporary American life, the publishing industry, celebrity book tours, New Age cults, get-rich-quick schemes, and promises of perfect sex."   —*Whole Earth*

PENGUIN

419

WILL FERGUSON is the author of several award-winning travel memoirs, including *Beyond Belfast*, about a 560-mile walk around Northern Ireland in the rain; *Hitching Rides with Buddha*, about an end-to-end journey across Japan by thumb; and *Canadian Pie*, which covers his travels from the Yukon to PEI.

Ferguson's novels include *Happiness™*, a satire set in the world of self-help publishing, and *Spanish Fly*, a coming-of-age tale of con men and call girls set amid the jazz clubs of the Great Depression. His work, which has been published in more than twenty languages around the world, has been nominated for both an IMPAC Dublin Award and a Commonwealth Writers' Prize, and he is a three-time winner of the Stephen Leacock Medal for Humour.

Ferguson lives in Calgary with his wife and two sons. Visit his website at www.willferguson.com.

ALSO BY WILL FERGUSON

FICTION
Happiness™
Spanish Fly

MEMOIR
Coal Dust Kisses: A Christmas Memoir

TRAVEL
Beyond Belfast
Hitching Rides with Buddha
Beauty Tips from Moose Jaw
Canadian Pie

AS EDITOR
The Penguin Anthology of Canadian Humour

AS SONGWRITER
Lyricist on the songs "Con Men and Call Girls, Part One,"
"When the Circus Comes to Town,"
and "Losin' Hand" on the Tom Phillips music CD *Spanish Fly*

419

WILL FERGUSON

PENGUIN
an imprint of Penguin Canada

Published by the Penguin Group
Penguin Group (Canada), 90 Eglinton Avenue East, Suite 700, Toronto, Ontario, Canada M4P 2Y3

Penguin Group (USA) Inc., 375 Hudson Street, New York, New York 10014, U.S.A.
Penguin Books Ltd, 80 Strand, London WC2R 0RL, England
Penguin Ireland, 25 St Stephen's Green, Dublin 2, Ireland (a division of Penguin Books Ltd)
Penguin Group (Australia), 707 Collins Street, Melbourne, Victoria 3008, Australia
(a division of Pearson Australia Group Pty Ltd)
Penguin Books India Pvt Ltd, 11 Community Centre, Panchsheel Park, New Delhi – 110 017, India
Penguin Group (NZ), 67 Apollo Drive, Rosedale, Auckland 0632, New Zealand
(a division of Pearson New Zealand Ltd)
Penguin Books (South Africa) (Pty) Ltd, 24 Sturdee Avenue, Rosebank, Johannesburg 2196, South Africa

Penguin Books Ltd, Registered Offices: 80 Strand, London WC2R 0RL, England

First published in Viking hardcover by Penguin Canada, 2012
Published in this edition, 2013

1 2 3 4 5 6 7 8 9 10 (WEB)

Copyright © Will Ferguson, 2012

"This house is not for sale" photo courtesy Kathy Robson

*Publisher's note: This book is a work of fiction. Names, characters, places, and incidents either are
the product of the author's imagination or are used fictitiously, and any resemblance to actual persons
living or dead, events, or locales is entirely coincidental.*

Manufactured in Canada.

LIBRARY AND ARCHIVES CANADA CATALOGUING IN PUBLICATION

Ferguson, Will
419 / Will Ferguson.

ISBN 978-0-14-317601-5

I. Title. II. Title: Four nineteen. III. Title: Four
hundred nineteen. IV. Title: Four one nine.

PS8561.E7593F68 2013   C813'.54   C2013-900116-6

Visit the Penguin Canada website at **www.penguin.ca**

Special and corporate bulk purchase rates available; please see
www.penguin.ca/corporatesales or call 1-800-810-3104, ext. 2477.

ALWAYS LEARNING   PEARSON

For Alex and Alister

419

Would you die for your child?

This is the only question a parent needs to answer; everything else flows from this. In the kiln-baked emptiness of thorn-bush deserts. In mangrove swamps and alpine woods. In city streets and snowfalls. It is the only question that needs answering.

The boy's father, knee deep in warm mud, was pulling hard on fishing nets that were splashing with life. Mist on green waters. Sunlight on tidal pools.

SNOW

1

A car, falling through darkness.

End over end, one shuddering thud following another. Fountains of glass showering outward and then—a vacuum of silence collapsing back in.

The vehicle came to rest on its back, at the bottom of an embankment below the bridge and propped up against a splintered stand of poplar trees. You could see the path it had taken through the snow, leaving a churned trail of mulch and wet leaves in its wake.

Into the scentless winter air: the seeping odour of radiator fluid, of gasoline.

They climbed down on grappling lines, leaning into their descent, the lights of the fire trucks and ambulances washing the scene in alternating reds and blues, throwing shadows first one way and then the next. Countless constellations in the snow. Glass, catching the light.

When the emergency team finally arrived at the bottom of the embankment, they were out of breath.

Within the folded metal of the vehicle: a buckled dashboard, bent steering wheel, more glass and—in the middle—something that had once been a man. White hair, wet against the skull, matted now in a thick red mud.

"Sir! Can you hear me?"

His lips were moving as the life poured out of him to wherever it is life goes.

"*Sir!*"

But no words came out, only bubbles.

2

Doors glide open, the sheets of glass parting like a magician's gesture as the West African air swarms in, a heat so strong it pushes her back into the airport. She shields her eyes, stands a moment as the bodies shove past her.

On the other side of the pavement, a chain-link fence keeps the riff-raff at bay. Riff-raff and relatives. Taxi drivers and waiting uncles. Shouts and frantic wavings, hand-inked signs reading TAXI 4 YOU and LAGOS ISLAND DIRECT. She is looking for her name among these signs. Even with the jet lag and nausea weighing upon her, even with the flight-induced cramps in her calves and the heaving cattle queues she's been corralled through, the customs officials who rummaged through her carry-on looking for stashed treasures only to throw her dishevelled belongings back at her in disappointment, and even with the sweltering air of the airport interior coming up against the blast-furnace heat outside, even with that, perhaps because of that, she feels oddly elated. *Calmly excited.*

Sweat is forming, the condensation that comes from colliding weather patterns. It trickles down her collarbone, turns limp hair damp and damp hair wet; it beads into droplets on her forehead. Somewhere: her name. She sees it being waved above the mob on the other side of the chain-link fence. But just as she is about to walk across, a voice behind her coos "Madam?" She turns, finds herself facing an armed officer in a starched green uniform, sunglasses reflecting her face back at her in a wraparound, panoramic mirror. "Madam, please. You will come with me."

It is almost a question, the way he says it. Almost, but not quite.

"Madam. You will come with me."

She pulls her carry-on closer: the only luggage she has. "Why?"

"Airport police, madam. The inspector, he wishes to speak with you."

3

The boy's father was speaking softly in river dialect, as he always did when speaking truths. "A father, a mother, must ask themselves this. If it gives the child a better life, would they? Would they die for their child?"

The mangrove forests were breathing. Wet sighs and soft lapping sounds. The boy's father, deep in tidal mud, was hauling in nets flopping with quicksilver as the boy stood on the shore, fishing spear ready.

"Remember," said the father, switching to English for emphasis as smoothly as one might switch from net to spear, "Kill the fish quickly. It is kinder that way."

4

"Laura? Are you there? It's—it's about your father. Please pick up."

The sound of a sob being swallowed.

Laura spit into the sink, scrambled to the phone.

"Mom?"

After they'd finished speaking, Laura hurried down the hallway, pulling on her jacket as she jabbed at the elevator button.

Outside, the night air was crystallizing into snow. She crossed a street empty of traffic, ran-walked down the hill.

The bungalow of her childhood was a stucco-on-stucco arrangement thumbtacked to the side of a steep street. A police car was parked out front, with Warren's brand-new Escalade hogging the driveway. It didn't matter; Laura had nothing to park.

When they were little, her brother Warren was convinced that the small nuggets of glass embedded in the stucco of their home were actually rubies, and he offered her fifty percent of the proceeds if she would collect them for him. "But I thought rubies were red," she said. "Don't be so picky," he replied. "They come in every colour, like Life Savers. It's why they're so valuable." So Laura spent an afternoon knuckling green glass from the walls. Fingers beaded with blood, she followed Warren proudly to the corner store, where Mr. Li offered them two all-day suckers in exchange—on condition they didn't mine their parents' stucco for any more gemstones. Laura considered this a fair return on investment; Warren was less enthused. He muttered angrily all the way home as Laura swung the empty plastic pail and moved the sucker back and forth in her mouth. She found Warren's sucker, still unwrapped, in his room several weeks later. He would try to sell it to her for a quarter the next time she got her allowance.

Inside her parents' wood-panelled living room: a police officer. Holstered gun and pale eyes. Those crocheted throw-cushion covers that had been there since forever. The knitted afghan draped over the back of the chesterfield (both the cushion covers and the afghan her mother's handiwork). And on the wood panelling behind: clunky oversized picture frames (her father's handiwork, both the frames and the panelling). Mall-bought oil-painted scenes of Paris in the rain, of Matterhorn in sunlight. Might as well have been paintings of Mars; her parents had never been to Paris or the Alps. And now her father never would.

Laura's mother barely noticed Laura enter; she was floating in place, scarcely tethered to the earth. Warren, standing to one side, fleshy face knotted with anger, had his arms wrapped tightly across his stomach. Warren, as bulgy as Laura was thin. Family photos always looked like an ad for an eating disorders clinic.

Warren's wife Estelle, meanwhile, was attempting, mostly in vain, to corral their twin daughters into the dining room and away from grown-up talk. Squirmy girls, mirrored reflections of each other, full of giggles and sudden solemn pronouncements. "Dogs can't dance but they can learn." "Daddy's silly!" "Suzie's dog can dance, she told me." Kindergarten tales and childhood non sequiturs. Warren's wife mouthed "hello" to Laura before disappearing into the other room.

Why would they bring their kids?

The officer with the pale eyes stood, extended his hand to Laura. Instead of a handshake, a business card. "Sergeant Brisebois," he said. "I'm with the city's Traffic Response Unit."

His card read *Sgt. Matthew Brisebois, TRU.* She wanted to circle the typo, add an "c." But no, not a typo. Something much worse.

"I deal with traffic fatalities. I'll be overseeing this investigation. I'm very sorry about your father."

No, you're not. Without traffic fatalities, you'd be out of a job. "Thank you."

"Can you fucking believe this?" It was Warren, turning to stare at his sister, eyes raw. "Dad drove off a cliff."

"Warren," said their mother. "Language, please."

"Your father appears to have hit a patch of black ice," the officer said. "It would have been impossible to see. Missed the bridge onto Ogden Road, westbound off 50th. It's an industrial area, and

— 7 —

he was travelling at high speed. Very high." *As if he were fleeing something,* Brisebois wanted to say, but didn't. Instead, he asked, "Where would he have been going that time of night?"

"Work," said their mother. "He was a watchman, at the rail yards."

"He was a teacher," said Warren.

"Retired," said their mother. "We were both teachers. Henry taught shop, I taught Home Ec. Henry was feeling—was feeling housebound, had started working, part time, as a night watchman."

"Would he have worn a uniform?"

She nodded.

"I ask because he didn't have one on. He was wearing"—Brisebois checked his notepad—"a sweater. Slacks. Loafers. The loafers came off in the crash. Would he have kept his uniform at work?"

"I suppose," said their mother, voice distant. "I just don't understand why he would be on Ogden Road in the first place. He always took Blackfoot Trail."

Brisebois jotted this down. "And did your husband wear his seatbelt? Generally?"

"Oh yes. He was very careful about that sort of thing." Laura's mother was holding a wad of Kleenex as though clutching a rosary.

"Mrs. Curtis, your husband phoned in a complaint a few weeks ago, said someone was across the street watching your house."

"Oh, that? It turned out to be nothing. Henry was up late and thought he saw somebody prowling under a street lamp. The police came, but—I'm sure you have a report."

The officer nodded. "We do. I'm just trying to ascertain if—"

Laura's brother leaned in, bristling. "Why are you asking these questions? This is bullshit."

"I'm trying to piece together what happened, and why."

"Why? I'll tell you why. Because this fuckin' city never clears its fuckin' streets after it fuckin' snows. That's why. Always waiting for a fuckin' chinook to do their work for them. Assholes. The snow gets packed in, we drive on ruts for months. Sure! Why pay for snow removal when you can wait for a la-di-da warm wind to come down from the fuckin' mountains and melt it. Well, it doesn't fuckin' melt, does it?" His voice was cracking in anguish. "Do you know how much I pay in property tax? Do you?"

"Language, Warren!"

"Sir, I understand you're upset. But I do need to—"

"A fuckin' shitload, that's how much. And what do I get for it? My father— The city, that's who did this. I pay my taxes, they raise them every year like clockwork. For what? You want to arrest someone, arrest the fuckin' mayor."

When Laura finally spoke, her voice was so soft the officer almost missed it. "Did they say what kind of sweater?"

Brisebois looked at Laura. "Sorry?"

"The sweater he was wearing, did they say what kind? Was it green, a green cardigan?"

"Um …" He flipped through his pad. "No, I believe it was blue. With patterns."

"What kind of patterns?"

"I'm not sure. It'll be in the accident scene photos, and the Medical Examiner's Office will have the actual sweater. Why do you ask?"

"I was just … wondering. It doesn't really matter. Not now."

Outside, the first whisper of a warmer wind was stirring, trickling down distant mountainsides, moving across the foothills. Above Ogden Road, the tire tracks in the packed snow would melt, first to slush and then to sludgy water. Traces of the accident would slowly vanish—except for one distinct streak of rubber, an extended skid on the asphalt where a second set of tire treads led toward the guardrail beside the bridge. Those marks would last a long, long while.

I'm asking you—
Who is dey mugu now?

5

Members of the collision reconstruction team had already gone through by the time Officer Brisebois arrived. They'd laid down tent cards for the GPS survey to follow, and under the glare of floodlights, their breath formed winter haloes.

He checked in with them first. "Colin. Greg."

The older constable, Colin, looked up, grinned. "Sergeant Brisebois. Nice of you to show up."

They never referred to him as Matthew. It was one of their few concessions to his higher rank.

Brisebois had been on call. "Pager was in my jacket. Jacket was in the coat check."

"Coat check?"

"I was at a show. Had to change in the car, if that makes you feel better."

He hoped that would be the end of it, but of course it wasn't.

"You can't sneak out of a movie? Flash your badge, demand a refund?"

"Not that kind of show."

Greg, the younger constable, laughed. "Don't tell me you were whooping it up at a peeler bar while we were out here in the cold."

"No, not that kind of show either."

Sergeant Matthew Brisebois had been at the city ballet's annual production of *Swan Lake*, his wife's ticket on the empty seat beside him. He sighed. Might as well get it over with.

"I was at the ballet. The wife and I, we bought season passes. Well, she did. For the both of us. Anyway, I had the tickets, seemed a waste."

"The ballet? What, like the *Nutcracker*?"

"No, not the *Nutcracker*."

"The nutcracker?" said the younger constable. "I think I dated her."

"Hell," said Colin. "I think I was married to her at one point." He looked at the cup of coffee curling steam in Brisebois's hand. "See you had time to stop by for a cuppa Tim's, though. We're investigators, we notice things like that."

"You brought some for us, too, I'm assuming?" asked Greg.

"I did. But I dropped it on the way down." Brisebois took a deep and intentionally satisfying drink from the cup. "So," he said. "What do we have?"

"Pontiac Olds. Came over the hill and then left the road—down there. Hit some ice from the looks of it. Driver missed the bridge, went over the edge of the embankment. Flipped, end over end, two, maybe three times."

"Oldsmobile?" said Brisebois. "That's a lot of metal. They don't even make those anymore; it's been, what, ten years at least. So … Male. Senior citizen. Somebody's grandpa. Am I right?"

Colin nodded. "Died on scene. He's still down there. I don't know how they're going to get him out."

"Was he belted?"

"Nope."

"You run the plates yet?"

"We did. Nothing on the vehicle. Not even a speeding ticket."

"And the driver?" asked Brisebois. "You run him through

PIMS?" This was the police department's updated central information system. Any previous contact with police, whether through an arrest or as a witness or in a report of any kind, from domestic disputes to noise disturbances, and the driver's name and background would pop up.

"Nothing much. He called in a complaint a couple of weeks ago about someone hanging around outside his home in the middle of the night. Turned out it was a bush."

A classic old-man complaint. *You kids get off my lawn!*

Snow was filtering down, phantom flakes melting on contact. Under the silent flash-and-throb of police lights, Brisebois and the senior constable walked over to where the car had careered off course, plummeting over the side. Tire tracks: leading off the asphalt, onto packed snow, and then—disappearing, into nothingness.

The fire department had parked a light truck on the bridge, and the spotlight was trained on the upside-down vehicle leaning drunkenly against a stand of poplar trees at the bottom of the embankment. Brisebois could see where the Olds had first hit, nose in, and then pivoted, rolling end over end. It wasn't like in the movies, where cars soared upward with a certain cinematic flair, sent off hidden ramps with their motors often as not removed ahead of time. In the real world, cars were front-heavy, and when one left the road it dropped—like a stone. An Oldsmobile? That would have been like driving a tank off the side of a cliff.

The touchdown point was a wet black bruise in the snow, shards of debris fanning outward. "Let me ask you something," Brisebois said. "From up here, where the vehicle first leaves the embankment, to where it hit, down there—from liftoff to touchdown, so to speak. That's more than a car length, wouldn't you say?"

"Yup."

They both knew what that meant: all four wheels had left the ground. The car had been airborne.

Brisebois looked up at the road that curved toward them. "Would be hard to work up a decent speed from there. Any sign of braking?"

"Not here, where it went off the road. But there's something farther back that you should take a look at. Something strange."

They headed up, toward the flashing lights of a police cruiser that blocked off the road at the crest of the hill.

"We found these when we first walked the scene," Colin said.

There on the asphalt, and already flagged with a numbered tent card—a second set of tire marks.

Brisebois crouched down, ran his flashlight along them. "That's a hell of a skid."

The other officer nodded. "We'll pull the drag sled, find the surface friction, calculate the speed. But just from looking at it, I can tell you, whoever left these marks was travelling fast and braking hard."

Brisebois looked down toward the bridge. "So … What do you figure? Same guy?"

"Maybe. But the tracks don't line up."

He was right. The tracks that ran off the embankment, missing the guardrail, were at a different angle than the tire marks higher up. "And if he did brake halfway down, that would've made it even harder to get up the speed he'd need to become airborne."

Brisebois ran the beam of his flashlight along the skid mark. "Whoever it was, they came to a complete stop."

Beyond the skid was a faint dusting of grit. This was part of the snowplow effect of a braking tire, pushing pebbles and dirt forward into its path. When a vehicle came to a hard stop, then rolled ahead, *through* its own debris … "We've got tread prints?"

"We do. Good ones, too. Greg already logged them, took pictures. They're faint, but very clear. Here's the weird part, though. Up ahead?" Colin angled his light low across the asphalt. "Do y'see?" The tread marks curved sharply to the left.

"The driver turned around."

"Whoever it was would have had to crank the wheel hard to make that," said Colin.

"So," said Brisebois. "This second driver comes flying over the hill, sees the first vehicle go over the side, brakes hard to a full stop, then pulls a sharp U-turn. Was the second car chasing the first one? Or did it turn around when it saw the accident, to get help?"

"Maybe."

"Who called it in?"

"The warehouse, over there." Colin pointed across the hill, to a distant line of docking bays under pooled light and falling snow. "Truck drivers, unloading their long hauls late at night."

"They saw it?"

"Heard it. We've got an officer over there taking statements. Don't imagine it will be much help, though. It was dark and they're far away."

Brisebois looked again from the skid mark down to the other set of tracks. The first driver: falls asleep, or has been drinking, or maybe suffers cardiac arrest, leaves the road, missing the guardrail and plunging over the side. A second driver: sees this happen, hits the brakes, comes to a stop, turns his or her vehicle around ... and leaves the scene. Why? Panicked? Maybe this second driver'd been drinking too. Or was driving without a licence, didn't want to call the cops. Or was there something else going on here?

The flatbed had arrived. Brisebois could hear its backup warnings beeping. Once the fire department got the driver's body out, the flatbed would haul the wreck to a reconstruction facility where they'd check the brake lines for tampering, begin the process of crossing items off a list, narrowing the possibilities.

Brisebois finished the last of his coffee. "I'll let you guys finish up. Measure the marks, calculate speed, all that fun stuff. I'll notify next of kin. Do you have an address?"

The other officer, Greg, grinned. "I did, but I dropped it."

"Guess I'll just look it up myself then," said Brisebois with a weary smile. And then, as he was about to leave: "Did you check for scrub marks? Down by the bridge, where the vehicle left the road, went over the side?"

"We did."

"And?"

"Just gets stranger and stranger."

6

A fan stirred the humidity, raising a breath of goosebumps across her skin. Her hair, still damp from her brief foray outside, formed unintentional ringlets, wet against her skin.

He had her passport.

Inspector Ribadu—"Please, call me David," he'd said, waving her to a seat across from his desk—was turning over the blank pages as though they told a story. And maybe they did.

Above his desk, on the wall behind, the national motto: *Unity, Faith, Peace & Progress.*

"All three in short supply," he joked, when he noticed her looking at it.

"Four," she said softly. She couldn't help it; when you see a discrepancy, you flag it. Four, not three.

He turned, looked at the motto as though for the first time.

"Oh no, madam. Only three are in short supply. This is Nigeria. We have plenty of faith."

He found the stamp he was looking for in her passport, and the stapled pages that were attached.

"A letter of invitation from the Nigerian consulate. Good, good. A mere formality, of course, as visitors are always most welcome. Often I say, why does someone need to be invited? In Nigeria, if a visitor comes to our door, even in the midst of night, we must welcome them in."

He smiled. Muscles bunching in his cheeks.

She sat across from him, clutching her carry-on bag and a sheaf of medical papers.

"I have my return ticket, and all the necessary inoculations." She slid the papers across. Her left arm still ached from the injections.

The inspector laughed, a low chuckle. "That's for your country to worry about, when you return." He rose, came around the desk toward her, and for a moment she thought they were done, but no. He was looking at her carry-on bag. "Sorry-o. May I?"

She swallowed. "Of course."

He took everything out one item at a time, laying them on his desk. When he came to the Virgin in-flight magazine, she felt her throat constrict. It was her good fortune, however, that the inspector had already seen this issue. He gave it only a cursory glance. "Excellent article about the wine country in France, yes?" He placed the magazine on his desk alongside her rumpled folds of clothes and assorted toiletries.

He surveyed the selection in front of him. "Only this?"

"I'm just here for two nights. I fly out again on Sunday. It's all there in the letter." She had explained this to the clerk at the consulate, how she'd won a ticket to anywhere, had always dreamed of Africa. She'd filled in all the necessary forms, had paid the necessary fees, had received the letter of invitation, as required, which Customs and Immigration had duly stamped.

Inspector Ribadu smiled at her. "Sightseeing, is it?"

She nodded.

"The Yankari Highlands, I imagine? To see our lovely elephants and baboons? Perhaps luck will smile and you will catch sight of some lions, very rare. This is West Africa, madam. We don't have the big-game safaris you might see elsewhere. But we do still have a few lions left, yes. And some hyenas. It's funny, madam. Visitors so often worry about lions, but it's the hyenas of this world one needs to watch for. They hunt in packs, hyenas. Lions hunt in prides. I like that," he said. "Calling them prides. No one ever speaks about a 'pride of hyenas.' Have you noticed that?"

"I hadn't, no."

"Wikki Warm Springs. Those are in Yankari as well. Very beautiful. I imagine you will be visiting Wikki during your stay?"

"I'm hoping to, yes."

"Ah, but that would be impossible. The Yankari Highlands are very remote. Much too far for the short time you have. Indeed, madam, I'm surprised you didn't know this before you came. With the short time you have available to you, you'll be lucky to get out of Lagos."

Lucky to get out of Lagos. Was that a veiled threat? She slid her hand into her skirt pocket. She had a fold of naira bills within easy reach, enough for an emergency but probably not enough for a bribe. But farther down, tightly folded in a small pouch she'd sewn into the lining of her skirt pocket: an American $100 bill. The international currency. *"Corruption at Murtala Muhammed Airport in Lagos has been brought under control. Do not, under any circumstances, offer bribes to airport officials."* Every travel advisory had stressed this, but is that what the inspector was fishing for? A payoff? She extracted the folded bill, slipped it into the palm of her hand.

"Such a shame," he said. "You have a visa valid for thirty days, but are only staying two nights. No husband?"

"No husband."

"So ... who supports you? You have a father, yes?"

"I support me."

"I see. In what line of work, madam?"

"I'm an editor—a copy editor. Grammar. Fact-checking. Indexes. That sort of thing."

"I see. A journalist, then? Here to do another story on the Heartbreak of Africa?"

"I'm not here on any kind of assignment. I'm here as a tourist."

"But you do work for magazines?" He picked up the in-flight publication. "Perhaps you are only pretending to be a tourist, to avoid the paperwork required of journalists? The visas and such."

"No!" she said, a little too quickly. "No, not magazines."

She saw him catch this, her sharp reaction, but he didn't connect the flash of panic to the magazine he was holding in his hand. He put it to one side absentmindedly.

"Newspapers, then?"

"Books, mainly. Biographies. It's—it's nothing."

"How can something be nothing? I suspect you are being too modest, madam. We all have our stories to tell, don't we? We all have our secrets. Sometimes the smallest detail can be of the utmost importance, don't you think?" He looked again at her belongings neatly arranged on his desk, the tampons and T-shirts, the tightly rolled socks. "No camera," he said.

"Sorry?"

"No camera. A tourist with no camera. When I see such a thing, it ... concerns me."

"My cellphone," she said. "It takes pictures."

"You came all the way to Africa to take photographs with a phone?"

"I was—I was going to buy a camera when I got to the hotel."

He turned back to the landing form that had been stapled into her passport. "Ah, yes. The Ambassador Hotel in Ikeja. It's very near here. You can see it from the airport. Splendid accommodations. I'm sure they will have shops which sell cameras and such, so that you may"—he searched for the right word—"*immortalize* your time here in Lagos." His smile softened, and he began placing her belongings back into her bag, starting with the in-flight magazine, flat along the bottom.

He'd missed it.

No explosives, no narcotics, no stash of money. It was something more combustible than that. And he'd missed it.

She quietly pushed the folded $100 bill back into her pocket pouch, unnoticed, as he finished zipping up her carry-on.

"There you go, madam. Enjoy your stay."

"Thank you. I will." She gathered up her bag, stuffed her medical papers into the side, hurried to leave.

"Madam?"

"Yes?"

"One last thing. Tell me, you hear of this problem we have in Nigeria? With 419?"

7

This is what her father had told her as he was leaving. This is what Laura's dad had said the last time they ever met. "You, I love."

Why would he say that?

"You, I love." She hadn't heard that turn of phrase in years.

Sergeant Brisebois accepted another cup of tea from Mrs. Curtis, who said, "It must be very difficult for you, dealing with this sort of thing every day. I'm so sorry."

Laura's mom, apologizing to a police officer for her husband's death.

—Is the wife a suspect?

—The wife is always a suspect.

The twins were trying to squirm their way out of the dining room. Warren had returned from the kitchen with a bag of Cheez Puffs, was fuming, as Warren was wont to do. And Laura? Laura was replaying it over and over in her mind: the last thing her father would ever say to her. *"You, I love."*

Brisebois had asked whether Laura's father was on medication, had been told no, not even Advil. He was now going over apparent incongruities in the route Laura's father had followed earlier that night. "Mrs. Curtis—may I call you Helen?—in situations like this, we like to compile a record of the last twenty-four hours." He had a map of the city open on the coffee table. "Your husband worked in the east rail yards, here, on Blackfoot Trail. Is that correct?"

Her mother nodded.

"But the accident occurred at Ogden Road. As near as I can tell, he was going the wrong way. Do you suppose he forgot something, had turned around, was heading home?"

"Maybe. I don't know."

Warren cut in. "Don't you think she's had enough for one night?"

"Of course," said Sergeant Brisebois. He finished the last of his tea, stood up and was buttoning his jacket when he asked, almost in passing, "Helen, you don't suppose there was any reason your husband might have felt his life was in danger, do you?"

Warren snorted. "Dad? Don't be ridiculous."

Their mother looked at the officer, tilted her head at the question. "Why would you ask such a thing?"

"No reason. It's just— The speed he was travelling, it seemed excessive. The medical examiner will perform an autopsy; it's standard in a case like this. They'll check blood levels for alcohol, look for lesions in the heart or evidence of a brain seizure. Perhaps your husband simply fell asleep. You said he was having trouble in the nights before this happened. Insomnia?"

Their mother nodded. "I'd often hear him up in the middle of the night, microwaving milk to help him sleep." She looked over at Henry's chair, then drifted again into that in-between world.

"Maybe that's all this is," said Brisebois as he pulled on his cap. "A case of driver fatigue. It's just that—there's a phenomenon we call scrub marks. These occur *inside* a tire track. When a vehicle is going at high speed and is then turned, forcibly, against its own forward momentum—even if the brakes *aren't* applied, there's this internal tension that occurs. You can see it: the vehicle is going one way, but the tires are being pulled another. We found very distinct scrub marks in the treads where your husband's car left the road. Now, if someone falls asleep, then suddenly wakes up and cranks the wheel, that will create scrub marks. But if that had been the case, your husband would have been trying to steer his vehicle back *onto* the road; the scrub marks would pull him *toward* the bridge. But your husband's treads pull in the opposite direction. Away from the bridge, toward the embankment."

Brisebois had released these details like depth charges and was watching their reactions carefully. The mother looked baffled. The son was eating Cheez Puffs from a bag and scowling. The daughter hadn't flinched, barely seemed to be breathing.

"So Dad was disoriented," said Warren irritably. He licked

his fingers, now stained with orange. "He steered the wrong way. What's your point?"

"We found a second set of tire tracks. This second set is back, higher on the road, halfway up. Those tracks stop long before the bridge."

Warren leaned in. "You think someone ran him off the road?"

"It's possible."

"I should have known! There's no way Dad would have been driving that fast! He was always a legal-speed-limit sort of guy. And the injuries he had, those were ..." Warren's voice trailed off.

Laura turned to her brother. "You saw Dad? You saw the—"

"Someone had to. And it sure as shit wasn't going to be Mom." He glared at his sister. "What the hell took you so long, anyway? I had to come all the way in from Springbank. You're just up the hill; you can walk down, for Christ's sake."

She'd been working late and had switched her phone to voice-mail because her father had taken to calling her in the middle of the night when he couldn't sleep. She'd had a deadline to meet and hadn't been picking up, and he never left a message. Just a series of clicks. It was only while she was brushing her teeth and had pushed PLAY that she heard, not her father's voice, but her mother's. *"Laura, pick up ... please."*

Laura's father: laid out under the sickly green of fluorescent light.

"You went?" she said. "You saw Dad?"

Warren didn't answer, wouldn't look at her, was keeping his eyes locked on the police officer instead, was refusing to blink, was denying sadness a foothold, was opting instead, and as always, for anger.

And in that moment, the years fell away—fell like feathers in a pillow fight and there he was, her older brother. Her big brother.

Warren Curtis, staring down the mean girls, forcing them to apologize to his little sister. Warren, sneaking into a slasher flick with Laura in tow, squeezing her arm, whispering at crucial moments, "Look away, look away *now*!"

Laura tried to catch her brother's eye. She wanted to mouth "thank you" to him the way his wife had whispered "hello" to her, but he wouldn't look, couldn't look. *If he did, he would start to cry,* she thought. *And he can't let that happen. He can't. Because once it starts, it never ends.*

"So that's what this is?" Warren asked the officer. "Some asshole joy riders figuring it would be fun to chase an old man down a hill? You better find those fuckers before I do."

"Language," their mother admonished, drifting back into the conversation.

Warren ignored her. "For Christ's sake, officer. I've watched *C.S.I.* Can't you run the tires through some sort of database, find these assholes?"

"Tire treads aren't like fingerprints," said Brisebois. "They change, constantly. You're dealing with rubber, which is a soft compound. A week later, even a day, and the tread marks will have been altered. A tire picks up a rock, loses a bit of rubber, forms a new crack, and the marks change. That said, yes, we can match marks that are *consistent* with a certain tire. But it's not like there's a central registry for tire treads. We can't find a vehicle based solely on its tires."

Laura turned to the picture window, saw the living room reflected back on itself. Her brother and her mother. The officer and herself. Her father, no longer there.

Language. Conceals as much as it reveals.

"You, I love." Why would he say that?

8

Mist on green waters. Children, waiting. Once the men had finished, the little ones would be called. They would scramble down with their buckets to collect the smaller fish that had been missed. That call would come soon; the men were moving quickly through tidal waters, backs bent, pulling hard on the nets.

The lagoon emptied into mangrove creeks, the creeks emptied into a channel, the channel into a bay. And the bay? Well, who knew where that emptied? Sea or sky? Or somewhere in between? "We live in a wet net, we are caught in it as surely as the catfish and prawns." This was how the boy's father had put it, speaking in their Delta dialect, finding patterns in everything as was his habit.

A sky heavy with the promise of rain.

From the grassy hillock above the lagoon, the boy watched the men moving through the mud-green waters below. The other children were lined up single file on the path behind him. "They aren't ready for us," said the boy, addressing the others as their designated leader. "We go'an wait up here, by the cannon."

9

Laura was outside in the cold. Officer Brisebois was trying to make eye contact, speaking quietly as the air around them turned to steam with every syllable.

"Will you be okay?"

She looked up at the apartment towers rising like bookmarks above the trees. *Will I be okay?* Will *we* be okay? That was the question.

Laura had offered to stay, but her mother had said no. Her brother had offered to take their mom back to his place in the suburbs, so that she wouldn't have to be alone, but she'd said no to that, too.

"I want to stay here tonight," their mother had said, her voice so faint it sounded more like a wish than a whisper. *I want to stay here tonight, in case he calls.*

They'd left her at the kitchen table, waiting for a husband who would never come home no matter how long she waited.

"I'll be fine," Laura told Brisebois. "We'll be fine."

"It's hard," he said. "Losing someone you're close to."

She turned, met his gaze. "You know what's harder? Losing someone you used to be close to. Someone you haven't been close to for a long time." *All those things that die with us, all those things that are left unsaid.* "He was a good dad."

The officer nodded. "I'm sure he was. I lost both my parents in the space of a few years. It's tough. Can I give you a ride somewhere?"

"It's just up the hill, I can walk." She pointed toward the two apartment towers. "Second building on the left. Third light in the top corner. That's me."

"There's someone waiting." It was more a question than a statement.

"Just the lamp." Then, with a half-laugh that died even as she tried to force it, "Not even a cat."

"If you need a cat, you can have mine," he said—too quickly. "Honestly, I don't mind. He's horrible. We're more adversaries than master and pet. You want a cat, I can drop him off tonight."

She tried again to laugh. "Thanks, but no thanks. Odds are, he wouldn't survive."

Brisebois looked at her. *Why would she say something like that?* "Well," he said. "If you reconsider, you've got my card. And if anything surfaces, anything at all. Your father. Anything. Give me a call."

I won't. "I will."

She started up the hill, then turned. "The last time I saw my father," she said, "he seemed—distracted."

Brisebois came closer. "Distracted?"

"Sad."

"Sad? Or distracted?"

"Both."

She said goodbye and walked back up the hill, lungs filling with cold fistfuls of air. Snow: sifting down, filling the cones of light that the street lamps cast, a snow so fine it felt like sand underfoot.

Laura lived in a shopping mall. This was how she described it, jokingly. Not jokingly. Her apartment elevators fed tenants directly into the Northill Plaza. Yes, there should have been two h's in the name, and yes, it spelled "north ill." Laura had to resist the urge to write in the missing consonant with a Sharpie every time she passed the mall directory. A mall with an apartment building attached, or an apartment building with a mall attached. It was the architectural equivalent of a zebra: black on white, or white on black? Residential on commercial, or the opposite?

Having the shopping centre directly below her should have been wonderful. The mall had everything she needed: a Safeway at one end, Sears at the other, a World Health gym, a Coles bookstore, a Laura Secord chocolate "shoppe" (Laura's namesake, according to her dad), a Magicuts hair salon, a food court, a pharmacy. Her building had a pool for swimming laps, and the professional centre included not only a medical clinic but an automobile insurance and registrar's office, should she ever need to register a vehicle, which she didn't. She'd auctioned off her parking spot online to cover her monthly membership fee at World Health, where she walked on treadmills and rode stationary bicycles every second day with a metronome's predictability.

Laura worked online—her daily commute was four paces from kitchenette to office alcove—so when the weather turned foul, as it so often did, she didn't need to go out. At all. It was easy enough to let the days slip by even when the weather was fair. At one point last spring, she'd realized she hadn't been outside for three weeks, and on her e-tax return under OCCUPATION, she had entered "Hermit." A faceless accountant somewhere had emailed it back, not amused.

Nine floors, two towers, no balcony. She entered her apartment and tossed her keys in the fishbowl, the fish itself having long since vacated the premises. Laura wasn't good at keeping things alive. Her ferns all but coughed and wheezed, and when she'd chosen the fish (a delicate little Beta) she'd felt like the Finger of Death selecting its next victim. She had once flirted with the idea of getting a cat, but it hardly seemed humane, keeping something enclosed so far up. Just as well. With her record, the cat would've developed some sort of feline leukemia on the trip home from the pet store and been dead by the time she got out of the elevator.

Laura rested her forehead against her living room window, breathed a soft fog onto the glass and then watched it slowly disappear. The Rocky Mountains were trapped inside the building across from her, dark peaks set against the night sky. *"You see, I'm falling too."* Her father on skates, falling. Again and again.

She'd chosen this apartment precisely because it lacked a balcony, to avoid the unsettling temptation that vertigo offered. When she was first looking for a place, she'd considered a spacious two-bedroom in a building high above the river. But as she looked over the edge of the balcony, she'd wondered how long she could go before climbing over and stepping off. How long she could have lasted before asking herself, "What would it matter?" And how much time would pass before anyone noticed she was missing? Any friends or colleagues she might claim were scattered across the country like spare change; they would have just assumed she was offline. But even as Laura asked herself that question, she'd known the answer: *Dad. He would notice I was gone.* He would be the first to sound the alarm. If her body had been swept down the river, he would organize the search party. Warren would find her, but her dad would be the one that led the way.

What if she didn't fall, though? What if she simply floated … away?

Laura's windows were aligned not with the mountains but toward downtown; they looked onto that sandstone-and-steel city below with its Etch-a-Sketch skyline, a city that was constantly erasing and rewriting itself. A cold city, exhaling steam. A city of CEOs and venture capital, of oil company offices hidden behind curtains of glass.

She could chart the price of a barrel of oil from her bedroom window by the turning of construction cranes along the skyline. When the price fell below some magical point, the cranes would slow down. And then stop. When the price rose again, the cranes would start up, spinning anew. Faster and faster.

The Heart of the New West. That's what they called the city. And from up here, it did indeed beat like a heart, like one of those stop-motion films of traffic pulsing on aortal avenues.

In the neighbourhood below, in a side street among other side streets, on the second floor of a two-storey apartment building, Matthew Brisebois was arriving home for the day. He brushed the snow from his boots, hung cap on peg, jacket on hanger, unclipped his tie, and turned on the television (pre-muted) for company. He stopped. Looked out at the room in front of him. What did he see? Walls, unadorned. A kitchen table that was also a dining room table that was also a desk that was also a mail sorting centre, with a laptop open, a pile of paperwork and a box of Just Right breakfast cereal beside it. Framed photographs, lined up neatly on the mantel. A fireplace that had never been turned on and the boxes from last summer still stacked in the corner.

As an investigator, how would he read this scene? Single male, mid-forties, divorced from the looks of it, and concerned about his fibre intake. If you sniffed the air, you might catch the scent of cologne and Windex. What you wouldn't smell was anything catlike.

He wasn't exactly sure why he'd lied to Laura about the cat. Maybe an attempt to gain her trust—he knew there was more to this accident than an old man on a sheet of ice—but that was explanation after the fact. Had she accepted his offer, he would have swung by the animal shelter, picked up a cat, used that as a way in. But she hadn't asked, and he hadn't gone.

He looked out at the twin apartment buildings on the ridge above. *Second building on the left. Third light in the top corner. That's me.* He would contact the insurance company tomorrow, inquire who the beneficiary was in the case of one Henry Curtis, recently deceased. And they would tell him; they always did. Any chance to avoid a payout.

He stood a long while watching that corner light. Watched until it finally blinked off.

> *Do you know who we are?*
>   *we are Mafia. We will FIND you and*
> *we will kill you*

10

Wet forests crowded the roadside. Broad leaves, heavy with rain, slapped against rooftops as the vehicles jockeyed for position. The tanker truck was bucking under its own weight, straining against its own momentum; the driver and his mechanic could feel its cargo of fuel pushing them forward as they drove across washboard surfaces and crumbling asphalt, windows down, grinning wide.

Joseph was gripping the wheel as though it were a life preserver and he was at sea. He had to yell to be heard over the noise of the engine. "Dreams Abound!" he shouted. "We are on our way!"

What could stop them? Nothing.

Nothing except— He geared down. "Roadblock ahead."

"Police?"

"Army."

11

You, I love. This is what Laura remembered: chuckwagons reeling around a corner, men in rippling silk shirts yelling hard, Stetsons flying, outriders in full gallop, hooves flinging up clods of dirt, the tinny cries of the announcer lost in the melee.

And then—one of the animals stumbled and the wagons took flight, wheels in the air, men tumbling upward, horses piling on top of each other. Laura's father, covering her eyes.

Had she seen that accident? Or dreamed it?

Memories of the midway. A Tilt-A-Whirl world of spinning lights and helium balloons escaping into the night sky. Laura, wearing a cowboy hat with a plastic whistle attached, and her father in full Western gear, meaning, in this case, a too-tight vest, a too-big hat, new cowboy boots, and no whistle. Wandering the midway was like wandering through a slow-motion pinball machine. Chimes rang and ricocheted. Ferris wheels turned and Gravitrons spun. Ring-a-bell tests of strength and guess-your-weight booths. Frozen bananas and deep-fried cheesecake. Light bulb lanes and tumbling milk cans. *"Throw a ball, win a prize! It's just that easy."*

With Warren off with his friends and a mother who didn't like crowds, it fell to Laura's father to entertain her.

But she was too small for the big rides and he was too big for the little rides, so the evening consisted mainly of her dad waving to her as she passed by on the Lady Bug Bugaloo or the Inch-Worm Express (a roller coaster that consisted of a single circle with a single bump).

While waiting in line for mini-doughnuts—moist and warm and dusted with cinnamon, the highlight of any Stampede midway visit—Laura had walked ahead, down the line, while her dad held their spot. She'd peered seriously at the menu-board options, decided after great deliberation to get the Big Bag, and was hurrying back when she kicked something underfoot. A twenty-dollar bill.

She ran, breathless, back to her dad. "Look what I found!"

Her elation didn't last, though. "Sweetie," he said. "It's not ours to keep."

So they went down the mini-doughnut line, asking everyone in turn if they'd dropped a twenty-dollar bill. One by one, everyone said no, till they got to a gaggle of smirking teenage boys. "Yeah," one of them said. "That's mine."

As she walked away, she heard them laughing.

"That wasn't theirs," she'd said, face in full pout.

"Probably not," said her dad. "But it definitely wasn't ours."

And somewhere in the gap between *probably* and *definitely*, her father had lost her, and the rest of the evening was ruined. As she walked, hand-in-begrudging-hand with her father through the fairway, with its toss-a-coin stands and dartboard prizes, she silently tallied the items she might have purchased with that lost twenty:

—a snow globe with a Mountie inside
—a bandana bedazzled with a rhinestone greeting of
   "Howdy, pardner!"

—an accordion-drop of postcards for Nana

—a pink cloud of cotton candy

—a glow-in-the-dark doodle pad poster proclaiming the
   Stampede the "Greatest Show on Earth"

—a small bear with Rumpelstiltskin-style granny glasses

—a plastic cowboy piggy bank

—a ticket to the All-Seeing Oracle

—an array of sparkly headbands and glitter lip gloss

The possibilities floated past on either side, as all the while she kept an eye out for the smirking boys who'd plucked that twenty from her father's hand. She never saw them, which was just as well. What would she have done? Trailed them like Nancy Drew? Confronted the leader with an accusatory stab of her finger?

Laura wasn't sure she'd ever really forgiven her father, though. Not inside, not where it counts.

12

A vein of lightning on the far side of the sky.

Storms without rain.

Winds without water.

She woke, and when she sat up, the dust fountained off her and the voice that had accompanied her once again stirred, once again whispered, *"Get up. Keep walking. Don't stop."*

13

There were three sets of tire treads from the Ogden Road accident to be sorted out: those on the upside-down vehicle at the bottom of the embankment; those of a car being steered forcibly off the road, through packed snow and over the edge—clearly belonging to the Oldsmobile below, but still needing to be confirmed; and the tire treads from the car that had braked hard and come to a stop, tires rolling through a dusting of their own debris as the vehicle turned to go back up the hill. The car that had been aiming for the guard-rail, but had stopped.

Sergeant Brisebois was at his desk with the accident scene photographs laid out before him, studying the stained sweater on the victim's body—*"Did it say what kind of sweater?"*—when the folder landed on his desk. "They match," said the young constable who had delivered it, a quick-talking woman from Collision Reconstruction.

"Which ones?" he asked.

"All of 'em."

"All?"

She nodded. "They're all from the same car, the one the victim was driving, the Oldsmobile."

Brisebois leaned back. "But the tracks didn't line up. The ones higher up and the other ones lower down—the ones that left the road and went over the side—they're at different angles."

"Be that as it may, the treads are the same. One car, one set of wheels."

She left him with this quiet revelation. The victim wasn't forced off the road, and he wasn't being pursued. At least, not by anything external.

Brisebois remembered something one of the other officers at the scene had said, Colin maybe, as they examined the route the vehicle had taken over the edge of the embankment: "He missed the guardrail by inches."

"Bad luck," said Brisebois.

"Bad luck," said the other officer. "Or good aim."

14

Laura's father was wearing the same sweater he always did, the one with the geometric deer on it, now looking a bit ratty, as though the deer were afflicted with some sort of woodland mange. He'd had that sweater for years; she remembered it from when she was little.

It was the last time she would see her father, though Laura didn't know that at the time.

"What happened to the green cardigan?" she asked. "The one I gave you last Christmas?"

"Oh, that?" he said. "I still have it."

"You never wear it."

"I do. I just—" He wore his deer sweater when he went to see her because he remembered how much she'd liked it as a kid, how she'd given each deer its own name even though the animals were identical. "I thought you liked this sweater," he said.

"I do, but it's getting a bit worn, don't you think?"

And—this is the awful part. He took it off.

"Dad, c'mon …"

"Oh no, it's okay." And he'd stood there in shirtsleeves, sweater balled in one hand. "So what are we having for lunch?"

They were at Northill Plaza. Laura had taken the elevator down, met him in front of the chocolate shoppe.

"My namesake," she'd said with a laugh. "Remember?"

"Sorry?" He seemed distracted.

"Laura Secord. The heroine on the chocolate box. You told me I was named after her. You said you'd won Mom over when you were courting with a box of Laura Secord's Assorted."

"Hmm? No. Not for Secord. Your great-aunt Ida, on your mother's side. Laura Ida. Not the chocolates, that was just a story."

"Yes, Dad, I know. I was only— So what do you feel like? Chinese? Greek?"

They had arrived at the food court.

"Italian?" she said. "Or Thai? Maybe Mexican?"

"Oh, I don't know. What do you recommend?"

"I had Opa yesterday," she said. "And I'm not wild about Edo of Japan. Let's see. There's Taco Bell. Manchu Wok. Seoul Express. How about that? It's Korean."

"Isn't that spicy? I don't really care for spicy food."

"I know, but this'll be fine. The kimchee they have is mild."

So they found a table and dined on mixed vegetables and mild kimchee. But their conversation seemed strange and disjointed. Her father's attention would drift away, then suddenly snap back into focus—though not always on the topic at hand. "You'll be fine," he said at one point, apropos of nothing. "Your mother worries about you, but you'll be fine."

"Mom worries about me? Why?"

"She thinks you should get out more, meet people."

Laura laughed. "That's what mothers do. They worry."

"But I don't," he said. "There's a strength running through you, Laura. Something Warren never had. A resilience. You get it from your mother, you certainly don't get it from me."

Dad, fishing for a compliment. "C'mon," she said. "You've got all kinds of strength."

"No," he said. "I don't. I thought I did, but I don't. You, though. That's a different story. I've always been so very proud of you."

Her father had helped her move the year she went away to university, driving across the prairies in a rented van: Laura immersed in earplug music, her dad aiming for the vanishing point ahead. Sunsets across open fields. A city glowing in the middle of it. "The Peg," he said as they circled in. "That's what they call it."

She'd stayed in residence the first year, and her dad had come back out to see her over Thanksgiving. "Your mom sends her best wishes—and this pumpkin pie," he said. Store bought, but still. Her mom was substitute teaching that week and couldn't come, let alone bake. But her dad had made the trip, and they had Thanksgiving together. He slept on the couch in the common room and headed back the next day, driving across the prairies toward that other vanishing point.

Laura had been struggling with an Introduction to Philosophy essay at the time, trying to somehow tie the absolutist moral philosophy of Immanuel Kant to both the emotive prose of the Late Romantics and Plato's Allegory of the Cave. The paper was a mess. After her father had left, though, she'd found something: in her open notebook, where she'd written out that ancient imperative, underlined forcibly for added emphasis as a reminder—*Let justice be done though the heavens fall!*—her father had written below it, in smaller letters, "Let Heaven be done, though justice falls."

She'd puzzled over this, her father's inversion of heaven and justice, of love and retribution, of forgiveness and reprisal. Was he just playing with words? He never played with words. *Let Heaven be done, though justice falls.* It was one of the few moments she remembered her dad ever being philosophical—if that's what that was—and it had stayed with her all these years precisely because it was so unusual. It seemed to offer a glimpse of something that lay below what she called his "dad demeanour."

Laura never did finish that essay; she was marked "incomplete," a verdict harsher than failure, in her mind. Even now, she carried the memory of that grade like a burden. *Incomplete.*

Laura had called home from the dorm every Sunday, sometimes with a forced joviality in her voice, other times sniffling with sadness. She spoke to her mom at great length about the minutiae of university life, the profs she disliked and those she could stand, the workload, the daily defeats, the small victories. With her father, though, it was mainly mundane: pleasantries accompanied by assurances from Laura that she was doing well, was knuckling down, studying hard. But if Laura's mother got to hear the detailed ins and outs of Laura's life, it was always her dad who got to say goodbye.

"Here's your father."

He would end the calls with "I love you." That way, he explained, "The last thing you hear before you go to sleep will be *love*."

She'd teased him about this. "Not love. *You*," she said.

"Me?"

"You. The last thing I hear is *you*. If you wanted to end it on love, you'd have to reword it."

And so it became a running joke between them. Whenever she phoned, the call would end with her father telling her: "You, I love."

It was something they shared throughout her Away Years, something she hadn't heard for a long, long while. Somewhere along the way, it had been forgotten. But when they'd said goodbye that day in the food court, he'd called back to her as she was leaving. "Laura?"

"Yes, Dad?"

"You, I love."

Why would he have done that?

15

There had been a boy at university. Not a boy. A grad student who taught one of her introductory English courses. There had been a baby as well. No. Not a baby. A shadow, a smudge on an ultrasound followed by protestations. "I can't be somebody's father. I can't. I'm not ready. I'll never be ready." Not that it mattered; Laura wasn't able to carry the child, and the entire incident had long been pushed down into the footnotes of her life. She hadn't told anyone about it. Not even her dad.

After university she'd been hired by Harlequin, proofreading romances. She'd later moved on to pocketbook police procedurals and then into the lucrative world of freelance copy editing. Memoirs, biographies, manuals. It was her job to impose a consistency of grammar, punctuation, to compile a style sheet of preferred spellings and usages for each particular project. It was decidedly unsexy, but it paid the rent (barely), even if it did come with certain challenges, mainly in the form of intransigent authors.

One particularly troublesome author had insisted on ending many of his sentences with ... nothing. No period, no question mark, no exclamation, not even an ellipsis. Laura had dutifully gone through and fixed these, adding a semicolon here, a period there, only to receive a barrage of incensed emails after the author had reviewed the pages. "How dare you!" the emails typically began. Laura had tried to explain to him that every sentence needed an ending, but the author had refused to accept this and had fought back with a passion worthy of a better cause. "Not everything has an ending! Open your eyes!" he wrote—using exclamation marks, ironically enough. After several testy back-and-forths, it became clear that it would be easier for the publisher to simply acquiesce. The reviewers then complained (inevitably) about the sloppy editing. "Riddled with typos," they said.

Did everything have an ending?

Poetry could end on emptiness, a disregard for proper punctuation being somewhat de rigueur among the poetry set. But prose? Biography? Her father's biography, uneventful till the very end— had it ended on the raised eyebrows of an exclamation point? The curlicue of a question left unanswered? The final summation of a period, or the stutter-marks of an ellipsis trailing off into blank paper …

Laura prepared indexes as well and was currently juggling several biographies, all public figures, all women—an athlete, a soldier (posthumous), a country singing star. Highlighting surnames and proper nouns, tallying Key Events and Honours, Earned. It was for a series titled Lives Lived. Indexes were tricky things. What mattered? Surnames, certainly. And cities. Specific locations (New York), but not general (kitchen). Do you group the subject's early jobs in advertising and marketing together? Or under subheadings labelled "Employment, Early"? Do you need a separate entry for "Advertising"? Or could you get away with using an artful "*see: Marketing*"? (Answer: No.)

It was not a particularly enjoyable task, indexing other people's lives. "Seems to me," she'd said with a sigh to her father on the phone one day, "that the most important aspects of someone's life are the very things not listed in an index." There were never entries for "memory," or "regrets," or even "love," in the lowercase. It was always "Education (post-secondary)" or "Awards (*see also:* Best Debut R&B Country CD by a Female Artist, Solo)." Indexes never seemed to get to the heart of the matter. There was never a heading for hope or fear. Or dreams, recalled. Smiles, remembered. Anger. Beauty. Or even images that lingered, glimpses of something that had made an impression. A doorway. A window. A reflection on glass. The smell of rain. Never any of that. Just a tally of proper nouns and famous names. And why only one life? Why not the web of other lives that define us? What of their indexes, their moments?

"I think," said her father, "you need to cut back on the espresso and try to get some rest."

— 39 —

She'd laughed and agreed, had taken the elevator down to the pool, had swum laps. Had swum until her eyes stung.

And now, here she was, still at her desk, still indexing other people's lives.

"You, I love."

Why would he say that?

16

A standard, paint-by-numbers biography begins with the subject's grandparents arriving from England/Ireland/Germany/Soviet Russia, then traces their humble beginnings as shopkeepers/ farmers/miners, *never imagining* (that's what forebears do, they go about their lives never imagining) that one day, their grandson/ daughter/son would grow up to become a world-famous/acclaimed/ notorious athlete/entertainer/politician/merchant of death.

With celebrity memoirs, this would be more self-aggrandizing, of course, and would usually start with a defining public moment. "As I sat in the audience, while [MAIN RIVAL'S] name was called to receive the award for Best Debut R&B Country CD by a Female Artist (Solo), I fought back tears, knowing that if I wanted to grow as an individual, I would have to reinvent myself as an artist/ woman/merchant of death." But after that, they too would settle into a straightforward chronology. *This happened, then this.*

The human memory is a salamander, though; it squiggles from point to point, slaloms its way improbably up walls and across ceilings. A ripple of colour, appearing and disappearing at the same moment, an orange head trailing a fluid blue body. Had she dreamed that? It seemed more memory than dream.

No story based on human memory was ever linear. Memories folded back on themselves. They clustered, they clotted. They arranged themselves not chronologically, but clumped together thematically. Betrayal. Ambition. Regret. Dismay.

One of the first things Laura did when she took over a manuscript was to start a timeline of events, to ferret out any internal contradictions and make sure everything lined up properly. But the events that followed her father's death defied Laura's best copy-editing skills. They were tangled and jumbled. They overlapped. They bled into each other: reds and blues, forming new hues and strange mixtures.

Try as she might, Laura couldn't sort these events into anything resembling a straight line. The devil wasn't in the details, it *was* the details. A memorial service to arrange. Relatives to contact. An obituary to write. And a mother too numb to help.

Somewhere along the line, Laura's father was turned into ash.

As for the obituary: "You're the copywriter," said Warren, doggedly erroneous. (No matter how many times she'd explained what she did for a living, he never got it.)

"I don't write copy, I edit it."

"Whatever. Just write an obituary, okay?"

It was an odd undertaking, the penning of obituaries. A life tallied up and charged by the word. What to leave out? What to leave in? The deceased's full name, certainly, with educational abbreviations, strung like semaphores behind it. B.A. Spec. Honours. Teaching Certificate (Industrial Arts), Athabasca University. A checklist of children and a spouse survived by (if applicable). Address and time of service. Donations in lieu of flowers. Flowers in lieu of attendance. A quote from someone wiser, more sentimental. "To every thing there is a season …" Obituaries weren't written so much as assembled.

"What does that even mean?" said Warren, baffled at the notice his sister had run in the paper. "Let Heaven be done, though justice falls."

"It's just something Dad said—something he wrote, a long time ago." Maybe he hadn't written that at all; maybe she had imagined it. But it was still a message. From their father.

Sergeant Brisebois had delivered the autopsy results in person, cap tucked under his arm as a sign of respect. He'd gone over the results as soon as they arrived from the Medical Examiner's Office. Cause of death: "Blunt force trauma." *No shit.* He didn't mention the fact that the tracks on Ogden Road had all come from the Olds, or that the investigation had expanded.

"There wasn't any alcohol in the bloodstream," Brisebois told the family. "No narcotics, and no sign of cardiac arrest, either. His heart was fine."

Laura heard this as: "He had a good heart." Laura heard this as: "He was a good man."

When Laura's grandmother had died, it had barely caused a ripple in the family; it was more as if their Nana had evaporated than expired. But with her father's death, everything clattered together, yelling for attention at the same time like Warren's twin daughters. Laura had handled the funeral and Warren handled the money, calling the insurance company, refusing to be put on hold, berating a series of administrators over payments due and procedures Warren deemed "unacceptable."

That was the first inkling that something was wrong. "The added coverage on your father's policy was too recent. It doesn't apply." This is what the insurance company told her brother. *Read the fine print, bozo.* As it turned out, their father had increased his life insurance in the week before the accident, more than doubling his premium. But a six-month waiting period was required before any added payouts could be claimed.

Their mother was now staying at Warren's house in Springbank, having finally accepted that their father was (a) never going to call to say it had all been a terrible mix-up, and (b) never coming home. (Even after his body had been incinerated, she'd expected him at any moment; it was only over the triangular-cut egg-salad sandwiches at the reception after the memorial service that she realized she was, indeed, a widow.) Warren's home was in a cul-de-sac amid other cul-de-sacs, and their mother, having packed only an overnight bag, spent most of her days in a flannel nightgown. Laura collected her mom's mail, kept it by the fishbowl in her apartment with a rubber band around it. "The mail can wait," she'd told her mom. But it couldn't.

Life insurance. Egg-salad sandwiches. Final notices. In lieu of flowers. The events continued to blur into each other, seemed to happen both at the same time—and separately. And then the ATM at Laura's mall swallowed their mother's bank card and nothing was ever the same.

Warren had taken their mother to see Laura, if only to get her out of her flannel nightgown. He'd dropped their mother off at Northill Plaza and she'd stopped by the bank at the mall to withdraw some money—she was planning to take Laura for lunch at the food court. It was a joint account she'd had with her husband, but when she entered her PIN the machine refused to give her any money or even to release the card. It held it hostage instead, with a message that read simply: SEE TELLER INSIDE.

Laura's mother fled instead. She took the mallside exit, past Shoppers Drug Mart and the Flight Centre to the lobby of Laura's building, pressed desperately on the buzzer.

"Laura, it's Mom. Please come down."

Together, they'd walked back to the bank and asked to see the manager. "It's clearly some sort of mistake," Laura said, using the definitive when she knew full well she should have been using the conditional.

The bank manager was pudgy and young, with Clearasil-pink skin and a tie knotted too tight for the overlap of his neck. He provided a bank statement. It showed a balance of (*$189,809.51*).

"What do these parentheses mean?" she asked, though she already had a sickened inkling.

"The what?"

"The brackets," she said. "Around the total. Explain those."

The bank manager blinked. "That means it's a negative balance. You didn't get the notice?" He turned to her mom. "About the default? On the house loan?"

"Loan?"

"The house loan. It's like a mortgage."

Her mother said, "We don't have a mortgage. We paid our house off years ago."

"Yes, you did," said the manager. "That's why your husband was able to arrange a loan. More of a line of credit, really, against the equity."

He showed them the paperwork for that as well. "Your husband," he said, sliding the papers across. *Your husband.* As though that explained everything.

Laura shoved the papers right back at him. "My mother didn't sign anything. This is a scam."

"Your mother didn't need to sign anything. The house was in your father's name."

"Why would the house be in—"

But her mother stopped her with a touch on the arm. "I was still in teachers' college when we bought the house," she said. "Back then, property was often in the husband's name. It wasn't unusual."

"But it's your house, too," Laura said.

"Um, actually," said the bank manager, "it's *our* house. The loan is in default." Then: "You should probably get a lawyer."

Laura could do better than that. "I'm calling my brother," she said, threatening him as though she were seven years old again. "You," she said, "are going to be sorry."

She sat there, staring defiantly at the bank manager, cellphone to her ear. But the days of her brother acting as protector were long gone, and when Warren picked up, he didn't let her get a word in. He'd been having his own runaround with the life insurance company. "They're freezing Dad's payout, 'pending investigation.' Can you fuckin' believe this?"

Laura turned away, lowered her voice, said, "Warren, we're at the bank. You need to come here right away."

"Dad took out an extra half-mill in added coverage just a week before the accident. And now the bastards are refusing to cough up any of it! Good thing the house was paid off."

As Laura tried to get her brother to listen, even for a moment, her mother asked the manager, "What about our savings?"

17

The following Monday, the police seized Laura's parents' computer.

After the fallout from the bank, her mom had made the mistake of contacting Sergeant Brisebois, thinking he was on their side. He was on no one's side; he was in the business of turning question marks into full stops, of explaining away discrepancies, of teasing out the hidden meanings in the seemingly innocuous and the apparently inconsequential. So when Mrs. Curtis called him, distraught, saying someone had stolen their life's savings, his obligations were not to her but to the larger narrative.

With Mrs. Curtis's approval, the bank had released her late husband's financial statements to the police, along with a list of transactions spanning the last six months. The balance in their chequing account had barely wavered. But their savings? Withdrawal after withdrawal, some in the hundreds of dollars, some in the thousands—money, bleeding away—followed by a final flurry of paperwork for a line of credit against home equity. The investigation had grown to include the possibility of financial crimes, insurance fraud, and possibly extortion.

—*Shall I stay on then? As family liaison?*

—*That's the plan. Call Lloyd at the Crown Prosecutor's office, get his advice. You'll want a standard warrant for the house and a production order for the hard drive.*

—*The widow's being cooperative.*

—*Get the warrants anyway. I've had sweet-smiling seniors suddenly get cold feet and withdraw their cooperation. What starts as a consensual search suddenly becomes a standoff, and next thing you know, you've got a suspect who's pissing backward, the arrest is tossed on a technicality, and the whole case has gone south.*

—*Understood. I'll contact the Crown right away.*

—*Sounds good. Keep me posted.*

And so it was, on the Chief Inspector's directives, that Sergeant Matthew Brisebois arrived at the Curtis home at 9:34 A.M. on Monday, accompanied by a district officer and two members of the Tech Unit.

Warren arrived soon after and was already in high dudgeon by the time Laura showed up. *How does he get all the way in from the burbs before I can even walk down a hill?*

"You don't have to give them the computer," Warren was telling his mom. "This is bullshit." Warren had a mouthful of beef jerky that he chewed like it was a wad of tobacco.

Who eats beef jerky for breakfast? There were days Laura forgot to eat entirely, but her brother had never had that problem. He was always chewing on something.

As the IT officers removed the hard drive and placed it into a protective carry case, Brisebois sat beside Mrs. Curtis, speaking softly, sipping tea.

"Matthew," she began, a waver running through her voice, "will this help us find out what happened? Will this help us find out who stole our money?"

"That's what we're hoping, Helen." She would have handed the computer over, even without a court-ordered warrant.

Laura had arrived still smelling of chlorine from her swim. She ignored Brisebois, asked her mom, "What are they looking for?"

"Kiddie porn and terrorist training manuals," said Warren with a snort. "These cops have got fuckin' blinders on. They think Dad was some sort of master criminal. Meanwhile, whoever drove him off the road is running free and laughing."

—*Is the wife a suspect?*
—*The wife is always a suspect.*
—*But did she do it?*
—*No.*
—*How about the son? The daughter?*

The officer with the pale eyes looked at Laura, the woman from the tower window.

—*The son? No. The daughter? She does seem … strangely removed from the situation.*

"Your father was sending a lot of money to people outside the country. Any idea why?"

"Dad never travelled," said Laura. "Who would he know?"

"We were going to travel," said her mom, jumping in to defend Henry. "Around the world and back again, it's what your father always said. The house was paid off, we had our pensions and some savings, our RRSPs. We were going to travel, going to see the world. Of course … we hadn't gotten around to the details of it yet …" Her voice trailed off. Laura watched the officer as he jotted this information down in his notepad. "How's your cat?" she asked.

"My cat?"

18

Laura's father, reading a bedtime story. Warren, too big for books, had wormed his way free, leaving Laura alone under her dad's arm as he turned the pages, slowly, deliberately.

"Rapunzel, Rapunzel, let down your golden hair!" he intoned in the sort of voice he imagined a prince might have.

Laura looked up at her dad. "Why didn't she climb down?"

Her dad looked back at her.

"The girl," said Laura. "Why didn't she just tie her hair to something at the top and climb down by herself?"

"You know," said her dad, "I never thought of that. I suppose you're right. She could have cut her hair when she got to the bottom."

"Hair grows back, right?"

"It certainly does," said her dad.

"So why didn't she just tie a knot and climb down?"

He frowned, considered the question. "I don't know. Maybe she was scared of falling."

"If she tied a good knot, it would hold her, even if she was scared." Then, with arms crossed, "This is dumb."

"Well, it's not a true story. It's a fairy tale."

But even fairy stories have to make sense, she thought.

Laura would later write a short story of her own when she was in elementary school, one about Rapunzel after her escape, running free with short hair.

She thought about that sometimes. About that other her, wondered what ever became of her. It happens so slowly, doesn't it? We surrender by inches. We surrender until one day when we're brushing our teeth, instead of Rapunzel plotting her escape we see a hermit staring back at us.

Warren, too big for books, had wormed his way out, leaving Laura alone under her dad's arm.

19

"Wait." This was Laura's mother stopping Brisebois as the officers wound up the last of the computer cables.

"Yes, Helen?"

"There is one thing. It's probably nothing, but I remember Henry said something about a message he got ... a message from Africa. Some sort of mistake, like a wrong number, but in an email. I never heard anything more about it, though."

20

They call us wizards for a reason. This was alchemy, not science. The IT officer knew this—knew it instinctively. He was navigating as much by magic as by prescribed protocol, by touch as much as by training. He was weaving his way into memory itself.

Memory was a holding cell, but the officer held the sorcerer's key that unlocked it, and dozens of deleted files now floated to the surface, emerging like ghosts from the hard drive. Email after email. Afterimages. Trails in the ether.

He had captured shadows in a net, had dragged them to the surface—and he smiled.

SUBJECT: Urgent Matter to the Attention of Mr. Henry
      Curtis. Please do not turn away!
RECEIVED: September 12, 11:42 PM

Complements of the season! With warm heart I offer you
wishes of good health from Africa. I am contacting you
today regarding an urgent business proposal, and though
this letter may reach you as a surprise, I implore you to
take the time to go through it carefully as the decision you
make will go a long ways toward determining the future
and continued existence of a young woman's happiness.

Sir, I am writing today on behalf of Miss Sandra,
daughter of Dr. Atta, late Director & Chairman of the
Contract Award Committee for the Nigerian National
Petroleum Corporation. As you may know, Dr. Atta died
tragically in a helicopter crash in the Niger Delta under
circumstances most suspicious. Miss Sandra's uncle vowed
to care for her, but he too has fallen afoul of government-
backed criminals. Her uncle was the executive chief officer
of the Niger Delta Development Agency, which works hand
in hand with the National Petroleum Commission to secure
quantities of Bonny Crude for export to OPEC refineries and
other ports asunder.

As might be imagined, between father and uncle,
Miss Sandra was able through God's will to amass
quite a sizable fortune. With her mother succumbed to
heartbreak and both her father protector and uncle killed
in the crash, Miss Sandra's life is now in grave danger.
Although only twenty-one and renowned for her beauty
she is unable to find a suitor, for she has been forced into
hiding by her family's high-placed enemies.

She has asked me to contact you—MR. HENRY CURTIS—for help. She cannot turn to the police, for the police are part of this murderous cabal. She is pleading on bended knees for you to rescue her from a hopeless future.

> With urgent regard,
> Victor Okechukwu, Attorney at Law

SUBJECT: Sorry.
SENT: September 13, 12:06 AM

I think you have me confused with someone else. Maybe check the address and try again.

SUBJECT: Apologies Mr. Curtis!!
RECEIVED: September 13, 10:49 PM

Oh! Many apologies, sir! I won't be bothering you any farther in this regard. Please say to no one the details of my previous correspondence, for I do not wish to imperil the life of Miss Sandra any more than it already is. Danger presses in from every side, as might be imagined.

I apologize with unreserved hindsight for intruding on your life. I was looking for Henry Curtis, graduate of Athabasca University, retired from the noble profession of teachering, a member in Good Standing of the Amateur Woodworking Society of Hounsfield Heights, subscriber of the Briar Hill Beacon Community Newspaper, husband of Helen, grandfather of twins, a highly respected figure in his community, known for his honesty and integrity. I apologize for this mis-sent mailing.

> With farewell,
> Victor Okechukwu, Attorney at Law

SUBJECT: Confused
SENT: September 14, 12:11 AM

Well, that's me all right. Except for the part about being highly regarded in my community (ha ha). I still think you've got the wrong person, though. I don't know anyone in Africa.

SUBJECT: But Africa knows you.
RECEIVED: September 15, 12:04 AM

So it is you! So happy to finally make contact with your good self. A colleague of yours in the Chinook Regional Teachers Union attempted to rescue Miss Sandra, but he failed in his entirety, I am afraid to say, as he told his spouse and friends, even the police!! Can you imagine such a miscalculation! Even after we advised him of the dangers posed by the henchman responsible for her father's slaying and even after we begged him to silence, he went blabbing to everyone and very nearly cost Miss Sandra her life. Clearly, we can not identify your friend for reasons of security, but fortunately, he gave us your name as a final act of appeasement in the hopes that you might succeed where lesser men such as he had failed.

But—it is also clear that he did not forewarn you or explain your role or tell you how we have placed our hopes on you, so I beg you our forgiveness and assure you that I will not bother you farther on Miss Sandra's behest. I ask only that you delete my previous correspondence and speak to NO ONE of this matter. It is not money she is asking for. Quite the opposite! She has plenty of money! She needs only a kind heart in a Foreign nation. But I can see you are too busy for her. I will explain this to her when next I see her.

> With sadness in my heart,
> Victor Okechukwu, Attorney at Law

SUBJECT: Miss Sandra
SENT: September 15, 11:02 PM

If not money, what does she want?

SUBJECT: A saviour
RECEIVED: September 15, 11:54 PM

It's not what she wants, but what she needs. She needs someone to *receive* money, not give it. I must explain the urgency of my tone, I think.

I have recently been diagnosed with prostate and oesophageal cancer and high blood pressure. Doctors have made it absolutely lucid that this disease is terminal.

I am in the know that the disease has ravaged my body and left me at the mercy of an endless cocktail of drugs that have been administered to me. These medications have gone a long way in alleviating the pains, but I still feel my life gradually ebbing away. I have tried with all the money I have to treat it, but to no avail. It has defiled all forms of medical treatment, and the doctors have now told me that I have only a few weeks in which to live.

It is too late for me, but not for Miss Sandra. As my final act on this Earth, I wish to save my beloved God daughter, Miss Sandra, the only child of my own childhood friend, Dr. Atta.

Please understand, she wants only the chance for a life of peace. Isn't this what we all wish? She was hoping to the point of heartbreak to start anew in your country. With her means, she would be independently wealthy and would be able to invest handsomely in your city. Perhaps you will advise her on such investment opportunities?

What Miss Sandra needs is simply this: to get her money out of the clutches of the Central Bank of Nigeria. A simple transfer of funds, nothing more. I can send you the necessary modalities asap. Time is urgent. If we do not move with utmost haste, her inheritance will be confiscated by the corrupt Nigerian government and their toadies in the military camp who want nothing more than to strip Miss Sandra. To strip her of her valuables and dignity, to steal her inheritance and then squander her future for themselves, most likely on harlots and nepotism. As a Christian preparing to enter God's Kingdom, as my God daughter's last remaining protector, I can not stand and see this happen.

My dear Henry (might I call you Henry? I feel a kinship
to you), we need to transfer Miss Sandra's money into a
bank account outside of Africa. That is all. Simply that.
We need to do this as discretely and as expeditiously
as possible. Even ravaged as I am with cancer, I would
happily do this on my own without asking your assistance,
but as a civil servant here in Nigeria under the Civil
Service Bureau of Conduct, I am not allowed whatsoever
to operate any foreign bank account. For this reason, I
need your help.

All you need to do is allow us to deposit the money. A
one-time transaction, which will save a young girl's life!
For your assistance I propose to give you a commission
of 15 percent of the total sum involved, which you shall
deduct immediately once the money is in your account.
If you decline, please tell us quickly so we may find
someone else.

As always, I implore you to exercise the utmost
discretion in keeping this matter completely confidential,
whatever your decision. We must beware of miscreants
and evil minded men who indulge in fraudulent activities
under false pretenses.

> With hope,
> Victor Okechukwu, Attorney at Law

SUBJECT: Miss Sandra
SENT: September 16, 12:14 AM

I don't know if I can help really. How much money are we
talking?

SUBJECT: TOP SECRET
RECEIVED: September 16, 1:19 AM

The amount, held in a floating reserve with a security
company, is $35,600,000 – THIRTY FIVE MILLION SIX
HUNDRED THOUSAND dollars US.

                With much sincerity,
                Victor Okechukwu, Attorney at Law

21

Outside: chinook winds dividing the sky, the clear blue pushing dark clouds forward in a single wide arc. Inside: Laura's father sitting on one of the mall's benches, staring at the ground, frowning thoughtfully.

Laura had just moved into the apartment above the Northill Plaza and was still stocking up on necessities—everything from electric kettle to toilet brush. Her dad had come to help. In this case, help meant "monetary donations followed by long waits."

"Can you hang out here for a sec?" she'd asked him outside Sears. "There are just a couple of things more I need to get."

"A sec" being an imprecise unit of measurement, she'd re-emerged from Sears a good half hour later with bags aplenty and found her father on the bench, staring at the floor.

"Fossils," he said. "Look."

She flopped down beside him, blew hair out of her eyes. "Sorry I took so long."

"There—do you see? Fossils, between the tiles." He looked around him. "Just here, though. Nowhere else."

Fossils? It took her a moment to figure out what he was talking about. Not real fossils, of course. Replicas, embedded in the floor around the bench. Decorative fossils.

Her dad stood up, smiled. "At first I thought it was, you know, something to do with the petroleum industry. Oil Town, and so on. But then I spotted the next one." He was excited, or as near to excited as her father ever got. "C'mon, I'll show you."

He hurried her through the mall to the next set of benches. "There, see?" He pointed to swirling patterns embedded in the floor tile. "Wind."

Sure enough. Semi-abstract clouds unfurling like storybook breaths.

"There's more," he said, rushing on ahead as she tried to keep up, all but dragging her bags behind. Her father was the sort of person who offered to carry other people's bags; the fact that he hadn't this time testified to the spell he was under. "See!" He pointed to where rippled designs emanated outward across the floor in concentric circles, as though a pebble had been dropped into a pond. "Waves," he said, not without pride.

"Um, you're right, Dad," she said. "Never noticed."

His eyes were bright. "It took me awhile to figure out, but the fossils are earth. Then we have air, water. The elements." His frown resurfaced. "Can't find fire, though. I walked up and down."

"Dad," she said. "These bags are getting heavy."

"Oh, sorry. Let me get those." By this point they'd almost reached the food court. "What would you like?" he asked. "My treat."

"I'm not really hungry," she said. "Though I suppose I should be. Chinese? Maybe Greek."

"Sounds good. I feel like Italian myself," he said.

So he ate his Sbarro and she her Opa, and they talked about her new apartment and its view of the city. Her father's gaze drifted upward to the skylight above them, and suddenly a grin appeared.

"I found it," he said. He'd been looking down, that was the problem.

She looked up, saw it too. A golden starburst around the skylight, right above the food court. Not fire, *sun*. Someone had gone to a lot of trouble incorporating the four elements into a shopping mall's layout. The evidence of something more.

"No snow, though," Laura laughed. "I always thought that was the fifth element, at least in these parts."

He thought about this. "Snow. That would be water plus air, minus sun to make it cold." Then, still glowing from their treasure hunt, "We got 'em all."

She wanted to say, "Not we, you." But instead she smiled and said, "We sure did."

22

A young man in a silk shirt, sipping spiced tea as he scrolls through messages in a cyber café. This is Festac Town on the Lagos mainland. A village within a city. A maze of streets folding in on themselves, with alleyways leading into lanes, lanes leading into dead-end turnarounds. You were always backtracking in Festac Town.

Inside the café: rows of computer screens. Hunched shoulders and cigarettes. A ceiling fan that rattled. The traffic outside: car horns and over-revved engines, broken mufflers.

The young man in the silk shirt had found Laura's father online through a forum used by retired schoolteachers, and had stalked him through cyberspace for weeks. And though the young man had other prospects he was even now kneading like clay—a business owner from Tallahassee, a pastor from County Wicklow—it was the retired schoolteacher, a plodding soul from the looks of it, posting comments on woodworking sites and online forums, and then commenting on the comments to his comments, posting his grandchildren's photos and giving tips on awls and the best way to solder a seam, who the young man now turned his gaze upon.

"I am a chimney sweep." This is what Henry would often declare.

"If I kiss you, will that bring me luck?" was Helen's response.

"Luck for me," he would say. "Not so sure about you."

I am a chimney sweep.

Henry had said it laughingly at first, and then with less good cheer as the months piled up. "A sweeper of chimneys. A purveyor of buggy whips. I make the finest whalebone corsets. I deliver milk bottles to your doorstep. I am a doctor who makes house calls."

As a high school shop teacher (ret.), he'd spent the better part of a lifetime acquiring skills that were no longer in demand. "Does anyone even teach shop anymore?" he'd asked his wife. "Outside of specialized vocational schools and such?" The skills he'd honed and had tried to impart to others were now considered "trades," not foundational knowledge.

"Oh, stop your moping," said Helen. Henry always took things too deeply. "You think shop is a dying art? Try Home Ec. There was a time when being a well-rounded homemaker was a point of pride. Now? Bread making, baking, sewing, they're just hobbies."

"Is that what we've come to? Hobbyists?"

"My grandmother used to pull her own wool and spin her own yarn. I wouldn't even know how. And I don't see you out working on our windmill and waterwheel, dear."

But that was exactly his point. Henry Curtis could take apart a carburetor and put it back together blindfolded, fully oiled and with the idle deftly set. But no one was making carburetors anymore; they didn't matter. His wife had excellent penmanship, but penmanship didn't matter either. Soldering irons and box socials. Carburetors and pie crusts.

"We're fading away," he said.

"Nonsense," she replied.

"We're disappearing, Helen. We're dissolving by degree and we don't even realize. In the morning, when I'm shaving, I'm surprised I can't see through my own reflection."

He'd always had morose tendencies; Laura got that from him. But since his retirement, the melancholy had only gotten worse. So one night, as the Disappearing Man poked about in the kitchen, looking for items that hadn't moved in twenty years, and before he could yell out "Helen, where's the …," she'd put down her magazine and called to him. "Henry," she said. "Let's run away together. Somewhere warm."

Having a project cheered Henry up. He went online, plugged in a few search terms—and was overwhelmed by the options available. So he turned to his Facebook friends instead. They in turn suggested "asking his community," so he'd posted a query on a forum set up for retired teachers. WIFE AND I ARE THINKING ABOUT TAKING AN EXTENDED VACATION. MAYBE A CRUISE. ANY SUGGESTIONS? *"Alaska was lovely." "The fjords of Norway. Definitely!! I can send you a link."*

I WAS THINKING SOMEWHERE WARM.

"Have you considered Africa?"

NEVER BEEN. WOULD LOVE TO GO. BUT I'M WORRIED ABOUT PIRATES HA HA.

"Your children would love Africa."

MAYBE THE GRANDKIDS.

"You have grandchildren? How fortunate! Are they old enough for a safari?"

THEY'RE ONLY FOUR AND A HALF. TWINS. HELEN (THAT'S

MY WIFE) WANTS TO TAKE THEM TO DISNEY WORLD BEFORE THEY
GET TOO OLD TO ENJOY IT. BUT I FIGURE I'M THE ONE TOO OLD
HA HA.

The young man in the silk shirt wiped his neck with a folded
handkerchief. Lagos never let you forget Lagos, that was the
problem. Even with the tea and the rattling fan to cool him, the
gummy heat outside had found him.

A dull-eyed laggard two computers down asked the room,
"How do you spell *inheritance*? My spellcheck doesn't know."

"You spelled it so bad even the dictionary don't know it? Dis
is shameful!" There was scattered laughter across the room, and
someone else shouted back, "Took two weeks for him just to find
the dollar sign!"

More laughter. Winston sighed. Sipped his tea. Lemon spiced
with ginger. Somewhere in the café, a radio was humming a song
to itself:

> *Oyibo, I'm asking you,*
> *Who is dey mugu now?*
> *Who is dey mastah?*

The din and ding of traffic outside. The smell of *suya* beef
and warm beer. The cyber cafés in Festac Town were as numerous
as *suya* stands and street hawkers. It was a long journey from the
young man's apartment, hours spent daily on *danfo* minibuses or,
when the go-slows knotted the streets beyond loosening, clutching
the back of an *okada* motorcycle taxi driver. A long journey, taken
daily. A necessary journey nonetheless, for the streets of Festac
Town were lined with shops offering internet satellite services
or, when the seats in those were snatched up, the less dependable
NITEL Network.

NITEL was a national service, and thus the cafés that operated on it were obliged to post "Wayo Man Be Gone!" notices on their walls. Some were more specific still: "No email extractors!" or "No mass mailings." But this was a mere formality, and Winston had never known any owner to prowl the rows of yahoo boys to try to protect some *oyibo* grand-mama on the other side of the world from trickery. As long as you slipped a few naira to the café operators, you could scroll through the internet unmolested.

Today Winston sat in front of a screen at the Cyber Hunt Net Trakker Café. The internet fees were higher here, but they came with endless cups of minerals and tea (not free of course; nothing was ever free in Lagos), with windows that opened onto the street and ceiling fans that swirled above, creating at least the illusion of a breeze. He'd sweltered in enough cinder-block cyber ovens just to save a few kobo to appreciate the influx of air, however muggy, that the traffic wafted in.

Winston had started his one-man enterprise with the simple purchase of some email extractor software. He'd begun by running random surnames through a search engine, hitting SELECT ALL, and then dumping the entire haul into the software, which then separated the email addresses from the rest of the text. Cut and paste these addresses into the bcc line of any web-based email, add a standard format letter— *"Dear Sir/Madam, I am the son of an exiled Nigerian diplomat ... "*—include a separate email address for them to reply to, and you were set. It was science, not an art. Winston knew that. The more messages you sent, the higher the odds of netting a response. This was brute mathematics at play.

A hard-working lad could send hundreds, even thousands of emails over the course of a single day. Could send them until his account was shut down by the server, with the inevitable message: *WARNING! You have reached your sending limit.* You'd then wait for responses to trickle in over the next few days, sent to the email address included in the message. (You didn't want them simply hitting REPLY because the original address was going to crash.) Those who replied, even if only to say "you've got the wrong guy," would receive a personalized message. But it was hard fishing nonetheless; a nibble so rarely turned into a bite.

Winston had realized early on that what these bulk mailings offered in sheer quantity they lacked in quality. It was disheartening to send out tens of thousands of pleas and receive only silence or automated messages in response. It was as though the world itself were ignoring you. Either people were becoming more astute, or spam filters were becoming more effective. Human folly being limitless, Winston suspected it was the filters more than any sudden increase in critical thought that was causing the problem. Spam filters were like ocean-going trawlers, dragging the sea floor with nets, swamping the boats and tangling the lines of independent fishermen who were, after all, only trying to earn a living.

You don't hunt prey with fistfuls of sand. You can't catch a cat by banging a drum. Winston knew this—and yet there they were: rows of bent backs wreathed in smoke, the yahoo boys throwing out mass-message formats into cyberspace. Carpet bombing, they called it. A truly inefficient use of time, he thought.

Winston was different. He'd abandoned the ploy of email extractors and mass bombardments and now spent more time up front, right at the start, sussing out targets, focusing his forays. Nor did he employ the intentionally crude, ungrammatical sentences, the almost laughable misspellings that telegraphed "Here is a rube with millions of dollars, easy pickings." These "formats," as they were known, targeted *stupid* greed, people who snickered even as they schemed to steal from who they thought were gullible

Nigerians. Winston was looking for intelligent greed or, at the very least, *thoughtful* greed. His approach was more … *refined.* That was the word he was looking for. Not for him the mass-mailing of blind formats. His was a surgical strike, not the indiscriminate firings of a machine gun.

More than anything, Winston considered himself a student of humanity, someone committed to his craft, constantly revising his pitch, sharpening his search tools. He employed business direc-tories. Annual reports. Online brochures. News articles. Even that old standby, the online Yellow Pages. You select your targets, fine-tune your format, make your move. Facebook requests and a few follow-up queries, and Winston could put together an accurate enough profile—age, political affiliations, church membership, niche interests—to slip inside the boundaries of trust, to cash in on a misguided sense of "community." *"As a fellow Presbyterian …" "As someone who also admires the works of Sir Arthur Conan Doyle …" "As an avid follower of your wedding bloopers blog …" "Dear Sir! I must say, your online essay on the songbirds of South Carolina captivated me. It has long been a dream of mine too to spot a gild-headed blue finch in the wild …"*

A great deal of preparation went into this, but once the targets were snared, they remained snared. And once hooked, it became a matter of playing them, of reeling in the line, overcoming their initial resistance, giving them slack at certain times, pulling taut at others. A city boy born and bred, Winston understood nonetheless that while some fish could be caught in billowing nets and others on baited barbs, some required spearing, outright and quickly. He didn't fish with line and hook, of course, but with words, with wonder. In this, the game was more like storytelling than blood sport. There were times when Winston felt as though he were a dream merchant or a movie producer, a scriptwriter, with the *mugu* on the other end cast as a character in a story, one staged solely for his benefit.

Or hers.

Female *mugus* were rare, but it happened. Hadn't a Hong Kong widow been bilked out of millions? A magnificent scam that made headlines only when those mealy-marrowed souls at the Economic and Financial Crimes Commission managed to track down the masterminds behind it and—instead of doing the decent thing and accepting a bribe—prosecuted them! They even returned the money to the old woman. Such fools! It saddened Winston's heart, the waste of it, all the hard work that must have gone into it, undone by meddling EFCC do-gooders who had no appreciation of the business he was in.

Hunter. Fisherman. Entrepreneur. Nollywood director. Winston saw himself as many things, but not as a criminal. Criminals lacked finesse. Criminals bashed people on the back of their skulls and looted wallets, rummaged through purses. Criminals murdered, but guymen seduced. Winston didn't take the *mugus'* money; they gave it to him, eyes clouded by greed, dazzled by dollars. *And when they give you their money, it doesn't count as stealing.*

Occasionally, Winston would be warned away from a chat site or an online forum, would see a posting on a bulletin board reading *"I am here ooooooo"* or *"Mugu guyman keep off!"* which told him someone else had staked out the site. It might be a fellow two chairs down from him for all he knew, but the protocol was to back off just the same—though guymen did occasionally get caught up in an online tussle over a particularly plump prize. A *"mugu* war," as they called it. Winston avoided these as well. They were counter-productive and only distracted from the task at hand: to snare, spear, snatch, and squeeze the *mugu*, the fool, dry.

Sometimes Winston would find a CV posted online, with street addresses and phone numbers given. That was especially useful when it came time to cut the *mugu* loose, to threaten their lives, family, et cetera. These exchanges usually ended in blubbering pleas from the *mugu:* "O, you have ruined me," "O, you have tricked me." Sometimes the blubbering turned into legal threats—more an annoyance than anything worth fretting over—and this was where a home address proved a boon. Attaching a simple Google Maps photo of the *mugu's* house to a note saying "We know where you live" was usually enough to shut down such nonsense. And even then there was little danger of any real legal action; it was more akin to swatting aside a fly. A minor annoyance at most, all those angry/sad/rebuffed/baffled emails cluttering one's inbox.

The real danger lay here in Lagos, in the sudden swoops of EFCC officers seeking to "rehabilitate" Nigeria's reputation. Interfering with hard-working 419ers, staging publicity-stunt raids and mass arrests. Winston had been caught in one such sweep—that was why he now moved from cyber café to cyber café, avoiding overnight stays and always scouting the quickest exit.

He started out as a yahoo boy, taking advantage of the cheaper prices to remain at the cafés overnight, long after the CLOSED sign had been turned and the door bolted. He'd never cared for the crude company of the other overnighters, though. The low laughs, the desperation disguised as camaraderie, the eye-stinging haze of cigarettes—*Was he the only man in Lagos who didn't smoke?*—the constant dull-witted banter, the tiresome obsession with the female form. Winston wasn't staying up all night to share lurid tales of sexual conquest, real or imagined; he had business to conduct, and the rambling discussions the other yahoo boys had about the best way to 419 a girl from Victoria Island into your bed was a taxing waste of energy. Winston had bigger plans than that.

He was no mere *wayo* man, a trickster, a huckster, a carnival conjurer. He was a true guyman, living by his wits, outsmarting the odds. This was what he told himself to buoy his spirits when he felt adrift.

There were times he thought he should make more of an effort to chum around with the yahoo boys, exchanging tips, sharing advice. He'd purchased his first formats from a yahoo boy, after all, a lengthy plea from the widow of General Abacha, almost comically inept in its structure and internal inconsistencies, but a start nonetheless. And after two hundred tries, it had paid off: a small payout from an engineering student in Edinburgh, only a few thousand pounds but enough to keep him going.

It seemed so long ago now. Winston waved for another cup of tea. The yahoo boys drank minerals and beer, but Winston was cut from a different cloth. Lemon spiced with ginger.

He forced a sigh back into his throat, scrolled again through the profiles he was compiling.

A city of millions, built on a swamp, on a series of stepping stones, on islands thick with humidity. The worst place to construct a metropolis, but that was Lagos. It defied common sense. Winston dreamed of streamlined cities, where action could follow plan smoothly and without the endless layers of *dash* and deceit that Lagos demanded. The yahoo boys were impatient—that was their problem. That was the city's problem, too; Lagos was always hurrying, always getting in its own way. The place needed less hustle, more strategy. There was so much energy expended daily over the most mundane of details—getting a haircut, paying a bill. Every transaction had to be wrestled to the ground, it seemed, every point of view debated in endless mind-maddening detail. These were the things that drained one's energy, dissipated one's profits. If only this energy could be better directed. *If we could walk in step, we could take over the world.*

But of course, the very strength of Lagos was that it *didn't* walk in step. Winston knew this; the city's weaknesses were also its wellspring.

We fall to earth like raindrops. Why did I have to fall here?

Winston dreamed of taking Nigeria's greatest innovation, the 419 scheme, to the next level, in Europe or the U.K., in New York or London. Not in sputters and sparks, with the usual street-gang syndicates and expat bone-breakers hired in America and Europe to shake down troublesome *mugus*—but something better, something bigger, something more *sophisticated*. It would be 419 on a corporate level, with managers and CEOs operating within the law, not outside it. It would be 419 painted on a larger canvas.

Even the best of the Lagos guymen had only scratched the skin; there was so much more to tap into. And yet … here he was, lost in Lagos, holed up in Festac Town, pecking out ridiculous messages to ridiculous *mugus,* dreaming—as always—of something more.

It would only ever be a dream. That was the tragedy of it. The raid that had nabbed him on Victoria Island had also tangled up his future. He'd been given a suspended sentence, was even now on probationary orders. With his passport suspended, he'd missed his sister's graduation from university in England, had been forced to make contrived excuses to his parents. The truth was, he was marked like Cain and would never be allowed to leave Nigeria. No visa, no hope of escape. The suspension would eventually be lifted, or so he hoped, but the damage had been done. He now had a criminal record, and the only way out was to smuggle himself into another country like a common refugee—which killed any chance of his building 419 on a truly international scale.

Perhaps he could land a sponsor, someone who wasn't related to him, someone who could act as his guarantor. Maybe he would meet a beautiful *oyibo* woman and charm her into marrying him? He laughed at this in spite of himself.

And so, there he sits, in Festac Town, typing fairy tales:

> Sir, I apologize with unreserved hindsight for intruding on your life. I was looking for Henry Curtis, graduate of Athabasca University, retired from the noble profession of teachering, a member in Good Standing of the Amateur Woodworking Society of Hounsfield Heights, subscriber of the Briar Hill community newspaper, husband of Helen, grandfather of twins …

23

Laura remembered something else her father had once said to her, years before.

It may have been at Christmas, maybe Thanksgiving. There was a fireplace and warmth, and he was looking past her when he said it. "Do you know what I fear?"

Home for the holidays. Her second year away? Maybe her third. The details were fuzzy, but not the feeling. Nutmeg in eggnog. The pop of wood knots in a fire. But no Christmas tree. Thanksgiving then? Snow outside. Had it snowed early that year?

Her mom had been at a school meeting and Warren was out, so it was just the two of them, with nothing much to say, happy just to sit and sip.

During one lull, he'd asked her the question, "Do you know what I fear?"

She didn't.

"As a parent? My fear is that when we die, we'll have to watch all those moments in our lives when we were short-tempered with our children, all the times they needed our love and we didn't give it, all those times we were distracted or in a bad mood, all the times we were angry or impatient."

"Dad," she said. "You were never angry. I don't think you ever raised your voice."

"Oh, there were times," he said. "You've just forgotten. Times when I brushed you or Warren aside instead of asking how your day was, those times I didn't listen to your stories. My fear is, when the time comes, I'll have to watch all those moments again. That they'll make us watch them before we can get into Heaven." He looked at her. "I'm sorry, Laura."

"There's nothing to be sorry about."

"But I am."

"Sorry? For what?"

"Just sorry. Sorry for the things I should have done, might have done, but didn't."

She should have said it then: *You were a good dad. You always did your best.* She should have said it, but didn't. She let the moment lapse into silence instead, let the silence pass into smoke.

24

My dearest Henry,

As perhaps you have been made awares, my childhood protector, Victor Okechukwu, has entered the hospital. I'm afraid his cancer has taken a turn for the worst. As his life dims he repeats your name and worries only about your commitment to this matter. Once Mr. Okechukwu's life has passed—as surely it must, I will have no one. I ask only for your assistance. I beg you on bended knees and with tears in my eyes.

Darkness and danger press in from every side. Until such moment as I am rescued,

> I remain as ever, yours truly,
> Miss Sandra

A grin from the boy in the silk shirt as he clicked-and-dragged an image of a Nollywood starlet with almond eyes and a tattered dress (in the role of a destitute daughter from a Lagos melodrama) and inserted it into his email. That a famed Nigerian movie star would pitch her woes to a distant *oyibo*, how could one not grin at such a thing?

Mugu fall, guyman whack.

Before the boy could hit SEND, though, a reply came back from his previous petition, a single note from the schoolteacher in Canada.

—*I can help.*

How easily a grin turns into a chuckle, and a chuckle into something deeper even than laughter. Winston leaned back and cricked his neck, sipped his tea, felt the burlap-sack burden that was Lagos grow suddenly buoyant, felt the netted entanglements of daily life dissolve. Sweeter than soft drinks, sweeter than tea.

But no sooner had he congratulated himself on the fine-spun nature of his fairy tale than a face appeared on his screen—not in, *on*. A reflection thrown back by the protective sheen the cyber café placed over its computer screens. A face. Not his. And before Winston could react, the reflection had reached out, had touched his shoulder. Police raid? EFCC sweep? Winston turned in a smooth swirl of silk, exiting the window on his computer screen with practised ease in one flowing motion. "Yes, bruddah?" he asked.

A thin man with swampy eyes, face bereft of expression. "Oga wants to see you."

Oga was a title, not a name.

Among the shadowmen of Lagos, Oga was "boss," Oga was "big man," Oga was "strong man." Rarely was there a hoodlum or crime syndicate head who didn't fancy himself as Chief This or Oga That. It was prestige through proxy, stature by mere word association.

The meaning of Oga. It did not escape Winston. Nor could he escape it.

Swampy eyes, a face bereft of expression. "Your Oga is waiting."

Winston blinked. "I don't have an Oga."

"You do now."

SAND

25

She dreamed of horses. Of wailing flutes and *tambura* drums. Of a rolling barrage of hooves, of horse and rider in full gallop.

It may have been Eid-el-Fitr, maybe Eid-el-Kabir. It may have commemorated the end of Ramadan or the prophet Ibrahim's sacrificing of a ram instead of a child. But in her dreaming, the horsemen of the durbar were out in full pageantry. Riders in scarlet turbans with swords drawn, sunlight sharpening the blades.

Horses, draped in quilted armour and adorned with falcon-feathered headdresses. Praise singers and footmen. The accolades of cannon fire and high-trilled voices. His Excellency the Emir looking on, languid under peacock feather fans, as the lancers line up, horses snorting. With a loud cry they charge, wave after wave, at breakneck gallop, pulling back only at the last moment, in clouds of dust and to the cheers of the crowds. A feigned attack, a test of mettle.

The emir never blinks; the horsemen never follow through. Instead, they raise sword and lance in a warrior's salute. A ritual of fealty, but one with an underlying message: *You have contained us; you have not conquered us.*

She dreamed of horses, woke to the sound of hoofbeats trailing away.

26

Laura's mother, on the phone. A tremor running through her voice. "Laura," she said. "They're ruling it a suicide."

"Who's they?"

The insurance company. Pending a final police report.

Jesus.

27

She dreamed of horses, woke to silence. Hoisted the jerry can back on her head, began walking.

It seemed she had always been walking, had been born of walking, could hardly remember a time when she hadn't been.

A young woman—a girl—layered in dust-muted indigos, clothed from forehead to ankle with only face and feet and hennaed hands visible, she moved across a parched and powdered landscape, the water balanced on folded cloth atop her head.

A dry land. It stretched out in endless arrangements of thorn bush and scrub grass. Boulders littered the ground like broken teeth, and the sun pushed down. The landscape reverberated from the heat like a horseshoe on an anvil still vibrating from the force of a blow.

Heat and thirst and sand.

The dry season had brought harmattan winds from the northeast that raked across the scrublands of the Sahel, carrying with it the taste of larger sands, wider deserts. When a sudden gust—as hot and dry as camel's breath—threw itself against her, it was the Sahara itself that gritted her eyes, made her cough. Trace elements of that encroaching desert, it collected like salt rind in her tear ducts.

She pulled her head scarf tighter, felt the water slosh inside the jerry can. It seemed as though she had always been walking.

Across the flatlands, the dry grass had been burned away, the fires set in the hope they might flush out bush rats and smaller prey. The ash cover the fires left behind might enrich the soil as well, might produce green shoots for grazing when the rains came—*if* the rains came, and not so hard as to wash the ash away entirely into the flood plains and saline gullies. There was a time when she'd helped guide these controlled burns; now she was walking through their aftermath, the thick grey ash coating her feet.

She had filled the jerry can at the last water hole she'd come to, but no matter how many times she'd rinsed it out, the water inside still tasted of gasoline. That was two days ago, and the can was already almost empty.

She had outwalked her own dialect, was deep among strangers now. Along the way she passed swaths of failed crops, sticklike in the soil, saw them as the omens they were. A soil grown too sandy for millet, and sparse grasses barely enough to support base grazing. The plains in front of her seemed to grow wider with the walking.

In the distance, a threadbare man in a threadbare shirt pushed a handcart that teetered with gourds along a parallel track, too intent on his load to notice a lone walker. The girl in indigo skirted the edge of a cluster of farm huts, the clay walls and thatched roofs eerily still in the lethargy of midday. She found the local water hole by following bone-ribbed cattle down to a swampy pond where she refilled her jerry can and then struck out across the scrublands toward the next cluster of rooftops. In the evenings these homes would glow with the light of charcoal burners, forming constellations across the plains. On occasion she would catch the smell of stockpiled yams baking in coals or a goat-head stew being stirred, and her mouth would ache for it and her stomach would whisper its faint, complaining plea.

It was a plea that would become more insistent as the days wore on, and with it came the counter-whisper, urging her not to stop, to keep moving.

The girl was chewing kola nuts to quell her appetite and was carefully rationing out the dried dates and cowpeas she carried in the folds of her gown. And all the while, that whispered voice spoke to her: *Keep. Walking. Don't. Stop.*

28

Ruling it a suicide.

The reed-thin insurance adjuster, another in a procession of pink-faced men who'd paraded through their lives since her father's death, sat at his desk in his pink-faced office, blandly unmoved by any of it.

Laura and her mother sat across from him, shell-shocked in the silence.

The pink-faced man spooned Coffee-mate into his Nescafé, drank with pursed lips from a chipped cup. One of Laura's authors was always adding details like that to his memoir—"A flake of dust had settled on her blouse," "A small, faded mustard stain was visible on his necktie." It was a world filled with slightly chipped cups and faintly furrowed brows, and Laura had highlighted these with the query: *"Would you really notice stuff like that?"* Now she knew. You do. You do. The reed-thin man with his hot-dog complexion was drinking Nescafé from a chipped cup, had measured it out with a coffee spoon, had stirred it while informing them that Laura's father, Helen's husband, had seen his life end not in a moment of skidded terror—which was bad enough to imagine—but in despair.

That second set of tracks.

Her father hadn't been able to go through with it, not the first time. He'd hit his brakes. Had sat there in the winter dark and then, slowly, had cranked the wheel and headed back up the hill for another run.

Sorrow as strong as a fist. It wrapped its knuckles around Laura's heart, squeezed it in a charley-horse grip. Laura's father, turning the car around. Laura's father, driving back up that hill. It must have been the loneliest ride of his life. And though she didn't know it at the time, everything that followed would come back to this: the image of her father turning the car around, and Laura wanting the people responsible to know what they had done.

—*You find those fuckers before I do.*

That's what her brother had said to Brisebois that first night, but as events played out, it would become clear that there was a misplaced pronoun in that sentence. Her brother should have said: *You find those fuckers before she does.*

29

Across the scrubland sands: a highway. Blacktop drawn like a line on a map. The girl in indigo turned, followed it southward.

She tried walking on the asphalt at first, but the heat of it seared her feet and she was forced alongside it instead, on the slower-going shoulders where the soil was as soft as sifted flour. Trucks rolled by in caravan, enveloping her in veils of harmattan dust and forcing her to steady the empty jerry can on her head. It had been easier to carry when it was full.

She walked herself in and out of dust.

Memories wavered in the heat. The past had become a mirage and the sun-warmed clay of her village was fading now with every step, with every gust of wind. The wives and uncles, the slow drift of cattle, the thump of millet in mortar: it seemed so distant, lacking as it did the substance and certainty of the walk, of one foot gliding in front of the other endlessly.

She was of the Sahel, from a clan rumoured to carry Arabian blood in their veins. The Lost Tribe of Israel. The descendants of Roman soldiers gone astray in the desert and taken in by Nubian riders—biblical tales and trade-route trysts put forth to explain the long limbs, the dust-coloured skin. But hers were a people born not of moonlight seductions or cast-off tribes, but of dust itself: a people given form from the very landscape they inhabited.

Who she was—and where she came from—was etched into her skin, was present in the delicate geometry of scars cut into her face, scars that both accentuated her beauty and identified her kinship line. The older wives had done their job well, and the lines they'd so painstakingly drawn—thin razored slices, with ashes quickly rubbed in to stop the bleeding and set the scar—had been the envy of the other girls throughout her childhood.

She wore her beauty like a map, and as she approached another crossroad cluster of buildings, jerry can on head, she pulled her head scarf in closer. Not so tight as to elicit suspicion, but enough to deflect it—she hoped.

Low-slung buildings, more mortar than brick, and a desultory motor-park market crowded the roadside, and as she threaded her way through the maze of stalls, her eyes would occasionally meet those of the Sahel traders. They would stop, would stare at her quizzically while she passed, trying to decipher the glimpse they'd gotten of the scars on her face, trying to read the story these told, trying to pin her in place. But hers was a small and dwindling clan, little known and often overlooked, and no one ever managed to unlock its secrets.

Her layered robes, indigo with scarlet trim, the embroidered sleeves of her *taqua*, even the manner in which her head scarf was draped—the style of loose knot, the way the folds fell—these too provided a map to who she was. Had anyone been able to read it, they could have charted the exact path she'd followed, right back to a specific wadi, a specific ridge, a specific village, even perhaps a specific home. That was the fear, that she would be unravelled, revealed.

She remembered outdoor schoolyard lessons as a child, under the spread of a shade tree, as the teacher spun a sun-bleached globe in front of them, the continents blurring into each other and then gradually separating as the world slowed. She felt as though she were walking on that globe now, turning it with her feet.

Her teacher had been from Mali, had stopped the spinning world at Africa, had pointed to the nook below the bulge, had said in mockery, "Here, in the armpit of Africa—Nigeria."

Her uncle fumed at this when he heard, stormed back the next day, demanded apology, and the teacher, suddenly deferential, acquiesced, speaking in a polite French that was both elegant and afraid. Her uncle had paid good money to put her and her siblings in a proper *lycée*, and he wasn't going to have them insulted by some mendicant Malinese schoolteacher.

"Africa is not an arm," her uncle explained on the walk back. He was speaking in Hausa, the language of business, not the French of the *lycée*. "Unacceptable! He should look more closely at his maps, that teacher of yours. He should look at the true shape of it. Africa is not an arm, it is a gun, and Nigeria is where the trigger lies." Then, slipping into his grandfather's dialect for added emphasis, "Anyway, we are not Nigerians, we are something else."

What was Nigeria?

It was the crosshairs of the world. You could look at any wall map and see this: North America on the left, Asia on the right,

Europe up top. Draw one line down the middle and another lengthwise and what would you see, dead centre? Nigeria.

What was Nigeria?

It was a net, loosely thrown, a name on a map, one created by the British to paper over the gaping cracks in the joinery. A conjurer's trick, where the many became one, a sleight of hand, like the tired magic of old men making coins disappear. "There is no Nigeria." This was the lesson her uncle had wished to impart. "There is Fulani and Hausa, Igbo and Tiv, Efik and Kanuri, Gwari and Yoruba. But Nigeria? That is only the pail we carry these in."

But she knew better.

She knew that the naming of a place helped bring it into existence. The naming of a location—or a person, a child—was a way of claiming them. Until you named something, it wasn't fully real. The trick to staying invisible, then, was to remain nameless. Without a name, you couldn't be pinned in place, couldn't be cornered or captured. The key was to keep walking, keep moving, keep heading south, out of the Sahel.

30

Dear Mr. Curtis!

I bring joyful news! The transfer has gone through! The money will be in your account tomorrow morning. All the necessary modalities have been arranged.

Perhaps I am running ahead of myself. First, allow me my introductions: My name is Lawrence Atuche, and I have been asked by my colleague Victor Okechukwu (who, as you may know, has taken ill) to oversee the transfer of Miss Sandra's estate into your bank account for safekeep.

I have attached the OFFICIAL REMITTANCE NOTICE from
the Central Bank:

> *To the Attention of Mr. Henry Curtis: Please be
> informed that as Head of the Administrative and
> Legal Reconciliation Department of the Central Bank
> of Nigeria, I have approved for immediate payment
> the sum of $US 35,600,000 (THIRTY FIVE MILLION
> SIX HUNDRED THOUSAND) into your account as
> listed on the application as submitted by one Victor
> Okechukwu. Once confirmation has been received
> and payment has been notarized, said funds will be
> transferred within 24 (TWENTY-FOUR) Hours.*
> > *With sincere wishes,*
> > *R. Bola Soludo, Director of Operations, CBN*

31

The tumbledown towns along the highway were closer together
now, larger, more dishevelled, more cluttered with life and
commerce. Tin roofs and square walls had replaced thatched roofs
and curved clay.

She searched out market wells to refill her water can, was chased
away as often as not by the other women. She learned to hang
back and wait. In the ebb and flow of people, she would find an
opening and follow an older woman in, unscrewing the corroded
lid of the can quickly, filling it with water and then disappearing
before anyone took note. As thirsty as she was, she never drank
until she'd put distance between herself and the well, walking as
swiftly as possible, the sudden strain of the water's weight both
reassuring and painful. Only when she was away from the crowds

would she allow herself a drink from the spout. The water turned the dust in her mouth to a slick of clay, and she couldn't escape the taste of fuel. But even then, the hardest part was to sip, not to gulp. Not to drink so quickly as to develop stomach cramps.

If she kept to the main road and larger centres, if she avoided the side streets and enclaves where outsiders were instantly noted, she might yet remain invisible. A young woman, a girl, barefoot with battered jerry can on head: other than the puzzled glances from Sahel traders, she hardly existed. She was certainly not worth the robbing, having long since divested herself of anything of value, the bracelets and the silver coins that once dangled richly from her robes— the birthright of her mother's kinship line—given up for food. Her family's history was now scattered across the Sahel: the *tsamiya* silk her aunts had bequeathed her, the burnished earrings, the polished beads and adornments, even, eventually, her sandals—all stripped away until she was left with only a few coins, a small bag of kola nuts, some cowpeas, a few final slices of dried yam, and her jerry can.

There were dangers other than robbery, though. In the motor parks and crossroad communities she passed through, when the sun collapsed in on itself and the earth began to cool, darker appetites surfaced. Sheen-faced truck drivers would huddle around oil-barrel fires, speaking in thick southern tongues, drinking illicit gin from mason jars as they eyed the world beyond their circles with a predatory gaze.

At those moments, she left the road entirely and walked out into the savannah, where the baobab trees formed elephantine shapes, their branches knuckling upward in arthritic angles. Acacia canopies provided parasols of cover. Termite mounds, taller than she was, were silhouetted like earthen minarets under the great dome of sky, and as night fell, a chill would set in.

The hyenas that had once roamed these savannahs were gone,

but human hyenas were on the prowl still, and even if she'd had any wooden matches, she wouldn't have lit a fire for fear of drawing attention. Instead she would unroll the long strips of tanned goatskin, as soft and supple as suede, that she kept folded inside her robe and would begin a methodical mummy-wrap of her legs. She would then pull the wide sleeves of her *taqua* across her chest as if in a funereal embrace, twisting the hems with her wrists until they were almost knotted. Even with her body heat turned in on itself, the warmth would seep out of the fabric during the night, leaving her to drift in and out of a shivering half-slumber. Alone, but not quite.

Hadn't the Prophet, Peace be upon Him, suffered harder trials in harsher climes than this? Hadn't He fled the city gates for Medina beneath similar stars and desert darkness?

Eventually, she would fall into something that resembled sleep, would dream, sometimes of horses, sometimes flamingos. It was more memory than dream; one from her childhood. The only flamingos she knew of were at Bula Tura, an oasis in the farthest corner of the outermost edge of her clan's widest range. Her family hadn't gone as far as Bula Tura for years, not since she was scarcely of walking age, in fact. It may even have been her earliest memory: Fulani nomads and Kanuri cattle drivers, camel caravans plodding past in slow-moving procession, and flamingos taking flight. The memories blended with those of other oases: of mangoes and African myrrh, of date palm and fire trees, of flowering jacaranda, the petals forming a mist among the leaves, and of water running clear and cool, gathered up with a laughing ease and flavoured with mint and crushed herbs. She woke with the taste of it on her tongue.

In the early hours, she would lie perfectly still to watch the stars blink out, one by one. It was a time of day when only the wind was awake.

She would untangle the knot of her sleeves, would sit up and slowly wind back the tanned goatskin from around her legs. She would shake the Sahel from her robes, would take a swallow of water, a slice of dried yam. Once, as she walked back toward the road, a lizard rippled through the dust in front of her—a flash of lemon and lime, yellow on green, appearing and disappearing at almost the same moment.

These early hours offered the thinnest sliver of opportunity before the rest of the restless world arose. Back at the roadside, she would move warily among the dens of drivers she had avoided the night before: sleeping bodies slumped in truck cabins or sprawled drunkenly on mats. If she moved carefully, stepped softly, she might find overlooked leftovers: *jollof* rice sticking to the sides of pots to be scooped with her fingertips and eaten hungrily, or sloppily discarded *suya* sticks with scraps of meat still clinging to them.

She fled these snoring roadside camps quickly, though, and would follow the highway south as the sun broke across the land. It was a sudden and immense heat, an oven door flung open, and the asphalt soon grew soft. The convoys of trucks that rumbled by left tire impressions in the blacktop as they passed.

Among her clan, the senior wives ran the household, the junior wives handled trade, and the men managed livestock: the selling and buying thereof. But the children, boys and girls together, would care for the cattle, making sure none wandered off or got stuck in sandpits. Only as they grew older would their roles slowly separate, girls milking the cows and harvesting millet, boys standing guard over land and livestock. Standing guard and—above all—grooming the horses.

As she walked, a memory surfaced, unbidden: a season of drought followed by heavy rains, which brought forth hordes of tsetse flies. Her family was forced to move the herd farther and farther afield to drier grasslands, trying desperately to avoid the flies and the sleeping sickness they might bring, travelling far beyond the grasslands, beyond the farthest outposts of her clan. So far, in fact, that she wasn't able to attend school that year. And when she did go back, it wasn't to the *lycée* but to the dustier outdoor tablet schools. The flies had cost her uncles their wealth.

Memories from that drought. *"Little one!"* Her brother calling to her frantically as a skinny longhorn ambled toward dense scrub. *"Run!"* And she did, stick in hand, as the steer lolled farther away from the herd. She hit the side of the animal with her stick, stopped it from escaping, ran so fast she tumbled headlong into a thicket of thorns. She remembered her brother soothing her tears afterward, picking out the barbs, saying, "You were very brave, very brave."

It was the highest praise possible in their language.

Her clan had not always been cattle herders fleeing flies. "We were ambush traders" was how they liked to describe it, eyes smiling. Ambush traders lying in wait for Arab camel drivers and Tuareg salt traders. "We negotiated with swords drawn." Caliphates and sultans were forced to kneel, emirs to bow down. Even the Seven Kingdoms of the Hausa had not been able to subdue them. Whenever armies moved against them, her clan would simply melt back into the Sahel.

The glory and wealth of the trans-Saharan trade routes— the gold and silver, the salt and slaves—had passed through her people's arid lands for centuries. Heaving caravans, laden with Sokoto leather and clothes of Kano blue, salt from Lake Chad, medicines from the Middle Belt, the spice and perfumes of Arabia, cowrie shell currency, silk rolls, Islamic scrolls—the caravans had all paid tribute, had all paid toll.

"We are horse riders of the Sahel," her uncles had reminded her. Riders, born of motion. And even now that the trans-Saharan trade was gone, even as her clan eked out crops from sandy soil and tallied their livelihoods in domesticated cattle, it was the horses that were still the pride of her people. Horses, pampered and groomed. Horses, as decorated and doted on as any bride. "The men love their horses," the women laughed, "more than their wives."

"Of course!" came the reply. "Our horses never scold us!"

On her first night of flight, she had slipped out of her uncle's home and hidden amid the outlying stables. The swish of tails and scent of manure both calmed and bestirred her; something moved within her on every shift and snort.

Once horsemen, now herdsmen. The royal indigo robes seemed threadbare and thin of late. A small people, crumbling underfoot like the soil. "If we are destined to disappear, we are destined to disappear." Those were the words they sang, handed down over generations, given voice, plaintive over the fields. "But if so, we will go with our swords drawn."

There were no hoofbeats of horses across the savannah now, not in pursuit or protection. There was only one foot sliding in front of the other, again and again and again. Only that.

Despair comes slowly, crawling its way up inside you until it threatens to overwhelm everything; it buckles the knees, makes you falter, makes you break stride. She felt drawn out, weak. Too tired to sob, or even sigh, she'd watch the next cluster of tin roofs and market stalls plod toward her, would feel hollow and defeated.

In those moments she would hold her hands *just so*. She would will herself forward until despair was replaced by something stronger.

She knew that if she could just keep walking, she could out-walk anything, could outwalk sadness, outwalk hunger, could outwalk whispers and bottled rage, could outwalk sha'ria law, could outwalk memory itself. In those moments she turned for strength to the Prophet, Peace be upon Him, and to God. Together, they would look into the wellspring of her heart, would know it to be pure, would guide her. And she might yet survive, Insha Allah.

At those moments, amid the thirst and headache heat, she would hold her hands just so, cupping her belly the way one might shelter a lamp in a wind. She would feel the flutter deep inside her—a stirring, a striving—and that too would whisper: *Keep walking, don't stop.*

32

My Dearest Henry,

Please do not endanger our endeavour. We must not give up! I understand with fullest appreciation that the hardest part has been keeping this wonderful news secret. But trust in the goodness of life and you will be rewarded! Utmost secrecy at this stage Mr. Curtis! As soon as the money has been transferred and you have taken your percentage, you may celebrate in high style with your wife and loved ones. Why not take them on that cruise you have always dreamed upon? I have heard so much about your kind nature from Miss Sandra and Victor. I only wish I could be there to see your wife Helen's face light up when you reveal the truth!

Perhaps some day we can meet and toast our friendship face to face.

With great happiness,
Lawrence Atuche, Professor of Commerce

33

On the far side of the sky: a slash of lightning, crack of bone.

Thunder without rain. It woke her from her sleep, brought with it the memory of other storms, more violent than this. Memories of lightning that snapped like a whip, hitting the Sahel repeatedly as a rider might in final gallop.

One such storm had left trees burning across the plains like torches; it was a memory so vivid it might not have been real, may have been fostered in folklore instead, in stories told and repeated until they became truer than memory.

Another flash of lightning, veining the night sky. The nights were cooler and better for walking, but the taboo was still strong within her. *Women who are with child mustn't walk after dark.* And just as well. The roads weren't safe. She had heard loud voices patrolling the highway, had seen the sweep of headlights. They weren't looking for her, just looking. But the threat was the same.

There were no burning bushes on this night, only bruised skies and a clouded moon. *I don't know if I can go on.* She whispered this to her belly. It was all she could do to sit up, to unwind the goatskin from around her legs. The harmattan dust fountained off her.

Keep walking.

It took her three tries to get the jerry can onto the folded cloth atop her head, three more to make the first step. She could see the curve of asphalt running through the hillocks, and as she walked down to meet it, she heard the scurry of something small and afraid in the underbrush.

At the blacktop she saw no sign of the night patrols, or slumbering truck drivers either, so no scraps of food to pick through. Only asphalt and—to the south—her destination. Zaria.

She had been able to see the city, low along the plains, for several days now, had been walking toward its minarets and mosque, had been laboriously rolling it toward her, trying to bring it near. But it never seemed to draw closer, always seemed to hover out of reach, an illusion born of wavering heat and a walking that grew slower and less sure with every passing day. The globe was getting more and more difficult to turn underfoot. As the sun crawled its way back up the sky, Zaria city appeared again, then disappeared, slipping behind distant hills and scrubland trees, lost to a foreground of thorn bushes and acacia.

The road brought her suddenly to an army checkpoint, and she caught her breath, steadied the jerry can. It was still early and the road was quiet. She started past the barrier the soldiers had rigged up—planks bound by hemp rope, laid across cement filled oil barrels—treading softly, eyes down. On the roadside, a single army lorry, painted a camouflage green better suited for the jungles of the Delta, was parked at a haphazard angle. Soldiers were sleeping on mats in the back.

She might have made it past, save for a young soldier who was squatting beside a small stove, boiling his morning coffee. He was startled by the sight of her and scrambled for his rifle as she hurried by. He hollered at her in the pidgin English that passed for a common language among those outsiders who couldn't speak Hausa or French. *"Hoi! Wetin dey for?"*

She kept walking. Heard him slide a round of ammunition into the chamber. A junior soldier, no doubt, given the rifle he was using. Not an AK-47 but a single bolt action, the kind her brothers had patrolled their cattle herds with.

The soldier's voice grew more frantic as she walked away. *"Wetin dey for? Get'in dis moto!"*

But she kept walking. She heard grumbled voices of other soldiers complaining and then the sudden sound of a vehicle approaching, braking hard—and a gunshot. She flinched, almost dropping the jerry can. With her arms held out, she turned slowly around, hoping it was only a warning.

They had already forgotten her. A large diesel tanker truck was slowing down, grinding gears as it came to a jerky stop at the barrier. The other soldiers woke and tumbled out, wanting to make sure they got their share. Not a gunshot, an engine backfiring. And a modern form of ambush trading. She spotted the senior officer striding up to the driver's window, an AK-47 in hand, authority in every step, and she turned, hurried on.

Moments later the truck rumbled past, draping her in a chalky cloud. She was once again invisible.

34

My Dear Henry,
    Regarding the transfer of funds into your account.
I'm afraid there's been a problem ...

35

As she walked into Zaria, the traffic increased, with battered cars and wheezing buses funnelling into the city. On the outskirts, she made a hesitant foray into a motor park that was crowded under an overpass. Hawkers with wares stacked high on their heads were moving among the trucks and long-haul buses, singing out their offers, haggling with passengers.

She had to be mindful of former *almajiri,* the street boys who roamed the motor parks and flyovers of the north in feral packs. The youngest sons of indigent families, the *almajiri* began as beggars and foragers, but often grew into full-time thieves and freelance thugs. By the time they reached their teens, many of them were already part of an ad-hoc army-for-hire. Extortionists and vote-rigging politicians alike relied on them. And no sooner had the fear begun to rise inside her than she spotted several of these former *almajiri* prowling the perimeter, planks with nails driven through resting casually on their shoulders. She ducked away before they noticed her, choosing the busiest crowds of people to squeeze through, fighting down the panic. Street boys were territorial, and a bustling motor park like this would be clearly demarcated, right down to specific bus stalls and taxi stands.

She needed to get deeper into the city.

The main road ran through the Sabon Gari, "the strangers' quarters," a sprawling neighbourhood that housed the city's motley assortment of outsiders and unbelievers: southern Christians and members of smaller pagan clans, Yoruba traders and Tiv day labourers.

Rumours of dark magic haunted the Sabon Gari, *juju* spells that could make one mad with blood lust. In the Sabon Gari, the stalls served millet wine and back-tavern gin with a brazen disregard for sha'ria strictures. Banners beside the doors advertised Gulder Beer and Star Ale with hand-painted signs above that read MERRY YOURSELF GUEST SPOT! and REFRESH YOURSELF COOL SPOT. Codes that even she could crack. Alcohol, although banned in the sha'ria states, was tolerated in the Sabon Gari enclaves. Though she was very much a stranger, she didn't belong in the Sabon Gari, and she knew it.

It was now late afternoon, and traffic was backed up, drivers blaring their horns in impotent anger. Queen Elizabeth II Road curved past the sha'ria courthouse, and her chest tightened as she went by, fighting the urge to run.

Directly across from the courts was the raucous clatter of a hotel bar. Sha'ria law on one side, Western sins on the other—each pretending the other didn't exist. She skirted the hotel grounds, where a muddle of foreign words leaked out from barroom doorways, punctuated with sudden bursts of laughter. These would be Nigerian businessmen from the Christian south, or traders from Ghana; there might even be a few pink-faced *batauri*, what other Nigerians called *oyibos*. She'd heard how these *batauri*, foolish and indiscriminate, would fling their money about as though it were dried petals. If she could find a *batauri* businessman basting in alcohol and blasphemy, she might be able to induce a few nairas' worth of pity money ... She edged closer, but a security guard spotted her and cut across, his path intersecting hers, his voice yelling out in anger as she quickly withdrew.

Beyond the hotel grounds, a heavy-set woman minded a fruit stall at a small market. Wealthy, given the quality of her head scarf and bracelets. She scowled at the girl but allowed her to come nearer. The girl pleaded softly, speaking Hausa, her voice dry with dust, palms held outward in supplication. *"Faranta zuciya,"* she whispered. *"Faranta zuciya ... "*

"Don'me?" the woman demanded. *Why?*

"Don'me?" said the girl. *"Don'me?"* In answer, she cupped her belly, looked back at the woman, eye to eye.

The market woman snorted at this, but then, with the slightest of movements, she gestured with her chin toward an overripe mango on the ground beside her stall. The fallen fruit, bloated with sweetness, was shrouded in a hover of tiny flies, and the market woman looked the other way as the girl retrieved its pulpy weight, water can balanced precariously as she knelt.

She crouched in a doorway, ate greedily, right down to the rind. The sweetness would get her through a few more steps, and as long as she always took that next step, she would never fall.

The day was seeping away. The clay and concrete of Zaria

glowed rust-red in the light of a dying sun. People were flocking home, trying to beat the darkness, and she followed them over the rail tracks and across a girder bridge above the milk-tea waters of the Kubani River.

She had entered Tudun Wada, the colonial section of the city, built by the British, its regal facades now faded. As businesses emptied for the day, chophouse light bulbs flickered on. *It's not safe here.* She could feel this in her belly, and she began to look for a place to hide. She found it along the water's edge, by the marshy shoreline of the river: undeveloped and littered with rubbish and small plots of planted maize. She threaded her way along squelchy grass, avoided voices and well-trodden paths, sought refuge in the burned shell of a Peugeot taxi where she curled herself in, to once again wait out the night.

All through the evening she heard laughing male voices passing by and then—the laughter was upon her. Voices outside the taxi frame. A pause, followed by the sudden sound of piss hitting the side of the car. She cupped her belly to calm it, as though the flutter inside might somehow give her away, and she waited for the moment to pass. The voices grew fewer and farther away until all she heard were whispered winds and the sound of a nearby goat ripping up grass.

She fell into sleep, like a body down a well.

36

She woke to beauty: the wailing cry of the *muezzin* calling out to the faithful from minaret heights.

She walked down to the water's edge and bathed in a hidden bend of river. Sifted through cobs of fallen maize along the shore. No way to cook them, and no time to let them soak in water to soften, but she tucked several into the folded pockets of her robe anyway, would chew on the kernels later if she had to; it might fool her body into believing it had been fed.

A soft light had settled on the musky riverside, and she followed a path back to the bridge. The sleepy streets were filling with worshippers, men in white robes and embroidered prayer caps.

The dusty rasp of a rooster could be heard across rooftops. She entered the Old City, its walls catching the morning light, the sun bringing a texture and warmth to its surfaces. These city walls had stood for a thousand years. Crumbling, true, but formidable still. Patched over and propped up, with goats now grazing atop and squatters perched in ragged tents along their mud-brown heights, the Zaria walls were more mounds than bastions. But they stood in testament to a past rich in war and trade. Amina, Queen of Zaria, whose walls these had been, had once controlled an empire that stretched as far as the Niger River. And wherever Queen Amina's armies moved, she had built walled cities, *ribat* fortresses, *birni* defenceworks.

"We were the reason they built these walls."

The voice of one of her aunts floated to the surface. The girl in indigo had been here before, at these walls, in this town. It would have been the farthest south her family had ever come, back when they were still trading and she was still a child. *It must have been on caravan.* From the flamingos of Bula Tura in the north to these crumbling clay walls encircling Zaria's Old City, the range of her clan's travels had been shrinking ever since.

She looked up at the walls, reached out, laid her hand against them. It surprised her, how cool they were to the touch. Powdery on the surface, but with a solid mass behind them. She remembered entering the Old City on the sway of camels, but it must have been horseback. The first daughter of a junior wife, she had been spoiled by the older wives, treated as a communal granddaughter. She remembered metal wares and cooking pots clanking against animal flanks, the bundled rolls of cloth and the singsong laughter of her aunts calling out. Laughing as they entered the gates. "They built these walls to keep us out. But we are here. We are here."

There was a time when her people had wrested control of the salt trade from the Hausa and the Fulani, from the Kingdom of Sokoto itself, had controlled the Sahel trade as far as Timbuktu. "The Sultans of Sokoto kept watch for the dust of our hooves."

Horse riders in a land of plodding camels. Lions of the Sahel. *We were raiders. Traders, unfettered and free. Walls cannot stop those who are free.* The words echoed in her as she walked through the Old City. But she knew as well as anyone that the lions of the northern savannah were long gone, lingering now only in folk songs and protected game reserves far distant. Her kinsmen had moved farther and farther away from the past, until the past itself was only a story, a distant murmur, like voices on the other side of a wall.

We count our wealth in cattle. But there was a time we counted it in gold.

Children chased a soccer ball across a vacant lot, robes flying, as grandmothers beat the night's dust from caked rugs. Mothers and daughters were hand-wringing washing in backyards as the *muezzin* call to prayer continued.

She followed the flow of white-clad men into a vast court-yard. These were the grounds of the Emir's Palace. A grand slab of prestige, the surface of the Emir's Gate was embedded with ceramic tiles—she remembered that, too, the intricate interwoven patterns as familiar to her as a dream. The lower courtyard was still in shade, but the slant of the sun had caught the upper mosaic, making the ceramics glow like illuminated embroidery. Like jewels embedded in a scabbard.

"Forward! Move forward!"

The emir's guards, leathery men in scarlet robes and turbans, stood at the gate keeping watch on the crowds. She was jostled from behind by young men hurrying past, and she steadied her jerry can, forced herself to become calm, took comfort in her own lack of significance. Swallows darted through as the crowds pushed toward the mosque. The mosque was directly across from the palace, and the minarets and dome were catching the light now as well.

She hadn't chosen this site by chance; she had followed the worshippers with intent. Keeping back from the main entrance, not wanting to overstep her bounds, she stopped at an alleyway instead, where footsteps and bodies were forced to slow down. She put her jerry can on the ground and stood, hands together, palms out, whispering a reminder to those who passed that almsgiving was as much a pillar of faith as prayer.

"*Zakat,*" she whispered. "*Faranta zuciya. Zakat.*"

The men who streamed by in billowing pants and flowing vests, the cloth pristine and white, were wearing their finest caps, snug on head. Most ignored her pleas or pretended not to hear. Some were annoyed, others irritated. But a few good souls dug into pouchlike pockets to hand her a few kobo or crumpled naira as they passed, careful not to touch her hand.

The sound of trumpets. A stir in the far court. The emir himself was making his way across from the palace to the mosque, a weekly walk through the crowded courtyard, his black turban seeming to float above the crowds. A cannon was fired to herald his appearance, a single reverberating boom. As a retinue of scarlet-turbaned guards forced a path in front of him, the emir clasped hands, accepted wishes of good health and longevity, nodded patiently at hurried accounts of matters personal and pressing, smiled in benevolence. For one mad moment she considered pushing through the throng of bodies and throwing herself on the emir's mercy—but the crowds were too thick and her body too weak. The courtyard of worshippers now emptied into the mosque, and she hoisted her half-empty jerry can back onto her head and moved on.

With Friday prayers came Friday classes. At a schoolyard in the Old City, boys in short sleeves and short pants and girls in long dresses, impeccably clean, gathered under a nearby tree, tablets in hand, laughing and pushing while their teacher peered at them over half-lens reading glasses, frowning them into silence. *"Ina kwana,"* he said.

"Ina kwana!" they chimed back.

Fulani girls, wrapped in head scarves as all girls were once they reached the walking age, hung back, shyer than the others, but the Hausa boys were boisterous and full of boasts. One of their classmates was struggling at the front, writing out a passage of scripture with grave determination. The others laughed at his efforts, and he grinned sheepishly until the teacher finally rose and waved the student away amid more laughter. As the girl in indigo passed, she heard the furious scratch of chalk on board, and the teacher saying *"See? As such."* This was followed by the sound of recitation, the children chanting out the words, the lessons growing fainter with every step.

Memories of her own tablet school instructions. Of wooden boards and Arabic scripture in outdoor schools. The various *malams* who had led the lessons, some gentle, some stern, all now fading as well. Geometry class and the laws of intersecting lines. The *malam* using a wooden compass, drawing a perfect circle on the chalkboard, and then using a measuring stick to slice across it, as clean as a razor. God's hand at work. She remembered the beauty of it, the clarity.

She belonged in a market; she was born of trade. Perhaps she might find an arthritic market lady who needed a sweeper, a stacker? Perhaps she might work her way up, minding stalls for the wealthier market ladies while they went about their errands. It was a wisp of a dream, like trying to catch wind in your hand, and she knew it. With no money to purchase a spot, no kinship ties or connections with the guilds that ran the markets, all she had was desperation and sincerity. And that would never be enough.

37

"Can you feel?"

She could.

"Embossed. First rate."

Laura ran her fingertips lightly across the letterhead.

She was in Meeting Room 2B at the Economic Crime Unit offices in the city's northeast.

Officer Brisebois was there, as was Laura's brother, her mother, and a pair of detectives: an older man, who introduced himself as Detective David Saul, and a younger woman named Detective Rhodes. Just Rhodes. No first name, apparently. The detectives didn't wear uniforms, but they might as well have: both were dressed in dark jackets and white shirts with starched collars.

Ice water in a pitcher. Cubes clinking on every pour. A wide table. Several thick folders. Flowers in the corner, petals too pink and leaves too green for this room. There was a window directly behind Laura, but the sunlight didn't reach the plants. They must be artificial; that's why they looked so healthy. Laura's dad had often joked that if anyone could kill an artificial plant, she could.

Behind the detectives, on the wall facing Laura, was a framed photograph: a black-and-white image of tree branches against a grey sky. An odd counterpoint to the plastic greenery in the corner.

The female detective was speaking.

"The only defence we really have with these types of fraud," Detective Rhodes said, "is education."

The detective was petite, fine featured, confident. She had a no-nonsense wedding band on her heart finger, would have chosen it for its durability, no doubt, thought Laura. The older detective—stone-cut face, close-cropped hair—wore no wedding band. Instead: a pale line where one used to be. Sergeant Brisebois had the same pale absence. Did they get together, Brisebois and this older version of himself? Compare tan lines, commiserate over beer about the decisions they'd made, the regrets they gathered?

"These are just some of the samples our department has gathered over the years."

Detective Saul passed a stack of pages across to Warren, who studied them as if they were ciphers in a puzzle he might yet solve. When no key revealed itself, Warren muttered and handed them off to his mother, who barely looked at them.

"Some are quite amateurish," said the younger detective. "Laughable, even, but a good many are almost, well, works of art."

The documents piled up in front of Laura. The headings on them were at once very specific and oddly vague: a Fund Management Agreement Form issued by the Central Bank of Nigeria; an International Remittance Voucher; invoices for expenses.

"Let's see," said Detective Rhodes as she passed the next batch over. "We've got a Certificate of Registration. Various tax receipts. A Foreign Exchange Application, signed and stamped. A demand for an overdue payment to the Nigerian Economic Recovery Fund."

On it went.

Bank processing invoices. Official contracts from the Niger Delta Development Commission. Various "Letters of Intent," affidavits, court orders, banking forms. All duly signed, duly sealed. There were elaborate Anti–Money Laundering Clearance

Certificates replete with flags and baroque borders, and equally elaborate Anti-Terrorism Certificates ("Under the Terms of the Revised National Security Anti-Terrorism Decree 25, Section B"). Each with a heavy APPROVED stamped across it.

"That last item is purportedly from Interpol," Detective Rhodes explained. "We have several of them, actually. This one here was issued—what does it say—'with the cooperation of the International Monetary Fund, certifying that the funds in question have no connections to any known terrorist organization.'"

"Interpol?" said Warren. "Tell me you've contacted them."

"We haven't."

"Why not?"

"Because there's no such thing as an Anti-Terrorism Certificate."

Laura's attention drifted back to the black-and-white photograph on the wall behind the detectives. The branches on the tree began to move. Only a faint tremble at first, so soft she almost missed it. Then a sway, a shift, and she turned around, startled, to check the window behind her. She saw the same branches outside. It wasn't a photograph on the wall opposite her; it was a reflection.

She looked at the branches moving on glass.

"Is that a mirror?" she demanded, her voice sharper than she'd intended. "Who's behind there? Is someone watching?"

This stopped the conversation in mid-syllable. The older detective turned, not sure at first what Laura was referring to. "No, there's no one back there."

But Laura wasn't appeased. "Is this some sort of—secret interrogation? Are we being watched?"

"Ma'am," said Rhodes. "There's no one on the other side. That's just a window onto a hallway. We don't interrogate, we *interview*. And that's not what this is. Frankly, we're here today because your brother has been badgering us. Lodging complaints, saying we aren't doing enough to catch the culprits who swindled your father. He wanted to see 'the evidence.' Well, here it is."

"Jesus, Laura," Warren whispered. "Relax."

"You're telling *me* to relax? You? Of all people?"

"Laura, dear." This was their mother. "Let them do their job. No one's watching. It's just a window."

"It looks like a mirror."

The detectives continued handing documents across the table, but Brisebois kept his eyes on Laura, watched the tension and anxiety draw the edges of her mouth tight—until, quietly, he slipped out of his seat and walked around behind the family to the main window. He closed the blinds. And as he did, the reflection across from Laura disappeared. The glass changed from mirror to window. A hallway emerged on the other side, empty.

They were right; there was no one watching. There was no one on the other side.

38

The market in Zaria's Old City had been a terminus of the trans-Sahara trade route, and even now a few camels loped by with knock knees on tethered strides. Spices and grains in every shade, lumpy roots and medicinal herbs, groundnuts and millet heaped atop woven display trays with umbrellas opened above to protect the wares from the worst of the sun. This was where she belonged.

Women moved through, heads balancing overstuffed baskets of produce, coarse gunny sacks of woven jute—both the women and their cargo bulging with sustenance and commerce. The girl envied the wealth of the market ladies, the confident sway of their hips.

Passageways twisted back on themselves, a maze that seemed to shift even as you entered. Gap-toothed smiles, low chuckles.

Ongoing feuds played out as she passed—market women hectoring the air between competing stalls, hand gestures flying every which way. Arguments were entertainment. Crowds quickly formed, and no one noticed as she slipped past.

There were Fulani saddles and leather harnesses studded with silver. The tables were swaybacked with goods. Millet and guinea corn. Mounds of yams, piled high, and pyramids of Benue oranges. Cassette players and tinny music. Grand displays of rubber flip-flops, racks of plastic sunglasses. Such abundance.

She walked across rickety slats, above sluicing drains that flowed with offal and runoff. Chophouse stalls lined the walk. Butcher blocks, splattered with blood and speckled with flies. Skewers of roasting grasshoppers hand-turned by sweat-dripping young boys. She passed racks of *kilishi* drying in the sun, the meat crusted with red pepper and delectable just to look at. She fought her way past *fate* vendors selling soups thick with couscous. Women stirred bubbling pots of *efo elegusi*—she could taste the bitter greens and melon seeds in the steam—and firepits simmered with *semovita* and pepper soup. She felt light-headed with hunger, ached for even a mouthful of *amala*.

Beyond the food stalls, in an open square, a band of acrobats were balancing on machete blades. Hand on jerry can, she pushed her way into the crowd. Where acrobats gathered, coins were tossed, and where coins were tossed, coins were lost. Contortionists vied for applause: young men standing with one leg thrown over their shoulders as casually as a scarf, while they just as casually ate great mouthfuls of fire and then spewed the flames above the crowd. Cymbals added an urgency to the proceedings. She turned her gaze from the spectacle, eyed the crowds instead.

And there, in among the sandalled feet, a crumpled bill, fallen loose. Twenty naira at least. Perhaps if she pretended to stumble, dropped the jerry can from her head, used it as a cover to bend down, reach out …

Was that stealing, or scavenging? She looked at her right hand, imagined it gone.

And in that moment, she realized she was being watched.

She glanced back, saw one of the emir's guards suddenly near at hand: scarlet turban, sun-seared features. He was looking at her looking at the crumpled money on the ground, and he now moved toward her. The dust of invisibility she'd worked so hard to pull around her had suddenly blown aside like harmattan sand. She turned to push away, heard the guard call out and turned back, choking on her fear. But when she met his gaze, his yellowed eyes were not enraged. Instead, they cast down at the naira. He nudged the crumpled bill toward her with his foot and said, in a heavy Zamfara accent, "You've dropped something."

It would normally be considered rude, moving an item with your feet, but here in this crowd, at this moment, it was anything but. He knew and she knew. He nodded for her to go ahead and take it, and she lowered herself into a half-kneeling stance, snatched the money up, whispered *"Na gode,"* and disappeared into the crowd.

She huddled in a doorway, pulled the other soiled bills from her folded pocket, flattened them out in her palm. Even with the coins she'd gathered outside the mosque, it was not enough for a full meal. But it would be enough for an egg and maybe a small bowl of *fura da nono,* yogurt mixed with millet, mixed with ginger. A woman at the stall scooped some out for her, waited for her to finish so she could collect the bowl. It tasted like the savannah after a rain. Yogurt for the child, millet for the walking, ginger for the courage.

And just when she thought she might yet make it, might stay in Zaria and work her way into a lower position at one of the market stalls, she heard a voice across from her. Male, asking her, *"Bede? Kanuri?"*

A toothless man wrapped in Sahel layers was addressing her, grinning wide, trying to read her scars.

Scars tell a story. They always do, and he gestured with his chin to her patterned skin. *"Dukawa? Dakakari? Aregwa?"*

His guesses were getting closer, were narrowing in on her, and she fled.

"Adarawa? Tuareg?" he called out. His voice became lost to street noise, but the shock of it echoed through her rib cage.

39

The Zaria dye pits lay beyond the market, near the edge of town. Here, rolls of cloth were soaked for days in a rich sludge of ash and indigo, the liquid fermenting to create a blue so dark it was almost black. Here, too, were the scarlet dye pits of the emir's guards, and the knotted patterns they called "Widow's Eye" and "Star in the Sky."

Royal colours were being brewed that day, crimsons that seemed to bleed from the fabric and auburns so warm they tasted of honey. She looked at her tattered robes, once a rich indigo themselves, looked at her wrists, thin and emptied of silver, felt the despair well up inside her again.

You. Must. Keep. Walking.

She filled her jerry can with water and left the city with a weight of dread upon her. Zaria was the farthest south she had ever been. Every step now would be a blind step off a tall wall.

She followed the road out of the city as the hills and scrubland opened up before her. Distant plateaus now rose in the distance; she was leaving the Sahel behind with every step.

She felt as though she had always been walking, had been born walking.

40

Laura Curtis, adrift in Room 2B, her mother and brother beside her. Detective Saul opened another folder and passed across yet another stack of papers.

"These are some of the actual documents your father received; our Tech Unit recovered them from the cached files on his hard drive. Your father had tried to delete them in the days just before his accident. He thought he'd cleared the memory, but— Here. Your father would have signed and scanned these forms, and then emailed them back to Nigeria as attachments."

Warren studied these pages with the same single-minded focus. "Look," he said. "Right here. This one's from Professor Kassory at the University of Lagos, Department of African Spirituality. And this one was sent by Joseph Sule, Senior Manager of the Credit Department in Abuja. How hard can it be to find these guys? Here's one on the letterhead of the Central Bank of Nigeria, signed by the head of the International Remittance Department himself. Look!"

"The Central Bank of Nigeria doesn't have an International Remittance Department," said Saul. "That's not what a central bank does. A central bank sets monetary policy; it doesn't chase down lost inheritances or charge fees to move money out of the country. These are counterfeits, every one of them. Counterfeits with forged signatures."

Laura caught that, the distinction between "counterfeit" and "forged." *Counterfeit:* a false item or document. *Forgery:* something altered to resemble an authentic item. A signature would be forged.

Plastic flowers would be counterfeit. Her father had been caught up not in a counterfeit world but in a forged reality, one that had been altered to appear as something else.

It was a nuance lost on her brother. "I don't know," he said. "These don't look like forgeries."

"Actually, they do. Counterfeit documents are often more elaborate and more official-looking than the real thing. A real document doesn't need to impress you with its authenticity; a counterfeit does." Detective Saul leaned in. "I doubt many people, Nigerians included, have ever seen an official document from the Central Bank or know what the letterhead of the Office of the Niger Delta Petroleum Commission looks like. Or if such an office even exists. An Anti-Terrorist Clearance Certificate? Anti–money laundering paperwork issued by the UN? Pure invention."

"The fees and documents," said Detective Rhodes, "are really only limited by the con man's imagination."

Warren turned a sour gaze on his mother. "You didn't know about any of this? You didn't happen to notice that, oh, Dad was receiving documents from the Central Bank of Nigeria?"

Rhodes answered for her. "Your father's credit card statements showed regular payments to Mailboxes & More. They have a store down in Sunnyside."

"I stopped by," said Officer Brisebois. "It's not far from my place, really. I couldn't open Mr. Curtis's mailbox without a warrant, of course, but the lady behind the counter told me not to bother. The box was empty." Then, to Laura's mother, "You wouldn't have any idea what your husband might have done with the original documents? The hard copies."

"The barbecue," she said.

"Pardon?"

"The barbecue. He made a fire a night or two before the—the

accident. I hadn't thought much of it at the time, but … he fired it up, even though the yard was full of snow. Said it was good to light it now and again, keep it from getting cobwebby." She looked at Laura, eyes wet. "I should have known something was wrong. We hadn't used that barbecue in years."

"But even without the originals, we've got a shitload of evidence right here," said Warren. "Messages sent back and forth between Dad and these criminals. Names, email addresses, phone numbers, the works."

Detective Rhodes spoke to Warren slowly, as if addressing a particularly slow-witted child. "They use free web-based email accounts, send out mass mailings—so many that they eventually get shut down. Now, it's true that our Tech Unit can sometimes and with great difficulty trace them back to a specific IP address. But even then, the messages might bounce across a dozen different countries first. All we can really say is that the emails your father received were *probably* sent from Lagos city, in Nigeria."

"I set up Dad's email account," said Warren. "His spam filter was on."

"The people behind these cons can get around spam filters. They prowl the internet constantly; it's what they do. They search classified ads, hang out in chat rooms, scroll through online directories. It's not that difficult to pull an email address out of the air. Spam filters stop a lot of it. But they don't catch everything."

"Okay, okay, I get it," said Warren. "The internet is anonymous, we know that. But look." He held up a sheaf of their dad's emails. "We've got lists of phone numbers as well. Surely you can trace the numbers or something, find out who was making those calls."

"We do have phone numbers," said Rhodes. "And no doubt your father sincerely believed he was speaking with high-placed bank managers and government ministers in high offices. But the area codes tell a different story."

Saul took it from there. "Nigeria is like the Wild West. The odds of finding anyone based on a phone number are almost nil." He slid the phone records over. "You see? The numbers all start with an eighty. In Nigeria, area codes that begin with eighty are for mobile phones, usually pay-as-you-go. You purchase minutes with no ID required, no background checks, no paper trail. The numbers, and the phones themselves, are more or less disposable. They're used and then discarded. Untraceable."

"Okay, okay," said Warren. "The phones may be disposable, but not the money. My dad sent more than two hundred grand out of the country. What about that? Someone had to sign for those payments. Someone had to deposit them into their account. If we find those accounts, we can freeze the money, maybe get some of it back."

"I'm afraid that's not possible," said Saul.

"Why the hell not?"

"Most of the money in this type of scam is paid by bank draft or wire transfer, usually using Western Union or MoneyGram. The funds can be sent to one office, then picked up at another. Anywhere in the world, really. Again, there's no paper trail, no background checks, no bank account numbers, no vetting process. Postal money orders, wire transfers, online payments: it's like sending cash."

"You might as well be stuffing an envelope with unmarked bills," said Rhodes.

"Police in Nigeria would have to nab a scammer at an actual agent's office," the older detective explained, "just as he was in the act of picking up cash with false ID in hand, and even then ... What? We don't have an extradition treaty with Nigeria. Even if we did, the people who collect the payments are usually low-ranking mules. And I imagine the police in Nigeria have more pressing matters to deal with than staking out the local MoneyGram to protect foreigners like ourselves from ourselves. It's the nature of 419."

Laura looked up, attention piqued as always by a new term. "Four one nine?"

"That's what they call these scams. The name comes from the section in the Nigerian Criminal Code that deals with obtaining money or goods under false pretenses. Any kind of fraud, really. It's entered the lexicon over there." Laura's renewed interest encouraged Saul. "Nigerians have a wry sense of humour," he said. "Four one nine now refers to any sort of ruse or swindle. A boy who tries to hide his report card from his dad will be accused of trying to '419' him. Girls who have a boyfriend on the side are said to be '419ing' the fellow. They've got pop songs over there that celebrate the wiles of the 419ers. Some of the more flamboyantly successful of these scammers have been elevated to folk hero status. But don't be fooled: 419 is a business. It brings in hundreds of millions of dollars a year. It's bigger than Nigeria; it's as old as sin. As old as desire. These 419ers, they prey on people's dreams. Average loss in a 419 scam is somewhere to the tune of $250,000—often more. The going rate for dreams, apparently."

"They're laughing at us," said Warren. "I can hear the fuckers now, living large on Dad's money. I tell you, if I find these assholes …"

"Not a smart idea," Saul replied. "The 419 business is intimately intertwined with more violent crimes. Narcotics, human trafficking, bank robberies, you name it. The syndicates that run the heroin trade in Nigeria often have their fingers in 419 as well. And 419 can be just as lucrative, but with less mess."

"You seem to know an awful lot about Nigeria," said Warren.

"I do."

Laura looked at the detective. "You've been there, haven't you?"

"I have."

"Lagos?"

He nodded.

"What was it like?"

"It was like looking into the future."

"That bad?"

He nodded.

"Here," he said. "Let me show you something." He produced a Google Maps version of West Africa. "Nigeria's here, at the bottom of the bulge. The Niger River runs through it, empties into the Atlantic Ocean at the Niger Delta. The Delta is a huge area, home to one of the richest petroleum fields in the world. It's also one of the most dangerous places on earth. The militants and local warlords in the Delta have declared war on the oil companies. You might have heard about it in the news."

They hadn't.

"Masked men," Saul went on, "in speedboats, attacking pipelines and oil wells, blowing up offshore oil platforms. The militants have been kidnapping and killing foreign workers with an unsettling ease as well. And not just workers. Any foreigner is considered fair game. In fact, oil, kidnappings, and 419 fraud are Nigeria's three biggest growth industries, and they often overlap. The Niger Delta fuels Nigeria's economy."

Literally, Laura thought.

"Lagos is over here." The detective ran his finger back along the coast. "Not in the Delta, but on the same coast. The city was named by the Portuguese. Means swamp or pond water or something. This entire stretch of shore used to be known as the

Slave Coast. It was dangerous even then. The early explorers wrote warnings on their maps: *'Many go in, few come out.'* If you were to show up today, start poking around, asking questions, odds are you'd end up in Lagos Lagoon with a surprised look on your face. For anyone thinking of making the trip to Nigeria to recoup their losses, my advice is simple: don't."

Laura now understood the significance of the empty hallway on the other side of the glass. The detectives were telling the truth. No one *was* watching. Why? Because there would be no more investigation, no follow-up. *They've already put Dad to rest. They're just walking us through the why of it.*

She looked at the older detective, said, "The money's gone, isn't it?"

He nodded.

The money. And her father too. "You're not going to arrest anybody, are you?"

"We'll forward what we have to the RCMP and they'll log the information, but—honestly? There's not much more we can do."

Officer Brisebois had been studying Laura's face. When he spoke his voice was soft. "No one," he said, "is going to be arrested."

41

Heavy rains had left Lagos steaming with humidity. On nights like this, even silk clung to the skin.

Cemetery Road makes a clean cut through the Lagos mainland. South from the Badagry Expressway, past the Baales Palace and the mosque, it takes a sudden turn, slicing across side streets before rejoining the expressway farther down. In doing so, Cemetery Road carves out a sizable stretch of territory, with the cyber cafés of Festac Town at one end and the bridges of Lagos Lagoon at the other.

Any headstones that might yet have stood along Cemetery Road had long been lost, buried by the false-front clutter of petrol stands and apartment block add-ons. But if you knew where to look—past the Ayodele Nursery School, where the road suddenly turns, and before it crosses Odofin Street—you'd find a high wall and wrought-iron gate. This slab of whitewashed cement, with its mausoleum-like entrance, might easily have been mistaken for the entrance to the street's namesake graveyard. It wasn't. It was the gateway to the International Businessman's Export Club, though it wasn't labelled as such. Wasn't labelled at all, in fact.

Winston waited as the thin man with the swampy eyes buzzed the gate, then turned to face the surveillance cameras.

The click of tumblers unlocking. And inside: a surprising sight. An open courtyard angled with luxury cars, their surfaces beaded with water, gleam-polished and parked in their own reflections. Even in the grip of a raw-throated fear, Winston passed this stationary parade of vehicles with something akin to reverence. Audi, Benz, Cadillac, Rolls—the names tripped off the tongue like honeyed sweets.

Boxes within boxes. Past the courtyard of cars, a second door, heavier than the first, and beyond that, another courtyard. High walls, no windows. Cobblestones stained with scorch marks, and the weight of heavy air trapped inside.

At the far side of this courtyard, another door, and once through it, a warren of interconnecting rooms—interconnecting buildings, actually—with corridors and angles that didn't quite line up. The thin man flowed through them with a singular grace, nonetheless. Down one hallway and up the next. Rooms adorned with art, African and otherwise, and in one antechamber waiting area a pair of languid-lidded women who watched Winston pass with an indifference that bordered on contempt. He nodded to them, but they did nothing in response. Not even blink.

Somewhere: the sound of someone coughing. The sound grew louder as they entered a passageway lined with mirrors and came to a final door. And then—the smell of mentholated balm and something sweeter still, like fruit, overripe, or blood on the back of the tongue.

"Oga, sir, I have him."

A large room, dimly lit. A wide desk. A face that was turned away, coughing into a handkerchief. Shoulders straining against the seams of a dress shirt with every hack, every gasp. The voice, when it came, was weak. Was strong. Was both. A wave of a hand, with back still turned. "Sit, sit." And then: "Tunde"—for that was the name of the man with the swampy eyes—"fetch the boy something iced to drink."

Tunde slipped away as Winston took a seat in front of the desk. A solid slab of polished wood glowing in the half-light.

The other man turned to face Winston for the first time. "Have you eaten?" Face like a fist. Eyes rimmed red.

Winston bobbed his head, tried his best to smile. "I have, sir, yes. Thank you for asking."

"I go by the name Ironsi-Egobia. They call me Oga, but please—'Mister' is fine. I do not dwell on pleasantries nor embellish myself with formalities. You are sitting too stiffly. Relax yourself, please."

"Thank you, sir." Winston let his shoulders loosen, ever so slightly.

"I have told you my name. You have not told me yours."

"Adam, sir."

"Ah, the first man. A good choice. You have been frequenting some of my cafés, haven't you, Adam? You always tip the cashiers, not too much, but not too little either. You tip—carefully. You never raise a ruckus, always maintain a well-mannered air. And you eschew the company of the yahoo boys. From this, I surmise you are educated."

"Yes, sir."

"College?"

"University."

"Here in Lagos?"

"Yes, sir." A lie. Not in Lagos, but educated still.

"So," said Ironsi-Egobia with a twitch of the lips. "You have done your parents proud, then?"

"I suppose, yes ..."

Ironsi-Egobia reeled away, covered his mouth with his handkerchief and coughed into it from the lungs, coughed so deeply and for so long that his face was clammy with sweat when he turned around again. There was blood on the handkerchief; Winston pretended not to notice.

Tunde had reappeared as silently as he'd left, with glasses of lemonade balanced on a tray and a silver bowl with a large chunk of ice inside. He passed the bowl across to his Oga, who picked up an ice pick that lay like a letter opener on his desk. Ironsi-Egobia stabbed at the ice, then dropped a shard of it into Winston's glass—with the same fingers that only moments before he'd been coughing blood into.

Do not hesitate. Drink. "Thank you, sir," said Winston, raising the glass to his lips. He wiped his mouth when he was done. "Very refreshing."

"This ice pick I am holding in my hand," began Ironsi-Egobia. "With today's refrigerator freezer cubes, who would need such a thing? Why do they still make them? A sign of ostentatious airs, that is all, like India ink and a nibbed pen. When you see an ice pick today, it is merely a symbol of status. And a weapon. Like a pen, also." He smiled, and in doing so, invited Winston to smile as well.

The ice pick in Ironsi-Egobia's hand now loomed very large, filling the space between them.

"I am from the Niger Delta," Ironsi-Egobia said. "But I was raised in Old Calabar, by the Jesuits, among the Efik. A beautiful town, Calabar. You know of it?"

"I have never been to the east, sir, but I know of Calabar, yes. A Portuguese colony in its day, I believe?"

"That's right. My name—my *real* name—is Michael, like the angel. But even that is not mine. It was gifted to me by the Brothers at the Seminary. The truth? I don't even remember my real name." He laughed at this, laughed until overtaken by coughs. Then, grinning, eyes watering, he said, "Don't you find that funny? A boy in a Christian seminary who cannot remember his Christian name?"

"I—I'm not sure." He looked to Tunde, but Tunde betrayed no hint of whether or not Winston should laugh.

"Ironsi-Egobia is the name I *adopted,* to steel my resolve, to bring myself fortune. To reward my ambitions."

Egobia was from the Igbo language, the language spoken in Port Harcourt and the upper Delta. *Ego* meant "money," and *bia* meant "come to me," making Egobia more an incantation than an actual name. *"Money come."*

And Ironsi?

"From the general," he explained. "A man of bone, a man of strength, a leader."

This would be the general who had taken power after the 1966 January Coup, the same coup that left Nigeria's prime minister dead and the regional premiers rounded up and imprisoned. This would be the general who was himself toppled in a counter-coup six months later, and then kidnapped, tortured, and killed. Some said he was tied to a Land Rover and dragged to his death. Others that he was executed in military fashion with a single bullet to the head. Still others that he died in an orgy of gunfire, his body almost pulped by it.

General Ironsi had been feted by Queen Elizabeth, and had been a UN commander in the Congo before making his lunge for power. Winston had seen photographs of the general—or rather, of the Queen with General Ironsi beside her, on Her Majesty's tour of Nigeria back before all the coups and counter-coups, when Nigeria was still part of the British Empire. That was the same year petroleum was discovered in the Delta. Perhaps that was why Ironsi-Egobia had chosen the name. Winston had seen the famous photo on top of his parents' living room dresser in a handsome frame of polished mahogany, knew the face of General Ironsi well.

"The name flows like palm wine, don't you agree? *Ironsi-Egobia.*"

Power. Money. Magic. "It does, yes," said Winston, feeling weak.

"General Ironsi was Igbo. The word 'egobia' is to harvest luck. The hyphen between binds them together. That is where I exist, you see, in the hyphen. It is where I reside. I came to Lagos as a young lad, looking to make my way in this house of mirrors." He smiled. "But I could find no exit. Everywhere I saw only my own face, my own hunger, looking back at me. So I searched for a hammer instead. And I found it. I trained under the chairman, under Ubah himself. I learned everything Ubah had to teach me—and more. I learned how not to get caught. I knew Anini before the Libyans got him. I ran errands for Tafa when he was still Inspector General of the Police, before he became known as Inspector General of Thieves. And when they caught Tafa in their net, I slipped free into muddier waters. Have you tried to spear a fish in muddy water? It's very difficult. When Nwude Emmanuel scammed the Brazilian banks for millions, I knew before anyone. And when they were moving in to corner Nwude, I knew that, too—knew it even before he did." Ironsi-Egobia leaned back, arms behind his head, as though considering the question for the first time. "How did I manage such a feat? How did I survive while others stumbled and fell? How did an Efik-Ijaw mongrel such as me, an orphan from the mangrove swamps, how was it I triumphed in a city as—*unforgiving* as Lagos?"

Winston wasn't sure if this was a question he was meant to answer.

"Ruthless integrity, that is how. My boys include Igbo, Yoruba, Hausa, Fulani. I don't separate, I ask only for their loyalty—and their honesty. Why? Because we who traffic in falsehoods must put a premium on the truth. You be 419ing?"

"Yes."

"Who for?"

"For none."

"I ask you again. Who is banking your efforts, who is it has been keeping you out of jail? Who is it has been creeping catlike into my territory?"

"None, sir."

"None? A freeman, then?"

Winston nodded.

"Do you hear that, Tunde? We have before us a freeman navigator, one who has chosen my cafés—*mine*—to ply his trade. We should be honoured!"

"Sir, if I have caused offence—"

"No, no," he said. "Not at all. *Know your way, no be curse.* Guyman brethren, we are one and the same." Then: "Your glass is empty."

Only ice left.

"Tunde, fetch some fresh." Another round of coughing, another blood stain carefully folded back into a handkerchief, another pour of lemonade, another offer of ice. "The Italians of Africa," said Ironsi-Egobia. "That's what they call us. Did you know that? They say we Nigerians are the Italians of Africa. But truly, it is *you* they are talking about. The Yoruba. You and your kin, you are the Italians. Your watch. Rolex?"

"A knock-off, yes."

He nodded, suitably impressed. "And a fine knock-off, from here."

"Thank you."

"The Italians of Africa. And the Igbo? The Jews of Africa, that is what they say. The Hausa and Fulani are even called 'the Arabs of Africa.' A ridiculous statement, because the *Arabs* are the Arabs of Africa. You hear this sort of nonsense constantly. Lagos is the New York of Nigeria. Abuja is our Washington, D.C., Port Harcourt is our Dallas, and so forth. But we were here first. Did not humanity pour out from Africa? Everything human—it has its origins here, all the good, all the bad. So, I ask you, Adam, first man, why are *we* the Italians of anything? It is the *Italians* who are the Nigerians of Europe. It is New York that is the Lagos of America. Dallas that is the Port Harcourt of Texas. More ice?" Another stab, another bare-fingered drop into Winston's lemonade. "You've heard the song, Adam, the one they sing, '419 Is Just a Game'?"

"I have, sir, yes."

"It is not a game. It is a business, and do you know what that business is? Retribution."

"Retribution?"

"Look at Brazil. Its wealth was built on the back of the slave trade. The slave trade fuelled their coffers, provided capital, labour.

Rich Brazilians enjoy a life they have inherited from unspeakable crimes. Why should we weep when a Brazilian bank is taken for millions then? Blood money, all of it. Slaves and diamonds, gold and oil. Even chocolate. It is all stained. Where would England be without Africa? England without Africa is England without Empire. The crowns of British royalty glitter with blood, with rubies and emeralds wrenched out of Africa. When you were in university, did you not study African history?"

"I—I studied commerce."

"Commerce bears the fruits of history, Adam. If we Nigerians are good at thieving, we learned it from the British. We may plunder bank accounts; they plundered entire continents. But I say to you: if distrust is stronger than trust, and hate is stronger than love, envy is stronger than adulation. And I assure you, we will take back our share of what was stolen. The banks in Europe and America— rolling in money like a pig in slop, they have grown fat on our misery. And they continue to grow fat even now. Where does the money from the Delta oil fields flow? Into offshore accounts, into foreign banks, back to the descendants of slave traders. Fat-faced *oyibos* fart like kings behind gated compounds in Port Harcourt, while the people outside live on table scraps and snot. Why should these bankers, these slavers—these *criminals*—not return some of their lootings to the continent they have helped impoverish? Justice demands it. God demands it. *The sins of the fathers shall be visited upon their children.* And not just the children, but the children's children as well. Read the Bible, it's all in there. Make no mistake, Adam, we are in the business of retribution. We are in the business of revenge."

Never mind that the manager of that Brazilian bank Ironsi-Egobia was referring to was Japanese. Never mind that the latest 419 exploit, reported breathlessly by the press, had bankrupted a

Taiwanese businessman. Never mind the widow in Hong Kong, taken for everything. Never mind that Nigerian 419ers preyed on their fellow Nigerians and targeted expat Nigerians as well, with bogus phone calls from bogus hospitals, demanding money for life-saving treatments for relatives. Any guyman worthy of the name would never limit himself to wealthy whites. A scammer will scam, as surely as a *mugu* will tumble. Race was not the issue; money was. Never mind, never mind. Winston knew not to mention any of this, and instead said nothing, wisely.

"Four one nine is not a game, it is a contest of wills," Ironsi-Egobia continued. "It is Nigerian cunning versus *oyibo* greed, and in such a tussle, cunning always has the advantage. Why? Because greed clouds men's eyes, fogs their gaze. Cunning focuses it. We are tax collectors, Adam. We charge a tax on greed. We should be congratulated, not prosecuted, and yet it is we who are called the criminals. Criminals! They talk about Nigeria's 'culture of corruption.' What of Europe's 'culture of greed'? What of America's? What of these *oyibos* agreeing to schemes that are so clearly illegal, were they to be true? Moving millions of dollars out of a poverty-stricken nation, profiteering on Nigeria's hardships? Are the *mugus* not criminals too? Aspiring criminals, but criminals still. Are they not accomplices as much as they are victims? This is what the fools at the EFCC fail to see."

The Oga turned to cough, but nothing came out, neither air nor blood. Not even sound. Winston could feel the undertow pulling at his feet, could feel his world being sucked toward darker, deeper currents.

"You go to church?" Ironsi-Egobia asked after a moment, breath rattling in his chest. "You are a churchgoer?" It wasn't really a question.

"Yes, sir."

"Anglican?"

Winston nodded.

A smile. "I won't hold it against you. You Anglicans—you are the Catholics of Protestants, no?"

A nervous laugh. "Yes, I suppose so."

"Listen to me. I don't care if you are Methodist or Pentecost, if you are a Baptist or a Witness to Jehovah, so long as you are devoted to God. Myself? I tithe to the church ten percent of everything I earn. Do you know why? Because I am a child of Abraham, I am following in his footsteps. When Abraham waged war against the Canaan kings, he turned over one-tenth of his spoils to the priests. And for this, he received divine blessings. Read the Book of Malachi, it's all in there, the Law of Tithing and the Story of the Abrahamic Blessing. But what many people miss is this: it wasn't Abraham's own money he donated to the temple. It was one-tenth of what he had plundered in battle. What he had stolen. And God blessed him for it. You ask why I tithe? That is why. You ask how I have survived, have thrived in this purgatory, this toilet of a city? That is how."

When they start quoting God, it is time to run. Run? Where? The door behind the Oga's desk led—who knew where? Even if Winston managed to elude the silent Tunde, he would enter a labyrinth, might well end up running right back into this room.

"I talk to you intelligently, because you are an intelligent fellow," said Ironsi-Egobia. "I can see that. So, here is what I propose. I will protect you, and you will tithe me. Will you consider this arrangement?"

"Of course."

Tunde finally stirred, rising as his boss stood. Winston did likewise. The meeting was adjourned as abruptly as it had started, and it ended with an extended palm, one still moist from the coughing, that slipped, with Winston's, into a forearm-to-forearm clasp.

Winston didn't even return to the cyber café to collect his umbrella, but fled instead, waving down the first motorcycle taxi he could, pleading with the driver, "Get me far away gone. Take me to the Island."

Winston was swept across the bridge to Lagos Island, didn't look back, moved his base of operations to the upscale cyber haunts of Allen Avenue. This made him slightly nervous, for he was only a few streets over from his own neighbourhood, and there was always the risk of running into a relative or acquaintance. But if he felt less anonymous, he also felt more protected. His daily commute was shorter now as well, and the boutiques and boulevards, the jewellery shops and nightclubs he passed every day were as familiar to him as a parental smile.

Dear Mr. Curtis,

I apologize for the disruption. Many legalities have arisen, but nothing which cannot be surmounted. The money will be in your bank account by week's end, I give you my personal guarantee.

It was said that Eschu, the Trickster God of Yoruba mythology, was buried somewhere along Allen Avenue. Not dead, waiting. That was the tale, anyway—it wasn't something they'd ever covered in Sunday school. But even if Winston had made the proper offerings, even if he'd known the correct manner in which to appease Eschu, it wouldn't have mattered. There were other gods in play.

Scarcely a month had passed and Winston found himself caught up in another police raid. They swept through the café with flak jackets and AK-47s, shouting in pidgin English and Lagos street slang, the chaos and confusion allowing Winston to exit his screen with a single click as the officers moved from workstation to workstation, yelling. They were looking for someone. It never occurred to Winston that the someone could be him. He was hustled through the back exit even as he tried desperately to bargain his way out. "Look, this is a Rolex, take it. I have money, I can pay."

Into an unmarked patrol car and then dropped off, not at a police station, but back again on Cemetery Road. The officers themselves buzzed Winston in, turned him over.

Ironsi-Egobia was holding a postal money order up to the light when Winston entered the room. "This is wonderful! Right down to the watermark. Look." He passed it over. "A sample from the finest forgers on Akwele Road. *Ikpu akwukwo*. True artists. Now, Adam—or may I call you Winston? We haven't seen you in Festac Town for some while now. You aren't shunning us, are you?"

"No, sir."

They had tracked him down. A city of thirteen million people, and he couldn't even find a hiding place.

"I'm sorry to hear about your recent arrest," Ironsi-Egobia said. "I protected you this time, paid your bail out of kindness. I'm not sure how long I can keep the police at bay, though."

Bail? Winston had never been fingerprinted, had never even reached the station.

"You can return the money when you are able," said the Oga with a magnanimous wave of his hand, as though that was what Winston was worrying about.

Run! Where? How?

Ironsi-Egobia held back a cough, and then looked at Winston with unblinking eyes. "We who traffic in falsehoods must put a premium on the truth. You ran. Why?"

"I was afraid."

"Of me?"

He nodded.

"Good. It's good you were afraid, you had reason to be." Ironsi-Egobia stopped again to cough. A dry raspy hack, bloodless this time. "I chose my name with great care, great forethought. And later, some of the 419 boys, I overheard them having fun with it. With their Lagos accents, I thought at first they were saying 'Iron Eagle.' But no, they were calling me The Iron Ego. Not the Yoruba *ego*, you understand, the English. I looked up the meaning. Did you know," he said, "that if you heat the human body fast enough, the skin will separate cleanly? Truly, it does. Slides off. Something to do with the fatty parts underneath melting quicker than the outside. Did you know that?"

When Winston spoke, his voice was barely audible. "No, sir."

"South Africans," he said. "They think they invented everything. Even something as ingenious as a Nigerian necklace, even this they try to claim. A humble ice pick can become a tool of persuasion, so too can a discarded tire and a bit of fuel execute the verdict. A bald tire, on its own? Merely some rubbish. But force it over the shoulders, pin the arms down in its grip, splash in a little petrol, and—well, you have a means of retribution. There is a beauty to it, a simplicity. The Rainbow Nation! That is what the South Africans call themselves now. Can you imagine such nonsense! Brown, black, and white. What kind of rainbow is that? And not even white—pink, like pork. Have you ever seen a brown, black, and pork rainbow?"

Winston shook his head, mute.

"Now, the necklace—that was invented right here in Nigeria. The trick is to split the tire, not down the middle, but lower, closer to one edge. You get a shallower scoop that way, but it is easier to force over the shoulders. Next, you have to add just enough fuel to get the rubber burning. Too much and the petrol is diffi-cult to ignite. Not enough and, well, you have to put up with the screaming and whatnot. If you manage it properly, though, both tire and body will burn beautifully, and the skin? It will fall clean away. It's quite a sight." And then: "I asked them, you know. As they were burning, I asked them, *What is my name?*"

The room began to tilt. Winston felt ill.

"You will pay me a tithe." This was no longer a matter of debate; somewhere in the silence, Winston had acquiesced. "Sixty percent to me," said Ironsi-Egobia, "plus ten percent to the catcher, and another ten percent to cover expenses."

"The catcher?"

"The guyman who sends the original format, the one who receives the reply. The one who first makes contact. He passes the *mugu* up, to a 'storyman.' That be you. When the time comes, you pass the *mugu* on to a 'banker.' The banker will arrange payments and will close the file when the time is right. The 'enforcer' will put the final block on the *mugu,* make threatening phone calls and such. We have freelancers in England and the U.S. for doorstop visits too, if we need them. But we rarely do. Winston, don't look so glum! Your days of mass mailings and email extractors are done! Finally, you can focus your talents properly. You won't need to waste them throwing blind formats, cutting-and-pasting letters, turning in circles. This is not some common shakedown. I'm not some area boy lying in wait under a bridge flyover, charging a toll with nothing rendered in return. I provide a service. Tell me, how many *mugu* you working, at this moment?"

"Three … possibly a fourth."

"Only that? Ha! I will give you that ten times over, I will make you rich and, most important, I will make sure no harm befalls you. I can ensure that you are never arrested again. Here, let me show you something." He slid his hand into the pocket of his shirt, withdrew a pair of reading glasses, and put them on. Peering through them like a schoolteacher, he opened a heavy, leather-bound book. So heavy, Winston mistook it momentarily for a Bible.

"The Nigerian Criminal Code: Revised." Ironsi-Egobia flipped ahead to a well-marked page; evidently Winston wasn't the first person to be on the receiving end of this recitation. "Section 419 of the Criminal Code: Obtaining Goods Through False Pretenses. *Any person who obtains goods or money through false pretenses with intent to defraud will be sentenced to a term of not less than five years' incarceration and*— Well, it goes on. Confiscation of assets, the freezing of bank accounts and so forth. But, and this is the part worth taking note upon: *Offenders can be arrested without a warrant only so long as said offender is found in the act of committing the offence.*"

He stopped, smiled at Winston above the lenses. "Do you see? This is why they always storm in, kicking up such a ruckus. They are trying to catch the 419ers in the act. The regular police are civil about it, you can slip them a bit of *dash,* settle things like gentlemen. But these EFCC rangers, they have been hitting the cafés in Festac Town and elsewhere with a singular lack of manners. That is what I am shielding you from. This is not some booth at one of my store-front shops where the low-rent yahoo boys congregate. That is not what I am offering you. I am offering you access to something much better. Not a cyber café, but a cyber *club.* A fully private establishment, members only, with bolted doors and mounted cameras. Even the most ardent of policemen and the most fervent of EFCC agents cannot simply charge in, willy-nilly, nor can they slip in by stealth, unnoticed. They must gain access, they must be buzzed through, signed in, properly verified. Plenty of time for the guymen inside to vacate the premises through other means."

It was clever. Even through his nausea and fear, Winston could see that.

"We are shadowmen," said Ironsi-Egobia. "The only thing we have to fear is sunshine, publicity. As long as we remain in the shadows, we will move as shadows do, across any surface. Show me the prison that can contain shadows! As long as we are plying our trade and collecting our dues out of sight, no one can reach us."

The Oga was right. And that was the problem. Winston didn't want to ply his trade in darkness, as though making money was something shameful. He wanted to do it openly, in direct light. Laws were malleable; surely they could be massaged and stretched, made to include 419?

"You will have access to the best forgers Lagos can produce. Legal wills and registered letters, birth certificates—and death—financial statements, diplomatic papers, documents from the Central Bank, stamped with the personal seal of the director. I even have printers who can typeset newspaper headlines, made to order, on real newsprint. *Millions missing from Delta oil contracts.' 'Foreign worker dies in ghastly car accident, leaves no heirs.'* Whatever story you wish to spin, we can provide the necessary documentation. We can even create mirror websites, showing great fortunes languishing in a Nigerian bank account in any name you desire."

That's what fortunes do in Africa, Winston thought. *They languish.*

What Winston wanted to say was this: "My passport is suspended. I have a criminal record. I cannot leave Nigeria. Help me. Help me and I will tithe you one hundred percent. I will tithe you one hundred and ten." The clandestine printing presses on Oluwole Street, the forgery mills of Akwele Road. If they could conjure birth certificates into existence, might they not conjure visas as well? Passports, even?

These were the things he wanted to ask, but didn't. It was reckless even to dream them. Because Winston knew that to arrive in London on a forged passport was to condemn your future self to life as a fugitive. You would never be able to work at your proper level, would end up, odds-on, arrested and then deported back to Nigeria, to languish, fortune-like, in Kirikiri Prison. You would end your days broken, would never, ever leave Lagos.

And why would his Oga help him flee the cage anyway? Winston was already imprisoned. Ironsi-Egobia was still speaking, but Winston barely heard.

"We buy cellphones in bulk. We have scanners and photo-copiers. Ink pads of every colour, envelopes of every size, postage stamps of every nation. We have chop and drink when you are hungry or thirsty. Girls, for the same. And if one of your *mugus* is so foolish as to show up, that is manna from Heaven. We will provide you with a driver, a bone man, whatever you need. We have lawyers on payroll and police the same. We have errand boys to pick up the payments when they arrive at MoneyGram or Western Union. If anything goes wrong, they are the ones to be arrested and beaten, not you. Think of it." He folded his glasses, put them to one side. "You can tell your stories without hindrance, with no one interfering. *Chop I chop.* That is what we say. You eat, I eat. *Chop I chop.* We don't stand on each other's shadows. You have only to pay your tithe to me, a fee to the catcher, plus ten percent for expenses—bribes and so forth. What could be simpler?"

… said the blind man to the diver.

Blood was back in his cough, and Ironsi-Egobia turned away, pressed a handkerchief to his face as though it contained chloro-form. Breathed through it—a gurgle in, a rattle out.

Winston was neck high in deep water now, was caught in the

grip of the undertow, could feel his head about to go under. And somewhere: the smell of gasoline, more a memory of something to come than anything real.

42

She'd grown thinner as her belly grew larger; it was as though the child inside was feeding on her hunger.

Were you to die out here, who would mourn? Who would perform last rites? But she already knew the answer to that: no one. Bones picked clean by desert ants, she and the child inside her would join the other skeletal remains that decorated the landscape: cattle bones with their elegant curves of white; the carcasses of cars, sun-brittle and bleached, abandoned on the roadside, stripped clean of everything worth taking. The asphalt was littered with the husks of such vehicles, testaments to the effect of sand drifts on drivers and the hazards of overtaking traffic on blind curves.

It was getting harder and harder to keep the globe turning. She could feel her footsteps start to falter, had been having trouble keeping the jerry can balanced. Arms as thin as bird bones. Eyes, half-shut. She was stumbling across the landscape now as much as she was walking, the last of her water sloshing back and forth.

I will die here, and who will mourn?

And at precisely the moment she was about to fall: the strangest of sights. A woolly ewe driving a motorcycle. The ewe passed by with a certain aplomb, chewing the air thoughtfully, looking rather regal. The girl almost laughed, would have, had she the strength— but then she realized the significance of this omen.

43

They were reconstructing her father's downfall in the same methodical manner they had reconstructed the accident itself: walking the family through it, step by step—though *stage by stage* might be more accurate, Laura thought. The narrative the detectives from the Economic Crime Unit were laying out for them resembled nothing so much as the Kübler-Ross checklist of grieving, albeit one that started not with denial but hesitation, then elation, and ended not in acceptance but despair.

The sun had shifted. Winter light, a low blue. There were no more reflections on the window across from Laura, only a hallway beyond lit by fluorescent tubes. The ice in their glasses had melted into nubs.

They were going over the emails her father had received, laying each one to rest in turn.

"Complements of the season!" That rankled her. It was a mistake that popped up several times, under various names: *"I complement you on your speedy response."* Laura had to resist the urge to correct the pages, to circle the error, change "e" to "i." *I complement you!* Maybe they did. Maybe whoever was sending her father these messages did complement him. Maybe they complemented each other.

"Do you see something?" It was Brisebois, zeroing in on the way Laura was studying one of the emails.

"No," she said. "Only errors in usage."

"Sometimes it's the widow of a dead general," said Detective Saul. "Sometimes it's a government official who's been secretly skimming money from the National Treasury or siphoning funds from Nigeria's National Petroleum Corporation. Or maybe it's a long-lost relative you've never heard of who deposited a fortune just before dying in a plane crash or a traffic accident. Sometimes it's a steamer trunk filled with hundred-dollar bills that have been dyed black in order to smuggle them out of the country—you just need a special chemical to clean them, and the millions are yours! It's really just pieces of cut-up construction paper, of course, with a few real bills hidden among them. Simple trick, really. It's like street magic, but with a much higher yield."

"People fall for that?" Warren asked.

"All the time."

"But whatever the variation," said Detective Rhodes, "the basic idea is the same: We'll send you a huge amount of money. All you have to do is deposit it into a bank account for us, and you'll get to keep either a healthy commission or all of it, in the case of dead relatives and surprise lotteries. No risk, no cost, huge windfall. It's a pickup line, basically. They just need to park their money in your account for a while. It's a hundred percent safe! No risk! Sure. That's what they all say—in the beginning."

Rhodes gave Laura a wry smile of sisterly camaraderie. Was she talking about criminals? Or men? *And why would she think I was with her on that? Because we're both women?*

Was this an interview technique? A way of getting around a suspect's defences, to make you think you had some sort of connection? (It was.) Were they taught this in detective school? (They were.) *Am I a suspect?* (She wasn't.) Not anymore, that is. This was the part Laura didn't know: her father had tried to move his entire insurance payout into Laura's name just before he died, but it had been disallowed by the insurance company. Sergeant Brisebois knew this. The detectives knew this. Laura never would. "No one," Brisebois had said, "is going to be arrested." What Laura didn't realize was that this "no one" included her.

Warren was shaking his head. "How could Dad fall for this?"

"It's easier to get caught up in this sort of thing than you think," Saul said. "You're made to believe that you're dealing with people of high stature in important positions—bankers, oil executives, top government officials, ministers, lawyers. All those names you saw forged on these documents. The Office of Attorney General. Economic Adviser to the President. Executive Director of the National Petroleum Corporation. It gives a sense of weight to the offer."

"There's an overwhelming sense of urgency," Rhodes explained. "You're told you have to act immediately. It's a seduction technique. They don't want you to make an informed decision. They want you to be rushed into it."

"They isolate their victims as well," Saul added. "Usually through some sort of sworn statement—often in the form of a legal-looking non-disclosure document. They always start by stressing the need for absolute confidentiality. They don't want the victim talking to family or friends or even spouses."

"They want to cut you off from the people around you," Rhodes continued. "It causes incredible strain on a person, carrying this enormous secret, this burden. As you can imagine."

"I suppose," said Laura.

"The victims I've interviewed?" said Saul. "They often say that's the worst part of what happened, more than the money they lost: feeling isolated from the people they loved. And when things fall apart, as they always do, it's like a sucker punch to the stomach."

No, Laura thought. *Not the stomach. The heart.*

"It's very easy to spiral into despair. So you have to reach the point where you accept what has happened, and can learn from it."

There it was. Stage Five in Kübler-Ross. How very textbook of them. But—what if you don't want to accept what happened? What if you want to hold someone accountable?

"The scammers shift the burden of trust onto the victims,

making them feel as though they're the ones who need to prove they're trustworthy." Saul held out one of the emails her father had received. "You can see it here, where they're asking him, *'How do we know you won't abscond with the entire amount?'* It changes the power dynamics, makes the victims feel pressure to prove their integrity, puts the onus on them instead. It also deflects suspicion." There was a pause. "It's brilliant psychology, actually."

"At the same time," said Rhodes, "they're feeling you out. Assessing your worth, getting a sense of how much they can take you for. That's why one Anti-Terrorist Certificate will cost $700 and another will cost $7,000."

"It's whatever the market will bear," said the older detective.

Warren nodded; he could see the economics of it. He did the same thing with his own clients.

SUBJECT: Transfer of Funds from CBN
RECEIVED: September 28, 9:47 PM

Mr. Curtis, we have hit a small snag. The Central Bank of Nigeria cannot transfer such a LARGE AMOUNT OF MONEY into any overseas account that has less than $US 100,000.00 in reserve. Can you confirm that this amount can be covered by you? Understand, this is PURELY FOR SECURITY REASONS. None of your money will or can be accessed by a third party, but I'm afraid that the petty-minded R. Bola Soludo, Director of Operations at the CBN, is being most troublesome. He has demanded I give an exact figure on fear of being considered some common swindler! I tried to make a wild guess at your savings, but the bank manager mocked me and said, "We have checked and know that is incorrect!"

Please help, as I am in a pickle.
> With much sincerity,
> Lawrence Atuche, Professor of Commerce,
> Lagos University

SUBJECT: Re: Transfer of Funds from CBN
SENT: September 28, 9:52 PM

Hi, 100 is not a problem. We own our own home. Plus we have RRSPs.

"We," not "I." "Our," not "my."

Laura noticed her father's choice of possessive pronoun and felt better for it. Whatever that pink-faced boy-man at the bank had said, her father had known it was her mother's house too. *Not his home, theirs.*

SUBJECT: Re: re: Transfer of Funds from CBN
RECEIVED: September 28, 10:07 PM

Thank you, my friend. That is excellent news! I shall hurry down to the bank right now. You should have the money in your account by waking hours tomorrow a.m.
> With great appreciation,
> Lawrence Attuche, Professor of Commerce,
> Lagos University

Laura looked up from the printouts. "The professor spelled his own name wrong. First with one 't' and then here with two." She passed the message to Detective Saul. "See?"

He chuckled. "You're right. Juggling so many different names and identities, you probably forget who you are at times."

"You see how they build up anticipation as well," said Detective Rhodes. "The money's coming! It's coming! At any moment! Just a tease, of course. It starts off as sunshine and butterflies, but complications arise. They always do."

SUBJECT: One final matter
RECEIVED: October 1, 9:37 PM

Dear Mr. Curtis,

Re: you're transfer of funds

I'm afraid there is one final, small problem ...

It is a minor issue, fortunately, and one easily resolved, but without putting this trifling matter to rest, we cannot move forward. The Central Bank of Nigeria has indeed confirmed that the funds are being transferred. Please see the link to the SECURE WEB PAGE (below) showing the account balance—in your name, to the full amount of $US 35,600,000. The transfer is done! It has only to be signed for and notarized and it will be complete.

You are, therefore, required to appear at the Main Office of the Central Bank in Lagos within two (2) business days to sign the required documentation. Miss Sandra thanks you for this in advance.

> Toasting our good fortune,
> Lawrence Atuche, Professor of Commerce

SUBJECT: Re: One final matter
SENT: October 1, 9:46 PM

I can't go to Nigeria on such short notice! I don't even have a passport.

SUBJECT: Re: re: One final matter
RECEIVED: October 1, 10:12 PM

Oh no! I was looking forward to meeting you in person and taking you for champagne and celebrations after the transfer went through. Fret not! I have just now spoken with the Bank and I am told that if you cannot appear in person, you may appoint an accredited barrister to act as your representative to sign the notarization process on your behalf.

The Central Bank usually goes through the Law Office of Bello & Usman. Mr. Usman is a fine and upstanding gentleman of whom I can personally vouchsafe as honest and efficient. There is a one-time fee of $US 900 for his services. I have asked Mr. Usman if he can't simply deduct his amount from the funds paid, but that is not possible as once the money is out of the country, he will have no guarantee of payment. I have told him you are a man of honest integrity, but lawyers are lawyers and they always play "by the book."

With many apologies,
Lawrence Atuche, Professor of Commerce

SUBJECT: Re: re: re: One final matter
SENT: October 1, 10:14 PM

Lawyers, eh? Same everywhere ha ha

"Your father signed a document granting power of attorney to the law office of Bello & Usman in Lagos."

"So why aren't you contacting them?" asked Warren.

"Because 'they' don't exist," said Laura. "Jesus Christ, Warren, what part of this don't you understand?"

"Language," said their mother, roused from her indifference.

"What if someone took them up on their offer?" Laura asked. "Flew to Lagos and confronted them face to face?"

Detective Saul looked at her. "People have tried that. They've gone over there and started poking about in the city's underbelly."

"And?"

"Like I said, they usually end up floating in Lagos Lagoon."

"But what if—what if you made them come to you, pretended to be an investor, say? Turned the tables."

"That's a dangerous game. You'd be on their turf."

"But couldn't you meet them on neutral ground? An embassy or something."

"Odds are, even if you made it out alive, you wouldn't get your money back," said Rhodes.

"What if," Laura asked, "it wasn't about the money?"

44

An ewe riding a motorcycle.

Only after the motorbike had passed did the girl in indigo see the driver sitting behind the animal, keeping the sheep propped up on the handlebars, peering over its shoulder at the road ahead.

She almost laughed, would have if she'd had the strength. Then she realized, *He can't be going far, this driver on his sheep-straddled motorcycle.* So she pushed herself forward, over the next rise of sandy hill. And there, a more remarkable sight still: a shining city on the plains, glimmering with light even at midday.

She had reached the end of the Sahel, had reached Kaduna. And she might yet survive, Insha Allah.

Lumbering freight trucks, loaded down like camels, rolled past. Men in flowing white robes flew by on motorbikes, ewe-less. And in the distance: the squat cylinders and intestinal tubings of the city's oil refineries, a complex so sprawling she almost mistook it for a city in its own right. She followed the pipelines into Kaduna.

Any fuel these refineries provided seemed to have bypassed local vendors, though. Long lines of angry vehicles were queued outside petrol stations—or at least those that were still open. She passed several that were boarded up entirely, with hand-painted NO FOOEL signs out front.

The fuel shortage had brought out would-be profiteers, young men selling plastic milk jugs and litre bottles filled with black-market gasoline. At one roadside stall she passed, a police vehicle had pulled over, not to issue a ticket but to haggle with the seller over the cost of a jug.

Kaduna.

The city was named for its river, and the river was named for its crocodiles. But the *kadunas* that had once floated like logs in the muddy waters were long gone, lost like the lions of the Sahel. She had never been to a city so big before, a million souls or more they said. Had never seen boulevards so wide, buildings so blindingly white. Grand architectural gestures loomed on every side: polished hotels and towering banks that proclaimed their wealth through the sheer gleam of their facades. Cinemas and chemists, billboards and barbershop poles that *turned*. And everywhere: traffic honking like bickering geese.

Preening, rooster-like buses, painted in flagrant greens and purples, veered past as loud-revving motorcycle taxis wove in and out, passengers clinging to their drivers' backs, bundles tucked tightly under arms. It seemed to be a city of bundles: bundles bulging, swaying, opened, emptied.

She heard half a dozen dialects and languages on the walk in, words shouted and sung, spoken and sighed; the city rang with their sounds, and even in her weakened state, it was exhilarating. In such a place, surely there was space for her.

But Kaduna was still Kaduna. A river of crocodiles, a city with teeth. The trick was to step as daintily as a bird picking meat from the gum line. Behind the Ostrich Bakery, she rummaged through garbage cans and empty sacks dusted with flour, uncovered a bag filled with sticky buns. The buns were furred with mould, but she carefully scraped them clean, ate the sour bread below.

Past the central market, she came to the edge of Kaduna's Sabon Gari district. These strangers' quarters, like those in Zaria, weren't marked as such, but were clearly delineated anyway. Muddy accents from the Christian south. Igbo traders and Yoruba. Nupe and Tiv. Families that might have lived there for generations but would always be looked upon as interlopers. She was one of them now.

45

What if it wasn't about the money?

Laura's question had given Detective Rhodes pause. What was she getting at?

But Warren had cut in before the detective's suspicions could coalesce. "We should sue Dad's bank for letting him send his savings out of the country! We should sue MoneyGram and Western Union. We should sue the goddamn Nigerian government."

Laura was going through the scanned documents. Her father's signature, granting power of attorney to an imaginary barrister hired to oversee the imaginary transfer of imaginary funds.

> Know all men that I, the undersigned, HENRY CURTIS,
> do solemnly grant exclusive rights and legal authority to
> DR. THEODORE USMAN, ATTORNEY AT LAW, to act in
> my place for the purposes of clearance and safekeep of
> said funds referenced No. 133-42.

Another one began:

> I, HENRY CURTIS, hereby authorize the Central Bank of
> Nigeria to remit the sum of $US 35,600,000.00 herewith
> into the following account …

The same signature he'd signed her report cards with.

"The lawyers' fees are usually the first payments the victim makes," said Rhodes. "But once it starts, it never ends. There are always last-minute unexpected delays, while the dream of the big payoff is kept dangling in front of you."

"This is why it's known as 'advance fee fraud.' The fees *are* the con," said Saul. "There are taxes to be paid, and levies, VAT and banking surcharges, then you need to cover *demurrage*—storage fees on boxes of make-believe money. There are the Anti–Money Laundering Certificates we showed you earlier. Transfer fees, processing fees, insurance registration fees."

"You're advised to keep track of all your expenses," continued Rhodes, "because supposedly you'll be reimbursed—with interest!—once the transfer goes through. Except, of course, it never does." Then, with an ingratiating smile aimed Laura's way, "It's like waiting for a guy to call the day after the night before."

"I wouldn't know anything about that," said Laura, a sliver of ice running through her voice.

"Well, you're luckier than the rest of us," Rhodes said with an easy laugh.

Detective Saul passed more scanned documents across the table, pages from a ledger, each entry carefully inscribed, down to the penny: her father, keeping a careful and no doubt scrupulously honest record of his expenses. As heartbreaking a sight as any lonely turn on a winter road …

Although she hadn't paid much attention to the other documents, Laura's mother looked at these, marvelled at the care Henry had taken with them. "He was always the one who balanced our chequebook," she said. "He was always the one who kept track of things."

"The more a victim puts in, the more they'll continue to put in," said Saul. "Until you end up chasing your own money, throwing good after bad, trying desperately to recoup what you've already lost. It starts a downward spiral that usually ends only once you've been bankrupted. Or worse."

"And if you start to flag, they push you harder," Rhodes added. "You feel like you're caught up in this swirling, clandestine affair. The con takes over your entire life. It's secretive and relentless—and all the while you're cut off from those closest to you."

Why didn't he say something—anything? Even once. Was that why he'd kept calling Laura late at night, hoping she would ask the right questions?

"The pressure builds," said Rhodes. "It builds and builds and never lets up."

They'd now reached the excruciating final spasms. "The scammers turn it around, start to claim that they're the real victims," Saul explained.

> Mr. Curtis, I have bankrupted myself and my family! I have had to sell my house to cover the gap in costs that you refuse to pay. Why do I help you if you can't keep your end of bargain?

"Sometimes they try to rally your sense of optimism."

> Mr. Curtis, God is on our side. You cannot abandon us now. Think of the girl, will you throw her to the fates?

"Sometimes they speak of justice, sometimes of despair."

> If you walk away now Mr. Curtis, Miss Sandra will have no alternative but to commit suicide, because I will not be able to protect her and she will most certainly not be able to withstand the demands applied from those nefarious souls who are circling even now, attracted by the scent of blood.

"Of course," said the older detective, "it's never the scammer who commits suicide." He regretted saying this even before the words had left his mouth, but the family seemed so numb by that point they hardly noticed.

> SUBJECT: You have destroyed me!
> RECEIVED: December 1, 11:59 PM

Mr. Curtis, I can no longer hide my outrage at you! You refuse to pay the final $US 20,000.00 needed to clear the money through customs, even though as you well know this is utterly the last payment required.

You are leaving me abandoned and betrayed. I have mortgaged my business, have gone into debt and sold my family possessions and heirlooms. I will lose everything because of you! I have covered the bulk of these costs and only $US 20,000.00 is needed on the receiving end. This is all that stands between me and abject destruction. Why did I ever trust you?

I have attached the records of my mortgage and the necessary bank payments—payments you were supposed to make! Payments I made on your behalf!

Why are you being so half-hearted in these matters, when millions of dollars and Miss Sandra's future happiness are at stake!!

> With disgust at your dishonesty,
> William Awele, Executor to the Estate
> of Dr. Atta, late Director of the Contract
> Award Committee for the NNPC

"There's always one 'last payment,'" said Rhodes. "They accuse the victim of being deceitful and two-faced. They attack, harass. They're incredibly persistent."

"And if the victim threatens to expose them?" Laura asked.

"Oh," said Saul with a smile. "They're ready for that."

SUBJECT: Your threats mean nothing! NOTHING!!
RECEIVED: December 7, 11:32 PM

Are you such a fool as that Mr. Curtis? You dare threaten
me??

You want to contact the police, do so! At this stage, I'm
thinking about contacting them myself. You understand,
this is illegal, what you have been doing. Trying to
smuggle money out of another country. You are an
accomplice to a crime, Mr. Curtis. You are a thief of Africa,
and you will be paid in imprisonment!

Go to the police and they will arrest you. How will your
wife and children feel then? How will you explain this to
Helen, to your grandchildren?

Send the money or face the consequences.

William Awelle

"Finally, when it becomes clear that there is no more money
to squeeze from the victim, the scammer suddenly throws him
a lifeline," said Saul. "They offer to resolve everything in one
swoop—to repay the victim his entire costs in a single move. They
essentially use the victim as a cheque-cashing service. They send
him a sizable cashier's cheque. Or a bank draft or corporate cheque,
even a money order, it doesn't matter. They tell the victim to cash
the cheque, keep half—which is usually more than the expenses
the victim has coughed up—and then send the rest to another
account."

"This is what happened with your father," explained Rhodes,
looking at Laura.

"The cheque arrives. The victim deposits it. The cheque clears,
so everything seems good. The victim has recouped his losses
and is happy to forward the remainder to another account. But
people misunderstand what 'clearing a cheque' means. The fact
that a cheque has been cleared doesn't mean it's legitimate. Your

local branch isn't an expert in forged documents. A bank will allow a cheque to go through based on its client's credit rating—your father's was impeccable—their many years as a valued customer, and so on. A bank can clear any cheque if they're confident they can recoup the funds should something go wrong."

"Your father was a client of some thirty years' standing," said Rhodes. "He owned his own home and had opened a line of credit against its value. The house acted as a guarantor against the sum."

"Let me guess," said Warren wearily. "The cheque bounced."

"That's one way of putting it. It was a forgery."

"Surely, for Christ's sake, the bank is liable."

"Bank tellers aren't fraud investigators," said Rhodes. "The cheque would have worked its way through the system to a central clearing house, would have been flagged and then have worked its way back. It can take several weeks before a phony cheque is caught, even after it's been cleared. And to put it bluntly, it was your father who committed the crime, not the bank. Unknowingly, but still. Your father," she said, "passed a forged note. He attempted to defraud his bank."

Good news! A fully certified cheque is on its way. You will recoup your entire loss, even while we await the final transfer. Deduct what is owed and return the rest. This is a way to get funds to Miss Sandra without the CBN getting their clutches upon it. Everyone wins! You will be repaid in full and Miss Sandra will be saved from a hopeless future!

"The bank will recover most of what it lost through the foreclosure and sale of your father's property—"

"My *parents'* property," said Laura, anger flaring.

Her mother put a hand on Laura's arm, said in the same

soothing voice her daughter had heard so often as a child, "It's fine, dear."

"Why didn't Dad just declare bankruptcy and be done with it?" asked Warren.

"He could've," said Rhodes. "But the end result would have been the same. Your parents would still have lost the house. The savings would still be gone. And your father would still have faced a criminal investigation into the forged cheque."

"Sometimes," said Saul, "when it's all over, the con men contact the victim *again*, this time claiming to be investigators from Interpol, or from the EFCC, Nigeria's Anti-Fraud Unit, intent on helping the victim track down the crooks and recover his money. For a fee, of course."

It was like watching a car crash in slow motion.

—*Egberifa.*

"There was," said Detective Saul, sliding a final sheet of paper across the table, "one last payment. It was on your father's credit card. The card itself was maxed out, but the payment went through. The transaction occurred just a few days before the—accident."

"An airplane ticket," said Rhodes.

This straightened Laura's posture. "Dad was going to Nigeria?"

"It wasn't a ticket *to* Nigeria. From. It was in the name of one Sandra Atta."

"She was coming here?" said Laura. "I thought she didn't exist."

"She doesn't. The ticket was never used. Someone cashed it, kept the money."

And the figure in the shadows, the one her father had called in a complaint about? "There was no one outside my parents' window, was there?" Laura asked.

"We didn't see anyone, no."

She should have felt relieved, but all she felt was sad. That these faceless criminals had been able to reach deep into her dad's mind and conjure up demons … On the day the flight arrived, her dad must have driven out there, to the airport. *He must have driven out there and waited—and waited.* In many ways, he was waiting there still.

Hi. Henry here. Please tell Miss Sandra that I will be at the airport on Friday to meet her when she arrives, just to make sure she gets to the right office and is given full protection as a political refugee. Don't worry, I won't let her be deported.

—Thank you sir and God bless! You are a good man.

"The final block is fear," said Detective Saul.

"They use your fears against you," Rhodes explained. "There's rarely any reason to send someone out in person to threaten you, though. It's mostly self-inflicted."

The final block is fear. In the weeks that followed, and throughout the events that ensued, Laura would remember those words. And she would ask herself: What if you denied fear its foothold? What if you refused to be afraid?

A final flurry of emails, fragments of messages hurled back and forth:

Do you love your wife?

—Of course I do.

Then shut up and don't cause problems. Do you understand? We are mafia. We will find you & we will kill! you. We will leave your life in tatters.

—You already have.

You will die. We know where you live. We will burn your house to the ground.

—What about the girl?

No response.

—What about the girl?

No response.

46

At the Katsina roundabout in Kaduna city, a massive tanker truck was parked like a beached ship, sides labelled in a hand-painted flourish: "Dreams Abound." Sweat-sheened truck drivers and long-distance bus passengers stranded for the night had shoved their way in under the awnings of the motor-park cafés, crowded their way along wooden benches, called out their orders across oilcloth countertops.

The girl stood outside, watched plate after plate of food-is-ready fare being dished out. Just 150 naira would have bought her a space along that counter. One hundred and fifty naira: it might as well have been a million.

She hung back at the edge of the motor-park perimeter while evening fell. She'd scouted a few possibilities, spots where the men were louder and drunker than most and would, she hoped, sleep more deeply as well. Inside a cement culvert, she lay down atop discarded cardboard and waited for the laughter to end.

Too hungry to sleep, she counted out the hours. One by one the pockets of celebratory gatherings went silent, and she crawled out under the blue cast of a swollen moon. Not a cloud in the sky for cover. *Women who are with child should not travel after dark.* But the night was not dark, and this was not travel.

Leaving her jerry can hidden in the culvert, she moved along the side of a sewage ditch, peering over it for any sign of roving boys or drunken men. Finally, with a deep breath, she left her cover and followed a path up and into the hyenas' den. A few flickers of flame echoed dimly inside the corroded oil barrels where the truck drivers had formed encampments, their vehicles packed in tightly on all sides as the men slumbered on mats. She heard heavy snores, crept closer.

She was hoping for the usual discarded *suya* sticks and mango rinds; she found much, much more.

Indeed, it was such a heart-catching sight she had to take a moment to calm herself. An entire flank of lamb, the meat heavy on the bone, was skewered above a firepit, the flesh charred and grown cold, glazed in its own grease. Bodies lay all around, but the hunger urged her on, deeper into the encampment. She stepped carefully, threaded her way among the sleeping bodies and piles of rubbish. Three or four steps and she would reach it. *This isn't theft,* she told herself. If she didn't take the meat, a stray dog or waddling rat surely would …

She took one hesitant step, then another.

But the world was not entirely asleep. Someone else was awake and watching her. And as she moved toward the fire pit, a figure took shape in front of her, stepped forward.

A smile emerged from the darkness. "What do we have here?" it asked.

FUEL

47

The sea had pushed the river back on itself, with the swirling saline blues curling into the darker greens of the Niger Delta. Tidal waters, deep among the creeks and mangrove swamps.

Just as smoothly, the sea had withdrawn, leaving sleek flats and rivulets flopping with mudskippers. The men moved quickly, stabbing and sorting as the first pelts of rain hit. They were tossing their catch into cross-hatched baskets slung over their shoulders, leaving the leftovers for the children to gather later. Men with backs bent, wet more from condensation than from sweat.

Some had staked out the backflow of estuarial waters with raffia fishing traps, straining the current for prawns. "Fewer than ever," they complained, to cries of agreement. "Fewer than ever, but enough still, Wonyinghi willing!," quickly amended to "Christ willing!"

The miracle of the fish and the loaves played out in more paltry terms that day: hundreds of croaker fish had arrived belly-up from the oil creeks farther inland, sheathed in crude and already rotting.

The boy was nine or ten, maybe more, maybe less; his parents hadn't kept track as diligently as they might, preferring to count out a life by the number of floods lived through rather than one's circuits around the sun. However one kept tally, though, he was still the eldest of the children, and he carried his rank with a firm but fair demeanour. That day, he'd led the little ones along the trail that ran from the back of the village, behind the church, all the way to the lagoon. They'd marched behind him in single file, arranging themselves naturally by height like waterfowl crossing a sandbar, plastic pails and enamel basins held one-handed on heads. Bellies in proud posture. Singsong voices, laughter.

Hardwood canoes were tethered together in the lagoon below, stranded temporarily on tidal mud. The few pirogues that did sport outdoor motors had them tilted up, their propellers useless at low tide.

With nets and fishing traps, the men moved through. Who knew but they might find a shark marooned in wet silt; it happened now and then, causing a riot of excitement and a circle kill. No sharks today, though. Only smaller fish and the fecund smell of the nearby mangrove marshes.

On those occasions when the tide rolled in a giant catfish, further nets would be thrown. Clusters of minnow-sized fish that flitted behind would escape, slipping free on the shallowest of trickles. And though these little fish weren't the offspring of the catfish, the boy's father saw patterns in this, too. "It is a parent's job to give its life for its children," he said.

From the path above the lagoon, the boy held up his hand, and the procession of children came to a halt. "Aren't ready for us," he said. The men would shout when it was time for the children to come running to gather any loose fish still flopping about. They'd have to hurry then before the tide snatched them back.

"We'll wait here," said the boy. "Beside the cannon."

The children lowered the basins from their heads, awaited further instructions. Even entangled as it was with netted vines, the cannon stood out as a local landmark. Cast in iron, the letters *HRH Victoria Rex* were raised along one side, like a welt on skin. The cannon marked the high point of the path—or what little high point there was. On its outcrop of rock, it still claimed a vantage point on the lagoon; the men below were caught in an ancient line of fire.

It had been trying to rain all day, and the overcast skies now finally collapsed. But the downpour didn't last. The rain soon turned to mist and the mist to steam, and still the men hadn't called.

The children had waited it out under large leaves, and when the worst of the rain had ended and the older boy said, "Okay then, go play," they broke formation instantly, squealing. The boys played at battle in the flattened clearing beside the cannon, wrestling in arm-lock posture, rolling each other into the wet earth. The girls played other games, hopping on one foot on matted grass as they sang precision phrases, trying to maintain balance and rhythm as long as possible, laughing when they stumbled, laughing when they didn't.

Beyond the cannon was the British graveyard, and as the little ones played, the older boy let himself drift toward it.

The names of the dead rolled off his tongue: *Manning Henderson, Esq. Richard Belshaw, Royal Gunner. Captain Reginald Louchland. For God and King. For Queen and Countrye.*

He could read the tombstones because they were in English— and though there might be some areas where they spoke only their local Ijaw dialect, out here amid the mahogany and mangroves of the outer creeks, English was their shared language. How else to speak to the Igbo traders or Yoruba priests? How else to cut across dialects of Ijaw so thick they were almost separate languages in themselves? English had been spoken in the Delta longer than this entity they called "Nigeria" had existed. The Ijaw of the Niger Delta had fought for the English king and against him, had mastered his language, had hosted his missionaries—had martyred more than a few. The king's language was taught in school, was used in the markets and at home, with conversations flowing from Ijaw to English and back again as easily as water might pour from one gourd to another. They spoke it properly as well, in low rich tones, with every word, every syllable, given equal weight, equal importance. Nothing like those reedy nasal inflections coming over the radio. Pale BBC voices, sickly and thin.

English had taken root in the muddy waters of the Delta as surely as the mangroves had. The language was theirs as much as it was anyone's, even if most children, and many adults, had never even seen an *oyibo,* as the Igbo traders called them.

The main evidence of *oyibos* in the outer Delta lay in the graves they'd left behind. The bones of the lesser dead were marked with simple wooden crosses that had long ago toppled and lay now in wet decay; you could mark their shapes in the moss that grew, green on green. But most were made of stone, hidden among the iroko trees, overgrown and blackened with mould. The boy was walking among English bones, past stone monuments to HRM's Royal Navy—*Gloria Filiorum Patres*—with the headstones of the Royal Niger Company alongside the older granite of the United Africa Company. *In Service to Greater Glory, 1895.* That was the year the British had fired on Brass Island. The boy's teacher had told them this, in among lessons on English grammar and Ijaw laws and the memorizing of multiplication tables. The English had rained down iron like an angry god it was said, had killed the Brass Islanders by the score for the sin of insolence. But the English had also lost lives that day. Their teacher had smiled when he told them that part of the story. "They die as easily as anyone," he'd said.

The English hadn't even taken the bodies home with them, but had abandoned them here instead. An awful insult to the English *duwoi-you* who were left behind, the boy thought. Without proper rites performed in your own village, how could you ever find rest?

You would be afflicted forever with wayward longings. Perhaps that was why the English had placed such large stones on top of the graves, to keep the souls underneath pinned down.

The other children, bored with their battles and chanted songs, had followed the older boy into the graveyard, curious and afraid in equal measure. He'd been dream-walking among the graves and had barely noticed the others tiptoeing in, but now—*something*.

The forest beyond the graves ... moved.

The wind? Or maybe he imagined it. The worlds of the *oje*, objects and the everyday, and that of *teme*, the spirits in between, were hard to distinguish at times. They got tangled up like vines, and it could be difficult to say where one started and the other ended.

The boy kept his breathing shallow, watched the forest. Waited.

The forest moved again.

And then—with a crash and a curse, wide leaves were flung apart and a figure emerged. A tall man with pink boiled skin, dressed in mud-splattered beige, strode into the clearing, followed by two men with normal skin. These two seemed nervous, and when they spotted the children they said something that was neither English nor Ijaw, and the boy knew why they were on edge. They weren't Ijaw, they were Igbo, far from the comfort of their own people.

The pink-faced man seemed oblivious, though. He paced out his steps, then slung a long bundle of wood from his shoulder and let the pieces fall into place, forming a three-legged stand onto which he screwed a small spyglass. He had rolled-up sleeves, buttoned back, and his forearms were fuzzed with light-coloured hair and freckled with spots. He peered through his spyglass with eyes as washed-out as he was.

The other two men—bodyguards, it would seem—took up position on either side of the pink-faced man as they eyed the children with a bluff of disregard. The little ones had crowded in behind their leader, and they all watched as this odd creature pulled out a notebook bound with a rubber band, snapped it open, and then wrote something in with a stub of a pencil. The pink-pale man then wiped his neck with a cloth, ran a forearm over his forehead. His hair was dripping.

Only then did the *oyibo* acknowledge the gaggle of children who had gathered. "Hallo," he said.

"You are an Englishman," said the boy, proud to have spotted it. What he wanted to ask was: Have you come to claim the bones you left behind? Have you come to take them home?

"You childrens, you are coming from the village, ya? On the other side?"

The boy nodded, and the pale man grinned. Teeth too big for his mouth. "Here." The man dug into a sagging shirt pocket, produced candies wrapped in wax paper. "Here. Go on."

To refuse it would have been rude, so the children shuffled up shyly as the pale man dropped the wrapped peppermints into their palms, one by one, as though dispensing medicine.

"*Dile,*" said the boy, apologizing for the reticence of his friends. "They think maybe you are one of the *duwoi-you.* An English ghost from the graves."

The man laughed. "Not English, no. And I sweat too much for a ghost, I think. Do you know a ghost with a face so red as mine?"

The boy laughed and the man smiled, and a strange pact was sealed.

The other children giggled as well, more from relief than understanding. The man leaned in, tapped the image of a shell sewed onto his chest pocket. "Not English," he repeated. "Dutch."

The boy asked, "Is it far? Dutch?"

"Very far. You know oil? Oil, ya? It is a curious sort of honey; it draws many kinds of flies. Afrikaners. Italians. Frenchmen. Texans.

Even some Belgians, if you can imagine!" He had ticked off the tribal names from his land as surely as the boy might have recited those from his: *Ogoni, Efik, Ibibio, Itsekiri, Opobo, Urhobo, Etche.* Some were friend and some foe, some kin, some adversaries; all were of the Delta.

The man looked at the trail behind the children, the one leading over the hillock and past the cannon. The lagoon beyond it was hidden from view. "Surely there were others," he said. "Chasing oil. Am I really the first?"

The boy nodded, and the man's face broke even wider still. More teeth emerged, an endless string of shells.

The children had seen the gas flares in the far distance, just as the fishermen in their village had seen their tributaries grow thick with sludge from upstream creeks. Everyone had known the *oyibos* were drawing closer, one gas flare at a time. The plumes of flame were now stuttered above the treetops, forming a dotted line heading straight for their village. And now, it would appear, the *oyibos* had finally come out from the shadows.

Oil.

The boy knew about oil. His mother cooked with oil: the red palm oil so much of their food was simmered in. The English had bombarded the Brass Islanders for that very oil, is what his teacher had said. It was Ijaw palm oil that the English had used to grease their machineries and run their cannon factories, to make their soap and their candles, even to feed their slaves.

But that was long ago, and it was a different sort of oil the *oyibo* was after now, the kind the boy's father wiped off his hands after working on the generator, the kind that seeped from riverbeds, the kind that was turned into the petrol that fuelled the motorboats, the kind that flared in the night. With so many *oyibo* mosquitoes needling into the flesh of the Delta, it was a wonder the entire place hadn't come down with malarial fever. That's what the boy's father said, and he was a storyteller not given to lies.

The Igbo guards were getting twitchier by the minute. They were expecting an ambush at any time it seemed, but the pale man ignored their unease, extended a hand instead. The boy clasped it, forearm to forearm, in proper Ijaw fashion.

"What is your name?" the man asked.

Everything that exists has a name. "Nnamdi," said the boy.

The Igbo exchanged glances. Nnamdi was not an Ijaw name. It was from the mainland, it was Igbo, as they were. The boy had been named in a fit of fervour by his father to honour the memory of another Nnamdi, the First President, a Father of Nigerian Independence. "It will bring him luck," his father had insisted over his wife's objections.

"The Nnamdi of his namesake," she'd reminded him, "was brought down by military coup."

The Igbo guards had taken a mistaken comfort in the boy's name, not realizing just how far into Ijaw territory they had trespassed.

Forgive us not our trespassers, thought Nnamdi. That was from Sunday school.

"Well, Nnamdi," said the *oyibo*. "It is very nice to be meeting you. I like your smile. And I hope any oil we find makes you very rich."

Oil was made from living paste. The boy knew this from school. Plants, animals. Anything that lived could be made into oil. Even Englishmen. Even Dutch. In Sunday school it was called "transubstantiation." They'd been made to write that out with chalk. Wine into blood. Or was it blood into wine? The grown-ups of his village had formed lines to drink this wine-blood when they attended church congregations, and Nnamdi wondered if the bodies of the Englishmen in the graveyard had transubstantiated into oil as well.

Perhaps it was the scent of English blood turned to wine that the Shell Man had been tracking through the forest, the way a hunter might stalk a wounded animal.

Voices on the far side of the hill, calling out.

"Someone is looking for you," said the man.

The men at the lagoon were shouting for the children, telling them to hurry before the next deluge hit. But the children were nowhere to be seen. They were in among the headstones, conversing with ghosts, and the fish were left unattended, mouths gaping, drowning in air, as the rains came down.

"We have to go," said Nnamdi, and the man nodded.

On Nnamdi's permission, the children scattered, running to gather their pails and basins. Nnamdi went as well, but he stopped at the crest of the hill and called back, on behalf of himself and the little ones, *"Noao!"* A greeting and thank you in the same breath.

The pale man waved back at him. *"Noao!"* he replied, pronouncing it funny.

Only after Nnamdi left did he realize that the man had never told him his own name, had chosen instead to keep it hidden, like a peppermint up a sleeve.

48

There were times when Nnamdi would wonder if he and the other children had dreamed that encounter. It seemed more myth than memory: the Shell Man with the Igbo guides and the spyglass. But the real asserted itself soon enough the following spring in a crash of timber and a toppling of trees.

Nnamdi had been playing with the younger ones among the tall stands of palm oil trees at the edge of the village, and the forests had again begun to move—but more violently this time.

A rumble, a splintering crash, and the trees beyond the clearing suddenly began to sway. A crack, like the sound of a bone breaking, sent the children running into one another as they fled. A machine pushed its way out of the forest, bulldozing a path. It was followed by a crew of men in beige uniforms, flanked by soldiers on either side, as another machine rumbled out, chewing up the debris the first had left. More and more men boiled out of the gap like ants.

Nnamdi turned to the nearest child. "Run!" he said. "Get the adults." But the adults were already on hand. They had come running at the sound of trees falling and were gathering now in growing numbers. The first machine cut its engines, and a diesel-tinted silence came over the clearing as the village headman made his way to the front of the line, walking slowly in flip-flops with a resigned posture, as though he'd been expecting this all along.

The bulldozers were operated by foreigners—Igbos, by the looks of it—and the village headman held a long conversation with the driver of the first machine, speaking in English laced with Ijaw, sweeping his hand from jungle to trail. But the men on the bulldozers had something greater than words. They had papers. They had papers signed by the Governor Himself. Papers that came all the way from Abuja, from the national capital.

"This is not Abuja," the boy heard the headman shout, hitting every word with a punch. "This is the Delta. This is Ijaw land."

First they came with handshakes and gifts, and then they returned with bulldozers and paper. This is how the story would be told.

The entire village seemed to have arrived by that point, and the people pushed forward in anger, carrying the headman with them. One of the soldiers slung his rifle off his shoulder and, with a practised, almost bored, sense of calm, fired a round above their heads into the sky, a sound so sharp it left a tang in the air.

Behind the bulldozers a jeep rolled in, wheels climbing and falling over the debris. In the open window of the jeep, Nnamdi could see an arm. It lay along the door and was tapping out a rhythm. It was the rhythm of waiting. An arm speckled with freckles, pale and pink at the same time.

49

Laura was cataloguing memories, compiling an inventory of loss.

Her father, skating.

An indoor arena in the blah days of winter. A faint haze, low along the ice. Crisp intakes of breath, echoing voices, other families.

Laura, at age eight. Maybe nine.

He was such an elegant skater, her father. Long strides, legs crossing effortlessly over each other. She lacked that grace, was afraid of tumbling, and as her dad circled wide and then reeled himself in, coming back toward her, Laura's skates suddenly went out from under her and she landed on her bum with a mighty *oomph*. Her dad stopped on a skid of shaved ice and laughed. Laughed without thinking. But when he realized his mistake, when he saw the tears pooling in her eyes—he fell as well. Got up, fell down. Again and again. Right on his bum too. Fell to make her feel better, fell to make her laugh, throwing himself down again and again. "You see," he'd said. "Daddies fall too."

What if it wasn't about the money?

50

Our Mother Who Art in Heaven.

Wonyinghi, the God above Gods, creator of everything that is and everything that shall be, sky-dwelling, removed from the mundane and the everyday, aloof, haughty even, yet always vigilant. She sits in final judgment on the lives below.

"We have all of us made our agreement with Wonyinghi, before entering the womb. Each person's soul"—the boy's father used the word *teme* here, signifying something halfway between the spirit world and the physical—"is summoned before Her prior to conception."

Each soul, each *teme,* was assigned its fate. "Whether it will obtain wealth and joy, whether it will be poor or rich, sickly or healthy, weak or strong, whether it will be fruitful or barren. It is all of it foretold."

Your entire life, laid out like a story. Your personality as well. Whether you would be *biye-kro,* resolute, or *toro-kro,* one who talked big but did not act; whether you would be a leader or a listener, a wrestler or a watcher, a king or coward, *olotu* or *su.*

Nnamdi and his father were mending nets in a blustery, mosquito-free wind. He was old enough now to help with this, was no longer playing chasing games with the younger ones.

"Sunday school doesn't teach you everything," his father said. "It doesn't teach you when you will die. Christ does not know this, but Wonyinghi does. She knows this because every *teme* also knows when it will pass away. This is part of the agreement. The *teme* agrees to the time of its demise, the exact moment it will leave its body. It is the body that dies, Nnamdi, not the *teme.* The *teme* moves on."

Depending on the nature of its agreement with Wonyinghi, a *teme* might enter another womb and be born anew. Or, if its sins have been many, it might limp off instead to lick its wounds in the Village of the Dead as a woeful ghost, an outcast. A *duwoi-you,* like those sad lost souls pinned down by stones in the British graveyard.

"Why does one woman bear a healthy child and another a

stillborn soul? Why do one man's wounds grow septic and another's heal? Why is one child fearless, another fearful? Why does this child sulk and the next chatter away like a trilling bird? It is their agreement with Wonyinghi."

It was very difficult to alter the agreement your *teme* had made with Wonyinghi. But the boy's father explained that it could be done. Your fate could be renegotiated through the employment of diviners, women (and sometimes men) who had special access to Wonyinghi.

"Theirs is a knowledge derived from dreams. They know how to cast lots, how to read the signs. They cajole lesser gods, petition greater ones. They know which rites to perform, which to avoid. They know which taboos have been broken, which laws of the village ancestors have been breached and how to make amends."

These diviners, the *buro-you,* were born into their role. It was something that emerged at an early age, an understanding of that in-between world, of how to distinguish between the real and the reflected.

Diviners stood in stark contrast to the darker medicine of the sorcerer, the *diriguo-keme.*

A diviner's hovel was easy to recognize. Tufts of hair and bits of feather fluttered outside. Tide-polished pebbles were piled by the door posts, clay urns and strange bundles sat out front. Nnamdi always slowed up when he passed such a place, cast his eyes downward, wary yet enthralled, listening for whispers.

No such markings warned of a sorcerer's abode. Theirs was the magic of vengeance, not justice. Poison, not persuasion. "The *diriguo-keme* operate in secret," Nnamdi's father warned, weaving shut a rip in the net. "They gather snake venom and stir up spells; they can even twist the weaker gods to their will." Unlike diviners, the women and men who became sorcerers did so by choice.

"No agreement with Wonyinghi ever includes evil," Nnamdi's father said as he wound in the last of the netting. "We are born good, we choose evil. Life forces these decisions upon us." And it often came down to that elemental struggle between *buro-you* and *diriguo-keme,* between diviners and sorcery. "The trick," said Nnamdi's father, "is to know the difference."

Thus ended the day's lesson. *"Time to go,"* the boy's father said. The sound of church bells had brought out his English.

The views held by Nnamdi's father were very different from those of the local minister. Or rather, *ministers.* There had been a succession of them. Mr. Baptist had stomped off the year before, abandoning his post and wishing ill will and lightning strikes on "ye of little faith." Mr. Anglican had failed as well, and now Mr. Methodist had stepped into the fray with a determined vigour and a thick Lagos accent. He'd landed in their village like a wandering *teme.* Among missionaries, it was apparently a point of pride to be posted in the "far wilds" of the outer Delta, in amongst the "remote" and "fearful" tidal Ijaw. Although, as the villagers liked to point out, it was Lagos and the rest of Nigeria that was remote and fearful, not them.

Mr. Methodist beseeched and behooved his congregation— his very words, "I beseech and behoove you"—to put aside their childish belief in diviners and sorcery. "Wonyinghi is NOT God Almighty! And Satan is not merely chief *diriguo-keme.*"

Of course not, thought the villagers. Satan was a serpent. That part made sense: a spitting cobra or a black mamba uncoiling in the shadows. But the lesser demons of the Bible? The various imps and minions? Surely those were *diriguo-keme.*

"You cannot assuage Jesus with a few twigs or with feathers cast by witchery, or with a leaf stem tied a certain way. Jesus is NOT another word for Wonyinghi, of that I most definitely can assure you. To begin with, Wonyinghi is a female. *A fee-MALE.*"

"But Jesus is all things! Is what you said." A few of the men in the congregation liked to torment the minister with their queries. The women were too polite to bait him. Poor Mr. Methodist.

"No," the Man of Cloth would sputter. "Jesus is—is a man like you or I."

"No one worships me!" a voice called out to laughter in the back. It was Ijaw laughter, a language the minister did not speak.

"Jesus is man and God. He is both."

"Woman as well?"

"No! Most absolutely not!"

And so on.

Nnamdi's mother would trudge to church every Sunday, dragging Nnamdi along like a captured mouse on a string. Mr. Methodist would then deliver his book-slapping sermons in rolling Lagos rhythms punctuated with loud exhortations. He didn't speak English in the proper Ijaw fashion, which made him hard to follow at times. You had to strain the flow of words as though you were trapping fishes. The Ijaw of the outer Delta had been speaking the King's English (now the Queen's) since the days of the palm oil trade, so to hear some fleshy-faced Yoruba pastor from Lagos mangle the language was hard on their ears. "We must be polite," his mother said, scolding her son for snickering. "He be tryin' his best."

Mr. Methodist had once been a wretched sinner himself. "I was lost in Lagos, but now am found! I was blind, but now can see!"

"Ah, but that be easy, gettin' lost in Lagos," one of the men said, not impressed. "It's very big Lagos, bigger than Portako, I am told. Anybody can get lost in Lagos. Is not a feat." Portako was the local name for Port Harcourt, the standard of all that was urban and enormous in the Delta states.

"But the streets in Lagos dey runnin' straight," someone else shouted back. "Man has to make an *effort* to get lost in Lagos. In the Delta, dey no street signs, no streets even! It is easier to get lost *here*. But getting lost in Lagos? That takes work. That is a true feat."

"You never even been to Portako, what you know about anything?" This was someone several benches back.

This was followed by a loud digressive discussion on the merits of creeks versus streets, and how one might best navigate the latter, at which point Mr. Methodist had to shout and pound a fist on his pulpit to regain their attention.

Wonyinghi may have been aloof, but the lower gods were not. They were everything that humans were, multiplied a hundredfold: petty and jealous, moody and mean, tender and kind. Nnamdi's father followed a lesser deity, an *oru* of the forest, one that calmed fears and protected children. He maintained a small shrine at the edge of the woods: tin roof and a dirt floor, carefully swept. The *orumo* of forests and the *owumo* of the river? "Reflections of each other," he explained to his son. "Like in your mother's mirror. But which is the real?"—and here he switched to English for emphasis— *"the tree or the tree in the water?"*

Nnamdi's father rarely came to church, and when he did, it was usually only in penance for a night of palm wine or a promise broken. It was Nnamdi's mother who needed assuaging, not Jesus Almighty.

And although Mr. Methodist may have cast Jesus Almighty as the greatest of all the *orumo* and *owumo*, greater even than Wonyinghi, Nnamdi's mother hedged her bets just to be safe. Hadn't she performed her own version of the *tenebomo* rites when Nnamdi had climbed his first palm-oil tree? It was no small thing, the climbing of palm-oil trees. Slip, and you might crash through the forest's lower canopy, bounce hard, break bones, dislocate shoulders, be left dead or, worse, crippled. After they'd climbed their first tree and cut their first bundle of palm nuts, the ones used to make cooking oil, many young men refused to go back up, choosing to tap wine palms instead—in leech-infested swamps, but on the ground at least. You didn't have to climb wine palms.

So the women in the village would perform the *tenebomo* rites after that first climb: to dispel fears and calm the hearts of boys on the brink of manhood. Nnamdi's own mother had taken part, kneading palm oil into his calves and thighs, his heart still pounding from the climb, as the other women moved around him in a slow circle, waving palm fronds up and down and whisper-chanting to him, *"You won't be afraid, you won't be afraid anymore."* He had felt his fears dissolve with every turn of the women's steps.

And didn't his mother quietly ask her husband to petition certain deities when she needed help, just in case Jesus Almighty's hands were full with other things? Whether to silence a rival at the market, or quell a rumour or cure a boil, when Jesus turned the other cheek it was time to call in the *orumo*. Hadn't Nnamdi's father always helped, never made a comment?

Love complicates a marriage. It tangles up everything, like a flotsam net in water, snagging paddles and poles alike. Best avoided, really. Nnamdi's mother was from another creek, where they spoke a dialect his father compared to talking with a mouth full of mashed yams. She had come to the market in Nnamdi's village and had never left. His father said: "When I met your mother, she was already my wife, she just didn't know it. We didn't *meet*. We found each other. She wasn't looking for palm oil that day, she was looking for me."

Nnamdi's mother always laughed at this, but she never challenged it, either.

51

Between spearing tidewater fish and keeping the village generators running, Nnamdi's father could have afforded to take a second wife, but he never did. Nnamdi's mother liked to say, "I am his senior wife, his junior wife, his favourite wife, his not-so-favourite wife." She would chuckle in that low rich way of hers, like the bubbles in a pot of pepper soup slow-boiling on coals, while his father smiled, crooked and quiet. Nnamdi had never heard his father laugh, but he scarcely remembered him ever not smiling.

Nor did his father dance.

Fetes were often staged for the *owumo*. The river gods, lurking in murky currents and hiding in the undertows, needed to be entertained, placated, and prodded—no matter how much the church officials objected. The village depended on it. And when the masquerade dancers with masks as long as their bodies, headpieces carved in the shapes of fish and fowl, moved to the heartbeat of drums in jerking steps and sudden starts, a form of elated madness took hold. Nnamdi had seen his uncle through the eye sockets of a mask, but his uncle wasn't really there anymore. A *teme* had taken temporary hold of him. "We become the masks we don." This was the magic of masquerade.

"Some of us are dancers, some diviners," his father explained. "It depends entirely upon the agreement we entered into at conception. But if we are quiet enough, we will hear it. We will hear our calling."

Some are drummers, some are weavers. And some are weavers of words. There was what you did to *live*—throw nets, grease generators—and what you did because you must. Nnamdi's father was a storyteller, and storytelling was something that chose you the way an *owu* might choose a priest, or a wife might choose a husband. And with property passing down through the wife's side, the choice of husband was every bit as critical as which *owu* you decided to honour. Did your future husband have other wives? Could he support other wives? And if so, what property did these other wives bring to the table?

Children played their own version of dancer and mask, holding up pieces of wood in front of their faces, chasing each other, shrieking and yelling, running to the gods, running from the gods. And when the gods had been successfully tired out and the heat of day had begun to subside, when the gas flares hissed and the winds shifted and a metallic taste filled the air, the children would gather around the adults in the main square.

Palm-wine music and moonlight tales.

In the muggy dusk, insects flitted about as birds staked out their noisy and competing claims to various treetops. The village's packed-earth perimeter kept the forest back and snakes at bay, but the crack of branch and rustle of leaf signified forest creatures whuffling about in the underbrush.

Adult voices, singing softly, the verses ending only when another song began. The children scooted closer. And closer. They would listen to the songs until one of them mustered the courage to cry out *"Egberiyo!"* which meant "Story!" The men would stop their singing and look to Nnamdi's father. With a practised sigh, as though accepting a great imposition, he would ask, *"Egberiyo?"* to which the children would cry, *"Ya!"*

Nnamdi's father did this every time, drawing out their excitement, until at last he would begin. The tales he told always started the same way: "Once, in times gone by ..."

The repertoire was wide-ranging: "The Tale of the Fat Woman Who Melted Away," "The Story of the Rooster Who Caused a War Between Two Towns," "The Boy Who Fell in Love with the Moon," "The Girl Who Married a Ghost," "The Story of the Young Woman and the Seven Jealous Wives," "Why the Bat Is

Ashamed to Be Seen at Daytime." It might take hours for his father to uncrate a tale, with many detours along the way, and as the children grew drowsy he would occasionally stop to ask, *"Egberiyo?"* To which they would reply *"Ya,"* to show they were still alert, were still clinging to the waking world.

Several years had passed since the *oyibos* had first arrived at the edge of the village. Compensation payments for the gas flares and the tarlike seepage from nearby wells helped pay for the monthly shipments of cooking oil from Port Harcourt. There was more time for moonlight stories now, just as there was no longer the need to climb palm-oil trees.

Wine palms were still being tapped, though. More than ever, in fact. But the milky drink was now distilled into gin—a stronger kick for young men with little to do. It might take eleven pails of palm wine to produce a single pail of gin, but oh, it was worth it, for the fire that was concentrated in that flammable drink was like swallowing thunder. These young men in their sweat-stained undershirts and loose-hanging shorts hung back from the story-telling, watching their own childhoods fall asleep to moonlight tales as they drank glassy-eyed from jars—drank in the orange shadows of gas-flare flames, to the hiss and sigh of escaping heat being drawn directly from the earth.

When the story was finished and his young audience was in slumber, Nnamdi's father would end with a final, forceful state-ment: *"Egberifa."* The story is over.

52

Moonlight tales and palm-wine music.

If nothing else, the oil company bulldozers had opened up the views. You could see gas flares above the jungle far into the distance, thin towers plumed with fire, the flames uncurling, illuminating the underside of clouds. One such tower had been built on the very edge of Nnamdi's village, and when the winds shifted, the air tasted like tin.

A humid swamp, exhaling fire, the Niger Delta was webbed with countless creeks and endless channels. But the Shell Men had found Nnamdi's village anyway, had tracked satellite photos and followed footsore surveys to get there.

They had changed the very nature of night. Nnamdi was now thirteen or fourteen and was having trouble sleeping with the eerie glow of gas flares and the heavy thumps underground. A muffled heartbeat in the earth below.

The oil men had cleared seismic lines through the jungle so that they could search for oil without drilling. They would carve out a grid, clearing the forest in strips, and then plant detonations at the cross points. In this methodical, mathematical manner they could read the shock waves that bounced back the way a diviner might read signs in the toss of sticks or the colour of a moon. The oil men could chart the unseen, decipher what lay hidden below.

These underground explosions had caused cracks to appear in the cement walls of Nnamdi's home, hair-thin fault lines that only got bigger. He would lie on his mat under the mosquito netting and listen to the dull thuds of Shell Men chasing the echoes of oil. He could feel the vibrations under his mat, would watch orange shadows play along the walls, would dream of hearts buried in oil.

There were times when Nnamdi scarcely seemed tethered to this world. "Your soul got lost in the clouds on the way down," his mother would scold. "You were entangled in stars at ya birth."

"Leave the boy in peace," his father would say. "It's the agreement he made before he was born."

"*Egberiyo!*" the children would cry.

"Egberiyo?" his father would reply.

Nnamdi's father had started to incorporate the gas flares and seismic surveys into his nightly narratives. "The Story of Lightning and Thunder," for example, was now turned upside down. Originally, Thunder had been an old mother sheep, and her son Lightning a ram; you could see tufts of their wool caught on trees, in the small clouds that formed after a storm. But now their arguments raged underground as well, flaring up in bursts of raw temper.

South of the village, more tales were unfolding. The oil companies were building a Road to Nowhere. The raised hump snaked its way through the squelchiest of the mangrove marshes, forcing a path from the clustered wellheads at the village edge to flow stations in far-flung swamps where only screeching monkeys and coiled snakes dwelled. Nnamdi and his father had followed this muddy scar a ways through the forest, had marvelled at the sheer determination of it. Work crews blocked their way farther down, though, with armed guards standing, rifles ready, behind mirrored sunglasses. So they never got to see the end of nowhere.

As they walked back, Nnamdi's father had pointed out how the roadbed blocked the water from seeping across. "Do you see how it's backing up on this side, and draining on that? The road is acting like a dam. This side will flood, that side will wash away. Not good for fish or forest." And so it proved. The wine palms died on one side of the road, and the fish drowned in the loam-rich waters on the other.

The cooking oil continued to arrive in ever larger tins.

Soon the lagoon behind the village was all but dead. Fishermen still made the trek, out of habit more than anything, pulling what few gaping mudskippers they could from the oil-slicked flats. Orphan fish, gills opening and closing, clogged with crude.

The diviners had failed; all their rattle-shaking dance steps and eye-rolling visions could not bring the bounty back. And try though they might to shift the blame onto broken pacts made with the past, these intermediaries of the gods had fallen from grace in the village. "The *owumo* have been silent. Why? Have they left us? Do you even know?" This was the accusation, unanswerable and spiked with venom.

In the lagoon, a shark had rolled in on one of the tides, already dead and covered in crude. This was taken as a sign, but of what? That the Shell Men were stronger even than sharks? That the oil was, as the elder members said, "the devil's excrement"? The tidal Ijaw had once cast a pall of fear across the lesser nations of the Delta; known as "swamp sharks," they had prowled the inlets with a predatory gaze. And now? Suffocating in crude. For some, the appearance of the shark was taken as an exhortation that they had lost their way. But no one would touch the carcass. It rolled away on the next tide, but every few days it would reappear, still coated in oil. It was a long time decaying.

New words had entered the village vocabulary: *pipeline, flow station, manifold.* Successive spills had left successively higher lines of tar along the mangrove shores and had spread into secondary creeks as well, forcing fishermen farther and farther into the mangrove swamps. Their canoes, carved from a hardwood that was even now disappearing under bulldozed paths, were not meant for deep water. The pirogues would sink as soon as they turned over, and more than one body of a fisherman had washed up, sheathed in oil as well.

The flare-offs had tainted the clouds, bringing down rains that itched and burned and left the plantain and palm leaves spotted with blisters. Children had begun coughing up blood, and village meetings became shouting matches. The village itself was divided into clans and the clans into larger *ibe*. Connected families were now accused of profiteering, of secretly siding with the Shell Men. And they were all Shell Men; it didn't matter whether they were *oyibos* or Igbos, and it didn't matter what the colour of their coveralls was or which particular tribal markings were sewn onto their chest pockets: Chevron, Texaco, Mobil, Agip, BP, Exxon. Total from France, Eni and Saipem from Italy. Even the NNPC, Nigeria's own National Petroleum Corporation. It was all Shell.

The Shell Men built a school (without teachers) and a health clinic (without doctors) and installed a pharmacy (without medicine): tidy-looking cinder-block buildings with corrugated tin roofs. They took photos of themselves clasping forearms with *ibe* elders, and when the lack of teachers, doctors, and medicines was pointed out, the Shell Men replied, "We build them, we don't staff them. Talk to the state administrators. Or send a letter to the national government in Abuja." But Abuja city hardly seemed real, that distant capital far removed from oil spills and gas flares. Shell? Shell was here, Shell was now, and the people's anger only grew.

So after the photographs had been taken and the soldiers had back-walked the Shell Men out of the village to waiting jeeps, the village was left to argue with itself.

"The health-care clinic has no roof!" people shouted at the members of the larger *ibe*. "How much dey payin' you?"

"No roof? And why is that? We all know it's you who stole it. Where are the palm fronds was once atop your house? How'd those turn to tin like so?"

"Not stolen, *taken*. That clinic was empty. No nurse, no doctor. Why let the roof just sit over nothing like that?"

"A nurse comes!"

"Once a year! If that. Once a year from Portako, nurse be coming to inject us with inoculate for everything except the oil.

Where is the inoculate for blood in the lung? For oil on the creek? For poison in the air? And now dey buildin' a brand-new pier with concrete pilings. Why? So they can land larger boats. You think those boats be filled with fish? Filled with medicine? *Ozu enini!* So ah'm askin' you again. How much dey paying you?"

It began with small acts of sabotage.

Sand in gas tanks, pilfered tools. The reaction this provoked was swift. Soldiers swept through on the Shell Men's behest, reclaiming tools and rifle-butting young men to their knees. Soon the soldiers outnumbered the workers. The oil crews were clearly on edge, landing at the village jetty at shift change with the precision of a military operation. When the village men tried to barricade the dock, the soldiers turned on them, torching the homes they'd decided belonged to troublemakers and plundering family supplies of plantain and breadfruit.

"You are caught between hammer and anvil," the officer in charge told the Ijaw men who watched, sullen and seething, as the soldiers moved through. Hammer and anvil.

"No," the men of the village replied. "It's not we who are caught between hammer an' anvil. It is you." It was less a threat than a statement of fact—and a warning.

Over in Warri, a mob had stormed the oil company compound, shattering windows and trapping the staff inside. And when the army fired tear gas into the crowds, the protesters—inured by now to acidic fumes—simply picked the canisters up and threw them back. The protesters finally dispersed, but only after leaving an empty coffin at the company's front gate.

In Nnamdi's village, however, any gestures would not be merely symbolic.

"Soldiers at their sides or not, the Shell Men be easy enough to kill. From the forest, we pick dem off one by one, collect their skulls, pile them in the middle of the village like yams on market day." These were the cries of young men, their anger stoked by gin. The older members of their *ibe* talked them down, but they couldn't stop events from escalating.

When torrential rains chased the crews and their armed guards from the village site, the workers returned the next day to find the scorched remains of bulldozers and jeeps toppled on their sides. The crew foreman walked through the aftermath. "How did they manage to set a fire in a downpour?" he asked, voice in a whisper. Maybe the *orumo* spirits had played a hand in it; maybe the forest had struck back.

Or maybe, with enough gasoline, anything will burn.

And that was when the Man from the Graves returned. It was the same pale-pink presence Nnamdi had encountered in the forest that day, no longer smiling, striding into a village council meeting forcefully and uninvited. He arrived during a heated debate over whether capturing the site foreman and setting him on fire would be enough of a gesture, or whether the entire crew needed to be doused and set alight as well. The man walked right in, along with an armed contingent of Mobile Police, the "Kill and Gos" as they were known. He took the floor without ceremony or proper modesty.

"I see angry young men," he said, meeting the glowering gaze of the gin drinkers at the back. "Young men with no prospects. No work. Come. We will train you, we will feed you, we will pay you." He turned to the older members of the *ibe*. "Give me the names of your finest youths and I will grant them employment. Give us your young men, and we will give you prosperity."

He left with the same sure stride.

"We don't want prosperity, we want clean water!" someone shouted in Ijaw, but by then it was too late. The Man from the Graves was gone.

53

They would prove no hollow promise, these Shell Jobs. The next night, as the elders mulled the matter over, compiling tentative lists, and the air outside hung with the smell of sulphur and sour gas, the children gathered in the yard, unable to sleep.

"Egberiyo!" they yelled.

Too old to sit at his father's feet without feeling childish, but too young for gin, Nnamdi held back instead, listened from a distance.

"Story!" the little ones yelled, but the story was never told, because the evening was interrupted: a sudden commotion, and the children were shooed aside.

The Man from the Graves had returned, armed with a clipboard and paperwork. A crowd followed him through the village in a hubbub more hectic than any masquerade of masks, and when they arrived at the council hall the entire village tried to cram itself inside. At the front of the hall, the man, flanked as before by his personal "Kill and Go" guards, tipped back a plastic bottle of water and drank deeply as the elder *ibe* members berated him formally and at length, listing each grievance in turn to a chorus of confirming shouts.

Fishermen had been compensated for ruined fishing nets (with many a rotting net hastily dunked in oil and then presented to the Shell company), but it was not enough. "You have taken our past; give us a future," they shouted in Ijaw. This was translated by the Igbo aides as "They want more money."

"Not money," the Man from the Graves said. "We have already given you enough of that. No more handouts. Jobs instead. Give a man a fish, and you will feed him for a day. But teach a man to fish—"

"We already know how to fish! What we need is for you oil men to go!"

He tilted back another long drink of water, waited them out. And in the sweltering heat, it was done: forms were signed, names written down. Many of the elder *ibe* members couldn't read what was written, but they made a great production out of poring over the papers anyway, frowning and nodding, making their X's to mark the spot. A long, laborious procedure, and as it dragged on, the pale man let his gaze float around the room. His eyes met Nnamdi's.

The Man from the Graves smiled. Nnamdi smiled back.

"I remember you!" the man said, and he stood and came around from behind the table to clasp forearms with Nnamdi. "I met this boy when I was still tramping about in the jungle," he told the others. Then, smiling at Nnamdi, "You were at the lagoon that day, keeping an eye on the other children ya? I remember you. You've grown very big! But your smile, it hasn't changed."

The final papers had been signed, and names were being called out. Young men came forward to receive their folded orange coveralls; these were the lucky ones.

The Man from the Graves called out to the *ibe* elders. "Is this one on the list?" he asked, referring to Nnamdi.

There was an embarrassed pause. Although Nnamdi's father was respected as a fisherman, a storyteller, and a healer of generators, he had married outside of clan lines, a woman from a lesser creek, a refugee from a village that had been reduced to rubble in the civil war and had never recovered. The *ibe* council hadn't even considered offering Nnamdi to the oil company.

"He's too small," they said.

"Small? Nonsense."

"Young. Too young, we mean to say."

"*Hetgeen?* That's ridiculous. Put his name down." Then, back to Nnamdi, "Would you like to work for us?"

Nnamdi looked over at his father.

Oil company jobs were coveted. There were rumours of men from other villages who'd been hired and were even now the subject of fantastical tales of wealth and lavish two-storey homes in Portako. An oil company job meant hard currency, health care, a wider world. Nnamdi's father felt the ground shift. His son would return with stories of his own to tell, would return with knowledge, would be able to advise the others on how best to deal with the *oyibos*. As the father, it was his decision to make.

"Well?" asked the Dutch man.

Nnamdi's father nodded.

And that is the Story of How a Smile Became a Shell Man.

54

They came the next day, lining up the young men they had selected for a cursory medical exam: checking for ringworm, using tongue depressors and small lights to peer inside them, into throats and ears, examining scalps and eyes. No one was rejected. Instead, the young men of Nnamdi's village were loaded into the back of pickup trucks and driven away. Family and friends followed this slow-moving procession through the village, but the farewell was strangely subdued: no shouts, no celebrations. Not even sorrow. Just the leaving.

A long bouncing ride along the Road to Nowhere took them through a chain-linked gate and then down to a pier where a passenger ferry lay waiting. The young men filed on board, into the hold, forming rows—but Nnamdi stayed up top. "It'll be choppy," the captain warned as he climbed past Nnamdi into the wheelhouse. "Could get wet."

Nnamdi smiled. "I don't mind."

As the boat pushed off, Nnamdi leaned into the wind, eating

air, feeling elated. He'd grown up amid the backwash of a distant sea, had watched that sea push its way into the mangrove swamps, had tasted the saltwater in its fish, had caught glimpses of something bigger between bends in the river. The village's fishing expeditions stayed close to shore and rarely skirted open water; there were too many dangers lurking about. But the boat Nnamdi was on now turned, followed a wide creek into a wider channel, and the sea ahead opened up in full view, like a heron spreading its wings.

The boat was pointed toward Bonny Island, a low silhouette nested in a cluster of lights. As they drew nearer, details emerged. Squat blocks of grey took shape, revealed themselves to be storage cylinders. Metalwork towers coalesced from the mist. Low-throated oil tankers appeared, bellowing for crude.

They passed offshore oil platforms—floating cities of light—as rain began to spit and Bonny Island grew larger.

The boat cut its engines and swung wide to glide in. Nnamdi could see the security fences and watchtowers surrounding the massive storage cylinders with the shantytown squalor outside. No tumbledown shacks for Nnamdi and the others, though. The boat slid through a gate and into a lock that closed behind them as another opened in front.

Bonny Island, at the mouth of the Delta, was the terminus of the Trans-Niger Pipeline. This was where all the threads came together, where the fuel was ladled into the empty holds of oil tankers.

Nnamdi would always remember that first chill of air conditioning. The a/c was like a *duwoi-you*'s breath on his skin. He'd felt this brush of iced air before, from the refrigerators in the village market, where a wheezing generator had rattled and coughed, keeping drinks cooled and the bitter greens from wilting. In the sealed buildings of Bonny Island, though, the a/c was more than a mere whisper; it was all-enveloping. Stark hallways, smooth as glass. Tubes of light unclouded by insects. Bunk-bed dormitories and strange, textureless food served in compartmentalized trays. No need for mosquito nets, because any mosquito that tried to find its way through the maze of hallways to the dorm-room bunk beds would have died from exhaustion before it arrived.

Stationed at Bonny Island, Nnamdi took motors apart and put them back together. He oiled bearings, cleaned cogs, replaced timing belts. The training wasn't much more than he'd already learned from watching his father coax yet another day of life out of the village's ailing generators.

The other young men from his village didn't fare as well. One by one, their ranks were winnowed down. One by one, they were pulled from mechanical training and placed in menial posts instead. Some on guardhouse duty, others on janitorial. Some did nothing except sweep floors, all day long. Some were sent as far afield as Portako, where they mowed lawns at the homes of oil company executives or unloaded cargo from dock to bay and back again.

In Nnamdi, though, the oil men had recognized something more. He was the only one from his group to go through the entire training as promised. And after his stint at Bonny Island had finished, Nnamdi was placed on a seismic crew, hand-cranking augers into the muck, boring holes into wet earth, placing the charges and patting the mud down, then unravelling the fuse wires quickly, back-stepping toward cover, sweating heavily in the heat. *Oyibo* technicians set off the actual charges, explosions more felt than heard, as Nnamdi wiped his face and guzzled that strange bottled water, devoid of taste and colour.

Though the crew was far from Nnamdi's village, they were still deep in Ijaw territory and had to be protected by armed guards. Mobs would gather at the blast sites, yelling death threats at

Nnamdi and the others in a dialect foreign to him. The intent was clear enough, though. *Traitors! We will find out where you live, we will track you down, we will kill you, kill your parents, kill your entire family.* The gunshots the guards fired overhead no longer made Nnamdi flinch.

After his tour of duty with the seismic crews had ended, Nnamdi was moved to a support station, where he kept the pumps lubricated and the diesel tanks filled. He learned new uses for old words. Delta crude, he discovered, was prized because it was "sweet" and "light." Catching a spray of crude oil in his mouth, he knew, was anything but sweet; having felt it soak through his coveralls and slide down his skin, he knew it wasn't light, either. Here, however, *sweet* meant "low in sulphur"; *light* meant "smooth and easier to refine than the sandy guck elsewhere"—even Saudi crude, which, Nnamdi was told dismissively, was very "sticky." He knew full well how the oil slicks in the Delta coated everything they came into contact with, killing off lagoons and forming a heavy sludge along the tide lines. But in this mirror world he'd entered, the smooth thickness of the Delta crude made it a prize to be coveted.

The oil in the Delta was near the surface as well. Indeed, it sometimes bubbled out unbidden. "Don't have to dig deep pits to get at it," one of Nnamdi's *oyibo* instructors explained. "Just stick in a straw and out it comes. It's what we call 'eco-friendly.' In Europe, and in America, where I'm from, they have tough laws about environmental stuff." The instructor laughed. "We could never do there what we do here. Bonny Light is very popular. It's a cleaner crude; that's why they go crazy for it back home."

Nnamdi continued his upward climb through the ranks, was promoted to a field crew, riding on fast-chopping speedboats under heavy guard, tacking into side creeks and tributaries, tracing the pipelines back to the wellheads and pump stations, climbing

ladders to run diagnostics. Simple enough work, checking pressure
and flow, ticking off a set list of boxes. There were pink faces everywhere, and Nnamdi was often presented as if he were a prized
possession. "From some backwater village in the outer creeks, no
less, and look how he performs!"

At night, lying on his cot in the company dorm, Nnamdi
would fall into dreams of pepper soup and moonlight tales, would
wake with the taste of both on his tongue.

And all the while, he was amassing money. Lots of it. Enough
to pour a proper cement floor for his parents' house, perhaps bring
in a new generator so his father wouldn't have to keep jerry-rigging
the old one, maybe a great fat refrigerator for his mother to stock
with Fanta and shaved ice to sell to the village. She could use the
income to buy a bright new headwrap and a giant pot for pepper
stew and maybe a goat to kill and a new radio, one that wasn't
hand-cranked but ran off a car battery, all that and a Sunday suit
for his father, for when his mother dragged him to church, and a
soccer ball for the schoolyard. Nnamdi would drift into sleep on
those thoughts, smiling.

But then the river caught fire, and that changed everything.

55

Like the other fishermen in his village, Nnamdi's father had been
forced to fish in the swampy side creeks where the brackish waters
held predators and parasites. On one such trip, his net got snagged
on something submerged and he slipped while trying to unhook it.
He came up sputtering, pulled himself back onto his canoe, swiped
the muddy water from his eyes.

That was all it took.

A thin worm uncoiled inside his blood, worked its way up into his optic nerve. First he went blind, then he went mad, then he got lost, and then he drowned.

The oil company had given Nnamdi time off and he'd hurried home, catching rides on a series of progressively smaller boats. He ran from the dock to his house, arrived to find his mother outside praying to the angels and *orumo* alike.

Nnamdi's father was sitting alone in the dark.

"Nnamdi?" his father whispered in a voice not his own. "Is that you?"

"It is, Papa."

Nnamdi's father fumbled for something: a fishing spike, the dim light catching the metal. He held it out for his son to take. "Quickly. Before the *orumo* find out. Tell your mother I went mad and attacked you, tell her that you had no choice. Hurry, Nnamdi. A final favour for your father. This story has taken a bad turn; help me end it."

But Nnamdi couldn't, he couldn't. "I will buy you medicine, Papa. I will find a cure, I will return." But there was no medicine, there was no cure, and Nnamdi would not return. Not in time to save anyone.

56

Back at Bonny Island, freighters with bellies as large as lagoons were lining up for Delta crude even as Nnamdi's father was buried in the village churchyard. His father's favourite wife threw herself on the dirt, sobbed until her chest ached. Nnamdi cried as well, calling out *"Egberiyo!"* again and again.

Those who die childless were wrapped in a plain mat and buried without a funeral meal served in their honour; they were sent into the afterlife hungry and alone. It was a tragedy beyond repair, to be buried childless, for without descendants you would never become an ancestor. No one would remember you, a *teme* lost between wombs, wandering in a daze through the Village of the Dead.

"I only gave your father one child," Nnamdi's mother said, speaking her Ijaw dialect. "Thanks to Jesus, it was enough. He doesn't have to go into the darkness unfed." But of course, she didn't say Jesus, not in Ijaw.

Nnamdi had purchased a refrigerator for his mother, had brought it in from Portako by boat, with a goat as well, but there was no longer any need for Sunday clothes for his father.

Nnamdi walked out to the shrine his father had kept at the edge of the forest. He swept the floor, sprinkled palm wine out front. He left for Bonny Island the next day, but he never arrived because by then the river was burning.

Crude oil had been spilling into the creeks beyond the lagoon for more than a week, spraying a mist of fuel that slicked the water's surface, light and sweet. A faulty valve, heat from a circuit, and the river burned for days, burned even after crews had managed to reroute the flow. You could see the flames against the underbelly of sky, the black wall of smoke spilling its ink across the sun. The river burned and burned, and when it was done burning, only blackened stumps and charred mangroves remained. Bodies, too.

After the river burned, there was a lull, part mourning, part planning. This was followed by a series of high-speed attacks. Across the Delta, flow stations and oil platforms were seized and foreign workers taken captive. A rocket launcher split one pipeline open; when emergency crews arrived, they were ambushed and then ransomed back to the oil company. When the next pipeline was ruptured, the oil companies let it bleed.

In Port Harcourt, bandana-masked gunmen swarmed a brothel,

taking expat oil workers hostage. They hustled their captives into the street, only to run into a police battalion; a gun battle followed, with officers and militants exchanging blind fire through the warren-like streets of the Down Below slums.

The oil companies pulled back behind secure facilities, closed down remote posts, sealed off several pipelines, and placed their foreign workers under "house arrest" in living compounds behind high walls in the restricted zones of Port Harcourt. Workers were airlifted to safety as oil production in the Delta squeezed shut like a constricted aorta, driving production down. The price of oil spiked on the world market. On the other side of the globe, tar sands operations rumbled back to life, began chewing up the oil-rich soil again. From Laura's window, she could see the cranes turning faster and faster.

And the young men from Nnamdi's village, those hired by the oil companies? They were sent home. Several of the attacks had clearly been abetted from the inside, the facilities targeted with a precision that could hardly have been coincidental, so all local workers were let go for reasons of "safety and security." Nnamdi was dumped unceremoniously on a Portako dock with a dozen others. They pooled their money, hired a boat, and made the long run out to the tidal creeks of their youth.

His year among the Shell Men had softened Nnamdi's speech, turning once-robust "deys" and "dems" into breathlike "theys" and "thems," the Ijaw in his English resurfacing only in moments of sadness or stress. At night, when he missed the starched beds and long hallways of the workers' dorms, Nnamdi would open his mother's fridge, close his eyes, and feel the cold air run its fingertips across his skin.

No blow goes unanswered. In response to the pipeline attacks, the Nigerian army unleashed full-scale "wasting operations" in the Delta, with the general in charge boasting that he knew "204 ways to kill a man." And not just men. Children, as well. And women. And *ibe* elders.

"Terror begets terror," the general explained. This wasn't his first foray into the Delta. He'd burned villages as a young officer during the civil war decades before. Had torched them so efficiently he'd been promoted up the ranks. "The Ijaw are a predatory race," he declared now. "How many of our ancestors have been captured and sold into slavery, or even eaten, by the Ijaw! The only thing they understand—the only thing they will ever understand—is might."

What followed was an operation so devastating that the government in Abuja eventually had to call it off, sickened by the reports that leaked back of entire villages razed and bodies left scattered along forest trails. The thump of helicopters in the night, the singed smell of goat carcasses, of plantain trees smouldering: it was—as they said in the Delta—"a gift for the flies." Bullet casings littered the mud like bronze coins.

The wasting operations never reached Nnamdi's village. Armies are nothing if not methodical, and the soldiers had worked their way outward, one creek at a time, starting with the city of Warri in the western Delta and then moving south from Port Harcourt in the east. The remoteness of Nnamdi's village, out there at the salt-rind edge of the mangroves, spared them the worst of it, but only just. They saw smoke rising from the villages upstream, braced for a hammer blow that never came.

The campaign had an unforeseen effect, the Law of Unintended Consequences being one of the constants of military action. As refugees fled the attacks, they poured into Nnamdi's village. Welcomed at first, and then resented, these new arrivals built their settlements on the mudflats outside the village, in shantytown camps that smelled of excrement and despair. The riverbanks were pocked with feces, the children naked and round-bellied, steeped in dysentery.

Through attrition more than anything, Nnamdi's village had become the central settlement in the outer creeks. On market days, goods from Portako appeared as though conjured, and the bags of rolled naira Nnamdi had amassed on the pipelines were soon almost worthless. Prices soared as a glut of currency continued to arrive, stuffed into suitcases and pillowcases. Nnamdi's mother had to charge tenfold now for her Fanta and bitter greens. Even then, the thin slice she took as profit had narrowed to a razor's width.

"Can you feel it?" she would whisper to Nnamdi from across the room as they lay under netting at night. "Something's coming." The creek was never meant to support that many people.

One morning, Nnamdi found an arm behind a chicken coop. What unspoken feud or dark rites had brought a machete down on that particular arm hardly mattered. Soon after, Ijaw militants swept in, gunning their speedboats and firing rifles into the air. Shirtless young men fuelled by anger and gin.

"Go!" his mother whispered frantically. And then, in Ijaw for added urgency, "They know you worked for the oil companies. Take the back path to the lagoon. Go!"

57

His father's dugout was still there, at water's edge, beyond the HRH cannon and the English graves. Nnamdi waded through the sludgy mud and righted the pirogue. He climbed in quickly and poled the craft out, into the current. He let the river take him as the sound of gunfire faded.

The forests were strangely silent. Nnamdi floated with the current, past the next village along the creek—or what remained of it. Scorched walls and blackened rooftops, the tin warped from the heat. A fresh attack from the looks of it. A few goats were poking about, and the dock lay in splinters, the planks like broken ribs. The body of a bush rat floated by, belly bloated and eye sockets emptied. The *teme* of the childless and of those lost between wombs were said to inhabit the Village of the Dead after their passing. Is that what this was? A graveyard of lost souls?

Nnamdi watched for any signs of life as he slipped past, of anyone who needed to be helped, but there was none. Only goats and silence. The mangroves beyond were criss-crossed with creeks hardly wider than his canoe. He poled into one of them, ducking to avoid the overhangs of vine while watching the thicker ones for signs of movement. Snakes dropped from above sometimes.

Nnamdi had stopped to wipe the sweat from his face when he heard—*something*. A faint sound, tapping out a message. It seemed to come from under the water, and for a moment he wondered if one of the *owumo* below was trying to signal him. But no. Not *from* the water, but across it. Muffled by mangroves, the sound ran low along the surface of the creeks: *thunk, thunk, thunk.*

Almost like a helicopter, but too slow in tempo. Yams pounded with pestle and mortar, but too metallic in tone.

Nnamdi poled his father's canoe away from the wall of mangroves, their roots twisty and webbed, and then glided quietly around the next bend and the next, switched from pole to paddle. A few strokes brought him into a stronger current, where a pipeline ran along the water, a dull metallic green, half-submerged.

Thunk, thunk.

Nnamdi followed the pipeline as it snaked its way through. The thuds grew louder, and as the pirogue slid around the next bend in the river, a flow station slipped into view. Almost immediately, Nnamdi realized his error. He tried to back-paddle, chopping at the water as quickly as he could, but the current had caught hold of him, pulling him forward. The water was too deep for a pole, so he tried arcing the pirogue toward the trees instead. If he could just reach the mangroves, he could come to a stop, then push himself backward and slip out of view—but no. It was too late. They had seen him.

There were four of them. Young men, backs streaming with perspiration, they were in a speedboat that had pulled up alongside the pipeline and were taking turns swinging a sledgehammer at a chisel held against one of the seams in the metal. Empty barrels and jerry cans stood at the ready.

One of the men had an ancient single-bolt rifle slung over his shoulder, and when he saw Nnamdi he whistled for the others to stop and then pulled his rifle from his shoulder, brought it up awkwardly, took aim.

Nnamdi was back-paddling harder now, fighting the current.

"Run and we will you chase you down!" the man with the rifle yelled in Ijaw.

They had a speedboat, Nnamdi had a canoe. It would have been a short hunt indeed. Nnamdi stopped paddling, held up a hand in greeting as his father's pirogue drifted in their direction. *"Noao!"* he called out, smiling. "I am looking for fish. Only that."

The man with the rifle let the barrel drop. He watched Nnamdi closely as he floated in. "I know you."

He was one of the other young men who'd been hired by the oil company. Nnamdi had met him on Bonny Island.

"Sure told!" said the young man, speaking in English now and grinning wide. "I know you."

Nnamdi smiled back, but by now the young man's grin turned into something else, something resembling a sneer. "I was mopping toilets when you was ridin' around in style." He turned to the others. "I was getting janitorial duties, while this one was sleepin' on big pillows, workin' in mechanical." He turned back to Nnamdi with a fury boiling in his bloodshot eyes. "Get out dis place before I shoot you!"

Nnamdi began paddling again in choppy strokes, desperate to get away. But the current kept pulling the canoe closer.

"Get out dis place!" the young man screamed. He slammed a shell into the rifle's chamber, pulled back on the bolt, fired a round into the water not feet from Nnamdi's canoe. The sound reverberated across the mangroves. Nnamdi flinched.

And then, and then, the current ... let go ...

Whatever *owu* had caught Nnamdi in its grip now released him, and he turned the pirogue sharply, steering it toward the mangroves that stood on leglike roots at water's edge. From there, he hoped he'd be able to pole his way upstream and escape.

The hammering on the pipe had started anew. Nnamdi looked at the knotted backs, the chisel set against the pipeline seam, the young man he'd met on Bonny Island. Had that all been a dream, Bonny Island? He thought about the number of toilets that young man would have unplugged, thought about hammers and anvils— and he stopped paddling.

Nnamdi's canoe pivoted slowly, began to float back toward the speedboat.

The men stopped and stared as he drifted in. But before a second shot could be fired, Nnamdi said, "You're doing it wrong."

His canoe bumped up alongside their boat.

"You can't get to the oil the way you're doing it."

They were hammering on a seam, but the pipelines were double-sheathed, with their seam lines staggered. "Even if you get through, there's another pipe underneath. And that one's steel. No hammer big enough for that. No hacksaw, neither. You can't tap into pipelines like you were tappin' a wine tree."

The young man from the Bonny Island dream narrowed his gaze. "What you knowin' about any?"

Nnamdi grinned. "I was workin' mechanical, remember? You need to find the main manifold." He pointed upstream, along the path the pipeline cut through the swamp. "Closest one will be that way. Find the manifold, and you will find the weak knee."

The others looked at him, still not sure how much to trust him. "Manifold?"

Nnamdi nodded. "If you go follow this pipeline, you're going to find a junction. Multiple feeders. The manifolds look strong, but they are just rivets and bolts, and any bolt can be broken. No one has been targeting them, so they aren't guarded—not like pump stations. Find the manifold and you can pry it apart easy as eels. Break the box and turn the valve to redirect the flow, and you've got your oil. It will take them days—maybe weeks—to trace the trouble and shut it down." He looked at the empty barrels and jerry cans stacked on the deck of their boat. "You're gonna need more containers. As many as you can find."

The young man he'd met on Bonny Island looked at Nnamdi with a narrowed gaze, his eyes like bullet casings in blood, and said, *"Noao."*

And that was the Story of How the Boy Became a Mosquito.

58

"Okay, the thing is, it's not that simple, there's a lot of factors in play, that's the thing …"

Warren was speaking quickly, his words tripping over each other the way they always did when he was trying to convince his little sister of something dubious. Like trading two quarters for four pennies. ("Four is more than two, right? So it's a good deal.")

Or jumping off the garage into a pile of leaves he'd just raked. Laura had spent three weeks with her ankle in a cast after that misadventure. Warren had been the first one to sign his name, with a great flourish of felt marker. It was the same signature he used even today.

The bank had begun foreclosure proceedings on their parents' home. Warren's lawyer had slapped the bank with an injunction— the investigation was ongoing, after all—but it was a stop-gap measure, and Warren knew it. They'd been dealt a losing hand, even if his sister couldn't see it.

"Our mother just got an eviction notice," Laura said. "From her own home!"

"Listen, here's the thing, for Mom to stay there, we're talking a deep six figures, we'd need fifty grand just to get our foot in the door, and even then, we'd be paying the house off for years—at above market value, I might add—and long after Mom was gone, we'd still be on the hook for it, and the thing is, it's not that great a house to begin with."

"It's our family home," she snapped.

"Was," he said. "Was our home. If you love it so much, why don't *you* buy it? You could move back in, take over the payments. I realize being a copywriter, or whatever it is you do, doesn't pay much, but you must have some savings, surely."

"I do, but not enough. Not nearly enough, and you know that. You're the one who's supposed to be this big successful businessman."

"I *am*," he snapped. "The payments on my Escalade alone are probably more than what you pay on your fuckin' apartment."

"It's not an apartment, it's a condo."

"You own it? You don't. You sublease. I helped set that up for you, remember? Call it what you like, it's an apartment. And that's my point. I have expenses that you can't even imagine. I'm already overextended, my assets are tied up, I've got investors breathing down my neck. I can't just pull fifty G from my ass, and I sure as shit can't buy back the house. Mom can move in with us at Springbank."

"What, in the basement?"

"Yes, in the basement. You have a better idea?"

"I do. You could use some of that fabulous wealth of yours to stop our mother from getting kicked out of her own home. You always said you were rich."

"I never said I was rich."

"You certainly act it."

"Not the same as being. It comes down to limited liability partnerships. I set myself up as a senior shareholder when I merged companies, but I should have been paying myself a contract salary instead of dividends, so when the market collapsed—"

"What are you going on about? Speak English."

"What I'm saying is, I don't have the money. Mom can stay with us if she wants, but the house we grew up in? It's gone."

Laura remembered the board games she and Warren used to play as children. Monopoly. The Game of Life. Snakes and Ladders. Sorry.

"Rubies," said Laura, her voice hard, sardonic, sad.

"Rubies?"

"We could pull rubies from the stucco," she said. "Pay the bank with that."

Her brother blinked, not understanding.

"When we played Monopoly, you always won." She said this as though it were an accusation.

"I cheated."

"You won when we played Sorry as well. You won when we played Clue."

"I cheated at Sorry. I cheated at Clue, too."

Clue always ended with the killer cornered and a bold declaration. *Miss Scarlet. In the billiard room. With a knife!* "How could you cheat at Clue?" she wanted to know.

"It was a three-player game, remember? We had to deal a dummy hand."

"So?"

"I peeked."

"Asshole."

"Language," he said.

59

When the tankers docked at Bonny Island, it could take days to fill them, even with the crude oil fire-hosing into the ships' cavernous bunkers. There was another sort of bunkering, though, one delivered not in a thundering cascade but through a thousand pinpricks: the illegal bunkering of the Delta, where mosquito crews tapped into pipelines to suck out the oil, filling up barrels scaled with rust, filling jerry cans and plastic jugs, even emptied tins of cooking oil.

A network of these black-market speedboats had fanned out across the creeks and rivers of the Niger Delta, ferrying illicit crude to waiting barges, which ferried it in turn to illicit oil tankers waiting offshore.

Enough mosquitoes can take down a heavy buffalo, can drive the animal mad and run it into the muck to sink. And the sound of this siphoning, of oil being extracted from veins, was driving the oil companies to distraction.

The Niger Delta was too vast, too wild, and too lawless for any single authority to stanch the loss. "The lifeblood of Nigeria," as the president called it, "was being drained away by ungrateful citizens." As many as 200,000 barrels of crude a week was what they were saying. "Which only leaves another million barrels for the oil companies!" was the response.

"It is nothing more than theft!" yelled the priest from his pulpit.

"They are the thieves, not us!"

"Thieving from a thief is still thieving!"

"And what of our forests? They is clear-cuttin' those as well!" The oil companies had leased their land concessions to lumber companies to clear for them, and the lumber companies had been stripping the hardwood forests bare and shipping the prized wood to Europe and America. "Where it's made into mahogany toilet seats!" someone shouted. "So that the *oyibos* can shit right through us!"

"It is still theft!" shouted the priest. "Thou shalt not steal!"

"Not theft, payment owed!"

But it was theft.

And payment owed.

Nnamdi could see that clearly enough. Having scouted the flow stations and pipelines with the oil-soaked bunker boys, having shown them the cleanest way into a manifold and the cleanest way out, he no longer had to run away when the militants came roaring in. They greeted him as an ally now.

AK-47s had replaced single-bolt rifles, and some of the more successful warlords had apartments in Portako, where they looked out at the gated compounds of the *oyibos* and plotted their own ascension into similar enclaves of luxury.

Unlike the salary he'd drawn from the oil company, the kickbacks Nnamdi received from the bunker boys was adjusted for inflation, rolls of bills bigger than his fist could hold. He bought his mother another fridge, and another. She stocked it with bottles of beer and flats of Fanta, and she lorded it over the older market women who'd kept her in her place for so many years. But she worried about her son, the only remaining shred left of her husband. Nnamdi was now giving advice on pipelines and manifolds to bunkering crews. "Is a dangerous game, Nnamdi," she whispered at night from beneath her netting. "Take cautions. Don't fall head-first into de crude."

"I won't," he promised.

But pipelines have a way of exploding. And as the bunker boys grew more profitable, they also grew more impatient, and they began using torch-cutters to get through, something Nnamdi had advised against. One night an entire flow station went up in a blossom of orange-crusted flame that sent half a dozen charred bodies floating among the mangroves.

The mix-and-match assortment of containers used to transport the bunkered fuel had given way to *zeeps*—square stackables made of plastic, easy to fill and easy to load. Speedboats soon sprouted second motors, and their drivers became increasingly reckless, weaving in and out, swamping those few canoes still casting nets along the currents. In some creeks, dozens of empty *zeeps* floated on oily waters. When overloaded containers fell overboard, they'd sink to the bottom and slowly leak oil until some magic balance was reached, at which point they'd suddenly bob to the surface like deliveries made from the other side.

It was palm gin and the weight of these *zeeps* that changed Nnamdi's fortunes. A particularly potent batch of gin had left men in a drunken stupor that lasted much longer than usual. With the *zeeps* too heavy to manhandle alone, the head of one of the bunkering crews had gone looking for Nnamdi instead.

He found him at his father's shrine, laying out leaves and whispering chants for the half-forgotten *oru* within. Nnamdi took small objects from a pouch, let them fall on the ground. Stopped to study the message they gave.

"Ya!" the foreman shouted, trying to sound brusque—but unnerved at the sight of Nnamdi caught in a trance, lost somewhere between *teme* and *oje*. "I need a strong back."

When Nnamdi had returned to the world of the everyday, he smiled at the man. "*Dile.* I was dreaming."

"Come away dis place. We are going to Mbiama."

Mbiama was infamous.

The national and state governments had launched a Joint Task Force aimed at hammering the bunker boys and black-market refineries into oblivion, and JTF boats now patrolled the main waterways. They fired with impunity and could not be bought off with bribes. Which is how Nnamdi ended up on a boat weighted to the water level with crude-heavy *zeeps* as it pushed its way through side creeks and unnamed channels, avoiding the main route, zigzagging toward the black-market boomtown of Mbiama.

The man who'd hired Nnamdi was yelling above the sound of the motor. "We are meeting an Igbo, a man named Joseph. I have not met him, but ah'm told he knows of you. A good person to have on your side. He is always on de lookout for a good mechanic. His last mechanic? A drunkard, left him stranded in the desert, is what ah'm told." The boat slowed as a cluster of smoke and ragtag buildings came into view. "Welcome to Mbiama!" the foreman shouted. "This is where road reaches water." Twin rutted tracks running through the jungle. "Drivers run the crude in from here to Portako."

Mbiama was painted with lights, strings of coloured bulbs that were draped from tavern to brothel. Girls in blue eye shadow and bruise-like rouge swished their skirts lazily at Nnamdi as he and the bunker crew foreman trudged up the dock, looking for a certain tavern. They found it, pushed open the screen door, went inside.

A fan stirred the humidity. Reggae music trickled out of a tape deck somewhere. Bodies were huddled around a table, speaking low. The entire place was swimming with sweat and ambition.

"I'm lookin' for Joe!" the foreman yelled. "Igbo Joe."

The man at the table looked up at them with clouded eyes. Heavy lids. A thick neck and beefy face. "You found him, bruddah." Joe extended a heavy hand to them, but shook daintily, in city fashion. No clasped forearms, just a hanky-handshake all around.

Igbo Joe was neither Igbo nor Joe. "I'm from up Onitsha way," he explained. "I'm Ibo, but no one out here can tell the difference." Joe and Nnamdi were down at the dock by this point, unloading the boat with the bunker crew foreman, wrestling heavy *zeeps* of bunkered oil onto a flatbed truck. "And my name is Joshua, not Joseph. Jericho, not de manger."

"What do I call you, then?" Nnamdi asked.

It was hard work, and they were sweating heavily. A *zeep* slipped from Joe's palms as he and Nnamdi hoisted it up, and it fell, slamming to the ground, almost rupturing.

"Christ and piss!"

Nnamdi grinned. "You want I call you by that? Or just be Piss for short?"

Joe glowered. "You the mechanic? The one worked for the oil men at Bonny Island?"

Nnamdi nodded.

Stray dogs were nosing through garbage. Music was bleeding from barroom doors.

"I'm driving this flatbed back to Portako," Joe said. "But after that, I'm takin' a tanker truck north, past Abuja. Fuel shortages up there, and I plan to cash in. I need a mechanic and a second driver. You could be both for a healthy slice. What do you say?"

Rare, something like that dropped from a vine so readily.

The bunker crew foreman handed Nnamdi a sweat-dampened fold of bills for his help, then headed to the closest bar for some "cool beer and warm women."

Nnamdi considered Joe's proposition. "Where exactly north?"

"Far," he said.

"How far?"

"The sha'ria states. In and out, very quick. I don't like to hang around up there. It's not—comfortable." He dug out a rag from his pocket, wiped his neck. "Ever been north?"

"Never been past Portako."

"Well, this is very far. Almost to the desert. The city we going to is named for crocodiles." He laughed, a broad, rolling timbre. "You from the Delta, you be used to crocodiles!"

"Never seen a crocodile."

"Oh, you seen plenty working with the oil company, I think." Joe looked at Nnamdi. "I have a buyer all lined up. You won't say this to any?"

Nnamdi nodded.

Joe smiled. "You want to know where we goin'?"

"I do."

"Kaduna."

60

There had been other manifestos, other battle cries. But this one was thumbprinted with blood, like a royal seal. Elders of the larger *ibe* and the leaders of outlawed Ijaw militants, their bodies painted white to stop bullets, eyes wild with narcotics and gin, had joined together, had issued their own manifesto.

It was nothing short of an Ijaw Declaration of Independence.

The Curse of Oil is destroying the Niger Delta. Foreign
companies grow fat, while we who live here cannot feed
our children. Corrupt leaders drive about in BMWs, while
we live in misery and starvation. By what right? This is
Ijaw land, Ijaw oil. The blood money taken from the Delta
pays for government mansions in Abuja and luxury hotel
swimming pools in Lagos. Enough!

There had been other manifestos, but this one was followed
by explosions, a series of timed attacks on wellheads and flow
stations that brought Delta operations to a stumbling stand-
still while emergency crews performed pipeline triage. The JTF
called in more patrols in an attempt to bring order to the growing
chaos.

The Oil Men run pipelines above ground directly through
our villages, they are flaring gas in the midst of human
habitation, they are leaving oil spills to seep into the ground-
water, are expropriating farmlands willy-nilly. Gas flares sour
our air. The flood plains are ruined. Crops have been razed,
and hardwood forests have been clear-cut with impunity.
Poisoned seas and burning skies. ENOUGH!

The militants of the Delta were nothing more than "gangsters
and extortionists," the governors of the Delta states had warned.
They were terrorists, and one does not negotiate with terrorists.

Oil from the Delta benefits everyone but the Delta man.
Where is our benefit? Where is our BMW? We are labelled
thieves, but who is the real thief?

"We cannot let the wealth of the nation be held hostage," said the army officer charged with bringing the militants under heel, his voice static-crackling over state radio. "We will set the Delta on fire if we have to. We will set it on fire, if only to smoke them out."

Enough of the gas flares and oil spills, enough of the blow-outs and bulldozers. Enough! All operations in the Delta must cease and the oil companies, together with their toady staff and Judas contractors, must withdraw henceforth from Ijaw territory or face the full brunt of our fury. You have been warned.

It was a good time to leave.

The *ibe*-backed militants had begun to branch out into other areas. Other endeavours. From gun-running and oil bunkering, they were now trading in narcotics and raiding the villages of rival ethnic groups. Towns farther inland had come under renewed attack—and not only from men in uniform. Caught between army and oil, between JTF and bunker gangs, entire creeks burned.

Splinter groups appeared, calling themselves Vigilante Councils and Liberation Armies, and people turned on their own like a snake swallowing its tail. New factions formed as old ethnic feuds bubbled to the surface. Most of the fighting was to the west, around Warri, or up near Portako. Nnamdi's village, crowded, unkempt, but still remote, had been spared the worst of it. So far.

Still. It was a good time to go.

Nnamdi sent word back to his mother, telling her he'd be gone a week, maybe more. It would take much longer than that, though.

61

Laura Curtis was looking through her reflection at the city below. From her window, she could see the river and the descending curved arches of the Centre Street Bridge looking like the trajectory of a skipped stone as it leapt across into the city.

At either end of the bridge, flanking the approach, were the For King & Country stone lions, chess pieces of Empire, suitably sombre at their posts.

A half-edited manuscript was waiting on her desktop computer, silent, insistent.

Laura had once again been working her way through someone else's life, flagging it for inconsistences, clarifying key events, compiling a timeline and style sheet. The author in question, a bombastic Czech with a massive comb-over (to judge from his author photo), had a habit of employing contradictory adverb/ adjectival arrangements: "calmly excited," "frantically tranquil," "expansively small-minded." She dutifully queried each usage, but when she came upon the term "oppressively free," it gave her pause. Could you be oppressively free? *Yes*, she thought, *you could*. Choices could paralyze you, overwhelm you. From that point on, she'd treated these phrasings as an authorial tic to be indulged, rather than an error to be fixed.

Her tea had gone cold in the cup.

She was staring through herself, was *actively ignoring* the manuscript that was squatting on the computer screen behind her. In the city below, emergency lights were catching the polished glass and clean angles of the downtown core. And she thought, *How beautiful it looks*.

Sergeant Brisebois was standing inside the blue and red wash of those lights. He was within a perimeter of yellow tape in an alleyway, a police cruiser at either end. EMS was there as well.

Through the space between office buildings, Brisebois could just make out the apartment towers on the ridge of hill above. Second building on the left. Third light, corner window. She'd shown up at the TRU office earlier that day, unannounced, asking to see the photographs of her father's accident scene.

"Are you sure?" he'd asked. "It's not pretty."

She hadn't flinched. Not at first. She'd studied them as though she were looking for something more than mere clues. One photo, then the next, until—

She'd looked up at Brisebois, smiling, eyes brimming. "Who knew?" she said.

"Sorry?"

"The sweater." She was referring to the knitted pattern visible in one of the shots. A geometric pattern. Not of deer. "Who knew my dad owned more than two sweaters?" The tears welled, but never fell.

"Ms. Curtis, we have a Victims Assistance Unit that can provide grief counselling if you need to—"

"Grief?" she said. "How about emptiness? Do you have emptiness counselling? Regret counselling? Things-you-forgot-to-say counselling?"

"Laura, if you need someone to talk to—"

"What I need is to be alone. Just for a moment. Please?"

"Sure. Care for a coffee?"

She did, but when he brought it in, creamers and sugar packet in one hand—"I wasn't sure how you take it"—she hadn't wanted it. She'd shoved the photographs back in their folder and hurried past him, trying not to sob.

He should have followed her. Should have caught up to her, should have asked, "Are you all right?"

But he hadn't.

She was up there now, standing by the corner window.

"Sergeant Brisebois? Homicide's here."

TRU had been called in. Reports of a vehicle on fire. It wasn't a vehicle that was burning, though; it was a man. A car had been spotted but it had sped away, leaving dark odours and a body behind. Not dead, but almost nearly. "Better call in homicide," Brisebois had said, even as EMS attended to the victim.

Brisebois looked at the smouldering garbage bags in the alleyway, the melted plastic and scorch marks, the reverse silhouette that had been burned onto the flattened cardboard of an alleyway bed: the blackened surface leaving the pale outline of where the body had been lying in a fetal position.

"Think he'll make it?" the homicide officer asked.

"It's unlikely. Third degree, most of the body. EMS said the skin had already started to separate."

Ambrose Littlechild. No fixed address. Originally a resident of Fort McMurray. Known to police. A panhandler, bottle picker. These details would come out over the course of the evening. Witnesses—mad, rambling, and unreliable; street people like Ambrose—had said there were four, maybe forty, maybe a hundred. Looked like college boys. "What does a college boy look like?" Brisebois had asked.

"Like not us."

The assailants had purred down the alleyway in a sports car, in a van, on bicycles, had found Ambrose sleeping, had gotten out, giggling and snickering, had tied him down, had knocked him out, had shouted, had whispered, had doused Ambrose with gasoline, had set him on fire.

On that point everyone agreed. He'd been set on fire.

"We tried puttin' him out with our blankets, eh? But those caught fire too."

When EMS had loaded Ambrose onto the stretcher, he was gurgling to himself in a language long lost, telling stories no one would hear. He lost consciousness soon after, as though consciousness were a balloon that had been let go, the string slipping from between fingers, trailing away.

Brisebois had walked the crime scene twice by the time homicide arrived, had located the cigarette lighter and the discarded plastic bottle in among the garbage bags. The sides of the bottle were clouded and the top was open, and when he crouched down he caught the sour-sweet smell of gasoline. He marked the bottle and cigarette lighter with a numbered tent card and moved on.

"So we're done, then?" asked one of his TRU officers. "Homicide's taking over?"

Brisebois nodded.

"You up for a drink?" The shift was almost over.

"No, you go. I have to swing by 7-Eleven, pick up some cat food. It's been a long day."

Red on blue, catching the tinted glass and clean angles of the downtown core. A corner light in the building above.

What was she doing up so late?

62

It took longer to organize the Kaduna run than Igbo Joe had expected—"A lack of bona fides," as he put it—and Nnamdi found himself in the shaganappi streets of the Down Below, Portako's waterfront slums. He was put to work tuning motors, and though he'd never formally trained as a car mechanic, applied knowledge was something of a Delta specialty, and he learned quickly enough.

The garage took up a whole city block. It was a metal building that curved like a culvert over oil-stained cement. Who had hired

Nnamdi and who exactly owned the garage was never clear; these things were always a tangle-work of overlapping claims and competing guilds. But dented taxis and traffic-afflicted minivans kept cramming in nonetheless as the mechanics hammered fenders and spot-welded seams, metal on metal, the sparks waterfalling down like fireworks.

Nnamdi slept in a cot above the repair bay and ventured into the crowded alleyways of the Down Below at night. The streets echoed with voices and the air was saturated with smells: everything from open latrines to the wafting steam of *garri* dumplings at full boil. Portako was an Igbo city, but you wouldn't know it from the mash of dialects and languages he heard along the waterfront. Nnamdi caught snatches of Ogoni and Ibibio, and a dozen variations of Ijaw, though none from the outer Delta.

Even if he never made the drive north, he could at least stay here, with roof and bed and work. One of the lucky ones. His father's *oru* at work on his behalf, he was sure.

His long wait ended with the pull of a curtain.

The threadbare cloth pinned across the front of Nnamdi's cot was flung aside with an energy only Igbo Joe could muster. "Get up, lazy man! Get up!" Joe sounded giddy. "Get up! She's here! And she is very much a beauty."

Nnamdi staggered awake, followed Joe down the stairs. A tanker truck now took up half the repair bay. It was a huge presence, with the taxis and minivans shoved against the wall to make space. Sheep making room for the dominant ram.

The truck's cab was sharply angled so it would fit, its cylinder tank sitting atop rows of wheels. "Needs a tune-up," Joe said. "That's for you to attend. Come, come. Look."

Joe was walking the length of the truck—it seemed to increase in size with every slather of praise he gave it. "Sixteen wheels! If one pops, you won't even feel it." The tire treads were bare, Nnamdi noted, but not yet bald.

"Sleeping quarters are behind the driver's seat, with space for food and baggage." Rusted hinges. A spiderweb of cracks across the windshield, and a cab painted in elaborate curlicues of green and gold, with a good-luck motto along the side: "Dreams Abound." Nnamdi squeezed around to the other side, and there in purple and orange was another message: "This Too Shall Pass."

"Oh, it will pass," Joe said when he saw Nnamdi reading the motto. "Everything on the road!" He slapped a heavy hand against the side door. "She's filled to the brim with bunkered oil, refined right here at Portako. The JTF shut down the operation, but not before we got our fuel! We're always one step ahead! You can't catch a shadow even with the finest net. Is what we say in Onitsha. This truck holds thirty thousand litres of fuel. One trip, and we won't have to work again for a year. The girls in the Down Below bars will see most of your money, I am supposing! A young man like you!" He laughed, grabbed Nnamdi by the shoulder, jostled him hard, taking his silence for concurrence.

A voice was calling out from the other side of the truck. "Joseph, my friend!"

"Ah," said Joe. "He's here."

"Who?"

"The Turk." With hand on elbow, Joe steered Nnamdi around the front of the truck. And then, with lowered voice: "He's not a black man, but he is still Nigerian, so be kind."

"Why would I not be?"

But Joe had already swept ahead in full Joe mode. "My friend, you have delivered the stars in a pail!"

The Turk was not Turkish. He was a Lebanese businessman whose family could trace their history along these coasts for

generations, and he ran several ongoing interests, illicit and otherwise, in the Down Below streets and warehouses of Port Harcourt.
The type of man who could grow fat in a famine, as they said. He
had long given up on trying to shed his misplaced moniker.

"Turk!"

"Josephant!"

The Turk met Joe halfway. He was a squat knot of a man,
and he gave Nnamdi a small bow of respect, palms held together.
"You must be the motor whiz magician Joseph has spoken of. On
the last venture north, the vehicle we'd arranged broke down in a
sandstorm, and the driver walked for days to the nearest telephone,
only to be stripped clean of everything by the time we came to
collect—both the driver and the truck! Joseph tells me you can
mend an aeroplane in mid-flight, a bus whilst it plummets—can
get it running before it hits the ground. He says you were the King
of Bonny Island, back in happier days, before these ... troublesome
times."

Nnamdi felt his heart race. Igbo Joe was given to embellish-
ment, but—"Yes," he said. "Most moto, I can fix." He'd never
worked on a vehicle this size. Before the cars, it had mainly been
motorboats and the occasional tweak at oil company flow stations.

The Turk turned to the tanker truck with a father's pride.
"Dreams Abound will get you there—and back, Insha Allah."

On a handshake, the deal was done. Joe and Nnamdi would
make the run north to Kaduna city with the fuel the Turk had
purchased, and would split the fee he was offering sixty-forty.

Selling oil in Nigeria seemed a little strange to Nnamdi,
though, like shipping salt to Mali, diamonds to the Congo, or salt
water to the sea.

"What do they need with Portako fuel? They have a refinery
in Kaduna," he said. He'd worked on some of the pipelines that

branched northward. The Kaduna Line. One of the lines that had been bombed, in fact. Bombed, but not destroyed, as far as he knew.

"True enough, Nigeria is floatin' on oil," said Igbo Joe. "The problem is not fuel, but delivery of fuel." He stretched the word out, making it sound more like *fool*. "There is no shortage of oil, bruddah. Only of cunning."

"They've got lineups across the north," said the Turk. "Those refineries have suffered neglect for years, have been struggling just to meet minimum capacity. So Abuja is now playing catch-up, shutting down whole segments for maintenance upgrades. It's causing … complications. Shortages, rioting, black-market profiteering. A terrible hindrance to the people. But I say to you, in life there is no such thing as a hindrance, only an opportunity. Trade is *movement*," said the Turk. "Sea salt moves north. Rock salt moves south. All of it salt, but what is important is that it moves."

"When do we leave?" asked Nnamdi.

"Now," said Joe. "Right now. The dry season. Best time for it. Can't risk the rains. The lands in the north are so bone dry, they don't know what to do with water when it does come. In rains, you have flash floods, roads that run like rivers. The earth becomes sticky clay, bogs down tires. No," he insisted, "I'll take heat and dust over floods and mud every time."

The Turk said his goodbyes with a flurry of handshakes and good-health salutations, and Joe stood, fists on hips, like a general surveying the battlefield. "We leave as soon as you're ready!" he said to Nnamdi. "We'll take turns—driving and sleeping, sleeping and driving."

This was, perhaps, the time for Nnamdi to mention a certain minor detail. "I'm not sure if this is a matter of concern," he said.

"But I have not operated a motorized vehicle before. Motorboats, of course. Certainly. But not trucks."

Joe looked at him. "You don't know how to drive?"

Nnamdi shook his head. "No. I understood it was more a mechanic you were after."

"A mechanic *and* a driver. Two in one. I can't drive all the way gone to Kaduna on my own. It is too far. Look. You know what a clutch is, what it does?"

"Of course."

"So. You gear up, gear down, keep your foot on the accelerator and the truck pointed down the middle of the road—we are big enough that others will get out of our way. Avoid the brakes, those will only slow you down. And if you can't find a gear, make one. That is all you need to know. I will get us out of the city, you take over once we are clear."

And that was that.

"I'll leave you to tune up the vehicle," said Joe. "I have to gather my belongings for the drive. It's a long road, but one with great riches at the end!"

It took Nnamdi half an hour just to figure out how to release the bonnet, and when he did he was startled to find that the entire front of the truck opened up, backward, from windshield to grille. Since arriving in Portako, the largest vehicle he'd worked on was a minivan taxi. He peered into the tanker's engine as though looking into a human chest cavity. He recognized the fan belt and not much else. After a few moments he quietly closed it up. "It looks fine," he said to Joe, whom he found upstairs stuffing a Ghana-Must-Go bag with loose clothes and mason jars of murky home brew.

"Good! Let's go!"

63

Nnamdi swung his own Ghana-Must-Go into the truck's cab. Grabbed hold and then launched himself up and into the passenger seat, the seat springs bouncing under him.

He was wearing Ijaw yellow, with billowing trousers and a loose-hanging smock. Joe frowned. "Will be cold wearing such as that."

"Cold?" They were heading north to the edge of the Sahara.

"You'll see." Joe wedged a final mason jar into the seat between them. "This will keep us warm. *Paraga*," he said. "A Yoruba concoction. Herbs and spirits, mixed together with tonics and such. I put some *ogogoro* in there as well for extra kick. Will keep you awake with eyes bug-open. Warms you from the inside out. If it doesn't kill you first!"

Joe started the engine and nudged the tanker truck out of the garage in fits and starts, cranking the wheel and squeezing it onto a side street scarcely wider than the vehicle itself. It was like poling a pirogue through the smaller creeks of the Delta. But with more traffic. They clipped a roadside vendor's stall, sending a pyramid of lumpy yams tumbling downward, and batted a parked bicycle to one side as pedestrians hurried out of the way in their flip-flop gait. Too slowly for Joe, who cleared a path with his air horn. He then forced his way into a go-slow, all but shoving the other vehicles aside.

"This lane is too crowded," he complained after struggling to keep the motor from stalling. So he pulled out, into oncoming traffic, to overtake a line of vehicles before veering back in. Once they got past the go-slow, they began to pick up speed, flying by shantytowns wreathed in smoke, and oil company compounds gated like luxury jails. Endless rows of roadside stalls crowded the street under great overhangs of trees. City and forest. Port Harcourt. Portako.

Every kilometre was a kilometre farther north than Nnamdi had ever been. *This is the farthest, and this and this. And this.*

"I saw you," said Joe, "last night, casting your stones, reading twigs and feathers." A small crucifix hung from the mirror; Joe had placed it there for luck. "You should attend church instead. Stop stirring up spirits that are better left alone. It's just folklore." The crucifix dangled between them, bobbed and leapt like a fish on a hook as Igbo Joe forced the truck into ever higher gear.

The *owumo* could be petitioned anywhere, and Nnamdi had brought several small items from the Delta to help him. "Was asking for safety on our journey," he said. "Only that."

"Well," said Joe. "Let's hope it worked. Soldiers, up ahead."

On the outskirts of the city, men in olive-green uniforms had blockaded the road, and vehicles were filing through for inspection. Joe had stashed a thick roll of naira in the glove compartment. "Peel off a few," he said to Nnamdi. After they'd paid the required "inspection fee," they were allowed to rumble forward. Not minutes down the road, and the police had set up a roadblock of their own.

Once they got past that, Joe steered them onto an exit ramp as the city fell away. The windows were down, and a soup of exhaust and muggy air swirled through.

"No a/c," Joe yelled. "But we have music."

He shoved a cassette into the truck's deck and Highlife filled the cab, swirling around them like an extra current of wind. Trumpets and trombones, metal drums and hand-clapping tempos. Highlife melted into *juju*, and *juju* into Afrobeat, with jazz and calypso, samba and gospel folded in for good measure, women's voices singing the chorus and the rich lather of male vocals out front.

"Fela Kuti," Joe shouted. "I saw him on stage in Lagos, years ago. Before, well, you know ..." Kuti had been injected with the

AIDS virus by government operatives jealous of his music. That was the rumoured truth, anyway.

The music rolled over them, joyous, felicitous, angry, alive.

"Yoruba music?" Nnamdi said, teasing Joe.

"Not Yoruba," said Joe. "*African.* True music, not the ooga-booga you have in the Delta."

Nnamdi laughed. "The drums of the Delta are the heartbeat of the gods! Show some respect."

"If that's the music of the gods, the gods need to take music lessons. A little more melody and a little less ooga-booga." Joe twisted the volume louder, and they were propelled across the landscape on Highlife and Afrobeat, in a quicksilver coffin labelled "Dreams Abound," eating air and grinning all the while.

They'd left the main highway and were bearing north through humid forests. Derelict vehicles littered the shoulders and the asphalt was pocked with potholes. It threw them back in their seats, then bounced them forward, Nnamdi clinging to the dash.

"It gets worse," Joe warned.

Nnamdi had counted a dozen wrecked vehicles in that first stretch alone. The tanker truck pushed on.

64

"So who got murdered anyway?" Laura asked.

A rainy day afternoon from long ago. Her big brother dealing out Clue cards.

"It doesn't matter who," he said. "Same guy every time. He doesn't have a name. Just roll the dice, okay?"

65

Paced out as regularly as accident scenes: roadblocks. Some were staffed by men in crisp black uniforms, others by sad-sack souls in tattered khaki. Some were in jungle camouflage. Others scarcely seemed like officers at all, looking more like forgotten sentries left to fend for themselves, wielding mangrove branches and brandishing snub-nosed pistols—the barrel of a gun being, as always, the final confirmation of authority.

A roadblock might be a simple pulley; it might be rubber tires stacked up with a plank across or a lone officer with an arm raised and an assault rifle on his hip. It wasn't the barrier that mattered, but the men behind it. And the guns.

Nnamdi peeled off another twenty-naira bill, passed it through the window.

"It's the least we can do," said Joe. "They are out there every day, standing in the heat, protecting our roads from rascals. The least we can do is buy them a canned Coke."

Nnamdi had already perfected what Igbo Joe called the "ten-kilometre-an-hour handshake," with Joe slowing down just enough for Nnamdi to lean out the window as a police officer stepped up on the running board to collect his fee.

"Always better not to come to a complete stop if you can help it," Joe explained. "They might start to dream up infractions to squawk about and tickets to write. Better just to shake hands as you go."

Army checkpoints were fewer, but scarier. The men at these sported AK-47s and flak jackets, and the senior officers were rarely assuaged with a handshake. They demanded to see Nnamdi and Joe's paperwork, forged letters from the Governor Himself that were duly handed over, duly mulled over, and duly returned. At army checkpoints, you always came to a stop.

Every town, no matter how dusty or down-heel, boasted at least one motor park where vehicles converged. Chaos, compacted. *Danfo* minivans, riding low on broken shock absorbers, and Peugeot taxis, overloaded and well-battered, wrestled for position. Ticket men argued over prices, dragging baggage onto bus roofs, dragging baggage off bus roofs. Passengers pushed forward—and were pushed back in turn by the ebb and flow of sudden surges. Long-haul coaches and ailing transport trucks wormed their way through the crowds, and in among them, a tanker truck from Portako filled with highly flammable, highly illegal, imperfectly refined fuel.

"We hunker here for the night," Joe would say. "Anywhere else isn't safe."

They would lock up their cab and climb down, ignoring the shrieks of taxi drivers who'd been blockaded by their rig, to head off in search of chophouse fare.

The food stalls in the motor parks were wedged in among the vehicles, with diners crowding along benches at tables bathed with exhaust. Women and young girls threaded through the mobs, enamel trays and tubs of food balanced on heads, calling out their wares in a singsong chant. Ragged beggars and lepers moved through—the crowds opening before them as they held up bandaged stumps, trying to scare people into flinging coins to avoid contact. When the lepers came, Nnamdi handed his kobo over, palm to palm, in proper human fashion, said, "God bless."

By then, Joe had staked out a spot for them at a *suya* stand. A shoe-repair tailor, calling himself Saviour of Soles, mended Nnamdi's sandals with a hand-cranked sewing machine while they ate. A tinker laid a handkerchief on the bench, carefully took Igbo Joe's watch apart, replaced a broken pin, and reassembled the timepiece in now-working condition.

"That," said Joe, "is the genius of Nigeria."

There was a rhythm to the road. After *suya* and beer, Joe and Nnamdi would return to their cab. Joe would challenge Nnamdi to a game of checkers. Nnamdi would accept, Joe would lose. So they'd play another round, and Joe would lose again. At which point he would pull out an *ayo* board instead. Thick wood with holes bored in. Joe would count out twenty-four seeds for himself and Nnamdi.

Nnamdi hadn't played *ayo* before, and Joe explained it with the same succinctness he'd shown in teaching Nnamdi how to drive: "You capture pieces by moving from hole to hole." A complicated game, in fact. But Nnamdi won nonetheless.

"Are you sure this is an Igbo game, Joseph?"

"I'm not Igbo, I'm *Ibo*. And my name is Joshua, not Joseph. And you—you are cheating. I don't know how, but you are."

Another round of *ayo*, and Joe would declare, "Let's go back to checkers." They did, with predictable results.

Joe would then drink himself into a stupor, and eventually to sleep, as Nnamdi lay awake on the front seat, listening to Joe snore and watching the moon refract across the cracks in the windshield. And then he, too, would drift toward slumber under a splintered sky.

"One does not drive after dark." This was one of the paramount Rules Almighty for driving in the north. "People live on the roads up here," Joe explained. "They treat it in the manner of a public hallway, with their huts like separate rooms. No street lamps, goats everywhere. Robbers, too."

When the police roadblocks closed down for the night, roving thieves took over. And no twenty-naira, ten-kilometre-an-hour handshake would save you from them. The police were at least civil, would drag a driver from a vehicle and beat him only if he deserved it, or if the officer was in a bad mood. But the night thieves, they would beat a fellow even if he'd handed over his wallet and watch.

Which was why a wrong turn on the wrong road could prove fatal.

Igbo Joe had made just such a turn. He'd exited the main highway too soon and hadn't realized it, taking what looked like a connector route into a low valley, only to find that the road soon narrowed into gravel and ruts. "A disgrace!" he said, still not realizing they were on the wrong track. "This is needing an upgrade. Some blacktop at least."

As night seeped in, headlights began flickering on. Or should have. Most of the vehicles around them seemed to be missing at least one light, often both. And with the road growing more pocked with holes, oncoming vehicles often veered toward them to avoid craters. The tension inside the cab rose. "Where is this exit?" Joe demanded.

"Perhaps we missed it?"

"Nonsense."

Joe hunched over the wheel, watching for potholes. Nnamdi watched for traffic farther afield like a sailor on a crow's nest, yelling "One-eyed!" for vehicles lacking a headlight and looking dangerously like motorbikes, or "blind man" if a vehicle was lacking both.

In the next town they found an exit. But it was the wrong one, curving west, not north.

"Love and piss!" Joe yelled, slowing down violently. "We take that and we'll end up back on the coast, in Lagos. Has our luck turned to vinegar? All we need now is to run into a Kill-and-Go patrol."

Nnamdi looked at the flattened scoop of the valley ahead of them. In the Delta, you might escape a mobile police assault by hiding in the jungle till the MOPOL unit passed. You could dodge the Coast Guard and JTF as well, losing yourself in the labyrinth of creeks and inlets. But here, under this open sky? On these open plains? Where would you hide? Where *could* you hide? A single body cast a long presence out here. Hunters could track you simply by the shadow you trailed, even in moonlight. You would have to run very far to escape.

Lost in the night, they needed to turn around, and soon. But where? The streets were too narrow for turning, so they rumbled on, looking for a gap. They found it in a schoolyard soccer field, where Joe made a sharp U-turn, leaning hard on the wheel, trying to avoid both the walls of the school and the jackknifing of the vehicle.

Checkpoints weren't always police or military; freelancers calling themselves "tax men" would sometimes shake down drivers for a "transportation fee." A toll, as it were. Indeed, any group might muster enough members to man a blockade. Border police (even deep inland), immigration officials (ditto). Agricultural and veterinary inspectors might also set up roadblocks to check for unlicensed vegetables and improperly secured livestock.

As Joe slowly brought the tanker truck back onto the road they'd just come down, a figure came running out ahead to throw a spiked roll of rubber across their tracks. Igbo Joe geared down, braking with both feet, barely stopping in time.

"Christ and vinegar!" he yelled.

A sinewy man in a thin undershirt called up to Joe. "I pray chop your hand-oh! Transport tax dis village. Where dis papers-oh?"

But Igbo Joe was in a foul mood, and he yelled down at the man, "What is the meaning of this! We are on official government business. A MOPOL patrol comin' soon behind us, arrest you quick."

"No Kill and Go out here. You is gone lost, I think, and dere is a fee for passing dis way. Village improvement tax."

Nnamdi looked around. The village could certainly use it.

"A tax?" Joe sputtered. "For using the road? Where is your gun?" he demanded. "I don't pay anyone till they go'an show me their gun. Where is your credentials?"

As Igbo Joe and the tax collector shouted at each other, Nnamdi slipped out the passenger side and, crouching low, ran up front and pulled the spiked roll of rubber aside. Joe had seen him do it, and when Nnamdi leapt back inside, Joe barrelled through, gears grinding.

The man in the undershirt was screaming at them in their side-view mirror, growing smaller, disappearing.

"We are free!" Joe roared.

Like shadows through a net.

It was late at night when they finally rumbled into the next motor park, their headlights scattering moonlit beggars picking through the rubbish. Joe and Nnamdi found a chophouse that was still open, pushed through the beaded curtains, sat on wooden benches, ate on oilcloth. Skewers of lamb and a savoury soup. Boiled yams and bony fish.

"Enjoy this last taste of the sea," said Joe, picking a hair-thin bone from his teeth. "Once we cross the Middle Belt, even dried fish like this will be hard to find. Just goat meat and millet after that. Even their beer is made from millet." He shook his head at the tragedy of it.

"I like goat."

"Not like this you don't. These are northern goats, raised on twigs and pointy grass. Just gristle and hide." A pause. "Will be good to be back south again."

There was a chill at night here as the heat of day gave way and temperatures fell from near-boiling to near-freezing. Nnamdi would be dressing in layers from this point on.

Igbo Joe finished off his broth, opened up his checkerboard on the chophouse table. "One more before bed."

Nnamdi sighed. "You never win."

"The only reason I never win," Joe said, "is because you never lose. That's the only reason. Now, let's play."

66

The next morning, Joe said, "You will drive from here."

They were having an early breakfast at a tea-bread-and-eggs stand. Pale grey omelettes and a fist of bread ripped from the heart of the loaf, served with tea that was boiled in sugar-milk and served in plastic mugs. "Waking up on sweetness." This is what Nnamdi's mother would say when she fed him nuggets of cane sugar in the morning. The Delta had never been so close. Or so far away.

"We'll bless the vehicle first, to be safe. You know, wash it in the blood of Christ before we go."

Joe tracked down a motor-park preacher to perform the service. A grey-stubbled man with a booming voice, he climbed onto the running board and, holding a Bible first to his forehead and then to his chest, intoned, "As you enter the north, may Our Holy Lord and Saviour Jesus bless this vehicle. Bless its cargo, O Jesus! Bless its alternator and its transmission! Bless its wheels that they may turn, bless its brakes that they may not fail, bless the fan belt and gears, O Lord, and see these men out safely again. Amen." He then walked around the vehicle, sprinkling water.

Nnamdi had cast his own prayers earlier, had clapped his hands to catch the attention of the now-distant *orumo,* had asked for benediction from the village ancestors that he might not crash the vehicle or become lost along the way. That he might escape, shadow intact.

The road continued to deteriorate.

Crumbling villages came and went, and the tanker truck splashed through rivers of raw sewage, then bounced across dry creek beds.

"Come rainy season, impassable," Joe said. "Becomes a muddy stew."

Nnamdi was gripping the wheel, eyes on the road, barely blinking, barely breathing. His first time driving.

"Speed up," said Joe. "A baby crawls faster."

Nnamdi swallowed down his nervousness, pushed a little harder on the accelerator.

"And don't swerve for goats like that," Joe said. "Go through them. It's the only way. We can hose off the grille later, but if we tip this rig on a swerve, all is lost."

The road began to undulate, rising and falling over hill and gulley, unspooling upward across the plateaued heights of the Middle Belt. With the altitude, the air grew cooler, and Nnamdi's ears popped. Then popped again.

"Tiv country," said Joe, pointing out the crops and slow movement of cattle below. "Farmers. They hop when they dance." Nnamdi waited for something more, but that was it. That was Joe's full summation of Tiv culture.

"I'm going to sleep," said Joe, and he crawled up into the bunk, pulled the curtain across.

Trails of smoke were rising from the Tiv settlements. "Are they peaceful people?" Nnamdi shouted back at Joe as he wrestled the wheel around a slow bend.

"The Tiv? I suppose," Joe replied. "Too busy hopping." He stretched out and was soon asleep.

From the thin air of the Middle Belt, Dreams Abound began its slow descent. Nnamdi could feel the immense weight of the fuel behind him, pushing the cab forward, and he fought against it, riding the brake pads, gearing down.

Joe was awakened by the strain of the truck fighting its own momentum.

"Don't use the brakes," he said, crawling back out of the bunk. "I told you, they'll only slow you down."

The outer savannah opened up, with rocky outcrops and a terrible emptiness stretching out in front of them. On the far horizon, a cloud the colour of dried blood had darkened the sky.

"Harmattan," said Joe. "We better find cover."

It was a race against the weather—and it was a race they lost, as the sands swept in, bringing the Sahel with it, turning day into dusk, dusk into night. They cranked up the windows and turned on the wipers, but the water that sprayed across only smeared the grit, didn't clean it off.

"Paraga and *ogogoro,"* said Joe as he unscrewed a mason jar, rolled down his window and hung out, into the storm, sand stinging his eyes as he reached to splash a chug of his mixture across Nnamdi's driver-side windshield. The dust slid away, left clear streaks in its path. "More than one use!" Joe cried with a laugh as he swung himself back inside. "Would'a been worse come rainy season. Dust is still better than mud."

Nnamdi wasn't so sure. The motor was gumming up; he could feel it growing sluggish. Harmattans and motor oil didn't mix well.

They entered Abuja city in the grip of a dust storm, headlights on, wipers flailing. Nigeria's national capital was clouded in a red haze, the government buildings outlined in rust. Nnamdi pulled over. "I can't do this. I'm driving blind."

Joe crawled across, took Nnamdi's place. The truck rolled down a wide boulevard strafed with grit till Joe found a motor park. It looked like a Bedouin camp, with vehicles shuttered and food stands closed tight.

"We'll wait out the storm here," said Joe. "And make Kaduna city tomorrow morning." His voice was strangely flat. Any elation he might have felt over their impending payday was lost in a sea of foreboding. "In and out," he said. "We don't linger. There's no drinking in the sha'ria states, you know. No taking of harlots or gambling."

Nnamdi said, "I wasn't planning on taking harlots. Or gambling. And I can go a night without drinking."

Joe grinned. "Well, I'm not one for gambling." He finished off the last of the *paraga*. "And just because it's not permitted doesn't mean it's not allowed. It's just—you have to skulk about so, like a common criminal in among the riff-raff and ruffians of the Sabon Gari."

"The Sabon Gari?"

"The Christian quarter. Every city in the north has one."

"*Sabon* means Christian?"

"*Sabon* means stranger."

The cab was rocking on the wind, sand hissing across the glass. Another round of checkers, another round of *ayo*—

"We should have been playing for money," said Nnamdi. "I would be a rich man by now."

Joe climbed up into the bunk.

"You're cheating. I don't know how, but you are."

"It is not cheating. It is cleverness."

"Cleverness is just another form of cheating. And anyway, if we played for money, that would be gambling, and gambling is forbidden up here." Joe rolled himself over and into sleep.

Tomorrow Nnamdi would clean the worst of the gunk from the motor. They would deliver their cargo of fuel, and then beat a hasty retreat, cash in hand. Nnamdi felt as though he had crossed an ocean, had reached the edge of the map, had climbed the tallest oil palm in the Delta.

As the storm outside thinned, he watched a red moon burn its way through the dust. And he smiled.

67

Fires were burning on the road to Kaduna. Vehicles, set alight. The fuel riots had spread, and mobs were smashing storefront windows and being truncheoned into submission. Broken glass formed diamond-dust patterns on the sidewalks, and a haze of smoke and harmattan dust hung over the city. The few filling stations still open were backlogged with cars, horns blaring their anger and frustration. Another riot seemed imminent.

"Let's hope they don't storm our truck, drain the tank," Joe said as they rolled down the debris-strewn boulevard. He tried to laugh, but it came out as a nervous giggle.

"They probably think it's empty," said Nnamdi.

"Let's hope."

Even in crisis, there was opportunity. Young boys moved through the angry mobs selling plastic baggies of water and packets of kola nuts. Black-market stands offered cloudy gasoline of dubious quality in plastic jugs and two-litre bottles. "Just enough to get to the next stand," Joe joked. "We are not selling ours on the black market, though. We are selling it right back to the government."

He turned the rig onto a wide side street, aimed it toward a fuelling depot ringed with razor wire and towering chain-link fences. "Illegal fuel to a legal depot." This was the brilliance of the Turk's scheme.

And it worked.

They handed over their paperwork, joined a queue of tanker trucks inching forward until it was, at last, their turn. Workers climbed up, opened the hatch and pushed a metal pole deep inside, drew out a sample to make sure they hadn't arrived with kerosene floating on top of well water. When their cargo had been filtered and confirmed, the coveralled workers threaded in a drainage hose, started up the pump. The sides of Dreams Abound rattled and banged as the fuel inside was emptied into underground reservoirs. Escaping fumes created a wavering mirage above the tanker trucks.

"We are rich," Joe whispered to Nnamdi.

They counted their money twice, couldn't stop grinning. By this point, dusk was settling over the city. "We don't want to be on the highway with this payroll," said Joe. He peeled off some bills for the night ahead, then wrapped the rest in a plastic bag and pushed it under the floor mat, in the space where the emergency brake had once been. "I had them remove it before I picked up the truck," he explained. "It was just taking up space." He slid the floor mat back in place. "Perfect!"

Once they'd manoeuvred the truck into the Sabon Gari motor park, Igbo Joe headed out for the night. Nnamdi stayed to watch the moon; by the time Joe returned, it had arced halfway across the sky.

Nnamdi was outside, sitting on the bonnet, leaning against the windshield, when he heard Joe coming, staggeringly drunk and singing loud. Joe was holding a bottle of gin above him like the head of a slain enemy. Shirt unbuttoned, belt the same. Nnamdi watched as he stumble-walked toward the truck; his legs appeared to be moving at different speeds. He proceeded to fall *upward*, into the cabin, if such a thing were possible, and then upward again, into the bunk.

Nnamdi had to laugh; how could he not? Igbo Joe—in defiance of every known law of gravity. Other truck drivers had been celebrating nearby, though not with quite the wholehearted abandon Joe had shown, his unease at spending time in the north having proven fleeting at best. The other truckers sat shoulder to shoulder around glowing coals, eating lamb off the bone and toasting their good fortune with millet beer. Nnamdi heard snatches of Yoruba in among the conversations, and he watched as the flames flickered out and the men fell away, one by one. He wanted the moon to tell him a story. *"Egberiyo,"* he whispered into the night, let his request float up and disappear.

The night before, Nnamdi had thrown stones while Joe lay sleeping. The message was as clear as it was confusing: *Something is coming.* But nothing happened.

The world was asleep when Nnamdi finally climbed down and came around the side of Dreams Abound.

Asleep, but not quite. Something was moving through the shadows.

Nnamdi stepped out from between trucks, smiled.

"What do we have here?" he asked.

A girl, eyes afraid at the sight of him, startled and searching for a way to escape. She'd been creeping toward the fire pit, and she backed up as he came nearer.

In the moonlight: scars, delicate and decorative, drawn across her forehead, framing the edge of her mouth, radiating outward from her eyes.

"Fulani?" he asked.

She shook her head.

"Hausa?" he said.

No. How to explain that she was of the Hausa, but not Hausa, that she came from a small band of horse riders who had once crossed deserts with gold and spices, salt and slaves, incense and myrrh. How to explain that walls had once been built to keep them out.

"Ina so in ci," she whispered, backing up farther as he came closer. *"Ruwa. Shinkafa. Ina so in ci …"*

"Sorry-o, I don't speak … *Kedu ka idi?* Do you understand Igbo?" If Hausa was the language of the north, Igbo was still the language of trade, and Nnamdi knew enough to scrape together a query. *"Kedu afa gi? Aham bu Nnamdi."*

She shook her head again. *"Ban fahimta ba."* And then: *"Hausa?"*

"No, no. Sorry-o."

"Français?" she asked. *"Moi, un petit peu."*

He shook his head. "English?" His accent had softened during his time among the Shell Men. "English?" he asked. "Do you speak it?"

A small nod. Her voice, still faint. "A little, some."

His smile turned into a grin. "So, the King's it is! Are you hungry, miss?" She was younger than he was, but calling her "sistah" seemed too familiar, "madam" too formal. "Are you hungry?" he asked again, making a gesture with his hand as though pinching off a piece of dumpling and then eating it. "Food? Yes?"

She said nothing, but he could see she was famished, and he climbed into the cab and dragged down his Ghana-Must-Go, rummaged through it. "I think I have some … You know *piti*? It's from the Delta. My mother makes them much better, but— Here. Take it, take it. I was saving them, now I know why."

He handed it over to her. Mashed corn and plantain, wrapped in leaves. "These are a little old. I bought them in the Down Below before I left, but still. Please, sit, sit." He waved for her to join him on the running board.

The food was sweet and glutinous and she ate desperately, with two hands, not caring.

"Piti," he said and smiled. "You like it?"

"*Na'gode,*" she whispered. *Thank you.*

He opened a bottle of Fanta for her, and she sipped it slowly to avoid cramping.

"*Na'gode,*" she said again.

"Where I'm from, in Ijawland, we say *Noao*. It means hello and thank you." He smiled. "Saves time. You know the Ijaw Delta?"

She shook her head.

"You know the pipeline? The oil?"

She nodded. She'd walked alongside it on the way into Kaduna, that pale green rope running low across the scrublands.

"Well," said Nnamdi. "Follow that line all the way south, and you will find my village. I live at the other end of that pipeline."

"*Akwai nisa?*" She should have known. His face had the dark sheen of oil, as though it had soaked into his skin. Just as hers had the colour of old clay, of dust, of sand and savannah.

"You still are hungry, I think," said Nnamdi. "I have some *akara,* too. You know *akara*? It's sweet bean cake. We eat it in the Delta. Wait a moment, I'll find some."

When she'd eaten her sweet bean and finished the last sip of Fanta, she returned the bottle and bowed her thanks to him, eyes averted as was proper. But when she got up to leave, the stiffness in her back and the slowness in her walk betrayed her. For the first time, he noticed the size of her belly, so out of proportion with the brittle thinness of the rest of her.

The Igbo believe we are born with two souls. Nnamdi had learned this from his father. It was similar to Ijaw beliefs. One soul leaves us when we die, the other walks onward. This second soul will attach itself to someone else, will protect them and in turn be protected. Nnamdi looked at the girl's feet, leathery and grained with dirt.

"Do you have a family?" he asked. "A husband, father?"

She shook her head. Only uncles.

"Where will you go?"

"Ina so in je ...," she began, then reworded it in English. "I need—I need be going far."

"I can take you there," he said, "to far away. Child, you are so tired. Why don't you rest? Come."

When she hesitated, he smiled at her. "No bad things will happen, I promise."

He had a beautiful smile, this boy. Even if he did have the sheen of the oil creeks about him. It was a smile one might risk trusting.

Nnamdi opened the truck door, swung himself in. She hung back.

"What do they call you?" he asked.

"Amina," she said, taking her name from the Queen of Zaria and the walls that had been built there.

"And my name is Nnamdi. See? We are not strangers anymore, so you may enter. You can have my spot, here on the seat. The springs are a bit soft, but still comfortable." He pushed aside empty bottles of Fanta and food-is-ready wrappers, embarrassed at the mess. "I must apologize. We don't get many visitors. We are bachelors, both, you see. Untidy by nature." He straightened out the frayed blanket he'd been using. "Here, child. Rest." Nnamdi poked his head through the curtain. "Joseph, move over!"

She stiffened at this. She hadn't realized there was someone else in the truck.

Nnamdi looked back and saw the concern on her face. "Don't worry. He's dead drunk." He made a drinking gesture, thumb like a baby's bottle, chugging it down, then pretending to burp. "Drunk, you know?"

He was trying to make her smile, but all she looked was worried. She held back, near the door, ready to run.

"Don't worry, he is a peaceful person." Then to Joe: "Move over, Joseph!"

A grumbled complaint, nothing more.

"Igbo Joe, move over-oh!"

"Drink my piss." Joe rolled onto one side.

"Mind your language, there is a lady present."

"A lady?"

"Yes, Joe. A lady."

"I'm too tired, you have her. And name's Joshua, not Joseph. And'm Ibo, not Igbo."

Nnamdi eventually managed to push Joe far enough over to squeeze in beside him. And with a whispered "Good night" to the girl, he pulled the curtain across.

"Noao," she whispered back, though Nnamdi didn't hear.

She planned to rest for just a moment and then slip away, perhaps with the blanket, certainly with a few more bottles of Fanta, but sleep engulfed her, pulled her down. Her limbs became heavy and her belly grew still. The child inside was sleeping too.

68

Nnamdi and Joseph woke face to face, with Joe reeking of sour nights and sin.

Nnamdi winced, rolled over, and went back to sleep.

Joe blinked, slowly realized Nnamdi was beside him.

"What in Chukwu ..." He crawled over his friend, pulled the curtain aside, and was about to climb down when he saw the girl asleep on the seat below.

He kicked Nnamdi awake. "What is this! You don't bring them back with you like some night-riding *mugu!*" Joe stepped out over the girl's sleeping form, checked under the floor mat from the driver's side. The money was still there, so Nnamdi would be spared a pummelling over that. "Nnamdi!" he yelled. "Pay the girl and send her gone!"

The girl stirred. The blanket had slid off, and even with her layered robes Joe could see the swell of her belly. It stirred up images of other bellies, other travellers in the night, other shelters, other strangers—and he cursed his Sunday school teachers with hellfire damnation and every manner of punishment. *Couldn't kick her out, couldn't take her with them.* She was going to cause them trouble, he could tell.

She woke, sat up, kept her eyes lowered.

Nnamdi slid down onto the seat beside her, the three of them now lined up like schoolchildren on a bench.

"You've met?" said Nnamdi.

Joe mumbled something about foolishness and trouble.

"Joseph, this is Amina. Amina, here is Joe. Igbo Joe."

"My name's Joshua, not Joseph. And I'm Ibo, not Igbo."

Nnamdi smiled, said to Amina, "Even scientists with the most advanced of technological equipment cannot tell the difference between Ibo and Igbo."

"You," said Joe. "Can eat the peanuts from my shit."

"We have a lady among us," Nnamdi reminded him.

Igbo Joe shot a look across the bow, didn't even bother addressing Amina. "What does she want?"

"Transport. Only that." He looked at her. "The next city?"

She nodded, and Joe slammed the keys hard into the ignition, made a noise low in his throat, somewhere between a growl and a sigh. She was going to be trouble, he knew it. "Abuja," he said. "Abuja city and no further." Then, with a wave toward the latrine ditch at the motor park's edge, "Easy yourself both before we go. We don't stop for toilets till we get to the capital. She can ride in the bunk, out of view. It will be our good deed for this trip. Nothing more."

Joe's edict banning Amina to the back bunk didn't last. Once they hit open road, he allowed her down, on the condition that she would scamper back up at the first sign of a roadblock. There were none. The police and the army had been called in to Kaduna, where the petrol riots had taken on a tribal taint. Neighbourhoods were burning, and the violence had spread to other cities, to the Jos Plateau and beyond.

But Dreams Abound had slipped free of the crocodile's jaws and the tanker truck was bouncing now, unburdened and barely tethered to the earth; had it come undone, it might have floated away like a mylar balloon, the kind they sold at street festivals and naming ceremonies.

"We couldn't have left her there," Nnamdi had said to Joe as they drove. "Not after I'd shared food with her and given shelter."

"I know," said Joe. *I know.*

Amina was relieved to creep down into the seat. The bunk had been tossing her about, and she was worried about the baby.

Nnamdi passed her a bottle of Maltina, the drink so popular in Portako—"A meal in itself," the ads said—and she felt it drain almost immediately into her child, felt the flicker of strength grow inside her even as she watched the flattened savannah roll by. Slowly, the savannah gave way to rocky outcrops and strange landforms. And birds. Hornbills with black wings and ivory beaks taking flight.

Nnamdi watched her. "Have you been here before?"

She shook her head. Every kilometre south was the farthest south she'd ever been. Only then did she realize she'd left her only possession behind: the battered jerry can of water hidden in a culvert near the motor park.

Nnamdi and Amina talked while Joe ignored them—loudly. Granite hills began to appear, pushing themselves out of the earth, and the road began to twist. Joe was leaning hard into the wheel on every corner.

"Zuma Rock," he said. "Up ahead."

A great stone loaf, Zuma Rock was a significant landmark; it denoted not only the traditional geographical centre of Nigeria—the "navel of the nation" as it was known—but also the border between the sha'ria states of the north and the Christian states of the south. Zuma rose up, rounded and sudden, on striated cliffs etched by a thousand years of rainfall and erosion. The ridges carved down its sides were the sort of lines that might be left by acid or tears.

"Finally!" said Joe. "We can drink beer and enjoy ourselves again."

"You were drinking beer before."

"But now we can do it openly."

"You *were* drinking openly."

"Yes, but I couldn't relax."

"You weren't relaxed? You seemed very relaxed."

Joe grumbled an insult in Nnamdi's general direction and said nothing more on the matter.

As they neared Abuja city, Amina climbed back up into the bunk. The white gates of Abuja soon appeared and they crossed through, into the nation's dreamlike capital. Open boulevards and shimmering hotels. Expressways that flowed without go-slows or entanglements. A government town, a showpiece where *oyibos* and British queens might be feted and fooled, Abuja was laid out like a blueprint, in a precise and orderly fashion; even the traffic signals worked.

"I don't trust any city where the traffic lights work," Joe said. "Do you know how much that slows drivers down?" He hated touching the brake pedal. "They don't even allow *okadas* in the downtown. What kind of city doesn't allow *okadas*?"

"But you hate *okadas*," Nnamdi said. The motorbike taxis, carrying whole families on their backs at times, were forever darting in and out of traffic in daredevil feats of boyish bravado, cutting off larger vehicles and snarling up traffic that needed no further snarling.

"I do," said Joe. "They are the curse of every truck driver. But that is not the point. No. Abuja is not Nigeria. Abuja fell from the sky. It is an invention."

The wide streets reminded Nnamdi of the air-conditioned hallways of Bonny Island. The city was basting in the heat, yet still looked cool to the touch.

"Did you know," Joe said, "when slums appear in Abuja, the government bulldozes them down to keep things pretty? An honest man does not have a fighting chance here."

Minarets and a church steeple appeared: the National Mosque and the National Church, squaring off from each other across Independence Avenue. Joe laughed. "They measured them down to the very inch, is what I heard, to make sure no side was favoured."

As the golden dome and minarets slid by on one side, the stained glass and cross on the other, Joe gestured with his jaw. "National Stadium ahead." The one shrine that united all: home of the Super Eagles. Igbo Joe watched it pass with unabashed reverence.

Abuja was oversized, its perspective skewed, from hotels to mosque, from church to football stadium. A person left behind in Abuja without friends or family would feel very small indeed, Nnamdi thought.

It needed to be asked. "Joseph," he said. "What will we do about the girl?"

"What we goin' to do? I tell you what we goin' to do. We are going to leave her. We'll drop her at the Jabi motor park, past the junction."

"We can't."

"*Can't?* We got her out of Kaduna. That is enough."

"She wants to work at a market. She told me this on the drive in. Abuja city, it's too controlled, you said this yourself. She won't make it here. They'll bulldoze her down."

"The Old Wuse Market. The New Wuse Market. Friday markets at the mosque. She can find work."

"She wanted to go far away. This isn't far away."

"They catch us with her in the truck, and what's gonna happen? They will search the vehicle, top to bottom. *Everywhere.* Is that what you want?"

"Exactly so," said Nnamdi. "It is too dangerous, my friend. Police and army everywhere. It's very risky, dropping her off in Abuja. Very risky for us."

Joe looked at him. "Are you playing me for a *mugu?*"

"Lokoja. We'll take her as far as Lokoja, fine, yes? The markets there are not ripe with police officers. Easier to disappear in Lokoja."

"Fine. You drive." Joe geared down, brought Dreams Abound to a halt at a roadside rest stop. "I'm hungry anyway."

Nnamdi turned toward the bunk to get Amina, but Joe said, "No. She stays inside. We're not taking her with us for chop. You can bring her back some food-is-ready. But she doesn't leave the truck."

They ate at the Mammy Market, in a courtyard where wandering musicians played flutes and lambs roasted above a central grill. Halfway through their meal, Joe realized they had left the girl alone in the truck *with the money.* "Finish your beer," he said, hurrying. "We have to go."

She was sleeping when they got back, and Joe felt vaguely silly at having panicked. He watched her sleep while Nnamdi went back to the food-is-ready stalls, returning with blackened goat cooked in mango. She woke to the smell of it.

As Nnamdi steered the truck back onto the highway, heading south, Igbo Joe and Amina changed places, with Joe stretching out in the bunk to sleep and the girl up front, eating. It was a hunger that grew with the feeding.

69

My Dear Good Fellow!

Colonel Mustard here. I understand you are looking for someone to invest money in your 100 percent risk-free Nigerian export business. Shame about the dead relative, though. He was a diplomat you say? Pip pip. I was once a member of the British Royal Commission myself, working in such far-flung spots as Upper Rubber Boot, Saskatchewan, and Nepal. I've got my chequebook open, pen in hand. How much do you want? Or should I just send you a blank note and let you fill in the amount?

With snooty good wishes,

Yours sincerely,
The Colonel

70

Stone markers counted down the kilometres to the next town, and the next. Small scenes flitted past: mud-and-wattle homes, children running, women queuing at a well.

The grasslands had slowly transformed into forest and the road had begun to rise, twisting upward in series of hairpin turns, touching the underside of clouds. The girl in indigo had never felt the effect of altitude on her ears before, had never seen such rolling landscapes. The air was cooler and thinner up here, and she felt light-headed and faint.

They had entered the Middle Belt, and on a sharp bend in the road, farmlands opened up below, with pastures and patchwork fields and clustered villages.

"Tiv," said Nnamdi to the girl. "They hop when they dance."

Dreams Abound hit a pothole, and the truck almost bucked itself off the road. When Nnamdi looked over to see if she was all right, he saw her cupping her belly, as though protecting a basket of eggs.

The Middle Belt rolled on and on, in sleepy turns and misted heights. Amina nodded off, leaning first to one side, hands still cupping her stomach, then to the other. The air had cooled, but as Nnamdi brought Dreams Abound down into the flatlands above the Benue River, the heat returned, as belligerent and insistent as ever.

She was still sleeping when they arrived in Lokoja. So was Joseph.

Nnamdi slowed down for a ten-kilometre-an-hour handshake at a police blockade, feeling nervous. But the officer who hopped up on the running board took the naira without a flicker of interest in Amina. Still, just to be safe, Nnamdi pulled the blanket over her before the next roadblock.

The mangled metal of past accidents marked the countdown to Lokoja. Nnamdi nudged the tanker truck into a motor park, killed the engine. He slipped out, closing the door quietly so as not to wake the other two. Cricked his neck, shook the stiffness from his legs, took a piss beside the truck. Across from the motor park, children were playing an indiscriminate game of football—the rules and rosters seemed to change on a whim—and their laughter and angry exhortations, their shouts of triumph and woeful cries of defeat rang out. Had he ever been that young? His mother had always said, "You were born an old soul."

Nearby, a few piecemeal food stalls constructed from leftover scraps of sheet metal were selling warm beer and dry *suya*. The main market was down by the river—he'd spotted it on the way in—and he walked toward it now along a path that took him through Lokoja's European cemetery. The area had once been a key crossing of the River Niger, and as such had inspired all sorts of imperial bombast. No cannons in Lokoja's boneyard, but lots of headstones leaning as though into a wind. Missionaries and mercenaries, soldiers and Royal Niger officers, lost among the weeds and rubbish.

The rubbish wasn't limited to the graveyard. It spilled out down the embankment to the riverbank below—the amount of rubbish, like the number of car wrecks, testament to a town's economic health. Wealth produced garbage as surely as food produced feces.

Nnamdi came at last to a grassy crest, and there it was, in front of him: the confluence of the Benue and Niger rivers. They'd driven through Lokoja at dusk on the way up, and he'd missed the full sweep of it, the two rivers sliding slowly toward each other with only a sandbar dividing them and then—not even that. Two different shades of clay combining, the muddy green of the Niger and the milky blue of the Benue. Not a collision but a soft blending, the Benue folding itself into the Niger. Hard to imagine that this was the same Niger that later splayed out into the vast and distant delta to the south. Had Nnamdi floated downstream from here into the labyrinth, he might have eventually reached his own village.

Cattle, rib-thin and looking for water, were being herded

along the riverside, goaded by the swish of switches and the click of tongues. On the Benue, a lone fisherman poled a flat-bottomed pirogue through shallow waters. The river had shrunk back from its shores in the parched heat of the dry season; it looked low enough to wade across. What might it look like after a heavy rain? The two rivers must churn into each other with something approaching passion. Nnamdi wondered if he was still thinking about rivers.

His father had told him tales of the Ghost King and his Igbo ferryman, Asasaba, who carried souls across a river of death to be reborn as shadows on the far shore. "It's why you must never tread on someone else's shadow," his father explained. "You never know whose soul it might contain."

Nnamdi followed the shoreline down to Lokoja's River Market, where aromas both pleasant and pungent mixed, and where voices shouted out above each other. Boats were lined up, with trade going on right at water's edge, the goods being ferried directly from bargemen to market women. Mounds of yams, knotted like driftwood and with the earth still clinging to them, were shovelled into burlap sacks. Other piles of them floated above the crowds, in basins and buckets balanced on heads.

Have we arrived at far away? This was a question that needed answering.

He retraced his steps to arrive back at the shaded graveyard. On the flat surface of a fallen headstone, he prepared to contact the *orumo*. He brushed dead leaves aside and removed a small pouch that hung around his neck, emptied it onto the granite slab. Rolled clay pellets, embedded with fragments of shell. A shard of bone, a feather tied with a strip of hide. He picked them up, held them in his palms, let them fall as they may. The reading wasn't clear, so he threw them again. And again. The trick with the *orumo* was to keep asking until you got the right answer. They were only ever guiding you from within, after all, and it was always your own heart you were reading.

Nnamdi thought again about the pale blue of the Benue, the dark green of the Niger; he thought about shadows and souls and stories left untold. And when he got back to the motor park, he started the truck and drove out of Lokoja without waking the others. Joseph continued to mutter and snore, and when Amina murmured in her dreams, Nnamdi *shhh-shh-sh'*ed her back to sleep.

71

At Onitsha, everything exploded.

Igbo Joe was seething. He'd woken while they were crossing the bridge over the Niger River, a soaring structure that jarred him from sleep by its very lack of bumps and thumps. By that point they were already past Lokoja, and he knew it. He crawled down, raining curses upon Nnamdi's ancestors and on those generations as yet unborn.

"Turn us around!" he yelled. "You son of Judas."

"Please, Joseph. I didn't want to waken you," said Nnamdi.

"Get over, I'm driving." They switched without stopping, Joe sliding across and Nnamdi scrambling under. They could see a roadblock coming up, and Joe snapped at Amina, "In the back. And stay there."

They rolled through with a ten-kilometre-an-hour, twenty-naira handshake; Joe knew that making a U-turn would only raise suspicions, invite a search. So he took his frustration out on Dreams Abound's throttle instead, pushing the truck to higher and higher speeds, overtaking traffic, forcing oncoming vehicles into the ditch.

Nnamdi stayed quiet. The forests were growing thicker, the air heavier. But at the Onitsha motor park on the cluttered outskirts of the city, Joe cleared a path with his truck, brought Dreams Abound to a shuddering halt.

He yelled back at Amina. "Out! Now! This is the end of the road for you. Off you go."

She crawled down, looked to Nnamdi.

"Can't we at least drive her in?" he asked.

"Drive? *Into Onitsha?* Are you feverish? The city is a goat's bladder. Go-slows and thievery, all of it. We drive into Onitsha, and we will come out the other side naked and on tire rims. In Onitsha, they will steal your eyeball from out of your head, and you won't even see them do it!"

"I thought you were from Onitsha."

"I am!" Joe roared. "I am from this place. Is why I know. *Mb'a.* We don't drive in. She can get out, take leg from here."

Nnamdi frowned. "That's a far leg. The markets are—"

"Onitsha is one big market! Lots to choose from. Fabrics, *juju*, meats, electronics. She can beg or trade her way into something. Look." He turned to Amina. "You just say *'A choro l'ga de market.'* Okay? Someone will point you."

"She doesn't know anyone," said Nnamdi. "In her condition, it will be hard to find her way. But I know people at the markets in Port Harcourt, in the Down Below."

"Out!" said Joe. "Both of you. Right now! Take your money, be gone."

"Bruddah, please. I'm only—"

"This is your plan? To go up Kaduna with petrol and come back with a girl? Get out! If you want to take a long-distance coach back, it's your matter. But I'm not ferrying beggars to Portako in the Turk's truck."

Nnamdi nodded. "Let me gather my things then." He pulled his Ghana-Must-Go bag down. "Oh, and Joe? Before I forget. The alternator? It's fit to seize up any moment."

Joe eyed him. "What did you say?" The Ijaw boy was bluffing. Or was he?

"The alternator. It's going to go. And the manifold is looking very shaky. I don't know if you will make Portako."

Nnamdi *was* bluffing. But Joe couldn't be sure.

"I was going to run diagnostics," Nnamdi said, "check the secondary junction panel readouts"—these were pipeline-maintenance terms—"and reset the gauges for pressure and flow."

Joe's eyes narrowed even more. "You're lyin'."

Nnamdi smiled. "Probably. But how you gonna explain it to the Turk, you kicking his mechanic out of his moto—just before it goes and breaks down. And all over a girl."

A smouldering silence filled the cab. Slowly, Joe turned to Amina. Each word he spoke was a lid on a boiling pot, barely containing the bubbling heat below. "Get. In. The. Back. And. Stay. There."

72

SUBJECT: The money

Is on its way.

> With finest regard,
> C. Mustard

73

Amina and the Turk were sitting across from each other on low soft chairs in the office above the repair bay, in a room crowded with filing cabinets and loosely stacked documents, the pages of which were curling at the corners in the damp heat.

The Turk waited for the tea to steep. "I used to own an inn," he said, "for travellers. Now I own other things." He filled her cup. "Jasmine," he said. "Tastes like one is drinking flowers, don't you think?"

In front of her was a tray with shwarma breads and kebabs crusted with savannah spices, flavours that came all the way from Kano.

"Please eat," he said, and she did.

It tasted like the Sahel.

The Turk poured tea into his own cup. "You seem to have bewitched our young mechanic." Then: "It is not safe here. Do you understand that?"

She nodded.

74

Dreams Abound had entered Port Harcourt under gunmetal skies on a road that twisted through thick forests. A paint-peeling billboard had welcomed them back to Rivers State, "Treasure Base of the Nation," but the first sign of the actual city was a glimmer in the sky: a glow above the trees. As Dreams Abound drew closer, the glow took shape, became a ball of flame uncurling. It reminded Amina of a blacksmith's forge. Reminded her of flame trees and lightning strikes. Of fires burning on the plains.

As the tanker truck thumped along, she'd climbed down into the seat beside Nnamdi and watched the world change in front of her.

In the Sahel, the baobab trees and the acacia stood stark against the plains; they broke the horizon, staked out their swaths of territory. But down here, everything was knotted together, vines running up electrical poles, leaves hanging from above. The ochre shades of the Sahel had been replaced by a dark wet green, dripping with condensation. Dust had turned to mud, just as church steeples had replaced minarets and fish-head soup had replaced beef at the roadside food-is-ready stands. Women moved past, baskets balanced, hips swaying. The hijabs and neck-to-ankle gowns of the north had given way to brightly patterned wraparound skirts with immodestly short sleeves and elaborate head scarves tied up in bows. The air was thick with the smell of mulch and mildew, and she could taste metal on her tongue.

"Natural gas," said Nnamdi, referring to the plumes of flame ahead. "A byproduct of oil. You can force it back into the ground, or try to catch it—but you need specialized wells for that. Easier just to burn it off. Sometimes, after the gas is flared, the rains that come down itch the skin. Kill the grass." He smiled. "You can taste it, yes? Like tin? In the air?"

She nodded.

The towns they'd passed along the way were carved out of the forest, and even Portako, a city of millions rising up in concrete blocks, was only barely keeping the jungle at bay. As they drove in deeper, helicopter gunships chuttered past, low across the treetops, soldiers leaning from the sides, gun barrels bristling.

Nnamdi could hear gunfire in the distance, and he looked at Amina. "Maybe it's best if you ..." She slipped back into the bunk, drew the curtain.

Young men roared by on motorcycles, shirtless shoulders draped with ammunition. Joe was fighting his way down Owerri Road to the rail tracks when he suddenly geared down, a clenched look on his face.

Nnamdi could see men on the road ahead. "Police?"

"Worse," Joe said. "Kill and Go. There's trouble in Portako."

It was less a roadblock than an ambush, the MOPOL officers dragging Joe from the truck and forcing him down onto his knees. They screamed at him for his papers, and one of their gun barrels pressed into his temple so hard it left an imprint.

Nnamdi had the roll of naira bills ready, but he soon understood that it wasn't what they were after. Carefully, with two fingers, Joe reached into his shirt pocket, retrieved the Turk's government-approved, artfully forged travel permits. The papers had been stamped with the same forger's flair, but the officer in charge barely looked at them. He wanted to know where Joe's loyalties lay, and he leaned in so close he sprayed spittle. "Dis moto chop-oh? En'la?" he demanded. *"En'la?"*

NDLA: the Niger Delta Liberation Army. Nnamdi's chest tightened.

Joe may not have been Igbo, but he spoke the language with a smooth fluency. The officer, on hearing his eloquent pleas and protestations of innocence, stepped back in disgust, waved him on. Had the MOPOL men dragged Nnamdi from the passenger's side and made similar demands, heard the rich Ijaw accent that was so impossible to disguise, things might have turned out differently.

Joe climbed back up, shaken but undefeated. "That's life in Portako," he said, attempting a laugh. He started up the truck, put it into gear. And then, with real laughter, he realized the MOPOL officers had forgotten to collect their *dash*. Not a single twenty-naira bill had changed hands. "That was the cheapest roadblock yet!" he shouted. The key was to claim any victory, however small. That, too, was life in Portako.

When they crossed the tracks on the Azikwe flyover and tried to turn right onto Station Road, thick smoke and burning tires blocked their path. Through the wavering heat, they could see a gun battle raging farther down: men moving across the road, muzzles flashing, the thud of bullets hitting walls. "Piss and damnation, this is an inconvenience." Joe forced the truck to a halt, cranked the wheel using his full weight.

They joined the stampede of traffic fleeing north along Aba Road instead. "We'll double back," said Joe. "Come in from the other side."

Their detour took them past luxury hotels and armed compounds, where foreign workers were holed up like bush rats.

"The Meridien," said Joe, referring to one of the grandest hotels they passed, now under sandbags and army protection. "The Presidential, too. I've been in both, in the lobby. It was like a waiting room to Heaven."

The oil companies had their own gated compounds, with high fences and armed guards. "I was behind those walls as well," said Joe. "Delivering goods. One place has a football pitch with grass as green and thick as a billiard table. Cricket fields and tennis. Swimming pools and a golf course. Do you know golf? A sport only an *oyibo* would play. You hit a little ball, then walk, walk, walk—or ride, ride, ride a little cart—until you find the ball, then you hit it again."

Through one gate, Nnamdi caught a glimpse of white bungalows lined up in rows. These too reminded him of the air-conditioned hallways of Bonny Island, only cleaner and emptier. Even with cricket fields and swimming pools, it must be a sad life, hiding behind high fences like that.

An SUV pulled out from another compound, a Nigerian driver behind the wheel and bodyguards hanging from the running boards. A necktied *oyibo* was ensconced inside, face looking boiled even in the vehicle's sealed a/c. He was shouting into a cellphone.

Joseph swung south, skirting the edge of the earlier troubles as he came back in on Elekeohia Road. Armed men at a police blockade rushed out to stop them, but Dreams Abound was close enough now to the Old Township that Joe crashed through instead, shattering planks and scattering officers. A few yells and the ping of gunfire against the back of the truck, and they were through.

"We have escaped!" Joe laughed.

Like water through a net.

They rumbled into the checkerboard lanes of the Old Township, past the brothels and bars of the Down Below. Even MOPOL didn't have the nerve to enter this area of the city, or attempt even a perfunctory sweep. Governor after governor had threatened to bulldoze the place, from water's edge right up to the Down Below slums, but none had mustered the courage—or foolishness—to try.

Igbo Joe bulldozed his own path through the alleyways of the Old Township, barrelling down jumbled lanes, forcing pedestrians and lesser vehicles aside with extended blasts from his air horn, taking out a chicken or two along the way, but otherwise leaving surprisingly little carnage in his path. "Portako people," he said. "Nimble-footed."

As he drove up to the garage, Joe pulled on the air horn until the work crew inside opened the doors, swinging them wide so the truck could enter. He leaned hard against the wheel one last time, bringing the tanker truck back to where it had all started. Dreams Abound barely fit—and had barely made it; the engine had been misfiring during the last stretch of road, shuddering in low gear, straining in high.

"It's good you tuned it up before we left!" said Joe with a nod at Nnamdi.

Joe had planned to send Amina on her way before the Turk arrived, but the Turk was already there, sweeping down the stairs from his second-floor office, smiling wide, arms out in peremptory embrace.

"My wandering boys have returned! You made it through the blockades! So much vexation, but you—you have come home to roost!"

Joseph and the Turk embraced. "What is happening in Portako?" Joe asked. "There are commotions everywhere."

"This, I do not know. I can tell you the city has been put under a curfew, but not a lockdown. Not yet. I have heard it said, too many foreign workers have been kidnapped. Some were pulled off a company bus here in the city—in daylight! Military versus rebels. Rebels versus police. Police versus military. Helicopters against motorcycles. Motorcycles against machine guns. And the Ijaw against everybody. It is all of the above and none of the above. The situation shifts daily, hourly, indeed. The important thing is, you have made it back—and that in itself is a blessing. I thought I had lost you both, to say nothing of the truck."

A creak of hinge, and a small figure appeared.

The Turk looked at Amina, then back at Joe. "What is this?"

And now here she was, in the office above the repair bay, sitting in silence across from the Turk with the taste of jasmine and the Sahel on her tongue.

Igbo Joe was hosing down the truck, clearing the caked-on clay from the wheel wells and scraping the worst of the bugs from the grille. Nnamdi was off spending his money. And the Turk was speaking to the girl.

"I used to own an inn," he said. "But there is little business in hospitality these days. Still, I miss my days as an innkeeper. We do what we must. Your tea," he said, urging her to drink. "Before it goes cold."

She nodded, sipped the last of it.

He had daughters of his own. "They say business is not kind, but why should that be? We can buy and sell without losing our way, can we not? It's not safe here," he added. "Truly it is not. I own half the warehouses on the Down Below waterfront, and even I cannot go above the Old Township without armed bodyguards. It is a sad state we have fallen to. Bloodshed in the north, revenge killings brewing down here. The Joint Task Force shutting down illegal refineries. Patrol boats lurking in the creeks, shooting bunker boys on sight. MOPOL trying to flush out Delta saboteurs. This city is not safe for someone such as yourself. You are Hausa, I presume?"

She shook her head.

"Good. What few Hausa as were here have fled. That you are not one of them may not matter, though. You are of the north, and we know what that means. Such a long history of animosity between Igbo and Hausa. Normally, it is kept on a slow simmer. But with everything that is happening now"—he sighed, a mix of sadness and resignation—"they may even target the likes of myself. Outsiders always get caught in the middle, you see. As I said, the Hausa and their families, and any Fulani who may have been working for them, have already been evacuated. But you—you can't go back, can you?"

"No."

They could hear someone running up the stairs. Nnamdi, returning, taking the steps two at a time.

"The gunfire is getting closer," he said. "But I eluded the worst of it. I have made it to the market. The supplies are loaded on a truck, ready to go! And me, still with money in my pockets!" He beamed.

The Turk smiled. "You and Joseph have made us all a great deal of money. You are to be congratulated. As for the girl," he gestured politely toward Amina, "she can stay here until the baby comes. We can clear a space for her in the storeroom, move some of the oil drums, let her sleep there. You would have to hire some sort of midwife, of course. But you have money enough for that, Nnamdi."

And after the baby came? What then?

Nnamdi had been thinking about this moment, had been thinking about it ever since he cast the stones in Lokoja.

"I have to get the supplies back to my village," he said. "My mother will be worried. And—you see," he turned to Amina, "in my village, I have an auntie who is a midwife."

Amina looked to the Turk, the Turk looked to Nnamdi. "I see," he said. "And you think the girl can make the journey? It's a treacherous trip, is it not?"

"If she can make the drive from Kaduna, I am sure she can manage a boat ride to the Delta. If she wishes."

75

Nnamdi hired one of the Turk's boats, a small outboard vessel with the name *Himar* painted on the prow. "It means 'donkey,'" the Turk said with a laugh. "Hopefully it will prove as stubborn, get you through."

He wished Amina and Nnamdi the best, but Igbo Joe was not quite so gracious.

"What!"

Joe had been tightening the lug nuts on the Dreams Abound wheels, standard maintenance after a long drive, and he now stood, wrench in hand, stunned, but not speechless. Never speechless. "What manner of foolishness is this? What kind of *juju* has taken hold of you? Christ in a well, has she cast a spell on you? You are going to take her—*her?*—to your backwater village? The creeks are filled with gunmen and police patrols. You will never make it, and if you do, what then? You think she will be adopted by the Ijaw? Eaten more likely."

"Joseph—"

"Come with me instead, Nnamdi. Give her some of your money, leave her be. You and I will reach new heights. Look. I am going to make another run, this time to Cameroon. To the border, anyway. Come with me, we will get rich together. And the women of Cameroon! Ah, the women. They make Nollywood beauty queens look like warthogs. The border is bathed in beauty. Come."

"I must get back to my village. I have been gone for too long a time."

Joe sighed, growled really. Turned to Amina instead. "And you? You want to go into that swamp? They're still cannibals, is what ah'm told. Several times, at night, when I heard this boy's stomach rumble, I caught him looking at me with a little bit of drool running down his chin. I slept with one eye open, I can tell you! Worried to wake and find him above me with a fork and some pepper."

"Sleep with your eyes open? You?" Nnamdi laughed. "You don't even drive with your eyes open. And anyway, we don't eat Igbos. Not enough meat on their bones. Just gristle and old skin." Then, realizing that Amina was becoming alarmed by this, Nnamdi turned to her, said, "Not to worry, child. No one will eat you."

"Not raw, anyway," muttered Joe. And then, to Nnamdi: "I can't believe you prefer to go back to that rancid swamp of yours rather than make money with me."

"We are kind to visitors," Nnamdi said to Amina. "Do not worry."

Outside, the gunfire was getting closer.

419

76

Joe drove them to the pier at Dockyard Creek in a loaded-down taxi cab he'd commandeered from the repair bay.

He insisted on helping Nnamdi load the supplies onto the *Himar*. The boat had a fibreglass hull with outboard motors, and they filled it mid to rear with cases of Fanta. Square tins of cooking oil. Tins of condensed milk. Sheafs of bitter greens. Dried-cod stockfish. *Garri* powder for dumplings. Cement for patching walls. Bottles filled with penicillin tablets. Hydrogen peroxide for cuts and petroleum jelly for burns, with ointments for the healing and gauze for the wrapping thereof. A box of flip-flops. Plastic bags filled with mosquito coils. New netting. A soccer ball for the school. Sunglasses and colouring books.

By the time the last of the supplies had been loaded, the boat was sitting dangerously low in the water. Joe pulled a tarp across, helped Nnamdi fasten the sides under spitting skies, shook Nnamdi's hand, forearm to forearm.

"If you have a change of heart, you can still make the run to Cameroon with me. I'll be leaving next month, before the monsoons."

"Maybe," said Nnamdi, though he knew his heart would never change; the stones had been cast a long time ago. "Maybe."

Harbour waters, thick with oil. Rain, beading on the surface. Joe, standing on the dock.

A cough and a stutter, and the motorboat sputtered to life. The Ogoni boy who was piloting the *Himar* backed it out of the berth, swung wide.

Nnamdi stood at the front of the boat, both hands raised in the air. "Goodbye, Igbo Joe!"

"I'm not Igbo!" he shouted. "And my name's not Joe!"

Long after his blood had turned to tar and the sores had spread, long after his immune system had collapsed and his body had

— 257 —

grown weak, Joseph of Onitsha would remember the Kaduna run he'd made with Nnamdi of the Niger Delta, would remember it fondly even as the lights went out, one by one.

Amina had never been on a boat before, and as it lurched below her, she gripped the sides fearfully. Nnamdi, however, stood straight-backed and strong, waving at the pier as Joe grew smaller and smaller.

"Noao!" Nnamdi shouted.

Joe was waving wide as well, back and forth with an open palm. By way of farewell he shouted, "I'll sit on your face with my bare ass yet!"

Nnamdi laughed, the boat turned, and they were gone.

Joseph and Nnamdi would never see each other again.

77

Language. Reveals as much as it conceals.

Laura had been thinking about compliments and complements. You're and your. Those distinct thumbprint misspellings and semantic blind spots that act as markers. Even as a copy editor, Laura had to stop and think whenever she came across "different from" and "different than," just as the vestigial "r" in the middle of "February" continued to bedevil her. She knew it belonged there—of course it did—but it still seemed like a typo. Were she ever asked to rewrite the dictionary, she would start with February.

"Complements of the season!" It was the sort of error a spellcheck program wouldn't catch. This wasn't a slip of the keyboard. This was something else. This was something you had to type in, every time.

Just a simple mistake? Or was it something more?

Perhaps it was a thread running through the air from Earth to emptiness, from satellite and back down again, across an ocean, over a continent, running along fibre optics before jumping through the air one last time, into a wireless router and then onto her father's hard drive. A thread running from here to there, from a bungalow in Briar Hill back to a distant locale Somewhere Else. *Complements of the season.*

78

The pilot steered the *Himar* along the shores of Dockyard Creek toward the main channel, where he nosed the small boat into the shipping lanes of giants.

Oil tankers were flushing their reserves in preparation for refilling their holds, and the channel was coated with the residual runoff. Those that were finished moved past, pushing swells of wave before them like dough under a roller and dragging a spreading wake behind. Whenever these tankers passed, the small boat Nnamdi and the others were on would lift a moment later, rising, then falling. The Ogoni pilot kept the throttle low. He angled across the crests as Nnamdi sat, face to the wind, and Amina clung to the sides.

Flat-bottomed pirogues, heavy with plantains and stacks of bundled firewood, were hugging the shore, their owners picking their way along with pole and oar, riding out the swells as best they could.

"My father," Nnamdi shouted back at Amina. "He had a boat such as that. I have it now."

They passed a derelict tanker, hollowed out and listing to one side, bleeding rust from its rivets. Flow-station platforms appeared as pipelines converged. Razor-wire outposts at water's edge, colours clearly marked: Chevron and Agip, Texaco and BP.

Nnamdi laughed. "Welcome to the Republic of Shell!" he shouted.

They passed a gas flare that vented its heat in the middle of a village. Vegetation on all sides had grown sickly and thin, but the women in the village were using the gas-fed flames regardless, laying out racks of cassava to dry and hanging their washing on the feeder lines, faces glistening from the heat. The pipelines carved paths through the forests, plunging in and out, across lesser creeks and larger ones, running along the surface like water snakes.

"Come rainy season, those pipes will disappear from sight," Nnamdi told Amina. He'd moved closer so he wouldn't have to shout.

She looked at the grey ceiling of cloud pressing down on them. The spattering rain and dripping forests, the wet breath of mist. *If this is not the rainy season ...* She pulled her head scarf closer.

"You can crawl under," Nnamdi said, referring to the tarpaulin. "If it rains."

If?

They had entered a steamy maze of waterways and tufted islands, and the *Himar* slowly began to pick up speed, its hull slapping the water as the rain pincushioned in, stinging skin like sand in a windstorm. *What have I done?* Fingers of water, everywhere. Endless passages. *What have I done?*

Nnamdi came back to sit beside her. "The water people, the *owumo,* they live below the surface. They look up at us and think we are the reflections." He smiled. "Maybe they are right. Maybe the *owumo* are real and we are the upside-down ones. The mothers, back in my village, they threaten children. 'Behave yourself, or the *owumo* will come get you! If you are bad boys and girls, they will snatch you.' But my mother? She would only say, 'Behave, Nnamdi, or *iyei* will come.' It means 'something.' Only that. She would never say what. Just 'something' is coming." He laughed. "That was always the worst, not knowing what—just *something*. Just *iyei*."

As the channel grew wider, the boat moved faster, cutting across the surface of that parallel world. On a lurch, Amina threw up into her mouth, spit the vomit over the side. Watched the waters blur past below.

79

You didn't get the money? Preposterous! I sent it by Super Express Rapid Overnight Air Mail, and have already received confirmation that someone picked it up on your end and cashed it. What is going on over there? Do you think I'm some sort of chump?

Sort it out and get back to me.

Col. Mustard

80

Bonny Island in the distance, glowing in a half-light of haze. Beyond Bonny Island, open water.

It was the first time she had ever seen the sea, but she felt no sense of elation at this, because she knew what it meant. She had run out of Nigeria to cross. She had come to the end of all roads, could go no farther.

The wind was stronger now, and the waves were beginning to curl. Thin lines of whitecaps on the horizon. The weight of open ocean in the distance. Offshore oil platforms floating on a grey sea, towers of fire, flaring gas. It made her think again of trees burning on the open plains.

Nnamdi pointed out the clustered lights and distant cylinders of Bonny Island's natural gas liquefaction plant. "What isn't flared into the air ends up there. I used to live on Bonny." Many lifetimes ago. "It used to be a slave port," he said. "The point of no return, is what they called it. The slaves, they would be brought to Bonny, and from there, ships would take them away. There is a freshwater well on Bonny Island where the men and women and children would have a final drink before leaving Africa forever. Even now, they say the water from that well tastes like tears. Some people say it is just the sea seeping in. Salt water among fresh. I'm not so sure."

Details were emerging. Bonny Island, coming closer.

"Of course," Nnamdi said with a grin, "we Ijaw were most commonly the ones doing the selling. If I was meeting Igbo Joe at that time long past, I might have thrown a net over him and sold him to the *oyibos*. We Ijaw captured and sold a lot of Igbos over the years. They are still mad at us about that. The Igbo were yam farmers back then. Easy to catch." He laughed, but the message was clear: the Ijaw had never been subjugated, never been enslaved. They had been the hunters, not the prey. The fishers, not the fish. Hammer, not anvil.

When he saw a flash of fear in her eyes, he tried to soothe her. "I am only making a jest. You will be safe with me." He looked out at Bonny Island. "You will like my village," he said. "We are kind to guests."

Naval gunships were on the prowl, riding low along the horizon.

"Looking for bunkering operations," Nnamdi told Amina. "They will board any ship with oil unaccounted for, even a tanker, and they will not let it go until they are well provided for. But no one is looking for us." He pointed at the forest. "My village is that way. In the outer Delta. There are seven hundred people in my village, and I am related to eight hundred of them."

He said something to their pilot and the boat veered, heading straight for shore. Amina gasped, convinced they would crash into the wall of mangroves, only to see a gap open up at the last possible moment. A trail of water appeared.

"Shortcut," said Nnamdi.

Their young Ogoni pilot, chin down, white shirt billowing, looked tense as they left the main channel and entered Ijaw territory. The Ogoni people and the Ijaw might have formed a tentative alliance in the Down Below slums of Portako, but out here, in the spiderweb of the Delta creeks, loyalties were less fixed. If this Ijaw boy and his captive—Hausa from the looks of it—were to turn on him, where would he flee, what would he do? Was he steering the boat into an ambush? The Turk had assured him otherwise, but in a swamp, assurances were as uncertain as allies.

They were now wending their way into the waterlogged heart of the Delta. Tidal estuaries. Brackish inlets. The sheen of oil on water, iridescent and beautiful. Like an insect's wing, Amina thought.

The mangroves pushed in on either side; the trees themselves seemed to be wading through the water, roots twisting their way out of the mud below. Low-hanging branches dragged across the boat, thumping the tarp and forcing the pilot to duck.

"If you see a vine moving," Nnamdi told Amina, "it's best you do too."

Storks took flight, wings leaving perfect circles along the water. On an overhead branch, a sudden shriek—and Amina scrambled backward.

Nnamdi said, "A monkey, nothing more." He could see the girl's shoulders shaking, thin and birdlike. "The monkeys out here have long tails, white throats. Always causing trouble. There is one monkey—a red one, with skinny arms, long hair. Very rare.

Professors from Lagos University have come here trying to catch it, and they have always failed. They even offered a reward! For a monkey! I have lived my life in this delta, and never have I seen such a monkey. But … maybe today is that day. So, child, keep your eyes wide. If you see such a creature, we must capture it at once. We will sell it to a zoo, then buy a big house and be rich."

She smiled, so faintly he almost missed it.

"Do you know how to catch a monkey?"

She shook her head.

"By being clever. If you put a pinch of salt between a monkey's eyes, he will go cross-eyed and not see you coming. A pinch of salt, between the eyes, and you will have him." Nnamdi imitated the cross-eyed fellow, staggering one way, then another. She had to hold a hand across her mouth and look away to keep from laughing.

Nnamdi passed her the canteen he'd filled back in Portako. "I think maybe you should smile more," he said. "It suits your face."

A rumble of thunder, and they made it through into the next channel. Thousands of dead fish were floating on the water, in among the mangrove roots, coated in oil. A charred forest. Blackened trees, charcoal vines. Sabotage? A gas leak, ignited unawares? A bunkering operation gone wrong? "I don't know," said Nnamdi when the Ogoni pilot asked. Anything would burn if you use enough fuel, even rivers. Nnamdi knew this firsthand.

Dusk on the Delta. The pilot leaned on the throttle, hoping to make Nnamdi's village before nightfall. He would sleep on his boat, then return in the morning. That was the plan.

But then Nnamdi looked behind them. "Something's coming," he said.

Another boat had entered the channel, in from the rear, moving fast. A speedboat, crowded with men, rifles raised.

The Ogoni pilot leaned harder on the throttle, and the *Himar* began to chop across the waves, almost taking flight at times, even with the cargo weighing it down.

"Can we outrun them?" Nnamdi asked.

The pilot looked back at the speedboat that was even now cutting across their wake. "We have twin outboard motors!" he shouted. "Forty horsepower. And we are heavy with goods. They have seventy-five horsepower. Maybe more. Can we outrun them? No, we cannot."

So the pilot spun hard, pointed the boat at one of the secondary creeks. "Perhaps we can lose them instead," he said. "Cat-and-mouse it among the creeks. Wait till nightfall, try to slip away."

"No," said Nnamdi. Running would only anger their pursuers. "Cut the motor, come around. We will see what they want."

"We know what they want! Blood!"

"Cut the motor," said Nnamdi. "It's our only chance."

The pilot killed the motor, turned the boat to face his fate.

"Is good you didn't run!" called the man standing along the speedboat's prow. "We would have gone shot you out of de water, used ya skulls for soup bowls."

They were taut-torsoed men, shirtless for the most part and streaming with sweat. One of them wore an orange Shell jumpsuit, unzipped to the waist and stained with something resembling rust. Three or four of them sported fresh scars across their chests, slits cut to insert protective potions under their skin. White tatters of cloth flew from their gun barrels. Egbesu boys, immune to bullets. Vaccinated against death.

"*Noao!*" Nnamdi said.

"*Noao,*" they replied, as their boat drifted up alongside. "We dey NDLA," shouted their leader. "What is your mission?"

"Going home, only that."

Their expressions reminded Nnamdi of the glazed stare of goat heads hanging in a butcher's market.

Glassy eyes, rimmed with red: hashish and gin, perhaps a little heroin to leaven the mix. One of the Egbesu boys pushed his way to the front of the speedboat, laughed, full-throated and loud. "I know dis one!" he said, pointing at Nnamdi.

It was his old friend, the boy from Bonny Island, the one Nnamdi had first taught how to break into a manifold. The young man had graduated from tapping pipelines, it would seem. An AK-47 rested in the crook of his arm and a leather belt of bullets was slung across his chest. A rocket-powered grenade launcher behind him leaned to one side. There was an oily sheen on everything: the men, the weapons, the boat. Nnamdi had seen such weapons on sale in the Down Below streets. A much improved arsenal, and a far cry from the single-bolt rifles of earlier days.

The rebels had cut their motor, and Nnamdi heard something small and afraid whimpering from below the other boat's tarpaulin. "That?" said the boy from Bonny Island when he saw Nnamdi's expression. "Just this."

The boy pulled back the covering, and below was a woman, hair-plastered with sweat, eyes terrified. An *oyibo* in khaki clothes. They hadn't bothered to bind her wrists. In a swamp like this, where could she possibly run?

"All the oil companies, all is under lockdown. Armed guards everywhere. So we raided a French facility, next creek over. Aid workers, is what they said—when they was dying. Workin' for oil either way. The men she was with, all died in de tussle. Found her hidin' under a bed. A handsome ransom for dis one, I think."

Amina looked at the pale creature, the frightened *batauri* cowering at the feet of her captors, saw herself in those washed-out eyes.

The boy from Bonny laughed. "I see you caught a woman of ya own. I would trade wit' you, but I thinkin' ours is worth a lot more."

Nnamdi forced a smile. "So be, so be. Not worth much, mine. Cost more to feed than to keep."

The pale woman looked at Amina. *"De l'eau,"* she whispered. *"S'il vous plaît. De l'eau."*

Amina handed her canteen across—the boys in the speedboat didn't seem to care—and the pale woman drank down the Portako tap water, gulping hard as Amina watched. After a minute, the men pulled the canteen away, tossed it back to Amina.

The woman kept her eyes on Amina as the men talked large and laughed loud. *"Aidez-moi,"* she whispered.

"Je ne peux pas," Amina whispered back.

"De femme à femme. Aidez-moi." She was holding back a sob. *"De femme à femme."*

"Je ne peux pas ... "

The men in the speedboat were demanding payment from the Ogoni pilot, a fee for the privilege of passing through their territory. "Coke, we want coke." At first Nnamdi thought they were demanding drugs, but no. They were eyeing the goods visible under the tarp. They were thirsty. "Give us Coke."

"Fanta?" Nnamdi asked, pulling back the covering. One of the Egbesu boys stepped aboard to claim it. "Wait," said Nnamdi. "The ones below are colder." He shifted a crate and dragged out a lower box, and with this simple gesture he unknowingly saved their lives: his, the girl's, the pilot's.

"A good man," they said, pressing the cold bottles against their temples.

The Egbesu boys started their motor up, and the two boats slipped apart like reflections separating. Amina and the *batauri* woman stared into each other as the distance between them grew.

The *Himar* moved again across the murky waters of the Delta. Nnamdi stayed silent. Finally, without looking at Amina, he said, "There was nothing I could do. I couldn't help her."

"I know."

"I couldn't."

I know.

In the gathering dark, they rounded a final bend in the creek to the sound of drums. The Ogoni pilot called to Nnamdi, but Nnamdi didn't know what it meant either. "Maybe a camp of some sort. It wasn't there before," he said.

Long white banners fluttered from tree branches like cotton bandages unrolled. Chanting and drums. And in a clearing, bodies painted with chalk, dancing in a grim gin-stoked frenzy, arms jerking, guns waving in the air. A round went off, and then another.

Amina felt the fear of a hundred days flood in. *Is this where it ends? Am I taking this boat to my own death?*

"What madness is this?" the pilot whispered, slowing down to glide past, hoping not to be seen.

"Not madness," said Nnamdi. "Egbesu. The Ijaw God of War. They have been inoculated, you see."

"Inoculated?"

"When you join Egbesu, bullets cannot harm you. They pass through your body like you are made of smoke. You can drink any poison, battery acid even, and not die. You are invincible."

"And if you do die?" the Ogoni demanded. "What then?"

"It means you have done something wrong, broken some commandment. If you die or are injured, the gods did not fail you. You failed the gods."

"And what are their gods telling them?"

"To fight. To drive the *oyibo* and the oil companies from the Delta. To make this an Ijaw state. To fight."

For the first time, the Ogoni pilot and the girl from the Sahel looked at each other.

"This ... is not good," said Nnamdi. "It means the time of talking has passed." There would be no more ultimatums, no more proclamations or press-conference manifestos. There would only be war.

Beyond the Egbesu camp, a familiar landscape of mangroves and small-scale cassava farms emerged. Houses floated past on shore, lit by coal oil and the occasional chest-rattling generator. Everything was backlit by the orange glow of gas flares.

"My village!" Nnamdi cried, pointing ahead, urging the boat on. "That tree—that tree there?" He was pointing to a trunk that formed a wide curve over the water. "I swung from that tree as a child. And that—you see, up the hill? Below the cross? Two lights close together? That is my father's house. Where I grew up."

Lights were blazing along the piers, bare bulbs dangling on extension cords. A city built on stilts. That's how it looked to Amina. Not a village, a city. A renewed wave of panic overtook her.

"You said—you said seven hundred people."

"Yes," Nnamdi said. "That's my village, in front. That, over there—" He pointed to the sprawling shantytown behind. Makeshift lean-tos and cast-off hovels. Huts made from mud instead of cement. Thatched roofs instead of tin. "That is not my village. That is the other side of the creek. Those are people from other villages that have been destroyed. Or abandoned. They come across at night sometimes, cause many kinds of mischief. But where we are going—that is my home."

To Amina, the demarcation seemed to exist primarily in Nnamdi's imagination; the two communities spilled into each other with only the faintest trickle of water between. She could see a church steeple above the crowded homes, the cross perfectly silhouetted by the gas flare beyond. A hand-painted sign near the shore read WELCOME TO NEW JERUSALEM.

The *Himar* bumped up against a broken-backed jetty, its hull scraping over submerged mangrove roots. Nnamdi and the pilot hopped off, pulled the boat in. "The oil company built this jetty; the rebels used it, the army destroyed it. But we can still land a boat here. We are good at landing boats."

As Nnamdi and the pilot unloaded the crates, word spread quickly, and a crowd of well-wishers came hurrying down, cheering Nnamdi's return.

Bare-bellied children scrambled near. "My cousins," he explained. They were holding up a rope on a stick. Not a rope. A snake—a cobra, impaled and dangling, dead. They were laughing, giggling, clamouring for attention, and Nnamdi congratulated them on their catch.

More faces, more forearm-to-forearm clasps, more people pushing in. Everyone seemed to be a cousin, or the cousin of a cousin. "And mine is a small family," he told Amina.

As the last of the boxes were unloaded, and as volunteers began lugging them up to Nnamdi's house, a murmur ran through and the crowds parted. A woman in flowing robes, regal in deportment, rich in laughter, came striding out.

Nnamdi's mother.

81

Scambaiting. This is what her brother was involved in. It was a neologism Laura hadn't encountered before.

"Payback," he explained. "For Dad."

They were at her brother's house in Springbank, and Warren was scrolling through website pages like a proud parent. He'd been eating Pringles as he typed, and the keyboard was sprinkled with crumbs.

"See? That one's mine," he said. "They posted it yesterday."

Winter had trapped Warren's kids inside. They thundered past, bickering on the fly. A muted television flickered, vying for attention: reality show contestants eating bugs, preparing sombre "tribal councils." Somewhere below, down in the basement, in her flannel nightgown no doubt, was Laura's mom. The prisoner of Springbank.

Laura drifted back to the one-sided discourse Warren so often mistook for conversation. He was explaining the concept of scambaiting to her. "There's a whole community of us," he said. "Like-minded people who are fighting back. We police the net, set up traps. The easiest way is to register dummy email addresses, turn off the spam filters, and wait. When these 419 weasels come calling, we take the bait. Instead of hitting DELETE, we reply. It's fuckin' hilarious."

Three-Stooges hilarious? Fingers-to-the-eye funny? Or celebrity-eating-a-bug funny? She remembered the prank calls Warren used to orchestrate as a teenager, before caller ID ruined that particular art form. "Ma'am, congratulations! You've just won CKUA's Chicken on the Run cash prize of *one hundred dollars!* All you have to do is cluck like a chicken for the next ten minutes ..."

Warren had opened his inbox and was grinning. "Y'see. Here's another one, just came in. *Dear Sir, I am the son of an exiled Nigerian diplomat ...* The trick is to answer with the most outlandish stories you can come up with, drag it out, waste their time, and then post the entire thing online. One scambaiter convinced the con men that he was a dying Belgian aristocrat, who was just ... about to ... send the money ... when—*croak!*"

Another 419 con man had been lured into a lengthy email exchange with a certain F. Flintstone of Bedrock, USA, "a town right out of history," who kept trying to pay with clams. Real clams. Another set of messages had been sent by one Captain Kirk, who agreed to send cash only on the condition that the people contacting him joined Starfleet Academy and sent signed affidavits that they weren't secret agents of the Romulan Empire.

"These morons actually printed off the forms, signed them, and sent them back," Warren chortled, "so Kirk kept making more and more demands. Handed it over to an associate named Lieutenant Worf, who started sending them letters written in Klingon. Some scambaiters have even convinced the con artists to send *them* money. Really! They'll say, 'I can help, but first you must demonstrate your sincerity by making a small donation of a hundred dollars to the Church of the Holy Turnip.'"

"They don't Google the names?" Laura asked. "Find out who Fred Flintstone and Captain Kirk really are?"

"Too greedy," he said with a snicker.

Greed versus cunning. Cunning wins. Where had she heard that? It came to her like a whisper from another room.

"They want it so bad," Warren explained, "that they never realize they're being played for fools—until it's too late. Then they go ballistic, start showering you with death threats and profanity. It doesn't matter. It still ends with us laughing at them, putting every-thing up on the web for the world to see. Here—check this out."

He opened a new window, clicked on a bookmarked page. A scambaiter from England had posted photos of a broken refriger-ator that he'd carted up and sent COD to a con man in Nigeria, who had paid the exorbitant shipping fees expecting—well, who knows? Gold, maybe. Certainly not a broken refrigerator. His angry response was laced with creative invective.

"Even better are the scambaiters who email the con artists to say, 'I'll be there Monday. Meet me at the airport! Wear a yellow hat with yellow shoes and yellow socks,'" Warren said. "One scambaiter got a Nigerian con man to fly to Amsterdam and had him waiting in front of a webcam outside a department store, standing around for hours like a moron. And if the con man emails back, demanding to know what's going on, the scambaiter responds by getting even angrier. 'Where the hell were you? I waited and waited!' Sometimes they'll send the con men to Western Union, and when the dupes email to say the money didn't go through, the baiter over here will fire back, 'Well, someone signed for it! Who the hell has been cashing my money orders!' Which sends them off on another goose chase. If we're lucky, they'll start fighting among themselves, accusing their partners of ripping them off."

Warren had moved on to another scambaiter site and clicked on the archives. "They call this the trophy room, where we post our latest conquests," he told Laura.

Photographs of young African men, some smiling, some not, some holding turnips on their heads or with their hands in a Benny Hill salute, some dressed in a bra and panties ("as a sign of your sincerity"), others holding up handwritten signs that read MY BOXERS ARE HOME OF THE WHOPPER or I SHOT JR!! or BEAM ME UP SCOTTY! NO SIGN OF INTELLIGENT LIFE HERE.

One man was holding a sign, purportedly in Swedish, that read:

IMAB
IGDO
OFUS!

Another had written out what he thought was the name of an international banking cartel:

I.M.A. Liberty Organization Savings Export Revenue

Warren was laughing out loud by this point. "Fuckin'
hilarious!" Laura, however, felt a queasy sense of—not sadness,
exactly. Something conflicted, the flutter of something trying to
escape. Warren scrolled down: rows and rows of photographs, each
one stamped OWNED! She'd seen photographs like that before. In
history books.

Warren kept opening new windows, cluttering his computer
screen with their overlapping views. "Wait, wait," he said as she
got up to leave. "Here's one I think you'll like. It made me think
of you."

Dear Chief Ogun,
    Delightful to hear from you old chap! I remember
my days in the Colonial Office of the Sudan quite well.
I was working with Professor Plum, who was studying
the aphrodisiacal effects of zebra hoofs on the wives of
British bureaucrats. I daresay Mrs. Peacock's husband
eventually murdered Professor Plum. In the library. With a
candlestick.

                    Sincerely,
                    Colonel Mustard, OBE

PS: I have copied your request to my assistant, Miss
Scarlet, at Corporate Living Unified Executives (C.L.U.E.)
who handles these sorts of money matters.

"Hooves," Laura said. "Not hoofs."
"What?"
"I'm going downstairs to see Mom."

"Wait. Check it out. Another rube has just joined the Church of the Holy Turnip."

On the muted TV screen across from them, the contestants had moved on to live worms and Laura had tired of Warren's game. Just as she was about to leave, though, she caught a glimpse of a message on Warren's computer screen that began *"Complements of the season—"* It stopped her, cold.

"Click on that one," she said.

The rest of the message popped up. A reply to Colonel Mustard from Chief Ogun. And there it was: *complements.* A common enough error, but still …

"Can I get copies?" she asked. "Of these emails. And the others? Can you print them off for me?"

"Which ones?"

"All."

"That's a hundred pages, at least."

"And the emails Dad got," she said. "I'll need those too."

82

"She can't stay here."

"She has nowhere to go."

"She can't stay here."

They were talking about her, whispering in Ijaw so she couldn't understand them. But she did. She knew what they were discussing, could hear it in the tension of his mother's voice, in the pauses between the words.

"You were always a dreamer. You never had any sense. What were you thinking, bringing her here? She can't stay."

"She has nowhere else to go."

Amina was lying on a mat with her back turned, pretending to sleep. Nnamdi had lit a mosquito coil for her, and she watched the thin smoke of it uncurl. Outside, heavy rains were coming down, rattling the roof. A small lizard scampered up the wall, its orange head trailing a fluid blue body.

They were talking about her.

"She can't stay here. She has to go."

83

The entire village had turned out to welcome Nnamdi home with cheers and laughter, drums and dancing.

"The prodigal son returns!" someone shouted. "Amen!" came the reply.

Women were waving palm fronds, men were beating out rhythms. Amina's senses began to spin. The Ijaw drums were so ... relentless, never stopping, never catching their breath, so unlike the lonely strings of the *goje* or the winds of the *kakaki* flutes, so unlike the music of the Sahel. The Fulani in the north were drummers too, but they never reached the hammer-on-anvil nature of the Ijaw. The rhythms of the Fulani drums were born of pounding millet, of women gathered around a hollowed mortar, turning music into food and food into music. These Ijaw drums were different: they were blood and fire, rain and thunder; they were the human heart after heavy work.

Nnamdi joined in with the dancers, leading one procession, following another. The dancers of the Sahel stepped as softly as a sigh, moving on the melody, not to the tempo, each step sliding forward, graceful, almost gentle. Here, the dancers were driven—propelled—by a muscular sense of purpose, movements that shouted out, men and women together, bent at the waist, feet rising and falling, arms carving patterns in the air with precise, slice-like gestures, the laughter almost an instrument of its own.

Amina felt faint. She had been standing too long. Nnamdi emerged from the joyous melee that was swirling around her, said, "Come away, you should lie down."

"But—is for you, this dance."

"Let's find a mat for you to lie on. There will be lots of time to dance later."

84

"She can't stay here. Look at her face, look at those tattoos."

"Not tattoos. Scars. And we must show her hospitality. Life demands it. We are Ijaw, and she is our guest."

"She speaks English like a simpleton."

"She speaks more languages than we do. She speaks French."

"She can't stay here."

85

Amina ventured out the following day, while Nnamdi was sleeping and his mother was away at the market.

Across from Nnamdi's home, a large iroko tree spread its shade in a central clearing, a communal living room of sorts. A sheet of corrugated metal provided shelter for a billiard table, and amid the click and clack of balls, men sat about on plastic chairs drinking the Fanta and ginger beer that Nnamdi's mother sold from her assortment of refrigerators. Amina tried to slip by unnoticed.

On the other side of the yard, a generator hummed. Old men and young children were crowded around the village's television set, watching the Super Eagles out-finesse yet another upstart collection of players. Amina's appearance broke the spell, though, and they stared at her as she passed—not in hostility, but not in friendship, either. It was more a puzzled curiosity, as though they were looking at an unusual bird and trying to identify it.

A lane led to another clearing, where oil barrels lay scattered about. Some had been upended and were being used as work-stations by women to clean fish or wash vegetables. Other barrels had been rigged with plastic sheets and funnels to catch rainwater. A hairdresser was plaiting a woman's hair in a doorway, and Amina hurried past, eyes down. The weight of their gaze followed her, though, and she began to walk faster.

The pathways between homes were muddy and crusted with shards of shells; it was as though the earth were embedded with diamonds. Corrugated rooftops, scaled in reds and greens, rust and moss, crowded in at sharp angles, the houses built this way and that, so close at times they almost touched. Open-ditch latrines. Swaybacked verandas. Windows without shutters, doorways without doors, and not a single privacy wall of any kind. Children and adults, men and women, intermingling with bare limbs and easy laughter. In a place like this, their lives must spill into one another's laps. No secrets. It wasn't possible. She felt the panic rising anew.

Past the football pitch, flattened grass framed by forest, she reached the farm fields at the edge of the village: small plots of land carved from the overgrowth, with the jungle pressing in from every side. Women were moving through, bending at the waist, slashing from the wrist, swinging machetes, clearing grass. Amina felt trapped. No horizon. No way to watch for the dust of hoofprints approaching. No dust at all. Only mud—and a wall of forest.

She'd slipped free of Nnamdi's home to scout a possible escape route, a place to run to if she had to. But now she'd come up against an oppressive backdrop of jungle, the green of it breathing in her face. The rolling rains of the night before had drawn earthy aromas from the soil. *When you pour water on a fire,* she thought. That was how the Delta smelled. Wet charcoal, water-drowned, but still warm. Always warm.

The very air had weight, texture. Fly strips of humidity, sticking to the skin. There was no reprieve. Any winds that did get through only stirred the heat, made it worse. Sweat trickled and dripped, but refused to evaporate. Even the trees seemed to be perspiring.

She retraced her steps to Nnamdi's house, defeated.

Nnamdi was up now, and he made her a cup of tea, stirring in condensed milk and extra sugar "for the baby." Gave her some of last night's fish, warning her to watch for bones. She was grateful, and she said so—*"Noao, Nnamdi."* But she was from the Sahel, and she needed lamb, not fish. The Sahel, where the soil crumbled between your fingers, turned to sand before your eyes. The soil here was dark and oily. It clung to everything. Her feet were stained with it just from the walk. Everything was so sticky, so thick. She missed the tastes and scent of the savannah, the clarity of its air. Most of all, she missed her family, her lost kinsmen. She was Amina the Incomplete. Without clan or caste, without that larger family, who were you? Just a singular thing. Unconnected and alone.

At night, she dreamed she had given birth and was holding her child only to have the wet earth of the Delta suck it out of her arms, leaving her nothing, not even bones.

She'd lie there, too tired to weep, listening to the sigh and roll of waves, the hiss of flames. Those flames never slept, even in the depths of night. During the day, Delta homes were so gloomy: cement walls with windows sheltered by great shelves of metal roofing. It kept the rain out—but also the light. At night, however, the interior of Nnamdi's home glowed from the constant fires of the gas flares. Amina wondered if she hadn't plunged through into the Otherworld, where light and darkness, day and night, were reversed.

"She cannot stay."

"I will throw the stones, ask the *orumo*."

"That? You do not need to ask the gods. You need to listen to your mother."

"I will throw stones. I will ask Papa."

"Your father is asleep in Heaven. Your mother is right here."

86

"Welcome to New Jerusalem." That was the sign that had greeted them when they first arrived on their donkey boat. Amina had thought it was the name of the village. It wasn't.

"Mr. Pentecostal, he put it up," said Nnamdi's mother, "to remind the Egbesu boys about dey one true God. Remind them of their churchly duties." The boys who painted their bodies for Egbesu on Saturday still attended church-hall revivals on Sunday.

Nnamdi's mother looked at her son, asked the only question that mattered. "Is it your child? The truth."

The truth?

This was a tanglement of a question, to be sure. Simple, on the surface, but snagged with detritus underneath. *Is the child mine?* Another way to look at it was to ask, Am I the child's?

As we move through this murky world, we all of us pass from protected to protector. Perhaps Nnamdi's walking soul had attached itself to Amina. Maybe Amina's had attached itself to him. So—was the child his?

He turned this question over, considered its many meanings. Turned it over like a tide-polished stone in the palm of his hand, and decided, yes, it was his child. His to watch out for.

"Is it my child? Yes, it is."

"The truth?"

"The truth."

Nnamdi's mother sighed. That changed everything. "Well, dey girl can at least change her clothing. And give her some proper flip-flops. Dragging her through the muck in tattered robes like that. Shameful."

Amina clutched at her head scarf defensively. "For me, I need have cover my head. I must to."

But Nnamdi's mother tutted away her fears. "You can still keep ya head covered up. I show you how to tie a proper *akede*. A headwrap. We'll find you a bright one. Flower patterns. Very beautiful. Maybe a matching *oshoke,* for the waist, maybe tie it over ya shoulder. You're so thin, will be lots of fabric left to work with. Now," she said with added weight, "some women wear very big *akedes*. Very big."

This was his mother's way of broaching the subject. The biggest and most elaborate headwraps were worn by *married* women. "The new minister, Mr. Pentecostal from Portako, can perform any type of ceremony." They could stay till the baby came, but her grandchild was not coming into the world to unwed parents—not when she was so active in the church.

"Mammy," said Nnamdi. "We need a midwife, not a minister."

His mother sighed the way only a mother can. "Fine. A smaller headwrap, then. But this matter is not over yet."

Lessons in the proper tying of an *akede* were only the start. Nnamdi's mother moved on to fish racks, demonstrating the correct way to weave dried stalks—under, over, twist, then turn—to create the plate-sized mats for fish to dry upon.

Fish unnerved Amina. In the outer Delta, people ate every part, served it with head still attached and the raisin-like eyes staring up at her. Could they not remove the heads first? There were fewer and fewer fish these days, and those that arrived had been netted far away in tributaries the oil companies had missed. But the weaving of fish racks was still an important skill to have. If the girl stayed.

Which she wouldn't.

"She has to go, you both do. You know that."

"She has nowhere to go."

"She cannot stay here."

Amina missed the taste of *miya yakwa,* the groundnuts and beef fried together, the wild onions and spices, the *yakwa* greens. It was all plantains and sugar cane down here, all cocoyams and cassava.

Palm oil and pepper soup. Banana leaves as pot covers, gourds used as mixing bowls. Everything was askew, even the manner in which the women cooked their yams, not pounding them with pestle and mortar, but burrowing them in coals, baking them until they became fibrous and tasteless. Having suffered this affront to yams over several meals, Amina showed Nnamdi's mother a trick. Shyly, with gestures more than words, she demonstrated how to mash the yams first and then knead in *garri* powder. A pinch of salt—three fingers and a thumb; two fingers was not enough, four was too many—a final knead and then a quick toasting, flipping it twice and eating it quickly, while it was still warm.

Nnamdi's mother chewed slowly, gave a begrudging nod of approval, but still refused to smile. Instead, she countered by showing Amina how to make a proper dumpling.

"Dip a dumpling into pepper soup and you have yourself a meal." She'd said this in Ijaw, without thinking—and then: "It's your husband's favourite."

She repeated this for Nnamdi's benefit when the three of them sat for supper. He pretended not to hear.

"The baby dance," his mother said. "She needs to learn that—*before you go.*"

The baby dance was used to rock a child to sleep or calm it when it was crying. "I carried Nnamdi on my back till his first tooth, making them steps. Even now, if I danced it a'front of him, the boy is sleepin' soon."

Nnamdi laughed. "Better than palm wine for sleeping. You have to soothe the child's *kro.*"

"*Kro?*"

"The power children have. It's very strong, *kro.* Children—they remember. They remember where they lived before they were born, how they died, why they were born again. When a baby cries for no reason, we say the child is remembering bad things. And sometimes, when a little one is learning to speak, it will tell us stories of its travels before it was born. Children remember these things. Growing up is a slow forgetting."

Travels before you were born.

Nnamdi smiled at Amina. "Your child has travelled very far, I think."

His mother caught this, the use of "your," not "our."

"Is why we say a woman who is with child should not walk near the forest at night," Nnamdi's mother said.

Amina's people had a similar directive. "We, too."

"It's because the *teme* from the other side recognize the baby inside," Nnamdi explained. "Might want it back."

"Just stories," Nnamdi's mother said. "Not real."

Stories, not real.

Nnamdi looked at his mother, puzzled. "Stories *are* real."

"You sound like ya father." Since his father's death, Nnamdi's mother had relied less and less on the *oru,* and more on the Bible.

"Can't you see the girl is scared?" she said. And then, to Amina, "Is only superstition."

"Superstition?" said Nnamdi.

She turned to her son. "When was the last time you been to church?"

"Every day. Papa always said, The world is a church."

"Girl," she said to Amina. "The reason you don't go walkin' in the forest is because of dey snakes. A pregnant woman, she can't run fast enough. That's why. And the baby dance works because of the swaying, not because of any such *kro*."

When a fish is pulled from the creeks with its gills still gaping, a fine filleting blade is used to slice a seam up the bottom. The fish is split open with a single motion and then left on the bottom of the boat with the others. As Nnamdi watched his mother bustle off to the kitchen with Amina in tow, he caught a glimpse of a filleting knife in his mother's hand, still wet and glittering with scales, both the blade and the hand that wielded it. It was not the fish's fault it had to die; that was just the way the river turned.

Only stories, not real.

Was that what his father had been reduced to? A story? Not real.

87

The Egbesu boys had been terrorizing the raggedy people on the other side of the creek, roaring in on speedboats, drugged up and feeling immortal, firing directly into the shantytown.

"They started with bunkering, but now just bandits," Nnamdi's mother said.

So far the Egbesu boys had kept their excesses to the other side of the creek, but the fear bled across nonetheless. The screams of women. The sounds of gunfire and laughter. Of things breaking in the night.

When he heard the speedboats coming, Nnamdi would hide Amina behind his father's trunk underneath a drape of dark fabric, with no telltale mosquito netting hanging above her. The Egbesu boys often used this netting the way spiders use a web, pulling it in on their victims, entangling them and then dragging them off.

Amina heard the women screaming across the creek. She knew why they were screaming.

The Egbesu boys had been camped outside the village for a week now. "When they leave, in comes the army, pretendin' to be in pursuit." The JTF would swoop in, tear up the place. "Worse than the rebels," his mother said. The soldiers would ransack storage bins. Burn homes. Between the Egbesu boys and the oil company security forces, between soldiers and the JTF, Nnamdi's village was no longer at the isolated edge of the outer Delta—it was caught in the middle of a war zone. The world had come to them, had kicked in the door and demanded entrance.

"It's not safe," his mother said. "If she stays here, someone will find her, and they will do harm to her—and to you. And to the child."

"The army is pinned down in Portako. They only make a show of force out here. She needs a midwife."

"She has to go."

"I will ask the *orumo*."

"Stories. No match for bullets."

Acidic rains had begun to gnaw through rooftops; the metal was scaling away in great corrosive scabs. Nnamdi followed the path past the health clinic, now used as a communal chicken coop, the floors inside splattered in fecal stains.

He almost couldn't find it, his father's shrine.

The forest had reclaimed most of the structure, with vines twisting through and grass sprouting in the cracks. Tin roof and a dirt floor. Nnamdi made a half-hearted attempt at clearing it, but he wondered if anyone was really watching. Silent gods. Overgrown shrines.

Every time he came home, it seemed the silence had only grown deeper.

The diviner's hut was abandoned: a few shards of bone and skin still hung outside, and a few animal teeth remained loosely tied, moving on the faintest breath of wind, but otherwise—empty. Wonyinghi hadn't chosen a new priestess in a long, long while, and even the lesser gods of the forest and the river, the *orumo* and the *owumo*, were only ever half-glimpsed and half-heard, like voices on a boat that has already departed.

Lately it seemed that only the angry voices of Egbesu and the clamorous calls of the revival-hall meetings could be heard. Both had grown louder, more strident, had shouted down the quieter voices.

Nnamdi threw stones. Gathered them up and threw them again. There was no response. Only the sound of a gas flare on the other side of the trees. He could feel its heat even here.

He moved on, crossed the trickle of sewage-fed runoff that constituted the creek on a hop and a jump, and then squeezed between the lean-tos and mud huts that were falling in on themselves.

Some of the men from the refugee camp were huddled around a car battery and a bowl of eggs, painstakingly piercing each egg with a needle and then sucking out the contents, spitting it into a pot for later. Other men would then draw battery acid out with a syringe to be injected back into the empty eggshells. Homemade puffs. They would be ready the next time the Egbesu boys stormed into their camp.

Nnamdi followed the path toward the gas flare, where the

green of the forest gave way to now-familiar anemic yellows and burnt browns. He didn't recognize these for the colour of drought, though Amina would have. The guava trees nearby had died, the wild pears had fallen, and the papaya hung bloated and grey, their skins stretched tight over swollen flesh. A gift for the flies.

He passed the roiling fireball where women in sunhats, faces running with sweat, laid out racks of cassava root to dry. Beyond the fire, the path rose. It was a landscape altered, the way things are in dreams. A bare knuckle of rock. The cannon, with its iron now corroded, as though it had been soaked in acid. And Nnamdi thought, *What a sad fate after so many years spent guarding a ghost empire.* The English graves beyond were no longer hidden in the undergrowth; the burning rains had stripped that away, and the blackened headstones stood exposed, looking corroded as well. It was only a matter of time before the stones would break and the *duwoi-you* below would finally slip free.

Beyond the graves, the ground was sodden with oil leaking from a feeder pipe. It trickled down all the way to the mudflats of the lagoon below.

"She cannot stay here."

But where else could she go?

A crash and a yelp, and an oil barrel suddenly appeared, cresting the hill and bouncing down, rolling across mud and yellow grass. It came to a rest at Nnamdi's feet and was followed a moment later by a swirl of curses, English mixed with Ijaw, and a stampede of young men following.

"Ah! You stopped it!" They shouted this with great relief, giving Nnamdi credit for what dwindling momentum and thick mud had actually accomplished.

They were boys from Nnamdi's village, slightly younger than he was, and they recognized him as the storyteller's son. *"Noao!"*

Their eyes were veined in red and their skin was a sickly shade of pale.

Nnamdi looked down at the runaway barrel. "You've been tapping oil," he said.

They shook their heads. "Not oil, gas. Before it reaches the flare-off." They gestured to the balled fire rising behind Nnamdi.

"Gas?" he said. "Natural gas?"

They nodded.

"You can't tap natural gas," he said. "It will kill you."

They laughed, answered in Ijaw. "We can, and we are."

Nnamdi looked again at the barrel, stepped away.

"Relax, bruddah. This one's empty. It had a leak. We are bringin' it back to fix."

"Gas, not oil." Nnamdi shook his head. "How?"

The leader of the boys tapped a finger to his temple. "Ijaw ingenuity," he said, and laughed.

They'd first tried splitting open one of the feeder pipelines, hoping to create an oil spill. The oil companies had improved their sensor systems, making it easier for them to detect a sudden drop in pressure. They were now able to quickly redirect the flow, which greatly reduced the amount that could be siphoned off. But the boys from the village figured that the Shell Men would still have to pay compensation for a spill. Or, even better, hire them to clean it up. You couldn't really clean it, not in among the mangroves. But you could skim the surface oil and collect your pay. Unfortunately, the oil companies refused to send in a crew, suspecting a trap aimed at snatching more workers for ransom. So the line had been left to leak. This was the spill Nnamdi had walked through earlier, the one that was now draining into the lagoon.

"Is a shame," the boys said. "Cleanup is good work. So we decided to go wit' natural gas instead. Gas lines are plastic, easier to tap because nobody expects it. We usin' the same drills we used for palm trees—remember? Remember your first palm tree, Nnamdi?"

"I do."

"That was a long time ago, wasn't it, Nnamdi? We were children then."

"We were."

"We thought we were men."

"We did."

The natural gas line ran below the water, feeding the flare. "We dived under, drilled a hole," the other boy explained. "The gas, it foams up soon as it's tapped. So we dived again, clamped on a hose—that was the tricky part. We ran the hose up onto land, attached a valve, and now it's easy. Like turnin' a tap on and off. We can fill anything that has a tight seal. Cooking tins, bottles, jars. Is not pure, but if we leave it sit a few days, it turns into kerosene. Problem is, it takes a lot of gas to make a little kerosene. We started thinkin', why not fill up oil barrels instead? So that's what we do, fillin' them up, then soldering them shut. Have to move quickly before it leaks out."

Nnamdi wasn't sure he'd heard right. "You solder them?"

"We do."

"But don't they—"

"Blow up? Yes, sometimes. You remember Samuel and Goodluck? The brothers? They burned up, both. A cousin with them, he lived, but better he died, I think. Eyelids burned off. Skin too. The brothers, they were loading a barrel and it slipped, scraped against the side of a boat, hit a spark. Enough fumes in de air to do it. Could see the explosion as far as Olobiri, is what I heard."

One of the boys was wavering on his feet. His eyes were milky and unfocused. It reminded Nnamdi of the glassy gaze of the Egbesu boys, but without the bravado or the gin.

"The hardest part is protecting your line from other boys. We have to stand guard twenty-four hours. Take turns, work it in shifts. But dey fumes is always leaking, from the hose or from the valve. So you inhale a lot of it. Gives you headaches."

Nnamdi looked at his sickly friends, grown wan and thin. "You have to stop," he said. "The gas will make you ill. It will poison you."

"It already has, Nnamdi." And then, in Ijaw: "It was our bad fortune, wasn't it, Nnamdi? To sit on top of wealth that others wanted. Why do you think the gods punished us like that? Cursed us with oil. Why?"

"I don't know."

"Do you suppose the oil is tainted by the souls of the Igbo and others that we captured? Do you suppose it's the blood of those, come back to haunt us?"

"If that was the case, my friend, the oil would make the *oyibos* ill as well."

"I think it has, Nnamdi."

Somewhere in the overcast, a helicopter was choppering through. The boys turned, looked toward the sound of it; it was a long time fading.

"Something's coming," they said.

88

When Nnamdi returned, his mother was patting out yam-and-cassava cakes and passing them to Amina to salt.

"And what have the gods been sayin'?" his mother asked.

Amina took the cakes out to the yard to place them over coals.

Nnamdi looked at his mother. "Tell me that you want her to stay. Tell me she is a guest, tell me she is welcome in our home. Tell me that, and we will go."

"She *is* a guest," his mother said. "But she cannot stay."

"Where, then? Don't say Portako. Portako is in turmoil."

"Not Portako. Lagos."

"Lagos? Among the Yoruba?"

"It's a big city, Lagos, with other cities mixed in. Ijaw and Igbo. Even Hausa. You have a cousin in Lagos. You can stay wit' him. He's a very important businessman. He will take care of you." She cleaned her hands, wrote it out on a scrap of paper. "Here. He was never given a proper Ijaw name, but he is relations still, and he will help you."

On the paper was a phone number, and below it a name: IRONSI-EGOBIA.

FIRE

89

She began by compiling a style sheet.

Complements of the season. A small mistake, and not uncommon, but it provided the thinnest of threads on which to pull, the way a tapestry might unravel. Or a sweater.

Laura first went through the emails her father had received from Nigeria, highlighting quirks of spelling and noting specific semantic tics. She was operating on the assumption that the various people who'd contacted her father—the dying lawyer, the desperate orphan, the crooked banker, the mafia thug—were one and the same.

The list grew and grew:

teachering
safekeep (instead of safekeeping—i.e., "we will deposit the money for safekeep")
We're in this in the all together.
vouchsafe (or is this a common term in Nigeria?)
modalities (unusual word choice, used here incorrectly? Check.)
we begged him to silence
points asunder
I am contacting you on _____'s behest. (instead of "behalf")

I can not stand and see (instead of "stand to see")

on bended knees (rather than "on bended knee")

in a pickle (common expression in Nigeria?)

by waking hours

with much sincerity (as a closing salutation)

caps on "Foreign" (though inconsistently applied)

discretely (instead of "discreetly")

use of "in [possessive pronoun] entirety" (e.g., "he failed in his entirety," "the plan was arranged in its entirety by him")

God daughter

made awares

a turn for the worst (instead of "worse")

Time is urgent.

it has defiled all forms of medical treatment (may be a one-off typo)

Author often begins an aside with an em-dash but then ends it with a comma (e.g., "Once Mr. Okechukwu's life has passed—as surely it must, I will have no one.")

we are mafia (also: "I am mafia")

we will find you and we will kill! you (internal use of exclamation marks)

you're (as possessive)

and of course:

complement (instead of compliment, but not vice versa)

Laura then turned to the emails her brother had printed off, starting with those from Chief Ogun. At first she was disappointed;

there seemed to be no stylistic correlation between them and the emails sent to her father. But that soon shifted, and she realized: There's more than one person involved. At a certain point, they'd passed Colonel Mustard on to someone else.

Was that someone else the same person who'd hounded her father and stolen her parents' money? The style sheets lined up almost perfectly; there were far too many points in common for it to be a coincidence. Laura began going through emails sent to other scambaiters. Each con artist, once you got past their cut-and-paste opening gambits, had their own eccentricities of style, their own pet errors. And when she came across one email from a supposedly love-struck swain to a scambaiter in California, Laura felt a rush of adrenalin: "Madame, we must focus on the money, even tho your compliments have set my passions on fire."

Madam with an "e," compliments with an "i." A different person entirely.

The longer any string of correspondence goes on, Laura knew, the harder it is to mask your identity. Hide behind fake names and online anonymity all you want, she thought; your true self is still there, waiting to be revealed.

In her corner apartment, high above the mall, Laura Curtis began to type:

Dear Chief Ogun,

I'm contacting you today regarding Colonel Mustard and his somewhat incoherent response to your initial business proposition. I'm afraid Colonel Mustard is getting quite old, and his mind is not as sharp as it once was. Please disregard any future emails from the Colonel. Instead, you may deal directly with me.

Sincerely,

She hesitated, only for a heartbeat, then entered:

Miss Scarlet   .

90

Nnamdi waited patiently for the coughing to stop. Amina, beside him, hands folded over her belly, eyes down, pretended not to notice the smell of rotting fruit, sweet and sickly, that seemed to be emanating from the esteemed gentleman in front of them.

"Cousins, then," said Mr. Ironsi-Egobia, voice weak. He folded his handkerchief to cover the stain, looked at his visitors with watery eyes, the whites gone yellow.

Nnamdi smiled at him, beamed really. "Cousins, sir."

They'd spent the last twenty minutes tracing the lineages and peripheral family connections that might allow Nnamdi to claim the catchall of "cousin." It had been like trying to trace a route through the Delta between far-flung communities at dusk, but they had done it, on a line that eventually led from Nnamdi's mother's village to a distant aunt and then back to the Catholic orphanage in Old Calabar.

Ironsi-Egobia reached into the breast pocket of his jacket, cream-coloured linen, freshly pressed but already crumpled, and retrieved a billfold. *He shows up here, stinking of the Delta, dragging some pregnant girl with him, making eye contact with me as though he were my equal.*

The boy hadn't even waited, but had sat down without being invited. Where was the respect in that? This was the problem with success in Nigeria: it brought out every relative and rat in a thousand miles, lining up with hands outstretched, demanding dollops of unearned reward.

Ironsi-Egobia smiled. "A fortunate day, then. When I was taken away without a name to be raised by the Fathers in Calabar, none of my relations came to claim me. None. The Fathers brought me back to the Delta. Did you know that? As a young man. They wanted to repatriate me. That's what the Fathers called it. But no one wanted me. And now, here I am in Lagos, a successful man, and my relations have come calling. A fortunate day indeed. So." He pulled a stack of five-hundred-naira notes from his billfold. "Allow me to welcome you to Lagos in proper fashion."

"Too kind, sir."

Nnamdi smiled at him, but Ironsi-Egobia was immune to smiles. "Tunde, come here a moment."

A thin figure appeared. "Yes, bruddah guyman?"

"Tunde, this is my cousin and his woman. Find a room for them." Then, to Nnamdi, "It will be nothing fancy, I'm sad to say. In Lagos, space is always at a premium." He passed the money across to the boy, then tucked his billfold back into his jacket pocket and stood up. They were being dismissed.

Nnamdi extended his hand. Ironsi-Egobia hesitated, then clasped it forearm to forearm.

"Thank you, cousin bruddah," said Nnamdi.

"What is family, if not this?"

Ironsi-Egobia turned, but Nnamdi stopped him. "Sorry-o. I hate to be an imposition, cousin. But this girl, she was hoping to have a stall in one of the markets, on the Island, sir."

"A stall?"

"Yes, sir."

"On Lagos Island?"

"Yes, sir. My mother had said you might arrange this for us. A stall with a small room behind to live in. As for me, I am a mechanic of some renown. Just recently, I have seen a tanker truck through from Port Harcourt all the way to Kaduna and back again, which as you know—"

"A stall? On Lagos Island?" Ironsi-Egobia could feel the arteries in his neck constrict. He had to fight the urge to strike the boy down then and there. "A market stall? *With living quarters?* On Lagos Island?"

Amina could see the rage that was coming. She touched Nnamdi's arm, but it was too late.

"Have you any conception," said Ironsi-Egobia, "how much a stall on Lagos Island costs? The market ladies have it sewn up. Do you have 700,000 naira in your back pocket to pay the fees? And you—a mechanic, as well? You might as well ask for the moon in a teacup. Do you think I am some sort of magician? Do you think I own the guilds? That I am made of money?" He glared now at Amina, at the scars on her face. "And you? Do you think I am some sort of Hausa cattle for you to milk? You want to slit my skin? Drink my blood? Is that what you want?"

Nnamdi was baffled and embarrassed. "No, sir. My mother, you see …"

Ironsi-Egobia fought his anger down. *He comes in here, stinking of the Delta.* "The girl. Her, I can find work for. Cleaning rooms, washing toilets. And you—I will find something for you. And you will pay back this debt, cousins or not. You understand?"

"Yes, sir." Nnamdi's smile was gone.

"Tunde will take you." Ironsi-Egobia scribbled down a name and an address. "The Ambassador Hotel," he said. "In Ikeja. Ask for housekeeping. Now go—go before I change my mind."

As they were hustled away, they could hear the coughing begin anew, deep bronchial rasps, wet with blood.

Amina didn't have her market stall, but she had work. And Nnamdi? He had a cousin protector.

"We are blessed," he whispered, as much to the child as to Amina.

91

"Hello, Mr. Driscoll? My name is Laura Curtis."

"Laura who?"

"Curtis. I was the copy editor on your book. We met at the launch."

"Of course! How are you, Laura?"

He didn't remember her, but they must have met. She was with his publisher, after all.

Gerry Driscoll, CEO and founding president of WestAir, was an upstart young cowboy who'd taken on the fat cats of the airline industry and won. Or at least, that was how he'd spun it in *Mavericks of the Sky: The WestAir Story,* his business memoir-cum-motivational tract. *"If you can think it, you can do it!"* Pliant airline regulators and a rejigged corporate tax scheme helped as well. *"In business, as in life, you must put yourself on the right side of history and then blaze a trail toward it!"* It was a book rife with exclamation marks.

"You gave me your card," she said. "At WordFest."

"Yes! Of course!"

He had no idea who she was. Laura had been hired to copy-edit *Mavericks of the Sky*: punctuation, grammar, the usual. The platitudes and bromides had been someone else's editorial responsibility. Laura and he had dealt with each other only via email, and amid the hubbub of the book launch, Gerry Driscoll, heady on wine and the sound of his own voice, had mistaken her for his actual editor. That editor wasn't there that night, but Laura was. It was one of the few outings she'd attended all year, so it may have stood out in more detail for her.

"You offered me a weekend getaway," she said. "Anywhere that WestAir flies."

Of course he had.

Mr. Driscoll was constantly comping tickets to people, both as a way of repaying social debts and, just as importantly, engendering obligations in return. After all, *a favour received is a debt unpaid!* He didn't remember this particular editor exactly, but it was easier just to give her the freebie than try to welch on the offer, especially when his as-yet-to-be-written follow-up—a memoir that she would presumably be working on—was titled *My Word Is My Bond!*

"Sure thing," he said. "Where would you like to go, Laura?"

"Nigeria."

He laughed. "I'm sorry, I thought you said Nigeria."

"I did."

There was a pause. "You know, I give out a lot of flights. Most people pick Hawaii or Cancun."

"Nigeria, please. Lagos."

"We don't fly to Lagos. We don't fly to Africa."

"But you partner with Virgin Air, and they do. The schedules line up. I checked. Four flights in, three flights out, every week."

Mr. Driscoll comped tickets through his partner carriers all the time, and they did likewise; it was one of the perks of being CEO. Certainly WestAir had flown in enough Virgin employees and families over the years, en route to Banff, to more than make up for it. He sighed. "Okay," he said. "If that's what you want. I'll put you through to my assistant, and you can work out the details with her. Good to hear from you, Laura."

"Thank you. And Mr. Driscoll?"

"Yes?"

"I'll need a hotel as well."

92

Dear Mr. Ogun,

I must apologize for the mix-up at the airport. Colonel Mustard and Mrs. Peacock no longer work for our organization; please ignore any further communications from them. I will be arriving at Murtala Muhammed Airport in two weeks' time, on Flight VS651 at 15:05.

I believe you and I have some unfinished business.

> With best wishes on behalf of
> Corporate Living Unified Executives
> (a division of Parker Bros.),
> Miss Scarlet

Laura was at the top of a tall tower, feeling empty and unafraid. When the CEO of WestAir had first offered her those tickets to anywhere, there hadn't been anywhere she wanted to go. If nothing else, she now had a destination.

She looked out her window, down at the city shimmering below, and slowly, she began to tie her long, flowing hair to a bedpost ...

93

The heat was making her queasy. "I'm sorry, but who did you say you were? Airport security? Police?"

He slid a business card across his desk. "EFCC. The Nigerian Economic and Financial Crimes Commission."

She looked at the card, embossed with name and number. "Well, Mr. Ribadu ..."

"David, please," he reminded her. "Up against Goliath, I'm afraid. The EFCC has been charged with addressing 419 crimes.

Bank fraud, advance fee swindles, cyber crimes, et cetera. Such activities are damaging Nigeria's reputation. They are hurting our chances with legitimate investors. When people hear the word 'Nigeria,' it is too often the swindle merchants and never-do-wells they imagine. Suffice it to say, these crimes have caused our dear country and its many innocent citizens a lot of embarrassment abroad. Of course," he held her gaze uncomfortably long, "when it comes to obtaining wealth through false pretenses, the white man is still the expert. I'm afraid the black man is an amateur when it comes to 419ing others. One might say, my entire country was obtained under false pretenses."

"I'm sorry, Mr. Ribadu, but I'm not sure what this has to do with—"

"We at the EFCC have been taking the hunt to the hunters. We have raided the cyber dens in Festac Town, we have rounded up the forgers along Akwele Road. We are authorized to trace emails, reclaim ill-gotten wealth. Indeed, madam, we have such powers as to confiscate assets, seize passports, freeze bank accounts. We can impound luxury cars, even take away the homes of 419ers. And, if we are not winning the war, we are at least harrying our foes. Unfortunately, every so often, some—shall I say?—*gullible* foreigner arrives and mucks things up, causing many sorts of trouble. It is precisely why we at the EFCC maintain an office here at Murtala Muhammed."

Laura hadn't even made it out of the airport, and already things were starting to derail. If it got nasty with Inspector Ribadu, she needed to know who to appeal to, who to go to above the inspector's head. "I'm still a little confused," she said. "You answer to the police?"

"The police answer to me."

I see.

"Am I under arrest, then?"

He laughed. "Arrest? No. We are having a conversation, that is all."

After he'd checked her documents and repacked her carry-on, Laura asked, "So … I'm free to go?"

"Madam, these gullible foreigners I mentioned, the ones who keep showing up at our airport, are lured to Nigeria. They are lured by the promise of easy money. But I assure you, it is skulduggery, plain and simple. These foreigners come to Lagos thinking they will claim a lost inheritance or take possession of trunks filled with money, dyed solid black with ink, so they are told. They are swiftly robbed by the 419ers. The lucky ones, at least. Some are kidnapped for ransom, some are tortured, some murdered. And we in law enforcement have to deal with the mess. The paperwork alone is very distressing. Embassies are involved, and so on. Wouldn't you say, madam, that it's better if these foreigners had never come?"

"I suppose …"

"You seem tired, madam. Such a long flight, for such a short stay. With the stopover in London, it must have taken, what? A day or more just to get here."

"Something like that, yes."

"And returning so soon. I dare say, you will probably spend more time in transit than you will here in Nigeria. A strange sort of holiday. Tell me. You aren't one of those foolish people, are you, madam? You haven't come to Lagos to reclaim your lost millions, have you?"

"No." *Not millions.*

"Well, you have my card. You may ring me any time, night or day, should any difficulties bedevil you. It's best you don't go to the regular police, and certainly not to some random officer on the street. Contact me directly instead. The police in Nigeria are woefully underpaid, you see. Mostly hard-working fellows, but some have been, how shall I say, compromised. Madam, we are cracking down hard on the 419ers. Please do not get caught in the middle. It won't end well."

He rose and walked her to the door, opened it for her with a gentlemanly grace. "Enjoy Lagos, madam. Enjoy the music, enjoy the food, enjoy the friendly nature. But please take care for your safety. Don't be fooled by smiles. Shady characters abound. Promise me you will take precautions."

"I will." *I have.*

94

He was younger than she expected—and handsome, though she noted this more with a sense of detached judgment than anything. She'd spotted him right away on the other side of the fence, holding up his sign: MISS SCARLET PLEASE. A crisp white robe with a matching cap that was tightly fitted and beautifully embroidered. He looked like a king, but called himself a chief, and as she crossed the sidewalk toward him he held his arms wide in a regal greeting. "Welcome to Nigeria!"

Such a low baritone from such a young man.

He watched her coming. On sage advice, he'd donned a full *babban-riga.* If you were going to present yourself as a Big Man of Africa, you needed to dress the part, and the *oyibos* were disappointed if you didn't show up looking like a Nubian potentate. But what of her? What effort had she made? Very little from the looks of it. She certainly didn't project the aura of a high-level liaison to an international banking cartel, what with her peasant skirt and wrinkled cotton top. Then again, *oyibos* were strange; everyone knew this. They didn't behave like normal people. "Treat them as you would children." That too was advice he had received. Children with money.

"Hello," she said.

He smiled, but not with his eyes. "Greetings! I am Chief Ogun Oduduwa of the Obasanjo, and I welcome you!"

He insisted on taking her bag as he ushered her through the pandemonium of taxi drivers and waiting relatives to a parked sedan. "Only this?" he said, referring to her sole carry-on.

Tinted windows, cobalt blue. A uniformed driver. A flutter of fear, pushed down, denied a foothold.

Chief Ogun Oduduwa of the Obasanjo opened the sedan's back passenger door for her.

"You seem awfully young for a chief," she said.

"A hereditary title. My grandfather and such. Please. Get in. We are parked illegally."

She stepped through the open door, into the sedan. The heat followed her in.

"I'm afraid the a/c is out," he said.

As she struggled with the seatbelt, Chief Ogun Oduduwa of the Obasanjo settled in beside her, her carry-on bag atop his lap. He had seen Miss Scarlet being whisked away by airport security earlier, had hung back and waited, ready to bolt had she reappeared flanked by officers. But no, she was alone. It had been a simple demand for *dash,* he imagined. Officers appeased and a woman set free.

She clicked the belt into place, straightened her skirt. Smiled at him.

"So," she said. "We meet."

"You have the money?" It wasn't a question, not the way he said it.

95

A cold snap, followed by wet snow piling up across the city, and now this: chinook winds moving in, melting everything, turning snowbanks to slush and revealing, like a tablecloth trick, a pair of bodies below the Bridgeland overpass.

Sergeant Matthew Brisebois trudged up the riverbank, through the slush and snow. Above him, on graceful arcs of cement, a procession of brake lights curved across the river, blinking red as they made their way over the bridge and into the city.

Another false call. No vehicle had been involved. There were no traffic fatalities for him to investigate—only bodies, and as such, the scene was beyond his realm of responsibility. He didn't know whether to feel relieved or disappointed, or whether to feel anything at all.

Under the overpass, patrol cars had blocked traffic in both directions, their lights washing back and forth.

"Drinking, from the looks of it," he said to the officer in charge. "Found an empty bottle of Jack Daniel's. And Baby Duck. Must've fallen asleep."

They had died propping each other up. Would have been a cozy scene, except for the dying part. *Some by fire, some by ice.* Where had he learned that? In choir, as a boy? In a song? He was tired. And try as he might to focus on the banter and jibes of the other officers, his attention kept drifting over their shoulders, up to the city skyline and a pair of apartment buildings on a crest of hill beyond.

The Curtis file was closed. So why did his gaze keep drifting upward? As he drove home along Memorial Drive, he leaned forward, neck craned, looking up at the corner apartment. The lights were out. The following morning, the lights were still out, and would be the next night as well.

Where do you suppose she went?

96

"You have the money, yes?"

Horizontal vertigo. If such a thing were possible, that was what she was suffering from. The airport off-ramp had poured them onto a cloverleaf and from there onto an eight-lane expressway, with the sedan veering across lanes to turn sharply onto another curl of asphalt, as she slid first against the door and then against Chief Ogun. The hotel was indeed beside the airport; she could see it from here. But there was a maze of elevated asphalt to manoeuvre through first.

"Do you have the money?"

"No, but I can get it," she said. "It will be waiting for me at the hotel." *Until they get their money, I'm the safest woman in Lagos.*

Chief Ogun smiled when he heard this. "Good, good." The smile became a grin, gap-toothed and wide. "And which hotel would that be, Miss Scarlet?"

"The Sheraton."

From the travel guide in her carry-on: "The Airport Sheraton in Lagos, Nigeria, is one of the most modern and secure facilities in West Africa. Its safety and amenities are well known, and the hotel remains the preferred choice of embassy staff, UN administrators, and visiting dignitaries. (See index for a full list of Western accommodations near the airport.)"

"Ah yes," said Chief Ogun. "The Sheraton, a fine establishment. I know the concierge."

She smiled. That would be worth noting if it was where she was actually staying, she thought. He didn't really think she was going to complete this transaction at her own hotel?

"We will be there in a quick jiffy," he said. "It isn't far."

And from curve to vertiginous curve, they came at last to the gates of the Sheraton itself. Armed guards. The flags of nations.

Manicured lawns and a three-tiered fountain, spilling water like a wedding cake.

As the sedan rolled to a stop—at the far edge of the parking lot, she noticed, away from any doormen or cameras—Chief Ogun turned to her. "Here we are."

Beyond the Sheraton, on the other side of the overpass, she could see the Airport Ambassador, the hotels like mirror images of each other.

A 747 was coming in, sunlight on white wings. She could feel the vibrations even from here.

Chief Ogun nodded toward the entrance of the hotel.

"I don't know the name of the person I'm going to meet," Laura explained. "I have to present myself, with my passport, to the front desk. The front desk will then page the person in question's room and the money will be brought down. I have to collect it in person, for security reasons. Silly, I know. But the international bankers I work for—the ones financing this—have become very concerned."

"Concerned?"

"About recent kidnappings."

"In Lagos?" he said, acting surprised.

"Yes. So, for my own safety, and theirs, we have had to keep everything anonymous." The lies she'd rehearsed were spilling out now, so smooth, so clean, they surprised even her. It wasn't enough to tell a lie, she realized. You had to believe it as well.

"Very wise. One can't be too careful," said Chief Ogun. "So, please pick up the money and then we will hurry down to the Central Bank. I will make you a millionaire by sundown!" The lies he'd rehearsed spilled out, so smooth, so clean. This was the first time he'd met one of his *mugu* face to face and he felt almost elated. It's not enough to tell a lie, he reminded himself. One has to believe in it as well.

"They're not going to let me bring the money out. You'll have to come in."

"But madam, I am not a guest at this hotel. They will treat me with suspicion. There are armed security guards throughout. Please, madam, you fetch the money. I will wait in the car."

"How do I know I can trust you?" she asked.

"Here, my business card." He fished one out of his wallet.

"Anybody could print one of those."

"Madam! Please. I am an upstanding citizen, an educated man. Look—" He dug out a snapshot of himself in university robes, arm slung around a woman in her middle years, a woman with the same broad smile.

"Your mother?" Laura asked.

"Yes," he said, tucking the photograph back into his wallet. "Now, please. Go fetch the money before the banks close."

He waited, but she didn't move.

"Can I see that photograph again?"

"Madam, please. We are parked improperly. Hotel security will soon rouse us."

"I need to see that photograph again."

He sighed. "Fine."

Laura examined the photograph carefully. "Your mother," she said, "is very beautiful. You have the same smile, the same gap in your teeth."

Chief Ogun laughed, embarrassed. "An unfortunate inheritance, I'm afraid."

"Well, I think it's very attractive."

"Madam, please—"

"Do you see this cleft, here, in my chin? It's faint, but do you see it? My father had the same cleft in his chin. I got it from him. That was my inheritance. Can you see it?"

Chief Ogun laughed warmly. "Oh yes, I see it. Very good."
Oyibos were so odd. "Now madam, at the risk of being rude, I must
emphasize again the urgent nature of our …"

It was as though she were outside a window watching events
unfold within. She didn't know whether it was jet lag or the
after-effects of her inoculations or the sleeping pills she'd taken
en route, or the fact that she was far from everything familiar
to her, but as she looked at this young man, this *thief,* she
couldn't feel anything resembling fear. Only a certain detached …
anger? Somewhere inside her, a voice was whispering: *Let the
Heavens fall.*

"Your father," she asked Chief Ogun. "Is he still alive?"

"Yes, still alive. Both my parents. I am blessed."

"You *are* blessed." And then: "I will need to meet them."

"Pardon?"

"Your parents," she said. "I will need to meet them."

"The bank—"

No. Not at a bank. Not in a hotel lobby. Here was something
better. Much better. "The banks can wait," she said. "I need to see
your parents."

"Why?"

"The men who are fronting this endeavour will need assurances from me that you are indeed a legitimate investor. That you're
not some sort of swindler."

"Miss Scarlet, I assure you—"

"They were going to drag you into one of the rooms, force you
to take a polygraph test—a lie detector. And if you failed, well …"
She lowered her voice. "Bam."

"Bam?"

She nodded. "These are dangerous people we're dealing with."
She could see the agitation in his eyes.

"Miss Scarlet, I cannot submit myself to such indignities, I am chief of the Obasanjo and I—"

"Listen, I'm on your side. I told them. I said, 'This is ridiculous.' But they insisted. So I asked, 'What if I were to vouch for Mr. Ogun personally?' And they agreed."

"Thank you, madam. That is most kind."

"Which is why I need to meet your parents. That way, I can report back that you're an honourable son of good stock. As soon as we do that, the investors will release the money."

Chief Ogun chewed his lip for a moment, then retrieved a cellphone from the voluminous billows of his robe, speed-dialled a number. No answer. He leaned forward, shouted something at the driver in Yoruba, and the driver passed his own cellphone back. Again, nothing.

"If you prefer to take a polygraph ..." Laura said.

"A moment. Please."

She half-expected his lip to start bleeding, such was the worrisome nature of his gnawing. Then: "Fine, madam. You may meet them, but only for a moment. Nothing more. I am adamant on that."

"A moment is all I need. A quick handshake, that's all. After that, the money is yours."

"Ours," he corrected.

"Of course," she said, playing along. "We're in this in the all together."

The driver put the sedan back into drive, pulled out of the parking lot, pointed them to Lagos Island. Laura had stepped off the balcony, would find out now whether she would float or fall.

The sedan's a/c wasn't broken. It was turned off, the better to addle the *oyibo*. Whites couldn't handle the heat, everyone knew that; they got flustered by it, distracted.

But now it was Chief Ogun Oduduwa of the Obasanjo who was getting flustered. As the driver eased them out of the Sheraton parking lot, he made one last attempt at changing the course of events, at controlling the narrative.

"Miss, it is twenty kilometres or more to Lagos Island," he said. "It will take us an hour, maybe more if we get caught in a go-slow. And even then we shall have to get to my parents' home at the far end of the island, out in Ikoyi. Why not simply *tell* your financiers you have met my mother and father? Vouchsafe my honesty."

She smiled. "By lying? I'm afraid I can't. They might hook *me* up to a polygraph test or inject me with a truth serum. I told you, these are dangerous men. I will meet your parents, shake their hands, and then we can turn right around and go back to the hotel."

"But Miss, by the time we get back, the Central Bank will be closed and—"

"If I meet your parents, if I look them in the eye, I will know whether I can trust you. If we do that, you can pick up the money tonight. We can meet again tomorrow morning, at the bank, to complete the deal."

Well, that certainly pleased him! "As you wish, madam. But only a quick handshake, nothing more."

"Nothing more."

They were sucked into traffic like a log down river rapids, the din and the odours hitting simultaneously: a fog of exhaust, the taste of diesel. Backfiring motors, broken mufflers, and the constant cry of car horns.

The lanes painted on the road seemed mere suggestions, rough guidelines rather than rules. A bus muscled past with passengers hanging on. "Movable morgues," said Chief Ogun. "It's what we call them."

A battered minivan forced its way in. Butter-yellow taxis fought back. Dented and dinged, they carried the scars of past battles. Three-wheeled Chinese *tuk-tuks* jockeyed for position alongside SUVs and Mercedes-Benzes. It wasn't traffic, it was an ongoing melee.

Laura held the seat in front of her, had to remind herself to breathe.

Cement buildings crowded in on either side, row upon row, cluttered with lean-tos out front. Boulevards lined with wilting palm trees. Humid and dusty at the same time.

Their window was down, and when a BMW pulled up alongside, she saw herself reflected momentarily in its tinted glass, her face rippling across, looking lost and small. As the BMW roared ahead, Chief Ogun's driver pulled into its slipstream, cutting off other vehicles, horn blaring.

"The Nigerian brake pedal," Chief Ogun said, referring to the horn and shouting to be heard.

A motorcycle squeezed in beside them, using the sedan as cover as he attempted to fit his motorcycle through a gap narrower than the actual bike itself.

"*Okada* boys," Chief Ogun explained, referring to the young motorcycle taxi drivers, unencumbered by mundane notions of their own mortality, who were weaving in and out of traffic, passengers clinging tight. "They saw off the ends of their handlebars to better fit between vehicles. Very ingenious."

"Doesn't that make it hard to steer?"

He shrugged.

The *okada* driver hit his own horn, a blast so loud it made her jump.

"The music of Lagos," said Chief Ogun. "The *okada* boys like to replace their usual toot-toots with air horns scavenged from trucks. It clears a route more quickly. As I said, very ingenious."

The *okada* driver, gunning his engine impatiently, spotted another opening and sped off into—and somehow through—the cross-hatched traffic ahead, defying both the odds and basic physics.

Ogun's driver grinned back at them. "If they ever have a World Cup of taxi drivers, I promise you Nigeria will win!"

The traffic ahead converged in an intersection where a broken street light, stuck on red, dangled from the cross wires like an eye from a socket.

What am I doing here?

The blare of horns grew louder as they worked their way past a recent collision: steam was rising from the crumpled hood of a taxi and oil was pooling below the rear axle of a BMW. It was the same BMW that had passed them earlier, the same one that had reflected her face back at her in its tinted glass. Its owner had gotten out and was waving his hands angrily. Onlookers had quickly taken sides in the matter, forming instant and passionate allegiances, from the looks of it.

"Traffic in Lagos can be fatal," Chief Ogun said to Laura. "Take a wrong turn, and someone will be waiting. General Murtala, the namesake of our airport and past president of our nation—he was murdered in a go-slow. The assassins walked up to his car, filled it with bullets. They have the vehicle on display at the National Museum. You can still see the holes." He nodded at the mob that had formed around the accident scene, the cries and recriminations. "Are you sure you wish to go to Lagos Island?"

"A minor snag," said the driver. "Very common in Lagos. Sometimes it leads to fisticuffs, but once past, we will be free."

Chief Ogun glared at him, but the driver was busy forcing his way through a gap he'd spotted, all but nudging bystanders aside at times. Bands of young boys had now appeared, taking advantage of the go-slow to jog alongside vehicles, knuckle-rapping the windows as they offered newspapers and baggies filled with water that bounced as they ran. "News from the world and water! Pure water! Pure water-o!"

"Tap water," said Chief Ogun, sitting back in his seat. "Filtered through cheesecloth. Best not to buy."

Other boys held up packets of batteries, fistfuls of pens.

"Power and pens!"

"Pure water! Pure water-*oh*!"

"News from the world!"

Behind a roadside boulevard, cement houses were packed in. In among them, a truly surreal sight—a home with a shuttered door and a message painted on its rolled-down metal slats: THIS HOUSE IS NOT FOR SALE. More such messages soon appeared. Some on shops: THIS PETROL STATION NOT 4 SALE. Some on unfinished construction sites, rickety with scaffolding: NOT FOR SALE!! One storefront had added a warning: BEWARE 419.

"That?" Chief Ogun said when Laura asked. "A blight on the good name of Nigeria, I'm afraid. Sometimes, when a family or business owner is away, crooked men will sell their homes and businesses out from under them. They pass themselves off as the true owners, sell fake deeds to the property, and then run off with the money. Property is very expensive in Lagos, so people feel they need to act fast to get a good deal. They often pay up front. And when the honest owners of the properties return, they find someone else living in their house. Can you imagine such a thing?

Losing one's house like that? The legalities of it can get very messy, as you might suppose. Sometimes the legitimate owners end up losing their homes in their entirety, even though it was they who were wronged. Best to put a notice up instead."

This house. Not for sale.

"And 419?" she asked, feigning innocence. "What does that refer to?"

"That I don't know about. Look ahead, miss. We are coming now to the Third Mainland Bridge. A feat of engineering!"

She could see the rise of the bridge ahead, the long line of cars caterpillaring across.

"Lagos is very flat. Built on reclaimed marshlands. A collection of islands, really, sewn together by bridges. The one ahead is the longest in Lagos, maybe in Africa. A marvel, don't you think?"

As they approached the bridge, the number of street sellers grew. Hawkers and hustlers, products and pleas. Men and women holding up their goods, calling out their wares. A dizzying inventory moved past. Some vendors held up trays filled with shoes, others with hats. Some were selling spark plugs, others sunglasses. Tubes of toothpaste, packets of laundry soap. Cigarettes. Nicorette. Gatorade and books—Bibles, mainly, and the Qu'ran. Fan belts and fans. And trouser belts. Racks of razor blades. Cartons of rum. Trinkets and toys and DVDs. Magazines. Pocket calculators. Neckties and nectarines. Flip-flops and alarm clocks. Ad-hoc barber's chairs and shoe repair stalls. Cutters moved through, brandishing nail clippers, and a tailor balancing a hand-cranked Singer sewing machine on his head called out to passing vehicles. One enterprising young man carried an array of toilet seats on both arms as though caught in an oversized game of ring-toss.

"In Lagos, we say that you can leave your house in your underwear, and by the time you get across the first bridge, you can be shaved, shampooed, and fully dressed, with polished teeth and a fresh manicure. And if you have forgotten your underwear, you can get that, too."

He wasn't kidding. She saw one hawker waving men's briefs on a pole, back and forth like a flag, saw another selling brassieres. (Hefty bosoms evidently abounded in Lagos, given the cup size of the bras on sale.)

"Do you have such a place as this?" Chief Ogun asked Laura. "Where you're from?"

She thought about this. "The mall, I suppose." Forget the bridge; it was the street sellers along the way who were the true marvel.

As the sedan made its way up the slow rise and curve of the Third Mainland Bridge, buses ahead of them slowed in order to pick up passengers, gearing down without coming to a complete stop.

"They are not permitted to *stop* for passengers on expressways or bridges," Chief Ogun explained. "But no one said anything about not *slowing down* for passengers."

From the rounded swell of the bridge, Laura could see thousands of makeshift shacks spread out directly on top of the water. It looked like an optical illusion, but no.

"The Venice of Nigeria!" Chief Ogun said with a grand laugh. "The Makoko slums. All of it built upon stilts. Ingenious, don't you think? A floating city, built piece by piece over generations. And do you see that cloud of dust over there? Those are the timber yards of Ebute Metta. The forests of the Niger Delta end up there, are cut and stacked and shipped to America and other such places."

Along the water's edge, flat-bottomed boats were moving through the tidal flats, poling across the thinnest veneer of water.

"Fishermen?" she asked.

"Scavengers. The main sewage line from the mainland empties there, and a lot of good things get washed out with the sewage."

Lagos proper was like a honeycombed hive kicked open. Everything was in motion, even the buildings, it seemed. The smell of fish and flesh. Narrow lanes and claustrophobic streets. And hers the only pink face in sight.

Wiry men pushed wheelbarrows through the traffic, oblivious to the cars and *okadas* that clipped past. Women with pyramids of oranges balanced on their heads followed, threading their way through with a grace Laura had never known—and all without dropping a single piece of fruit. *How did they manage that?*

"I will tell you one thing," Chief Ogun said with a laugh. "God is a Nigerian! I promise you, only a Nigerian could make order out of such chaos. There is Africa, and then there is Nigeria. There are cities, and then there is Lagos."

Car exhaust was making Laura light-headed as the city swirled around her. Parrots in hand-twisted cages. Dead rats strung up on a stick. As traffic slowed, a young boy dangled one such collection of limp rats through the window. Chief Ogun shouted at him, and the rats were quickly withdrawn.

"They sell rats?"

"Not rats, rat poison. They want to show you how effective their products are."

With the car barely able to move, they were now besieged by beggars. The blind and the broken, the bandaged and the battered, the dustbinned of life, palms out, singing their sorrows. "Please for me, blessings please."

Laura began rummaging in her pockets, but she had no coins to give, only Nigerian naira bills whose exchange rate she didn't completely understand—that, and the $100 bill folded tightly in her skirt pocket.

"Don't," Chief Ogun said when he saw what she was doing. "Once you start giving, it never ends."

The next street brought the sedan into a shadow realm of soot-stained lanes. Narrow passageways splintered off under corrugated rooftops that almost touched overhead. Smoke uncurled and new smells drifted in: tanned goatskins, burning sticks.

"*Juju,*" Chief Ogun explained. "Black magic. Older gods."

Every *mugu* was driven through the *juju* quarter in Lagos at some point, he knew, and Chief Ogun had given his driver explicit instructions to that effect. It helped jostle the *mugus'* minds, unravelled their judgment, made them more suggestible. More pliant.

He watched her taking it in: the fetishes that hung in bunches like shrivelled grapes outside grimy stalls. The animal paws and accompanying heads. The reptile skins, splayed and stretched. The chameleons in cages, and snakes as yet unskinned. Albino boas sliding over themselves behind clouded glass. Elephant tusks. Leopard hides. Rows of teeth strung together.

"Crocodile teeth. That is what they claim." He laughed. "But all and sundry know they're just canines taken from stray dogs. It's all good fun, madam. Potions and poisons, and what have you. Would you like to stop and get out? Purchase a souvenir of Africa?"

Laura shook her head, was having trouble forming the sound necessary to say "no."

Just as well. Christian though he was, and immune to such superstitions, the *juju* quarter unnerved him, too, and he was relieved to put it behind them.

Ash filtered down from mounds of smouldering garbage, piled two floors high at times. But none of it seemed to settle on the people. Everyone was so tidy, so well turned out in crisp shirts and starched blouses, the women with headwraps artfully tied like the bright bows on Christmas packages. No one drooped, even in this muggy heat.

She looked down at her own creased cotton skirt and canvas sneakers—*Avoid open-toed sandals and never get into a taxi without first making sure the air-conditioning works! (Traveller's Tip #37)*. She felt lumpy and dishevelled, sloppy and sweaty.

Men in impeccable white robes and women with equally impeccable smiles. And behind them: a stack of burning tires. Bucket-throws of smoke billowed up. It smelled the way blood tasted, and for a heart-skipping moment, Laura thought she saw someone inside the flames, burning, a single hand raised almost in greeting, fingers trailing smoke. When she looked again, it was gone.

And now the acrid smell of burning tires was overpowered by something worse: the wet thick odour of human feces. Pools of urine in littered lots. Open sewage, running through drains and ditches. The reek of it folded around her, filled her mouth. She held back a reflexive gag. "Can we—can we roll up the window? Please, the smell, it's too much."

The Chief smiled sympathetically at her discomfort. "I apologize. It is very bad. But I must say, we Africans do not produce nearly the amount of stool and waste that you do in America. You just hide yours better."

"Please ... I can't."

"If we roll up the windows, you will melt."

At last, they came into an open square and Chief Ogun signalled for the driver to pull over. Minarets and their ornate domes were catching the light of the late afternoon, creating a well of shadows below. "The south is Christian, but we have many Muslims also, especially here."

He fished out his cellphone, dialled a number. Again, no one answered.

Across from the mosque lay not a market so much as a city of shops and stalls. Women, everywhere. "The market ladies of Lagos Island," Chief Ogun said. "Very strong. Even the police are afraid of them." He redialled the number. Waited. Still no answer.

Chief Ogun chewed on his lip. Then, with a sudden resolve, he said to the driver: "Take the Ring Road."

He'd been buying time, Laura realized, taking them the round-about way, trying to figure out what to do with her. And she thought to herself, more with a detached curiosity than with any real concern: *Is this the last day of my life?*

98

"So," she said. "You rescue people?"

Brisebois was still in uniform, nursing a wounded beer at the Garrison Pub in Marda Loop.

An accident on Crowchild Trail had been wrapped up and he was now trying to make small talk with the woman next to him. Full lips. Hair, teased high and dyed an unnatural shade of red. A smoker from the sounds of it—and interested in him, apparently. Or at least in the uniform.

"I get called in after an accident," he said. "I try to figure out what happened."

She blinked. "So ... you rescue people?"

He paid for his drink and left soon after.

It would stay with him like an accusation: *You've never rescued anybody, you've never saved anyone.*

99

It was a remarkable transformation. The city of market women and *juju* vendors had given way to one of skyscrapers and bold designs.

Chief Ogun's driver had forced his way onto progressively wider thoroughfares until they'd finally reached the Ring Road, a broad sweep of freeway that circled Lagos the way a leopard might circle its prey. At times, the expressway left the earth, and they were suddenly suspended in mid-air over open water.

High-rise office towers rose out of the cat's cradle of electrical wires and telephone lines that netted the city.

"Magnificent, yes?" Chief Ogun shouted to Laura above the wind that was sweeping through the open window. As much as he hated Lagos, he loved it, too. How could you not?

Oil company office buildings were shimmering in the half-light. An Anglican cathedral, lit up with spotlights. A stadium. A slum. Stained-glass windows and crumbling colonial buildings. The city flickered past like images on a Zoetrope.

"There—do you see it? The NITEL building. Tallest in Nigeria, maybe in Africa."

In Lagos Harbour, tankers were lining up, silhouetted in smoke. And somewhere out there in the haze, close enough that you could taste it, the sea.

The wind tossed her hair, forced her to squint. But it didn't drown out the radio, not entirely. It was playing a jangly, uptempo tune:

> *Oyibo, I'm askin' you,*
> *Who is dey mugu now?*
> *Who is dey mastah?*

And in the background, female voices rising in chorus:

419, guyman game,
419, all the same.

Chief Ogun leaned forward, said something, and the driver changed the station. Coming through the static now: Highlife. The good life. Upbeat and buoyant. Laura felt as though the car might leave the elevated highway entirely, might bounce free and float upward into the evening sky.

The feeling didn't last, though. As the road curved down, it swept the sedan in toward a bottleneck of off-ramps and intersections. The backlog of vehicles came up so quickly that their driver had to veer into oncoming traffic to avoid it, cutting back in a moment later. Only then, with great reluctance and to the accompaniment of blaring horns from all sides, did he apply his brakes.

Chief Ogun pointed past the freeway that segregated one side of Lagos Island from the other. "It's getting dark, we have to keep moving."

He yelled something up at the driver.

"Awolowo Road is backed up completely, sir," the driver replied. "Perhaps we cross over to Victoria Island, come back in again on Falomo Bridge?"

"That will add an hour at least! No, we'll fight our way into Ikoyi. Take the next ramp, we'll cross under instead. We'll take the flyover below Independence Bridge."

"But sir, there are rascals afoot. If we get caught down there, it will be bad news for us."

"Take the ramp. We will be fine."

And they almost were.

They peeled off from the rest of the traffic, with two wheels up on the sidewalk, and then sped down, past the cluttered shantytown shacks below, and came speeding in under the overpass, around a corner and—a chain. Across the road.

They almost hit it, with the driver two-footing the brakes and Laura and Chief Ogun thrown forward, then back.

A band of shirtless boys appeared, spiked sticks resting on their shoulders as casually as one might carry a cricket bat between pitches.

Laura watched them approach the car. "What's going on?"

"Area boys," Chief Ogun said. "Hoodlums and thieves. They charge a toll for crossing whichever corner of Lagos they happen to claim as their own. Please, say nothing." Then, to the driver: "Pay them off. Don't argue or negotiate, just pay."

The driver handed a fold of naira through the window, and the boys took it with a nod. But then they saw Laura in the back seat.

"You no say you hab' de *oyibo* wit' you!"

Suddenly the toll went up tenfold, and the area boys grew belligerent, leaning in and grappling with the driver, trying to pull open the car door. Laura's mouth went dry. Even when Chief Ogun threw more money their way, they weren't appeased. They'd blocked the sedan with their bodies and bats, and were now rocking the hood.

Laura began digging around frantically in her skirt pocket for the $100 bill. She understood none of what was being said, just that she was in danger. But then, just as she was about to thrust the bill through the window, Chief Ogun yelled something at the area boys and their demeanour changed. He repeated what he'd said, punching the air with his voice, and she saw the boys' resolve falter. *"Area faddah, Ironsi-Egobia!"* he shouted.

The area boys stepped back, let them pass.

Chief Ogun wiped his forehead with folded handkerchief and puffed out his cheeks in long exhalation, gave Laura a wan smile. He didn't look quite as handsome as he had before.

"I apologize, Miss Scarlet," he said. "These ruffians are usually more polite than that."

Beyond the flyover, they entered the leafy avenues of Ikoyi, where the sidewalks were lined with cafés and upscale boutiques. Chief Ogun spoke again, trying to lighten the mood. "Lovely, don't you think? Ikoyi was once its own island. But the marshlands were filled in, and now we are attached. Like Siamese twins."

"Attached?"

"To the rest of Lagos Island. The working man's neighbourhood, Obalende, is just there."

On Chief Ogun's instructions, the sedan turned off the main drag onto a side street. Up one, down the next, past small bistros and shops. They entered a warren of alleyways and narrow lanes, and Laura soon lost what little bearings she'd had. Were the driver and Chief Ogun taking precautions against a possible police tail? They were speaking to each other in their language, so Laura couldn't be sure. She looked behind, could see no sign they were being followed. Then she realized what was going on. *They're trying to disorient me, so I won't be able to remember where we went.*

They entered a back alley and came at last to a high wall with broken glass embedded along the top and tendrils of razor wire twisted above. A heavy metal door with an intercom. Chief Ogun turned to Laura with a severe look on his face.

"Nothing, do you understand? Nothing about who you are or why you are here. If you say so much as one word about our arrangements—one word!—the deal is dead. My parents know nothing about this. It is highly secretive, do you understand?"

She did. "Yes, absolutely."

"We say only hello and goodbye. Nothing more. Is that clear? And it is taboo to speak of my chieftainship. Instead, you must refer to me by my … conventional name."

"Which is?"

"Winston."

She gave him her word. Only then did he let her out of the car. Laura stood to one side as Chief Ogun pressed the buzzer.

The intercom crackled. "Hello? Who is this?"

"Mama, is Winston."

"So late? Something's wrong!"

"I have a friend, please come the back way, give greetings."

"The back? Why you aren't coming to the front, properly?"

"Mama, please."

"Don't move. I'll get your father. *Marcus! Is Winston out back, in trouble it seems.*"

Winston sighed. A moment later a light bulb in a mesh cage came on above them, a deadbolt turned, and the door opened. A small woman appeared. She had a robe pulled in around her, and her husband stood beside her in a button-down shirt. A handsome man.

"Son?" he asked. "What is the meaning?"

When Winston's mother saw Laura, she smiled. That same gap-toothed grin.

"And who is this young lady?" she asked.

"Mama, Papa. This is a colleague of mine, a businesswoman from North America, who wants quickly to say hello. And she has, and now we must go." He gripped Laura's elbow to steer her back to the sedan, but Laura pulled away, extended her hand instead.

"It's very nice to meet you, Mrs. ..."

"Balogun, Mariam. And this is my husband, Marcus."

A round of greetings and handshakes followed, as Winston tugged more firmly on Laura's elbow.

"So your last name is ... Balogun?" Laura said. "Not Ogun?"

"Oh no," the mother laughed. "Ogun is the Yoruba God of Iron, in folklore."

"Really? I must have misheard. I thought Winston said Ogun. The God of Iron, is it?"

"Yes, iron. And markets also. Where blacksmiths would ply their trade. Just folklore."

Winston was growing more insistent. "Visiting is over. We have to go."

"Winston!" His father gave him a stern look.

"Sorry-o, Papa. But truly, we must go. Now."

The father peered at his son, took in the flowing *babban-riga* robe. "Winston, why in devil's name are you dressed like that? Where is your white shirt and necktie?"

But before Winston could answer, the conversation had galloped off without him. His mother was clasping Laura's hand between two palms and asking, "So, how is it you know our Winston? He has never mentioned a girl, never seems to have time to spend with ladies. Too busy, you see. It worries me." She might have been dubious, her son showing up with an *oyibo* woman in tow, but this wasn't some exchange teacher he'd brought home or, God forbid, a journalist doing another story on the Heartbreak of Africa. This was a proper businesswoman, even if she did dress a little, well, sloppily. "Do you work in international finance as well?" Winston's mother asked. "Imports and exports? That sort of thing?"

"In a manner of speaking."

"Mama," said Winston. "We are going now. Goodbye."

Laura again yanked her elbow free from Winston's clasp. "He hasn't told you about me? Shame on you, Winston." And then, looking past them, into the yard: "What a beautiful garden."

Winston's father stepped to one side so that she could better admire the view. "Just a hobby. A small garden. I have some eucalyptus, some mangoes, a small pear tree—Do you see it? There, in the corner."

"It's beautiful. May I come in?"

"No! She has to leave, Papa. We have no time. Maybe tomorrow."

This drew a sharp rebuke. "Where are your manners, Winston?"

"I would love to see your garden," said Laura. "If it's not an imposition."

When a visitor comes to your door, you must welcome them in. "Of course you may. Come, come. Is this your first time in Lagos?"

"It is. I've just arrived."

"Miss Scarlet," said Winston, "if we don't leave immediately, all is lost."

Exactly.

"Don't listen to our son. He's too impatient. Come, come."

"We have to go. Right now!" Winston was dismayed, almost begging. "We must go. I absolutely insist." But it was too late for that. His parents had opened their door, and the *oyibo* had slipped through it, into the garden.

100

Ambrose Littlechild was a long time dying. He stirred briefly at one point, chuckled to himself, eyes closed, then slipped free. The nurse on call had contacted "Sgt. Brisebois, TRU" as the first officer listed on the medical report.

He'd started to say "I was only the responding officer, not the—" but stopped himself. "I'll be right there."

Not that it mattered. By the time Brisebois arrived, Ambrose had departed.

"He didn't say anything?" Brisebois asked the nurse. "No hint of who did it?"

"Not a word."

While the medical staff prepared their reports, Officer Brisebois kept Ambrose company in the silence that envelops a room after someone has died. When they wheeled the body away, Brisebois lingered a moment by the window. He could make out the silhouette of the apartment towers across from him, closer now than from downtown.

The corner apartment. Lights still off, windows still dark. It gave him a vague sense of unease, though he couldn't say why. After she'd asked to see the accident scene photos, she'd pushed past him, distraught. She had rejected every offer of counselling, of coffee, of conversation. The widow had her children for support, the son had his wife and his anger, but where did the daughter turn? Brisebois wondered where she was at that particular moment, wondered if she was sitting in her apartment with the lights out and whether he should stop by to check on her.

He never did, but if he had, what would he have found? An empty room, an open window, a knotted tress of hair hanging from the bedpost.

101

"I call this the conservatory," said Winston's father, proud and a little embarrassed. Mangoes hanging heavy and ripe, all but begging to be bitten. "A modest arrangement, but a pleasant mix, I think. Those are date palms by the wall, and beside them, that's the eucalyptus. This underperforming fellow is a jacaranda. When they flower, they are very beautiful, more of a northern tree, really. If it gets much larger, I will have to prune it into shape. But that's unlikely. With these high walls, we don't get enough light." Broken glass and razor wire lining the tops. "Unsightly, I know. But we need to keep the rascals out."

Winston was standing on the threshold of the back door, having refused to step into the garden.

His mother gave him a disapproving look. "Where is your hospitality, Winston?"

"Even with the walls, Lagos creeps in," Winston's father continued with a sigh. "Sometimes, when soot blows in from the mainland, I have to dust these flowers. Can you imagine? Having to dust flowers!"

They came to a raised bed of dirt. Folded petals of white and red. "This is the one little bit of the garden my husband allows me," Winston's mother said with a half-laugh. "Roses, imported from England. It's dark now, but in the sunlight, they glow."

"They're beautiful," said Laura.

"I'm leaving," said Winston.

Laura ignored him. Looked instead to the house beyond the garden. Ivy-clad. Handsome walls. Solid. Colonial.

"A lovely home as well." She took another baby step forward, inched closer. *Mother-may-I?*

"This old pile?" His mother wouldn't take the compliment. "Old and damp, like my husband. If he put the same effort into its upkeep as he does into this garden, we'd be living in a palace!"

Winston was trying to wrap things up, but Laura had no intention of leaving. She thought she might ask for a glass of water, maybe a chair to rest upon. But there was no need.

"Have you eaten?" Winston's mother asked. "You must be famished."

Laura smiled. "I am a little hungry, yes. But I wouldn't want to impose."

"Nonsense! Come, we'll feed you."

Laura turned, called back to Winston. "Would you bring

my bag?" And before he could sputter an answer, she'd slipped inside.

"But the driver is waiting!"

"Pay him and send him on his way," said his father. "We have company."

Large leather chairs to sink into. Pastel paintings of the English countryside to admire. Formal family portraiture framed on the wall. Their studio-lit, canvas-cloud backdrops made her think of the Sears photo studio back home.

"We call this the drawing room, though TV room is perhaps more accurate."

They had a giant pedestal-mounted television screen, and Laura sat across from it, facing her own murky reflection.

"High def," Winston's father said. "Fifty-four-inch plasma. A Sony." He pronounced it *sonny*. "Winston bought it for us."

"Did he now?"

Winston was sulking on the couch beside her, saying not a word as his mother bustled about in the next room, assembling a tray of food for their guest.

"Oh yes," said Winston's father. "He had it shipped in from America. I still don't know what half the buttons on the remote controller do."

Winston muttered something about reading the manual, kept his arms crossed over his chest, said nothing. Loudly.

His father ignored him. "Something to drink, miss? Perhaps a glass of Moët or Rémy Martin? We have Guinness, as well. Canned, of course. And Scotch eggs to go with it, if you'd like."

"I'm so jet-lagged, a drink would go right to my head."

"My wife will soon be in with tea. *Mariam!* Our guest is going to faint from hunger."

Winston's mother appeared with a silver tray laden with grapes and cheese cubes and Ritz crackers fanned out like playing cards. She poured a cup of Earl Grey for Laura and offered a tin of condensed milk to go with it.

"Thank you so much," said Laura.

But this was only his mother's opening volley. The food kept coming as though on a conveyor belt: avocado cocktails, cold creamed pasta from lunch, mushrooms basted in wine sauce from supper, apples diced with almonds, sugary cakes and cinnamon rolls, and even the Scotch eggs, as promised.

"Shall I warm up a meat pie? We have kidney and mashed peas. Or maybe a small quiche? We have canned pears as well, imported from Portugal."

"But you have pears in your garden."

"Not sweet enough," said Mariam. "Nigerian pears tend to be starchy."

"Nigerian pears are fine," said Winston. He leaned over, spooned some creamed pasta onto a plate, grabbed a Scotch egg. His sour mood was slowly lifting as he resigned himself to a meal with his parents. Even if he didn't get the money tonight, he could still stage an ambush tomorrow, have the money robbed from him in front of her, turn himself into a co-victim, maybe accuse her of being in on it, threaten her with arrest.

Winston's mother clucked again at his attire. "I don't know why Winston met you at the airport dressed like that. African robes, that silly cap. He has expensive silk ties he could have worn."

"Well," said Laura. "For what it's worth, I think he looks dashing."

His mother beamed. "You hear that, son?"

Winston said nothing. Ate his Scotch egg.

The lights in the house began to flicker, and Winston turned to his father, sighed. "Shall I start the gen?"

"NEPA has been like this all day. It should pass."

The lights flickered again.

"NEPA is the national electrical power authority," Winston explained, speaking to Laura for the first time since they'd sat down to eat. "It stands for Never Expect Power Again."

"Don't listen to my son," said the father. "He's disrespectful. NEPA is much improved. It's been completely reorganized."

Winston scoffed at this. "Yes, it is now the Power Holding Company of Nigeria, PLC. Which means Problem Has Changed Name, Please Light Candle. Even with the name change, everyone still calls it NEPA. NEPA this, NEPA that."

"Winston," his father said. "Don't insult our national institutions in front of our guest. She will get a bad image."

"But you complain about NEPA all the time!" he said.

"Not in front of guests."

The lights flickered again.

"Shall I start the generator or not?"

"It's the dry season," his father said. "Water levels are low. There's not enough hydro power to support the grid. But NEPA is doing its best. The power usually goes out only when it's getting dark."

"At the very moment we need it!" said Winston.

"It goes out because of the power surge," he said, ignoring his son. "Everyone selfishly putting on lights at the same time. Some people leave all their lights on just to show off! This is why we have a backup generator that runs on diesel."

And on that, the house was plunged into darkness.

Miss Scarlet. In the drawing room. With the night.

A disembodied voice, Winston's mother: "I'll go."

Laura sat, waiting in the darkness. She could hear Winston breathing. Then a rattle, a cough, and the lights flickered back on. Winston was staring at her, hard and unblinking.

"Finish and go," he said, voice low. She pretended not to hear.

Winston's mother returned, having somehow conjured a fresh pot of tea en route to the generator. She topped up Laura's cup. "You must be so tired."

"A little. I haven't checked into my hotel yet. That's why I asked Winston to bring my luggage in."

Her carry-on was next to the couch, beside him.

"That's all you have?" his mother asked.

"That's all I need."

"And the traffic to the Island?" asked the father. "No trouble?"

"No trouble," said Winston.

"Well," said Laura. "We did run into some problems under one of the bridges."

"Area boys," said Winston. "It was nothing."

"Area boys," said his father. "*Yan daba* is more like it. 'Sons of evil.' Lazy Nigerian youths. No ambition, no moral compass."

"They didn't cause you any grief, did they?" asked Winston's mother.

"No," said Laura. "Winston took care of it."

"I paid them off, it was nothing."

"Shameful," said his father. "Deeply shameful. These young people don't want to work, they're looking for easy money, the quick fix. They have no patience, they want everything fast. For them, it doesn't matter how you get money, only that you get it. And once they have the money, they expect everyone to bow down to them like a golden calf, even if they haven't earned it."

"Papa," said Winston, weary of what he'd clearly heard many times before.

"The problems in Nigeria trickle *up*," said his father, "from our youth, from our schooling, from a lack of proper parenting that infects everything, tainting our national esteem, poisoning our national institutions. I tell you, what we need in this country is another War Against Indiscipline, like we had under General Buhari."

"Papa, don't even joke about such a thing!"

"Who's joking? I will say it: Things were better under the generals. These area boys and their *yan daba* allies should be put to the gun! It's shameful that a visitor, a lady such as yourself, is robbed in daylight on her first evening in Lagos. It was better under the generals!"

"Even Abacha? He bled us dry. Trickle up? Under General Abacha, the badness pissed down! The fish rots from the head— you always say that, Papa."

"Winston!" said his mother. "Such language! A guest is present."

But Winston refused to budge. This was clearly an argument they'd been having for years, given fresh vigour by Laura's presence.

"Have you forgotten, Papa? How General Abacha treated the Yoruba, how he persecuted us? We are only now waking up from that nightmare."

"It was still better then."

Winston's mother steered the conversation into calmer waters. "First time in Africa?"

Laura nodded.

"Oh, that's very exciting. Did you get a chance to see some of the city on the drive in?"

"I did. The *juju* market certainly made an impression."

Winston's father was instantly affronted. "The *juju* market! By Jankara Hospital? Winston, why on earth would you take her through there?"

"The traffic was bad."

"Not five minutes ago you said the traffic was fine!"

"Did our son show you a bit of Ikoyi?" asked his mother.

"He did. I got quite the tour of the back alleys and side streets."

"The driver," Winston said, cutting in before his father could build up another head of bluster, "he got us lost."

"You live three streets from here!" his father said. "How could you let yourself get lost?"

Laura smiled. "I didn't know you lived so close to your parents, Winston. How sweet. You must remember to give me your address."

And for the first time, Winston caught a glimmer of the larger game she was playing. Just an inkling of what was really going on here, but it was enough. "Best we go," he said. "It's getting too late."

"But I haven't finished my tea."

His mother offered Laura another sugary cake. "You must come back in the daylight," she said. "Ikoyi is very different from the rest of Lagos Island. This was once the G.R.A, you see. The Government Reserve Area, set aside exclusively for Europeans. Our home was originally built for a German diplomat, so we are told. There are many homes much lovelier than ours. The embassies and the more expensive hotels are on Victoria Island. But Ikoyi is quieter, more peaceful. Many of the foreigners in Lagos have homes here in Ikoyi. So if you ever move to Lagos, we might be neighbours!"

Laura turned to Winston. "Wouldn't that be something? You and me, neighbours. What do you think, Winston?"

He said nothing. Glared.

"You have to understand," Winston's father said to Laura. "Lagos was never colonized. This was British territory, under the dominion of the British monarch. We had the same rights as British citizens. The rest of Nigeria may have been conquered and cobbled together, but not us. Sometimes I think we should separate, create our own city state."

"And where would we get our oil, Papa?" Winston gathered his robe about him, bristling with annoyance.

Winston's mother leaned in, as though confiding a secret. "Our Winston has a degree in commerce, with a minor in political science. He went to university in Ibadan. His sister Rita is there now, doing her post-graduate work."

"You must be very proud."

"We have always valued education in Nigeria," said the father. "Or at least, we once did. This is the problem. So many top-notch universities, so few opportunities. We have a surplus of educated young men and women coming out of their schooling with no careers waiting for them at the other end. Educated and unemployed: it's shameful."

The tea was done. Winston's father served up a tall glass of berry-red bitters mixed with tonic water and topped with a fresh slice of lemon.

"Chapman's," he said, referring to the drink. "Very expensive, hard to find. Winston buys it for us by the crate."

"Does he?"

"He's very successful," his mother said. "*Very* successful."

"Winston spoils us," his father conceded.

"He's a good son, then?"

"Oh yes." Mariam's eyes shone. "And he will make someone a wonderful husband. How about you? Do you have children?"

"I don't."

"Don't?" said Winston's mother with a sad, maternal smile. "Or can't?"

"I find that one usually leads to the other," said Laura.

"Mariam," scolded her husband. "Don't interrogate the poor girl." Then: "So, no children. What does your husband think of this? There is medicine you can take, you know."

"No husband."

Winston's mother smiled again. "I see. Single, then? Winston, why haven't we heard of her before?" She lowered her voice to a stage whisper. "He's always so busy, you see. But I ask you, Who is too busy for a family? And yourself, dear? Busy?"

"I suppose I just haven't met the right person yet."

"Myself as well!" her husband roared. His wife laughed, swatted him on the arm, then turned back to Laura with a sudden, focused intent.

"Do you see the photograph, by your elbow? That's Bishop Akinola. We know him."

Laura turned, admired the photo. Wasn't sure what to say.

"We're members of the Anglican Church, you see. And yourself? Anglican? Episcopalian?"

"Um, no."

"Catholic, then? Anglicans and Catholics are not so far apart as it might seem."

"Not Catholic, no."

"Surely not Baptist!" Both parents laughed.

"No, we're— Well, I think my grandparents were Methodist, but then we became United. I'm really not sure, exactly. It wasn't a big part of our house, growing up."

This baffled them. How could God not be a big part of any house?

Laura sipped her berry bitters. Marital status, now religion. Had she entered into marriage negotiations without realizing it?

"This," said the mother, "is Winston as a child." A photo album had somehow materialized.

"Mama, don't. You're embarrassing our guest. We have to go."

Laura turned a page. Winston in grade school. Winston missing a tooth. "Look at you. You're adorable." Laura smiled at him, as sweet as any sugary cake. *He's thinking: I will have to kill her now. I have no choice, she knows far too much about me.*

"And your papa?" Winston's father asked. "Is he too in the export business?"

"He was, in a way. He exported his savings—to Nigeria."

"Pardon?"

"You've heard of 419?" she asked.

"Everyone knows 419. A terrible plague on our nation."

Laura looked across at Winston, and this time she wasn't smiling. "You don't realize how fortunate you are, Winston. Both your parents, still alive." Then, turning back to Winston's father: "My dad died because of 419. He was killed by Nigerians."

"Oh no."

"Oh yes. I'm afraid it's true. It's why I'm here. I don't work in exports. I'm working with—" She had intended to say the police, but she now went one better. She fished out Inspector Ribadu's card, slid it across to the father. "The EFCC. In fact, I met with them when I arrived at the airport. My father had his savings stolen, he lost his home, his life. My mother is living in my brother's basement now. And the man who was responsible for this needs to know. He needs to know what he has done, he needs to make amends. I have come to Nigeria to find him. And Winston's been a big, big help with this."

"How will you manage it?"

"I've traced the emails, the money transfers."

"Well," said Winston's father. "I hope you find the miscreant."

"I already have. I found him before I even arrived. Among all the millions of people in Lagos, I have located my father's killer. And I have something to show him. Would you like to know what it is?" She turned back to Winston, met his gaze. In his eyes: panic, fear, bottled rage. It was the look of a man being driven off an embankment, a man falling through darkness. "Winston," she said, "would you be so kind as to pass me my bag?"

And there, between the glossy pages of an in-flight magazine: police photographs of an accident scene. Her father's pulped features, face smeared, a mouth filled with blood, soft flesh ruptured, an arm dangling, barely attached.

Winston's mother gasped, but she couldn't look away. Nor could her husband. No one ever can.

"Winston," Laura said, her voice softer now. "I think you need to look at this, so you will understand why I have come all this way."

When he spoke, his throat was dry. "We should go."

"Yes," said Laura. "I suppose we should."

"We are so, so sorry about your father." Winston's mother had tears in her eyes.

"I hope you catch the *yan daba* behind this," her husband said. "I hope they send him to prison a long while."

"I'm sure they will." Laura slid the photo back between the pages of the magazine, collected Inspector Ribadu's card, returned it to her pocket. "I hate to end on such a sad note," she said. "You have been very kind to me. I would like to send you something from Canada, a small gift when I get back. Maybe some maple syrup or some cookies."

"Oh no," they protested. "No need. It was truly a gift just to meet you."

"Well, at least a postcard." She got out a pen. "Maybe you'll come to Canada someday and visit me."

"We would love to. Winston has had some visa problems. He was supposed to go to London last summer, but there was a mix-up with him getting out of the country, red tape and such."

Laura smiled. "Well, I'm sure I could vouch for him, if he came." She passed her pen over to Winston's mother. "May I have your address? And your phone number? And Winston's too, of course."

"Of course. We are on Keefi Street. Winston is just off Awolowo. Here, I'll write them out for you."

Winston watched it unfold as though from a great distance: his mother carefully writing out both her address and his, passing it to the *oyibo*, the *oyibo* entering the information into her cellphone, hitting SEND.

"There," said Laura. "I've sent the addresses and phone numbers to myself, and cc'ed my office. It went through, so everyone now knows where I've been tonight—if they need to find me. Isn't that something? All that information, instantly sitting in people's hard drives on the other side of the world. And look, my cellphone takes pictures as well." She snapped one of his parents, then turned, said "Cheese!" and caught a frame of Winston glaring at her. She emailed those off as well. "As a memory of my visit," she explained. "So. I have pictures of you, I have your names, your addresses, waiting for me in my inbox when I get home. Isn't it amazing, what technology can do?" She looked at Winston, smiled. *Kill me now, Sony boy. Let's see you try.*

Mr. and Mrs. Balogun agreed that technology was wonderful these days, magical, miraculous, even. They offered Laura wine and chocolates. And she took another sip, had another bite.

"What a lovely young lady," said Winston's mother.

102

She'd come in by the back door, but was leaving through the front.

Winston's parents stood waving on the doorstep as he and Laura walked down the street toward the sedan that was waiting under a street lamp.

As soon as they were out of sight, Winston turned on her.

"What is the meaning of this?" he demanded, more fear than anger in his eyes.

In Laura's experience, when people asked what the meaning of something was, they usually already knew.

"The meaning of this? You need reminding?" She dug into her carry-on bag and pushed the photo of her dead father into his face, forcing him to step back to get away from it. "Give me back my father, and we'll call it even."

Winston pulled ahead, walking faster, leaving her behind. "Crazy woman. I have nothing to say to you! Find your own way home."

She called after him. "The EFCC will be knocking down your parents' door with a battering ram first thing tomorrow morning."

He spun on this, came back, stabbed a finger at her. "Do not dare!"

"You're a thief and a murderer."

"Hold your tongue, or I will cut it from your mouth. I am not a thief, nor a murderer. I am an entrepreneur!" He all but shouted that last phrase out. "And you are no longer welcome in my country. Go home, madam. We are done."

"Done? We haven't even started."

He stomped on, with Laura in harrying pursuit. "Give me back my father, you thief."

He turned again, livid. "Is this what you want? Reparations? From Africa? Justice—*from Africa*? Nigeria is not your playground, madam. Africa is not some sort of—of metaphor. Go now and be gone, madam. Go home, before something terrible befalls you."

"Give me back my father, give me back his house, give me back his sweater."

"Your father died from terminal greed, madam. There's no medicine for that."

She stepped in closer, not giving an inch, surprising even herself with the ferocity of her anger. "My father," she shouted, "was not a metaphor! Give him back to me!"

"You're crazy." He turned, continued walking.

"Your parents have a giant-screen plasma TV."

He stopped. "So?"

"I don't have a giant-screen plasma TV."

"Oh, so because my parents are African, they are not entitled to such comforts?"

"Not because they're African. Because you're a crook."

"And the crooks in your country? They don't own giant-screen TVs?"

"Give me back my father!" She was screaming now, was weeping. Her rage spilled out, hot against her face. The stucco bungalow, the modest savings, that sad little tally sheet that was her father's life, gone. "Give me back what you've taken, give me back what you've stolen!"

They had arrived at the sedan. Winston opened the door. "Get in," he ordered, and then, to the driver, something in Yoruba, something about Ironsi-Egobia.

Laura ran.

Ran through the humid night. Ran, crying. Not from fear or anger, but from the crushing weight of what had been lost. She hadn't cried at her father's funeral, but she was crying now as she ran, aiming for a brightly lit street corner with Winston in pursuit.

"Wait!" he shouted, dress shoes and flowing robes slowing him down. "Stop now, and nothing bad will happen."

Some *okada* boys were purring their motors outside a café, waiting for fares. They heard the frantic footsteps, saw the weeping *oyibo* woman running toward them, bag bouncing, an angry man in full robes chasing her.

She ran up to them, gulped air. "I need—I need to get back to my hotel."

Winston stopped, saw the circle of hostile faces staring back at him. He said, between gasps, "Miss Scarlet, please. Come now. We will talk about this."

But the *okada* boys narrowed their gaze, squared off, putting themselves between Winston and the woman.

"Mistah bruddah," they warned Winston. "You go take your *babban-riga*, disappear. Lady here be fine wit' us."

"I wish, just to speak with her a moment."

"Speakin' time is done, mistah *babban-riga*. You go disappear." One of the drivers turned to Laura, spoke in an accent so thick she could scarcely follow what he was saying. "Is no need cryin'-oh. I get you home—safe as."

And so he did.

103

The phone in her hotel room was ringing.

She had arrived on *okada* wings, the driver angling in and out of traffic as she clung to his shoulders, eyes clenched shut, carry-on bag wedged between her belly and the boy's back. She'd paid him all the naira she had on her, not knowing if she'd shortchanged him or grossly overpaid. She supposed the latter, but it didn't matter, just that she was here. Safe.

The Airport Ambassador Hotel & Suites. A voluminous lobby with walnut wood and superfluous lamps. As she checked in, the man at the front desk had said, voice as soft as lather, "We were worried about you, madam. Worried something might have happened. You hadn't checked in, and your flight landed many hours ago." The Airport Ambassador Hotel & Suites, on the other side of the overpass from the Sheraton.

"I was—delayed."

"And your luggage, madam?"

"Only this," she said, keeping the carry-on close to her.

The hotel was self-contained and hermetically sealed, with air-conditioned air wafting through and piano music trickling out from somewhere. A business centre, a conference room, shops that sold aspirin, a pool, a full-service bank offering foreign exchange and wire services, even tennis courts. Indoor, of course, to avoid the heat.

The ding of elevators. Long hallways. Numbered doors counting down slowly to hers. The slide of a card and the click of a door unlocking. It was all so comforting, so secure.

She entered a darkened space. Those first stumbling moments in a hotel room were always a scavenger hunt of light switches and dimmers, and as she groped her way through, she asked herself, Why must they always make hotel rooms so hard to illuminate?

The phone was ringing.

She fumbled with a reading lamp, stared at the telephone. The only people who knew where she was staying were Inspector Ribadu and the agents at Customs and Immigration. Had she let the name of the hotel slip when she was talking with Winston's parents? Her head was swimming, and she couldn't remember.

The phone rang and rang.

The motorcycle taxi boy. She'd told him where she was staying. Winston must have overheard.

When she finally picked up—

"You are dead! Do you understand, madam? Dead! You have written your own obituary."

It was Winston.

"We are mafia! We will ruin you, we will leave your life in tatters! You will die in Lagos!"

"Tell your mom and dad I said hi."

She hung up. Took a deep breath. The phone rang again almost immediately, and this time she was ready.

"Winston. Listen. When you scream like that, it's hard to understand what you're saying. You seem upset."

"Fuck you, madam! *Fuck you!* We will find you, and we will kill you!"

"You've already found me. But—more to the point, I've found you. I have the emails you sent my father, a record of the money transfers. I know who you are, Winston. I know where you live, I know your sister's name, I know where she goes to university. I know where your parents live. I've got their phone number. I have everything I need. So. Shall I hang up and call the EFCC? They will destroy you, Winston. They will destroy your life, they will destroy your family. They will seize your assets, they will freeze your bank account, they will confiscate your passport. Your parents will probably lose their home. They will certainly lose their son. Are you listening now, Winston?"

A long silence passed between them. When he spoke, his voice sounded distant, hollow. "Your father was not my fault."

"My father was nothing *but* your fault."

"What is it you want then?"

"I want a bear with Rumpelstiltskin glasses. I want a stucco bungalow with wood panelling in the living room and orange shag carpets in the den. I want my father back. I want a snow globe Mountie and a ticket to the All-Seeing Oracle. I want a piggy bank shaped like a cowboy. I want postcards for my Nana." She was reaching back through time now, was wiping the smirk off the face of a teenage boy at the Stampede midway.

"I don't under— I can't …"

"Then give me back the money you stole."

"I don't have it."

"Bullshit. Bring the money to the Ambassador Hotel tomorrow morning. The banks are open on Saturday. I checked. Do that, and I will leave. I will fly home, and you will never see me again. Do that, and I won't have you arrested. Your parents can keep their garden and their plasma TV, and they won't have to visit their son in prison."

She dropped the receiver into its cradle, followed the cord back with her hand, unplugged it from the wall.

The car tumbled through darkness, end over end …

In the hum of a silent room, Laura Curtis stood at the window, looked out through her own reflection. Airplanes were landing and escaping, lights blinking. An air traffic control tower stood silhouetted against the night sky, the searchlight on top turning and turning.

104

Winston waited for the coughing to stop. *Begin with the assumption that he knows everything, that he already knows the answer to every question he asks.* The coughing trailed off into rattling breaths, a final wheeze. At first, Winston had suspected that the constant hacking and facial sweat were more a manifestation of suppressed rage than an actual affliction, but blood on a handkerchief, the whites of the eyes gone jaundiced—could even rage do that?

Ironsi-Egobia looked up at Winston. "And?" he asked.

Fear was a worm in the heart, a tremor in the chest, a flutter in the bone. "There were … complications."

"Complications? Is that what you're calling it?" Ironsi-Egobia leaned back from his desk, and as he did, his face fell into the umbra of shadow beyond the overhead lamp. He became a voice. "Tell me, Winston. Do you believe in God?"

"I do."

"At the seminary in Old Calabar, we were taught that God sees everything. Do you believe such things?"

"I do, yes."

"Do you want to end your days in Kirikiri Prison? Do you want me to end my days in Kirikiri?"

"No, sir."

The Oga leaned into the circle of light, and when he spoke he did so with great deliberation, putting equal emphasis on every word, every syllable. "We who traffic in falsehoods must put a premium on the truth. I will ask you this only once, and you will answer truthfully. Do you understand?"

"Yes, sir, I do."

"Winston, where is the money?"

"It was—it was a trap, sir. A fiendish trap. No money."

"No money? Or did you pocket it?"

"No, sir. She's connected to the EFCC. She—she knows my name."

"Does she know *my* name?"

Quickly. "No."

"Come closer, I want to look in your eyes."

Winston did as he was he told, and Ironsi-Egobia leaned toward him in the way someone might for a kiss. "If you lie, Winston, I will know. So I ask you again. Does she know anything about me?"

Winston shook his head, mute with fear.

Ironsi-Egobia nodded, pressed a handkerchief to his mouth. He held back a cough, held it till his eyes began to water. "Tunde," he said at last.

Winston hadn't realized Tunde was there till the man stepped out from the corner. A thin figure, almost feline. A shadowman.

"Yes, bruddah guyman?"

"Go now and fetch me the Ijaw boy."

105

It rained every night it seemed, even though it was supposed to be Lagos's dry season. Scalding heat during the day, then sticky and wet come evening.

With the rains, the sewage in the gutters rose and mixed with rubbish to create a diarrhea-grey sludge. Cholera waters, people said. "Wait till the monsoons," she was warned. "The streets of Iwaya will swim."

The neighbourhoods of the city spilled one into the next; she and Nnamdi were caught on the mainland somewhere between Tatala and Iwaya.

"The monsoons," the other women warned, eyes on her belly. Dysentery. Typhoid. Malarial fevers. "It's the dying season for children."

But there were children everywhere, lugging heavy pails, running errands, playing games. If the street was thick with sewage, it was also thick with children.

It had taken them twelve hours in a crowded bus across washboard roads to get from Warri to Lagos. They'd had to find a way past Port Harcourt, and it had cost them. They spent most of Nnamdi's savings just to get out of the Delta; what the police hadn't taken, the army had, and they'd arrived with only what Amina had managed to hide under her robes, wrapped tight to her belly. No market stall with living quarters waiting for them, no mechanics guild for Nnamdi to join. They hadn't even made it across the bridge to Lagos Island. Nnamdi was disheartened, but Amina remained unbowed. She could see the future—*their* future. Like a sword raised. Sunlight on silver.

Lagos itself was a marketplace, a crossroads of caravans and kingdoms, and in among the swirl of colours, among the Yoruba blues and Igbo reds, she knew there was room enough for indigos and other savannah dyes. She would find a way in to the markets of Lagos Island, and she would bring Nnamdi with her, *sunlight on silver.*

Ironsi-Egobia's swampy-eyed associate, Tunde, had found a place for them in a cement-block building patched over with cardboard and corrugated metal. They shared a room with two other families: twelve people, sleeping in shifts with only a tattered curtain dividing genders, a communal latrine out back, a wash basin and kerosene stove in the hallway, an alleyway for washing clothes. Laundry was draped like banners from window to window. And everywhere: the footfall of children running, flip-flops slapping air.

The latrine sluiced into an open gutter that was crossed with planks. It ran just outside their window, and the smell of it kept her awake at night, with Nnamdi lying on the other side of the curtain, breathing softly. Sometimes she would hear him stir, would hear him wake and tiptoe outside to sleep on the stoop to escape the smothering air within. He'd been warned about the city's malarial mosquitoes, but they had only the one sleeping net, and he had given that to Amina. "The baby needs it more than I," he'd said.

Even with the cesspool slumber and crowded quarters, Amina counted them among the lucky. They had a roof, a kitchen, a place to sleep. They weren't under plastic tarps amid smouldering rubbish, they weren't picking through refuse for food. She even had a chair, where she could sit and rest her back while wringing the washing.

On Amina and Nnamdi's street was a small shrine to the Yoruba god Lyamapo, deity of the womanly arts—including the art of childbirth. The other women in her building had urged Amina to pray at the shrine or at least lower her eyes when she passed, and though Amina demurred, out of fidelity to her own faith, Lyamapo watched over her nonetheless: a goddess reclining, children at her feet and three sets of arms reaching out, offering up the Three Essences of a Woman's Life: advice, blessings, and regret. Sometimes Amina thought about the French hostage, the woman they'd discovered on the boat trip to Nnamdi's village, wondered if she was still out there, lost in the Delta, begging for water. Wondered if an *oyibo* god was watching out for her as well.

The people on their street moved aside for Amina. At first she thought it might be her belly, so round and taut, barely contained by her wraparound gowns. Then she thought it might be the story etched on her face. But as she passed, she would hear whispers of "area faddah," which could only mean Ironsi-Egobia.

Tunde had told Nnamdi that their benefactor had begun his ascent right here, in the mainland slums of Iwaya, before crossing the bridge and staking his claim on Lagos Island. Even the hoodlums who swept through, bullying families and shaking coins from the wretched and the wounded, gave a wide berth to the building Nnamdi and Amina were in.

No work for Nnamdi, still no word from Ironsi-Egobia. Nnamdi couldn't afford mechanic's tools to set himself up as a freelance footwalker, shilling his services in go-slows and off-ramps. He could do nothing except wait on his cousin's word.

It was Tunde who drove Amina out to the hotel that first day. She watched the airplanes coming in low across the skyline on the drive up, saw the hotel in the distance. It looked partly like a palace, partly like a hospital. A fountain out front, spilling water. A lobby so large it trapped echoes. And *batauris* everywhere, what Nnamdi referred to as *oyibos*. The place was infested with them, faces pink and bloated.

The air in the hotel was as cold as ice water. Amina marvelled at it while Tunde and another man haggled over her worth. She couldn't speak their language, but she knew the man was complaining about the size of her belly. It took some time to find a uniform that fit her, and the one they gave her was so large the hem had to be taken up. Amina never came in through the lobby again after that, entering instead through the staff door, frisked by security every time she left.

Tunde drove her in only that first day. After that, she made the long walk to Makoko Road every morning to climb into a *danfo* headed to Ikeja. A forty-minute ride, longer if she got caught in a go-slow.

On Amina's first full day of work, the woman in charge of housekeeping took one look at her belly and put her on toilet-and-mirror duty. This was actually a gruff piece of kindness on the woman's part, sparing Amina the heavier work details. Instead of flipping mattresses, she would wheel a bucket and mop down the hallways, with Windex and spray bottles holstered beside, ahead of the larger linen carts and the Hoover maids that followed. "Don't want de baby poppin' out early. Would have to put her to moppin' floors too!" said her supervisor with a large laugh.

The hallways in the hotel smelled of medicine, and the beds were as tall as tables. (She couldn't imagine sleeping so high up without feeling dizzy.) She was taught to knock before swiping her card to let herself in. Still-life arrangements of other people's lives: neckties hanging from chair backs, emptied bottles lined up on the dressers, tangled bedsheets as though a battle had taken place.

The a/c in the rooms made her forehead ache—"You will get used to it," Nnamdi warned, "I did"—and her pay went directly to Ironsi-Egobia; she never saw a single time sheet or work stub. Management had set Amina up with a hotel bank account—all employees had one—but what little money she was able to deposit came in the form of tips left behind by departing *oyibos*. Loose bills tossed aside like lint from a pocket, they were gathered and tallied, divvied up and carefully allotted by the housekeeping staff at the end of each shift. Barely enough to feed herself, let alone Nnamdi—or the baby inside her that was pushing ever outward, impatient to arrive. A headstrong child, she knew that already. Headstrong and hungry.

Amina worked in advance of the other cleanup crews, and, by God's grace, fortune would sometimes smile: a half-eaten sandwich, consumed quickly, or a neglected side salad; a tip of two fifty-naira bills, where one would do. She would extract one of the bills and pocket it quietly, but she never touched the American dollars or British pound coins, on the chance that security would find them on her when she left at the end of her shift and inform housekeeping that she'd been skimming. It wasn't stealing, she told herself; the guests never said who the tips were meant for. *First in, first fed,* as the saying went. And anyway, security checks weren't looking for naira; they were looking for silverware and *oyibo* wallets.

Amina was saving up these small windfalls so that she could pay for a midwife when the time came. She'd already spoken to several prospective women on her street and had amassed almost enough for the fee. She was stockpiling water as well, bringing a plastic bottle in to work every day and filling it with tap water before she left. The water smelled of bleach, and she couldn't drink it unless it was boiled with pepper as a soup. But Nnamdi wasn't as picky, and would take a bottle of hotel water with him when he left in the mornings.

A mechanic without tools, Nnamdi hadn't spoken with his cousin protector since that first day in Lagos. When he'd broached, with Tunde, the possibility of a small advance so that he could buy the equipment he needed, to be repaid with interest, of course, the man had flown into a rage. "Ingrate! He has given roof to you, is that not enough? Go now and scavenge a livelihood from the lagoon. You're Delta born, should be used to that."

And so, after seeing Amina off, Nnamdi would make the long walk through labyrinthine streets, through the Hausa quarters and the Igbo, past the prostitutes' town and forgers' alley. Down to the water's edge in the slums of Makoko, a city built on stilts. Constructed piecemeal from scrap wood and tin, the shacks were perched above the black and brackish waters of Lagos Lagoon downstream from the main sewage feed. Makoko teemed with activity, was ripe with life. Replace untreated sewage with raw crude, and he might have been back home, in the Delta.

A few kobo in coins gave Nnamdi the use of a flat-bottomed pirogue for a day. The first boat had leaked so badly he'd turned it around and come back. "You are trying to kill me," he shouted to the man he'd rented it from as he slid the vessel back into its makeshift berth. "And you aren't even married to me!" The man had laughed and, charmed by Nnamdi's smile, had relented, giving the young Ijaw the use of a better boat and a longer pole.

Nnamdi would punt his way along the tidal mudflats near the sewage outlets and the runoff points, dreaming of stashed coins and lost earrings, finding none.

Past the sawdust sludge of the Ebute Metta timber yards was a dumping ground where mountains of rubbish collapsed in on themselves, tumbling at times into the lagoon. Feral children had staked out the high ground, scavenging for copper wire and brass fittings, for tin and rubber, anything that might be sold to the scrap dealers, and every new truckload of rubbish brought swarms of pickers rushing forward. Nnamdi had watched the struggle from the pirogue and soon learned that he could come in from the water instead, pole right up to the edge and sift through what had already been sifted. Very little was left. A flattened can here, a broken-strapped rubber flip-flop there: they lay on the bottom of his pirogue like a paltry day's catch of fish. Nnamdi's eyes would drift up to the long line of cars snaking across the Third Mainland Bridge, sunlight flaring on their windshields.

On the other side of the lagoon, high-rise buildings rose up, hazy in the distance. Lagos Island. Would he and Amina ever get to the other side of that bridge? Had they come so far to fall just short?

Nnamdi had been casting stones, looking for messages. But the *orumo* and the *owumo* hadn't followed him to Lagos. Their voices had been lost somewhere between There and Here.

The few naira Nnamdi made from scavenging scrap hardly paid for the canoe, and as the days went on he found it harder and harder to make the walk to the water's edge. He would prepare Amina a breakfast of corn porridge and fried plantain, perhaps boil her a bowl of Nescafé, and then see her on her way, deeply ashamed to be living off her tips.

At night, when Amina's legs were throbbing and her back was aching, Nnamdi would reach a hand through, under the curtain, would rub her belly and sing softly. Ijaw lullabies to calm the child inside her. "I have so many stories saved up," he would say. "So many stories to gift you with. You must be strong so you can hear them." And he would whisper the Story of the Girl Who Married a Ghost and the Boy Who Fell in Love with the Moon.

Amina had seen the feral children from the windows of the

danfo minibuses as she passed, pauper kings atop fetid mountains. She felt her own child trying to escape, turning this way and that, pushing against the walls of her body. This was the future she feared: to have walked so far only to contribute another child to the pile.

And so, when Ironsi-Egobia finally sent for Nnamdi, Amina was elated. She would remember that, how happy she'd been when Tunde had arrived and told Nnamdi to come with him. How beautifully Nnamdi had smiled when he turned and looked back at her.

106

"Do you have the money?"

"Understand," Winston said with a pleading sincerity. "I am putting my life in jeopardy just by meeting with you."

Laura stared at him. "Do you have the money or not?"

They were sitting in the hallway outside the hotel swimming pool. Winston hadn't wanted to meet in the main lobby, hadn't wanted anyone at the front desk to see him. So Laura had chosen this busy nook instead. Guests flitted past in bathrobes as the cleaning staff wheeled their carts up and down patterned carpets.

"Please, miss," he said. "Listen to reason. For your own safety and mine, it's best you give up on this mad quest. Go home, madam. If you don't, I fear that someone may die."

"Well," she said. "It won't be me."

A tight smile. "You can see into the future, then? You can glimpse what is coming?"

"Listen, I'm not leaving this hotel until I get the money. If you wanted to kill me, you missed your chance."

"I do not wish to kill anyone, miss. But I can no longer protect you."

"Protect me? I'm not asking for your protection. I'm asking for my money. Now. Do you have it or not?"

"Miss, please—"

She started to get up.

"Wait, wait. Yes. I do."

He passed her the satchel that was sitting beside him. She opened it, riffled through, not bothering to count it. "It's in naira. And it's not enough. I asked for American currency."

"It's all I have! Everything. I was at the bank all morning. I cashed everything I had. There was no time to convert."

"It's not enough." It didn't really matter how much he'd brought; it would not have been enough, would never be enough.

"Wait, wait." He slid a thick manila envelope from his inside pocket. "This was what I was going to live on."

She leaned in, smiled with all her teeth. "Asked your parents to sell their plasma TV, did you? The one my dad helped buy?" And then: "Still. Not. Enough."

"But miss—"

"Open your wallet. I want to see how much you have."

She took it all. A thick sheaf of naira. She even claimed the kobo coins that were worth only a fraction of a cent. Only when he offered his St. Christopher medal, his Rolex watch, and his Ray-Bans did she feel she had reached the bottom.

"You can keep the watch and the sunglasses." She considered taking the medallion. "And you can keep that as well. Wait here. I'm going to the business centre to see what the exchange rate is."

"I have nothing left I can give you. You understand, my life is in danger. Please. Help me get out of Nigeria. I have had some troubles getting a visa, due to a past misunderstanding. Sponsor me and I will come to your country, I will work hard, I will bring my parents over. We will contribute to your nation. I will pay you back five times what I owe."

An educated young man, brimming with ambition and business acumen? He certainly would contribute.

"Help me get out, miss. It's the only way I can make amends. If you leave me here, I will be beaten and massacred. You have taken every scrap of money I have. Help me get a visa, and I will pay you back tenfold."

"Fivefold is fine. Let me deposit this, make sure everything goes through, and then we'll talk about getting you a visa."

"Thank you, thank you. You won't regret it."

He was still sitting there, hopeful and buoyant, when security arrived.

Laura had unpacked the stacks of high-denomination naira at the hotel bank counter. She'd set aside a fold of bills for the taxi to the airport the next day, but had given the rest to the teller to be counted and converted, had filled in the forms and presented the bank with her passport number. It was unusual for naira to flow the other way, but not unheard of; this was the Airport Ambassador Hotel, and business deals were consummated here every day. By hotel standards, it wasn't even that large an amount. Large enough to require government notification on the forms Laura dutifully completed, but not large enough to raise alarm. There were millionaires staying here, after all. The teller stamped the necessary forms, obtained the necessary signatures from the necessary office managers, gave Laura a confirmation slip.

"So the money's now in my account? Back home?" she asked the teller.

"Yes, ma'am."

"Are you sure?"

"Yes, ma'am."

Laura walked across the lobby and asked one of the doormen to summon security. When the guards arrived, she informed them that a young man had been harassing her whenever she went to the pool. "He was threatening me, making sexual advances. I suspect he's not a guest at this hotel. I think he may be a thief."

Laura watched as the guards manhandled Winston through the lobby and out the door even as he pleaded with them, eyes searching the lobby, frantically looking for her. *Goodbye, Winston.*

She'd won, and yet—

She felt, not triumphant, but only alone. No bursts of confetti appeared, no balloons rained down. No champagne. No Dad, either.

She had a drink at the hotel bar, something frothy and sweet, and then slipped into the comfort of chlorine, taking long, slow victory laps in the swimming pool. Exhale, inhale. Breathe out under water, breathe in above. The crawl, the breast stroke, the butterfly. As she swam, it entered her mind, fleetingly, that perhaps she shouldn't have wired the money home quite so quickly, that having sent Winston's funds out of the country, she now had nothing to bargain with if things turned bad. It was a thought that sank as quickly as it surfaced, though, and she flipped over, floated on her back, eyes closed, leaving slow spreading waves in her wake.

The ride through Lagos the day before had left its mark on Laura in the form of prickly heat. Sweat, trapped in her pores, had formed small blisters along her neck and forearms, and the itch only grew worse with the scratching. She'd applied soothing creams she'd bought in the hotel pharmacy, but the rash still bubbled and burned below the surface. She felt as though she were stewing in her own body, and after her swim she stood for a long time under the changing-room showers, letting the water wash over her.

Laura patted herself dry, wrung out her swimsuit, had another drink in the hotel lounge as the television above the bar played images of riots with the sound turned down. Petrol shortages in Abuja. Ethnic violence in Jos. Beauty contestants in Lagos. A tickertape of headlines scrolled along the bottom of the screen as an officer in battle fatigues spoke into a mike, his mouth chewing the words in silence. Behind him, bodies were being loaded onto a Coast Guard vessel labelled JTF, militants and hostages alike, according to the tickertape, all of them draped in oilskin.

It was evening by the time she got back to her room, wobbly on margaritas and missing her dad. It took three swipes of her card to open the door and several more miscues to reach the bathroom. Why must they make hotel rooms so dim? She hung her swimsuit over the shower bar to dry, splashed water on her face, studied herself in the mirror. *This is me in Africa.* She had pulled it off, had made it out alive, would be heading home tomorrow.

It was only then that she realized someone else was in the room. As she stepped out of the bathroom, she sensed it. There was a phone beside the toilet. She might have barricaded herself inside and called down to security, raised a mighty tumult. But she didn't. Instead, she did what anyone else might have done. She said in a loud voice, "Who's there?"

Housekeeping staff? A radio left on at levels so low you could hear it only when things were completely quiet?

It was none of those. It was a smile, with a boy attached. He was sitting on a chair beside the window under the half-light of an early moon. He was holding what looked like a letter opener, but wasn't.

Laura Curtis had fallen through to the other side, into that counterfeit world she'd helped create. *Miss Scarlet, in the bedroom, with an ice pick.*

"Hello, madam."

107

Cousin guyman had leaned in so close Nnamdi could feel each puff of breath, could smell the sweet sticky smell of blood in Mr. Ironsi-Egobia's lungs.

"You've speared fish?" Ironsi-Egobia asked.

"Of course, cousin. I'm of the Delta, we grow up spearing fish."

"Such is so. It's like that now. One, two, through the gills, twist it wide and let it bleed. One, two—and everything you want is yours. The market stall, the mechanic's tools, a future for your child. The only thing required is this: one, two, and walk away."

Everything we need. Nnamdi had tossed the stones, had looked for guidance, but there was none coming. He was on his own.

And so was the *oyibo* woman.

108

Laura, throat dry. Voice a whisper. "Is this about the money?"

His smile turned sad. "It's always about the money, madam."

The young man sounded resigned to what was going to happen. He'd sat in the darkness long enough for the nervousness and fears to dissipate. All that was left was this: he and her, and a task that needed doing.

When Laura spoke, her voice wavered. "Did Winston send you?"

He sounded puzzled. "Who is Winston?"

"He's … a business associate."

"No, that is not why I am here. Please, madam." He gestured to the chair across from him. "I wish to tell you a story."

109

Palm wine and moonlight. Sleepy children and a tale wrapped within a larger story.

Nnamdi's father was lulling the young ones into slumber:

"Once there was a hunter who had many friends. Everyone enjoyed the hunter's company. They enjoyed his drinks, his dancing, his food. But most of all, they enjoyed this: the hunter always paid. He paid for everyone. He paid for the palm wine and the pepper stew, he paid for the drummers, he paid for the music, paid for the sweets. He always kept the dancing going when the others had begun to tire. Everyone liked him, and the hunter carried on in such a manner until, sad to say, one day his money was all gone. So he asked his friend, *'Please give me twenty kobo so I can buy some corn.'* But his friend said, *'Not give, lend.'* And this friend demanded the hunter's gun as a guarantee. *'When you pay me back, I will return your gun.'* Now the hunter, he needed his gun to hunt the animals to sell in the market to make the money to pay back the twenty kobo to his friend. But his friend was firm on this. He took the gun and he warned the hunter, *'I will be at your home tomorrow morning to collect payment. If you do not have it, I will keep the gun as mine.'* So the hunter went to see his friend the leopard, and he said, *'Please, I need twenty kobo to pay my debt.'* The leopard agreed to lend the hunter the money but warned him, *'I will be at your home tomorrow. If you do not have the money, I will take what I want.'* The hunter hurried now to his friend the goat and asked for money to pay the leopard. The goat lent the money, but he too said, *'I will be at your house tomorrow to collect.'* So now this hunter, he went to the bush cat to get money to pay the goat to pay the leopard to pay the friend. *'I will be at your house tomorrow morning,'* the bush cat said. *'And if you are not there, I will take what I wish.'* So the hunter asked the village rooster for money to pay the bush cat to pay the goat to pay the leopard to pay the friend, to get his gun back. The rooster gave him the money, but warned as well: *'I will come at first light, and if you do not have my money, I will take what I wish.'* The hunter agreed to this. But the next morning, he woke before everyone else and scattered the last of his corn on the ground outside his house. Then he hid behind a tree and waited. Soon after arrived the rooster, crowing for payment. Finding the hunter was not at home, the rooster said *'Fine, I will eat his corn then.'* As the rooster was pecking at the corn, the bush cat arrived and, seeing the hunter gone, decided to take the rooster as payment. The bush cat was eating the rooster when the goat arrived. Angry that the hunter was not there to pay him, the goat charged the bush cat, knocking him into the forest to die. The goat began to call for his money. But the leopard was now on his way. He heard the goat's bleatings and he followed the sound all the way to the hunter's home. When he found the hunter gone, the leopard pounced, taking the goat as payment. As the leopard was eating the goat, the hunter's friend appeared, carrying the gun. Seeing the leopard, he quickly took aim and—*pa-dang!*—he shot the leopard dead. At which point, the hunter jumped out, angry and shouting. *'You have killed my friend the leopard! You will be punished!'* The other man was startled, and he begged the hunter for forgiveness. *'I did not know the leopard was your friend! Here, have back your gun. Your debt is paid. Let me go.'* After the other man had gone, the hunter skinned the leopard, cooked the meat, and sold the skin in the market. And that was the end of that."

110

"Miss," said Nnamdi. "Don't you think it would have been better for everyone if the hunter's friend had let him keep his gun? Had not demanded repayment so fervently?"

When Laura spoke, her voice was so faint it almost dissolved into the air between them. "I've done nothing wrong," she said.

"Why are you here, madam, causing such mischief?"

"My father."

"Your father sent you?"

"No, my father died."

"I'm sorry to hear this. My father also died. How did yours?"

"He fell."

"Mine drowned."

"He didn't fall," she said. "He was pushed."

"Mine too."

For the first time, she recognized the beauty of the boy's smile. Saw in it a sliver of opportunity. If she could establish a human connection with him ... "I'm sorry about your father," she said. "We've both suffered, it seems."

But this only puzzled him more. "My father—he suffered. I was very sad. But it was my father who died, not me. Soon, my wife will give birth, and I will become a papa myself. Do you have any children?"

She shook her head.

"That is a shame, madam. Because then you would understand what is going to happen. My father said the test of a parent is to ask, *Would you die for your child?* Until you can answer yes to that question, you are not ready to become one. But, madam, I think the greater test is, *Would you kill for your child?*"

"Don't," she said. "There's no need."

"Every day," he said, "I see children picking through mountains of rubbish. *Mountains,* madam. My child will not crawl through rubbish. I think that is every parent's wish, don't you? That their children do not have to climb through rubbish."

"Wait, no, don't. Listen—here. I have …" She dug out the bill she had in her pocket. She unfolded it now for the first time, hands shaking, and offered it to him. "A hundred dollars. Take it, please, as a gift. I'm—I'm not going to the police, I'm not going to the EFCC, the only place I'm going is home. Please, just let me go home."

"A gift?"

"A gift."

One, two, in and out, let it bleed and walk away. Ransack the room, make it look like a robbery, opening drawers, flinging belongings this way and that. But just make sure she dies.

"Don't," she said when she saw his expression change. "You can't. I'm—I'm pregnant." It was the only card left to play.

This took him aback. "You are with child?"

"Yes, I found out just today. If you kill me, you'd be killing my child, too."

Nnamdi smiled. "I would wish you a heartfelt congratulations, madam."

"Thank you."

"But we both know you are not with child. It is a ruse, madam. You are simply trying to 419 me. We both know this."

111

Amina was waiting in the stairwell with a change of clothes for Nnamdi. But when he appeared, there was no blood. A clean kill? Or no kill at all? *If we go down, we will go down, swords raised.*

"Here," he said, palming the bill into Amina's hand. "One

hundred dollars. That's a midwife and swaddling, that's an electric fan, a cradle."

"The *oyibo* woman?"

"Gone."

"Gone, dead?"

"Gone soon. She will be leaving first thing in the morning and will be making no more mischief. She promised on her papa's soul." He was out of breath.

"But guyman will be asking—"

"Only just you and me knowin'. We tell guyman faddah she never showed. Tell him she was already gone away home. Now, hide the money quick, so it can't be found."

He ran down the stairs, two at a time, feet clattering echoes all the way. He'd answered his own question. He might die for his child. But he wouldn't kill.

Nnamdi tossed the ice pick down a stairwell laundry chute as he ran, heard it bounce metallic against the sides as it fell. It would be discovered in among the hotel bedding that night, when the laundry was dumped into the washing bins, but by then it wouldn't matter.

They were waiting for Nnamdi when he reached the lobby.

As the door clicked shut behind the young man, Laura had scrambled to shove the chain into the slot. She'd turned the deadbolt, hands palsied with fear.

She was having trouble breathing, felt the panic come in waves. Hands still trembling, she'd called down to the front desk, had said, "I've just been robbed. He's on his way. Hurry. You might catch him."

And they did.

112

"Sit down there." A shove.

His face was badly swollen, with one eye puffed shut. But he felt thankful nonetheless; he'd been plucked free of police custody just moments before they were going to start breaking bones.

Hotel security had yelled one question at Nnamdi, again and again. "Who let you into the room?" They wanted to know if he'd been working alone or in tandem with others.

"Door was unlocked, sir," Nnamdi said through a mouth full of blood. "I let myself in, alone, sir." It was the truth. And even after he was carted off by the police, and no matter how hard they hit him, he never wavered. *The door was open. I let myself in.*

Surveillance tapes from the hotel showed Nnamdi slipping in, and this was enough for the police to convict him in advance of any trial. Had they rewound the tape further, to several hours earlier, they would have seen a cleaning girl enter the room with extra rolls of toilet paper, might have noticed the door not quite close as she left, might have noticed it held open—ever so slightly—by a deadbolt, half-turned. But it would never come to that. As abruptly as Nnamdi had been arrested, he was released. The officers tossed his belongings back at him, not even bothering to steal the few kobo in coins he had before dumping him out the back door.

A car was waiting for him.

And now he was here, in a crumbling courtyard that smelled of petrol. High walls, no windows.

A familiar cough. "Gently, gently. There is no call for any roughhousing. Fetch the boy some water."

Nnamdi squinted at the figure moving toward him. "Cousin guyman?"

113

She wouldn't leave her room, so they came to her: investigators with the Nigerian police, speaking in hushed, almost hallowed tones, offering her the tea and scones and sympathy that the concierge had sent up.

"We've caught the rascal," the officer in charge assured her. "We will question him over the weekend, assess his story, probe for accomplices. You will need to come down to the Ikeja police station on Monday morning, make a formal statement, identify the culprit."

"Monday? I can't."

"I'm sorry, madam, but you must. Bring your passport."

"I can't. I have a flight to catch. I'm heading home tomorrow."

"Oh, madam, I'm afraid that is out of the question."

They're not going to let me leave. I'm never getting out of Lagos.

"Did the boy mention any accomplices?" they asked.

After the investigators had left, she locked herself in again, dug out Inspector Ribadu's card. And if I do call him? They may very well find out about the money I transferred home. May even accuse me of 419. But if I don't call him ...

She paced the room, secure for now behind her deadbolt and chain. When she had outpaced the worst of her anxiety, exhaustion set in, and she lay down on the bed. This had been no random robbery, she knew—the story about the leopard and the hunter, the warning to go home and cause no further mischief. The boy hadn't known who Winston was, though; his puzzled look seemed genuine. But who knew what alias Winston was using? She should have said "Chief Ogun," and she berated herself over that. *I should have said Ogun.*

Laura ate her dinner from the minibar fridge—cashews and chocolate bars and screw-top wine—and watched the searchlights on the airport towers turning. Just when she'd resolved to call the EFCC and come clean, the phone rang. It was the police officer who had interviewed her earlier.

"Madam, you are free. You may go home. I just require your flight times and information, in case of last-minute complications."

"I don't have to come to the station, identify the boy who robbed me?"

"There is no need, madam. He died in custody."

114

Ironsi-Egobia dragged a chair across the cement floor of the crumbling courtyard. Aluminum legs, vinyl seat: he turned it backward, sat across from Nnamdi, his heavy arms folded on the chair's back.

"Can you read?"

"Yes."

"Did you read the newspapers yesterday?"

"No, sir."

"The United Nations has reported that the average life expectancy in Nigeria is 46.6 years. As of today, I am 46.7 years." A smile surfaced, wide and magnanimous, like an invitation to an embrace. "You see? I have already bested the odds." His low belly laugh turned into a bronchial cough, and then into blood. He wiped his mouth, continued to laugh.

Ironsi-Egobia's men shifted uncomfortably behind him. They were not used to hearing him laugh.

Slowly, Ironsi-Egobia's expression changed. He looked at Nnamdi. "I was there, you know, in the Delta, when the army burned Odi to the ground. I lost my mother, my father. I even lost my name. The Fathers at the seminary in Calabar took me in, raised me among the outsiders, taught me the gospel. Turn the other cheek. Love thine enemy. But they also taught: *An eye for an eye*. Last year, I tracked down the colonel in charge of the Odi offensive; he's retired now. I removed his eyes and fed them to him, and then I relieved him of his teeth. It was ... biblical. Understand, this was someone who had once bragged that he knew two hundred and four ways to kill a man. I showed him a two hundred and fifth."

Ironsi-Egobia stopped again to cough blood into his handkerchief, and when he stared at Nnamdi his eyes had the wet look of someone who's been choking on a bone. "Among the Igbo, they say *A lizard who wages war with the landlord ends in death*. But I say to you, landlords die like any man. Lagos is a city of landlords, and I arrived here, in this city, with nothing but my will. I had no cousins to coddle me, no relatives to needle with outlandish requests. I fought my way into Ajegunle, and I fought my way out. I battled for control of the Mushin crime dens, and I crushed the area faddahs on Akala Road one after the next. I bought those I could, killed those I could not. And when the Yoruba mobs attacked Ijaw slums, I fought alongside them because they were the stronger ... Then I turned on them, devoured them whole. On Odunlani Street, I organized the ragtag boy-men into something like an army. I added discipline to their ambitions, put a fear of God in their souls." He turned to his shadowmen, said, "Is this so?"

Mumbled "Ya" and "Is so" replies.

Ironsi-Egobia returned his attention to the boy, lowered his voice. "Now, the Igbo, they have something they call *ekpawor*. It's a kind of medicine. Very strong, I have seen it work. They ferment it in earthen pots with every manner of item thrown in. Bones, skin, spoiled gin. Sometimes even there are rotting eggs floating in it. When someone drinks the *ekpawor*, it enters their soul, and they are compelled to speak the truth. And if they have done wrong, they die. Now. If I gave you *ekpawor* to drink, what do you think would happen?"

"I—sir, I don't know how to answer."

"This is the problem, isn't it? In life, the cure we require so often kills us. But do not worry. I have no Igbo medicine for you to drink. I have only a request."

"And what is that, sir?"

"The truth. Only that." He leaned in, levelled his eyes on the boy, looking for facial tics and other small tells. "We who traffic in falsehoods …"

115

The pimple-like blisters along her neck were burning. Her hands were trembling and her head felt light. She had trouble keeping the receiver to her mouth. "Died in custody? How?"

"Madam, I will pass you over to my associate. He will take down your flight information and answer any questions you may have."

The second man carefully recorded Laura's flight number, departure time, the confirmation code the airline had given her.

"But I want to know what happened to the boy who robbed me," she said. "The one you arrested."

"He escaped, madam."

"Escaped?"

"Yes, madam."

"But the other officer said he died in custody."

"Yes, madam. He died in custody, and then he escaped."

116

The latest bout of coughing had stopped, and Ironsi-Egobia looked at Nnamdi and sighed. "It cost me a lot of money to get you out. Much more than the hundred dollars you stole."

"I didn't steal it, sir."

Another sigh, this one almost a growl. "It's the lying that frets me, not the thieving. I cannot allow people to see me as *toro kro,* someone who speaks big but never acts."

"Dile, cousin. *Dile."*

"It's too late for Ijaw apologies. I know how little those are worth. So listen to me now, and answer me truthfully. I will only give you the one chance. Did you tell them my name? Did you tell them anything about me?"

"No, sir."

"Did you tell *her* my name?"

"No, sir. She called the hotel police quick when she saw me. There was no time. I ran."

"I see. No time to kill her, but time enough to rob?"

"No, sir. I didn't rob her."

"She sayin' you took a hundred-dollar bill. So, I'm asking you: Did you thief it? The money? Are you trying to play me for a *mugu?*"

Did he thief it?

Nnamdi turned this question over in his mind, considered the many varied meanings of taking, of stealing. A robbery? No. He didn't take the money, she gave it to him. It was a gift, she'd said as much herself. "I didn't thief it, sir."

Ironsi-Egobia turned to the others. "He's lying. Tie his arms down. We will beat the truth out of him."

They wrestled Nnamdi's arms behind his back, bound them tightly.

Ironsi-Egobia called out, "Tunde!"

Tunde scattered Nnamdi's possessions across the rusted lid of an upturned oil barrel. "This is what he had on his self, guyman faddah. Was no hundred dollars."

"Of course not," said Ironsi-Egobia, holding back a cough. "The police pocketed it."

The Oga went over to the barrel, examined the items. A bus stub. Some licorice. A few kobos' worth of coin. Some clay pebbles, embedded with bits of feather and bone, shards of shell and stone. Ironsi-Egobia picked these up, rolled them in the palm of his hand. "My, my. What do we have here?"

Then, to the others: "Do you know what this is?" They didn't. *"Buro-you,"* he said, speaking a language he had long pretended not to know. He was surprised how thick it felt on his tongue. "*Diriguo, buro-you, owumo. Ha! Buro-keme, buro-keme. Igbadai.* We have a diviner in our midst! A fortune teller."

"Oh no no," said Nnamdi. "I'm only a simple Ijaw man—"

"A simple Ijaw *boy*," he corrected. "You are no man. You are a swamp rat who thinks he can charm his way into a finer fate. And let me tell you, a diviner who denies he is a diviner is not much of a diviner. Mumbo jumbo. That's what the Fathers at the seminary called it. *Mumbo jumbo.*" Ironsi-Egobia stared at Nnamdi, his eyes lit as though from within. "But you and I, we know better, don't we, Nnamdi? Tell me, can you see the future? Can you see your own fate?"

"Sir," Nnamdi said weakly, "I'm not any sort of—"

But Ironsi-Egobia had already turned away. He gestured to his men, who wheeled in a tire. One man followed with a jerry can of petrol.

Ironsi-Egobia turned, smiled at the boy. "You are to be congratulated! You're going to join the ancestors. You will be among the *opu duwoi-you.*"

Nnamdi looked up, tears welling. "But sir," he said. "Who will take care of the girl?"

Ironsi-Egobia steadied his gaze on his cousin. "The girl did what was asked of her. She may continue to work at the hotel if she wishes, till the baby comes, and after as well. It is ... beneficial for me to be havin' her there. *She* may still be of use. I cannot say the same of you." *You come in here, stinking of the Delta.*

The men wedged the tire over Nnamdi's shoulders.

"Do not bury me childless," Nnamdi pleaded. "Do not bury me wrapped in a ragged mat, no food offered. I beg you, cousin, you must not send me hungry into the afterlife, for I am not childless. You understand? I have a child."

They poured gasoline over his head as though anointing him with oil. It pooled in the tire and stung his eyes, forcing them closed and making the others laugh, for it looked as though he were crying tears of petrol.

Ironsi-Egobia leaned in, spoke to the boy one last time; it seemed only fair to share the truth at such a moment.

"Do not feel bad," he said. "I was never going to let you live." And then, closer still, so only he and Nnamdi could hear, *"Egberifa."*

117

Nnamdi was lying on a woven mat, legs sore and heart still pounding from the climb. The women of the village had gathered, and his mother was kneading palm oil into his legs. She was whispering softly in his ear, *"You won't be afraid. You won't be afraid."*

118

A locked door, a dark room, and hair too short for the climbing.

She lay on the cumulus softness of hotel pillows, trying to will herself to sleep. When that failed, she rolled onto her side, watched the thin band of light below her door. She tensed up every time the shadow of footsteps passed.

How had that boy gotten past security; how had he managed to enter a locked room? Who had let him in? Winston? But how? She was breathing in shallow sips, jumping every time a distant elevator dinged or a cloud of murmured voices passed. She jerked in fear when the a/c kicked in, jerked just as fearfully when it suddenly shut off. Twice she crept across the room to check the chain in its slot, the bolt on the door, only to return more unnerved than before. The sole comfort she took was in the sound of airplanes landing and leaving.

And then—another sound.

Not a sound.

The echo of a conversation, resurfacing from her first moments in Lagos: *"Where are you staying, madam? The Sheraton? A fine establishment. I know the concierge."*

And there it was: the why of it, the how.

I know the concierge.

He wouldn't have known the concierge only at the one hotel. He would have known them all, would have made it his business to know. Would have known the concierge here as well, at the Ambassador. And in that instant—even with the police having been called in and hotel security everywhere—she realized just how much danger she was still in.

And yet.

Knowing this calmed her nerves. She was in danger, and had to plan her escape with care. She had to focus—and from focus came resolve, another word for courage.

On the other side of the city, in a quiet kitchen on a quiet street, Inspector Ribadu was waiting patiently for his tea to steep. Had she called, he would have come; had she called, he would have helped. But his phone never rang.

119

When Nnamdi didn't return, Amina knew something had gone horribly wrong and she set out for Cemetery Road to buy back his life, to try to renegotiate his fate. The child inside her was stirring, was straining against her, and she whispered admonishments to calm it. *"You must wait just a little longer."*

She herself waited more than an hour in the outer hallway of the International Businessman's Export Club before Tunde finally appeared and gestured with his jaw for her to follow. Through a series of heavy doors, past sullen eyes, deeper and deeper into shadowman land.

Ironsi-Egobia was waiting for her, and he didn't bother with pleasantries. "What is it you want?"

"Please," she said, offering the $100 bill on outstretched palms. "Please, sir, release him to me."

And the crowds yelled out for Barabbas. "He was a thief and a fibber."

"A dreamer, sir."

"A diviner, a witch."

"A boy. Just a boy."

Ironsi-Egobia looked down at her belly. "He was man enough for some things." He leaned in, stared into her eyes until she was forced to look away. "He. Was. A. Thief."

Only then did she catch the past tense. Her world began to collapse inward, clay walls tumbling into sand.

The rage bubbling within Ironsi-Egobia brought forth a new spasm of spackled coughs, which he held in with a stained handkerchief.

Amina was shaking. "Please, here is the money. Please give him to me."

But there was no him for the Oga to give. "He died well, if that is a comfort. He died well and was buried with proper rites." This was a lie. Nnamdi's body, charred and stumped, would bob to the surface of Lagos Lagoon several days later, where it would ruin the view from several fine homes on Victoria Island. It would float there for almost a week before it finally disappeared. Fell apart or carried away on the tide, it was hard to say. But the curtains on Victoria Island stayed closed until then.

They have left me nothing, not even bones.

"Keep the money," Ironsi-Egobia said with a generous wave of the hand. "The boy paid for it with his life. Tunde, take her home."

When she tried to stand, her legs gave out, and she had to be helped. *Emptied of everything, even tears.* She staggered again, every breath coming out as a dry heave. This wasn't the story she was meant to be living. *Sunlight on silver.* Not this.

Loss demands repayment, and she turned back to Ironsi-Egobia, spoke in sobs. "The *oyibo*. She has to die too. Don't let her to live."

This *batauri* woman, this boiled-faced *oyibo*, lacking in grace, acting like an oafish house guest who knocks over furniture and then tries to leave without paying. This *oyibo* couldn't be allowed to twist the story like that and then walk away unharmed. Loss demands repayment.

When Ironsi-Egobia spoke, his voice was unnaturally calm. "Do not fret. The woman will die. I give you my word."

120

Laura woke to the sound of church bells.

Across the airport suburb of Ikeja, across Lagos, across southern Nigeria and West Africa, women were hurrying about in their Sunday best, tying up their elaborate head scarves, pirouetting into wraparound skirts, draping their shoulder shawls just so. Men were donning dress shirts and Sunday jackets. Little boys were buttoning up their vests, and girls were adjusting ribbons and satiny bows as the church bells beckoned like songbirds.

The voicemail messages from Winston had piled up during the night. So many she'd been forced to unplug the phone again. She listened to them now in bed, the messages by turn plaintive, indignant, angry, hurt. "My life is in danger. Do you understand? You have caused all sorts of consternation. They have killed the boy. They will kill me too. You must help me. I need to get out of Nigeria. Only you can save me. It is in your hands. You have taken my money, please don't claim my life as well. Miss, I beg you." Message after message. Variations on a theme.

She let the voicemail play on while she showered. When she got out of the stall, the bathroom mirror had clouded over with steam. *The Sheraton Hotel? I know the concierge.* He did this. He killed the boy with the beautiful smile, *not me.*

Laura chose the DELETE ALL option on the hotel voicemail—and in doing so, saved Winston's life, though she would never know this. Later, when they came to check her voicemail for messages and clues, they would find none.

Laura peered through the peephole with its fish-eye view of the world, listened at the door, took a breath, and then stepped out quickly into the hallway, hurrying toward the elevators.

A cleaning woman, tremendously pregnant, was pushing a cart toward her. Their eyes met as they passed. She looked … *familiar* to Laura. As though they had met somewhere, long ago. Had been separated at some point.

The cleaning lady stopped, cried out at Laura's back. "For why?"

Laura turned around, looked up and down the hall; there was no one else there. "Sorry?"

The cleaning lady came toward her, anger and sadness in every step. "For why?"

"I'm sorry, I don't—oh my God, who did that to you?"

Laura was speaking about the scars on Amina's face. Amina said, "It was for you to die. Not him."

The *batauri* woman, eyes so pale, skin the colour of boiled lamb, hair the colour of drought, was startled—and confused—by Amina's tears.

"It was you, woman," said Amina. "It was you did this. The boy, coming in your room. The boy, he let you live." She pointed to her chest. "He was mine. And he is died. For why?"

In the turmoil of that moment, Laura never heard the elevator doors open, never noticed the lone man who stepped out or the polished shoes that were now striding toward her.

It was the concierge. "Madam, we were worried about you." He shooed away the cleaning girl as though she were a stray cat, then turned to Laura. "You weren't answering your phone, so I came to check on you, to make sure everything was all right."

"I'm—I'm fine, thank you." She looked down the hallway. The pregnant girl with the scars on her face had disappeared. Had she been a hallucination? "I was on my way down. To see you, in fact."

He smiled, but not with his eyes. "Well, then," he said. "Why don't we ride down together?"

He escorted her to the elevators, held out a hand for her to enter. Pressed the button for LOBBY. The doors closed them in. "Will madam be extending her stay?"

The lights on the panel were counting down the floors.

"No, I'll be leaving today. I'll be back to check out and gather my bags. I'll need a taxi to the airport."

"Of course, madam. I will make the necessary arrangements. What time shall I say?"

"Um, one? One o'clock."

"Certainly, madam."

The door opened onto the lobby, and he held a hand across the door to keep it from closing. "One o'clock, madam. I will make sure a driver and a car are waiting for you."

121

One o'clock.

Tunde watched his reflection in the smoky grey of the hotel's glass doors. His reflection parted every time the doors opened, every time a gaggle of *oyibo* businessmen elbowed their way through in a swirl of air-conditioned mist. Tunde had started as a taxi driver, several lifetimes ago, driving a battered Peugeot 504 on Akala Road, but he'd never worn a uniform and had never driven a sedan this sleek. Until now. He smiled at himself—at the chauffeur's cap and jacket, the creased trousers—smiled as his reflection disappeared, then reappeared, with every exit, every entrance.

The area boys were waiting too, under the airport flyover, and better armed than usual. Hatchets and chains, mainly. *Wait for the signal.* Ironsi-Egobia was in his office, phone on table, waiting for word from the concierge. Winston was pacing back and forth in his apartment, waiting for a call from Miss Scarlet. They were all of them waiting. But the lady had vanished. Miss Scarlet was gone.

As the doorman waved a crumpled yellow taxi over, she'd told him she needed to pop out for a bit, would return to the hotel soon to check out. But when she climbed inside, she'd leaned up to the driver and said, "I've changed my mind. Take me to the airport instead."

As the clock ticked past one, then started the slow sweep toward two, the concierge began to worry. He eventually sent the cleaning girl in to check.

Amina entered on a knock and a soft "Hello?"

The room was still. The curtains were drawn and the windows were closed. A lamp was standing in a pool of light. Bedcovers, twisted into a fitful knot. A carry-on bag, open on the desk, rolled items of clothing beside it. Underwear and stockings. A compact mirror.

The bathroom door was closed.

Amina could hear the fan running, could see light below the door. She called out again, her voice sounding unnaturally loud. Tried the handle. Locked.

The housekeeping staff could open locked bathroom doors if they had to; it was easy. A simple push with a metal pin, and the door would pop open. Amina popped the lock, hesitated. She knocked again, pushed the door inward.

No one.

Amina turned off the fan, stepped inside, was startled momentarily by her own reflection in the mirror. On the bathroom counter: a toothbrush leaning in a glass, a half-rolled tube of toothpaste, bottled water, scattered items. A hairbrush with filaments of gold, faintly visible. Just wisps, really, barely there.

A bathing suit was hung over the shower rod, and the shower curtain was drawn. Amina pulled it aside, heart tightening in her chest. The bathtub—was empty. The room was empty. The *oyibo* woman was gone.

The concierge was waiting in the hall, hands clasped behind his back, face clenched.

"Well?"

"She is gone away."

"No luggage?"

"Luggage, yes. The woman, no."

The concierge stormed in, rifled through Laura's belongings. Everything was there. Everything except: passport, cellphone, ticket, woman. He rushed out, pushing past Amina, hurrying to the elevators, shoes hitting the carpet. But by then it was too late.

Far.

Too.

Late.

122

WestAir Flight 702 dropped through the overcast, down to a city of sandstone and steel. Cold rains and winter grey. Laura stared through the drizzle at that strange place called home.

—Nothing to declare?

—Nothing.

Back at Murtala Muhammed Airport, before she lined up at security, she'd thought about stopping by the EFCC office to see Inspector Ribadu, to tell him "I have seen lions and I have seen hyenas, I have seen hunters and I have seen crocodiles. And I never left Lagos." But she knew their conversation would only lead to questions, and those questions would lead to more questions, and she needed to remain invisible.

Only when the airplane had lifted off from the tarmac in Lagos did she fully exhale. And as the plane banked toward the sea, she sent a song back to the city below. It was a song she'd heard on the radio during her ride through the city: *"419, play the game; 419, all the same."* And threading through it, a question: "Who is the *mugu* now?"

In the taxi to the airport, she had slid the creased photograph from her skirt pocket, had methodically ripped it up. "Do you have somewhere I can throw this?" she'd asked the driver. "Certainly," he said, and he'd taken her fistful of tatters and reached his arm out the window, letting the pieces fall from his fingers. She gasped and turned, watched her father cartwheel away.

A three-hour layover in London, then a long flight across a wide ocean. And now Laura, falling through the overcast. Rain on the window and a long line of brake lights far below, moving down Deerfoot Trail, going home. She stared out the window until her breath fogged the plastic and the runway came up to meet her.

123

When Laura first arrived back at her apartment, she walked through it turning on lights. It felt as though she'd been gone much longer than she had. She undressed, stood in the shower a long while, eyes closed. Changed and then went down to the food court for supper. But when she got there, she felt addled and distracted, couldn't choose between Greek or Korean, Chinese or Thai, and she retreated to her apartment instead, locked herself in. The yogurt in her fridge was still fresh; it was as though she'd never left. *No one even knew I was gone.*

Emails in her inbox. Queries from publishers mostly. A follow-up to *Mavericks of the Sky*. And the messages she'd sent to herself from Lagos: images of Winston's mom and dad waving at the camera, of Winston scowling. She hadn't thought to take a single photo of the city itself.

Laura tried to focus on her work, but was having trouble concentrating. She took the C-Train to 7th Avenue, a bus to Springbank, walked down to her brother's cul-de-sac.

Warren was out, but their mom was there.

"I got Dad's money back," Laura said. "Not all of it. Some. As much as I could."

They were sitting at the card table in her brother's basement, across from the furnace room.

Her mother barely seemed to notice what she'd said.

"Tea?"

"The bank in Nigeria finally released it." Should she tell her mother that she'd been to Africa and back? It barely seemed real even to Laura. "There was a lot of paperwork involved. I didn't get enough money to buy back the house, not entirely. But it's enough to stop the foreclosure. Maybe we can use it to make a lump-sum payment against the debt, start paying back the rest slowly."

Her mother poured Red Rose into china cups that Laura recognized from her childhood. Those burnt orange mugs that were standard issue in all 1970s bungalows.

"You know," her mother said after a long pause. "I never really liked that house. It needs a lot of work. The roof needs to be reshingled. The boiler needs replacing. And without your father, it feels a little empty. We were talking about selling it anyway, finding something smaller. I've settled in here now. I can hear the footsteps upstairs and know I'm not alone. But I can be alone when I want to, oh, you know, talk to Henry. The twins come charging down every day to say hello." She smiled, then confided, "They tire me out. It's wonderful when they come down, just as wonderful when they leave. Milk for your tea?"

"But—the money. I don't think you understand what I went through to get it."

"You keep it. It's what your father would have wanted. Warren is fine, and I need so little. You have it."

"But, Mom, it's not my money."

"The tea," her mother said. "Before it gets cold."

124

Cold tea and fever dreams.

Laura felt as though she were lost in her own bedding, tangled and suffocating, and she woke to find herself marinating in sweat, sheets clammy, the pillow as damp as her hair. Her head ached from neck to temple, but she couldn't rally the strength required to get to the medicine cabinet and swallow any pain-numbing tablets. She lay there instead, felt the bed shift below her, tilting one way then another as sunlight slowly filled the room.

When she finally did stagger to the bathroom to wash down some Advil, she immediately threw it up, and she spent the rest of the day bent over the toilet, feeling as though her stomach was being turned inside out like a Safeway bag. The fever came in waves, the shivers turning to spasms, the spasms knocking her to her knees every time she tried to stand.

A thin face in the mirror. Fever dreams, strange visions. Flamingos lifting off, flames in a forest. Her father, cartwheeling away.

The emails started soon after. Threatening, begging, cajoling, insistent. She wasn't sure how he'd tracked down her address, but when she tried blocking him, he simply slipped back in with a new identity. When she was finally strong enough to stand, she hobbled down to the IT Computer Centre near the food court, asked if it was possible to block an entire country, or even an entire continent. She wanted to ask if they could block memories as well.

"Easier for you to change your address," they said.

She did that, but he found her anyway.

"YOU HAVE PUT MY LIFE IN DANGER!!! You have RUINED me!"

And then: "Sponsor me. Get me out of here. I will repay you tenfold. A hundredfold. I would be a great asset to your nation. I am hard-working. I have ambitions. Bring me over, I won't disappoint. It is only paperwork that stands between me and my dreams."

She ignored him as best she could. Tried to go back to indexing lives and copy-editing textbooks. Couldn't. *You have ruined me.* And all the while, the money sat in her bank account, quietly breathing.

125

Nausea and night sweats brought a skewed sense of perspective. It felt as though she were going to slide off entirely at times—off the edge of the bed, off the edge of the world.

Warren had been badgering her, demanding more details, wanting to know when the rest of the money would be released. She let the phone go to voicemail in the other room. She'd collapsed into bed after returning from the mall's medical centre, where the doctor on call had scolded her for not coming in sooner.

—*I couldn't walk.*

—*You should have called someone.*

—*Who?*

Blood tests, Malarone treatments and heavy doses of quinine, dire warnings about organ failure and a poisoned liver. "It can't be malaria," she insisted weakly. "I was never bitten. Not a scratch." The doctor's litany of dangers blurred in with her brother's financial tirades; the two seemed intertwined. She put her hand to the side of her head. "Winston, please," she said, finally answering the phone. "My head is pounding."

"Warren," her brother said.

"What?"

"My name. It's Warren. That's the second time you've done that."

And in that moment, she realized that Winston Balogun of Lagos, Nigeria, only son of Marcus and Mariam, brother of Rita, was right: he *would* be an asset to Laura's country. She could picture Winston here perfectly, in this city, with her brother, could picture him thriving.

And now. Days later and she was back in Springbank. At Warren's dining room table.

Her brother was armed with glossy printouts and pie-chart diagrams.

"Until the banks release the rest of the money, and who knows how long that will take, right?, we can't just leave what we do have parked in some low-interest chequing account. That's for chumps, is all I'm saying, so take a moment and look at these figures instead, that's all I'm asking. Give me access to that money and I'm telling you, Laura, I can double our investment in sixty days, and we can still get Mom's house back. Everybody wins."

Everybody wins. She thought again of Winston, back in Lagos.

Just a matter of paperwork. Forms to sign. A declaration as guarantor.

Laura went down to the basement, sat across from her mother in silence.

"Why did he do it?" she asked.

"Your father? Oh, I suppose he felt trapped, got bogged down in despair."

"Not the accident. The con. Why did he fall for it? It wasn't the money, was it? Tell me this whole thing wasn't just about the money."

When her mother spoke, her voice was soft. "I don't think it was the money, no. I think it was the girl. I think your father wanted to be a hero to someone, just once."

The car tumbled through darkness, end over end.

126

"Another transfer, Ms. Curtis?" The tellers at the bank knew her by name now. "You can transfer some into my account, if you like! Just kidding. Nigeria, right?"

Laura nodded. The fever had left her paler and thinner, and she still felt weak on her feet.

"You didn't fall for one of those internet scams, did you?" the teller asked with a laugh.

"No," she said. "I'm sponsoring someone. Trying to get a visa for them. It's complicated."

Laura had been wiring money to Lagos in larger and larger batches. There were endless rounds of forms to fill out and paperwork to submit, with every transaction requiring additional fees. Everything seemed to be in order now, though, which was good, as she had no more money to give.

And so it was that Laura Curtis found herself at Arrivals Gate C at her city's international airport. She'd maxed out the last of her credit cards to pay for the ticket and now stood waiting as the passengers filed off, bleary-eyed and yawning, some waving to relatives, some striding forth with purpose, others alone and looking small. A young man in a tailored suit came out, grinning wide in all directions, searching the crowd for someone. Not Laura.

Laura was waiting, but not for Winston. She was waiting for a girl with scars on her face and a child on her hip.

In Lagos, Inspector Ribadu was working late. He leaned back, eyes closed, various and assorted files open on his desk.

At the International Businessman's Export Club, Tunde was napping in a chair, and Mr. Ironsi-Egobia was coughing blood.

And Amina of the Sahel? She never got off that plane, because she never got on it. She'd cashed the ticket as soon as it arrived for her at the hotel. Had kept it along with all the other money Laura had forwarded to her.

Laura waited till the next flight landed, and the next, then drove back into the city under chinook skies.

In spite of herself, she smiled. The money was gone and would never come back, and yet—she couldn't help but feel her father would have been proud of her nonetheless. And later that evening, as she sat at her desk, indexing lives, the intercom in her apartment would ring. It would be Matthew Brisebois, asking if he could come up, if she might buzz him in. The only question remaining was whether she would.

127

Computer screens, lined up in rows. Bodies huddled in front of keyboards, pecking out messages. A young man in a silk shirt, lost in the labyrinth. He is sending emails into the ether, distress signals and fairy tales. *"Dear Mr. Sakamoto, I thank you for your kind response."* A young man in a silk shirt, dreaming impossible escapes.

Down the hallway, the coughing had stopped. Not that it mattered. That young man is typing still.

128

Nnamdi's mother is calling out.

"Slow down, Nnamdi! Slow down."

And here he comes running, his little legs powering him through the crowd, dodging rackety carts and head-balanced basins.

"Nnamdi! Not so fast!"

He has outrun the men from the mosque who are chasing after him, breathless and laughing at this bundle of determination they call a boy.

Nnamdi tumbles upward into his mother's arms. She sweeps him in, asks, as she always does, "Are you hungry?" A sweetened slice of plantain and some dried mango, and off he scoots, past his mother's countertop display of *kilishi*, past trays of dried meat dusted with savannah spices, past the thick folds of indigo laid out on tables, past it all and through the beaded curtains behind. Onto his bed, where his play clothes have been laid out for him.

"Nnamdi, fold your good clothes. Don't just let them fall in a heap!"

But he has already reappeared, shirt misbuttoned and tail untucked, wearing short pants and a very large smile.

The Lagos women laugh. Such a big smile on such a little boy. They tease his mother. "Nnamdi? That's not a Hausa name."

"I'm not Hausa," she says. "And he was named for his father."

129

The car finally came to rest at the bottom of the embankment, leaning against a splintered stand of poplar trees under falling snow.

Sirens and lights followed.

The would-be rescuers came down on grappling lines, leaning

into the angle of their descent, boots crunching through glass and snow.

The driver: an elderly man in a blue sweater, face pulped, white hair matted with blood.

"Sir, can you hear me? Sir?"

He tried to speak, but no words came out, only bubbles, and something that sounded like love.

Sign on a Lagos wall

Notes toward an index

anger

beauty (*see:* scars)

courage

distances, crossed

distances, imagined

dreams (sleeping)

dreams (otherwise)

dust

dry season

earth

elements (*see:* dust, earth, fire,
     wind, snow, mud, oil)

falling

fire

fear

hello (*see also:* thank you)

hesitation (*see also:* resolve)

hope

laughter

love

memory

mirrors (*see also:* windows)

mud

oil

rain

resolve (*see also:* courage)

sadness

scars (*see:* beauty)

silence

smiles (with eyes)

smiles (without)

snow

spring (*see also:* dry season)

thank you (*see also:* hello)

waiting

walking

whispers

wind (chinook)

wind (harmattan)

windows (*see also:* mirrors)

winter (*see also:* spring)

L.C.

AUTHOR'S ACKNOWLEDGMENTS

The police investigation described in this novel is based on interviews, information, and contacts provided by a number of people, whose kindness and assistance are greatly appreciated: Bob Evans; Brian Edy of the Calgary Police Commission; Emma Poole at the Media Relations Unit; Chief Crown Prosecutor Lloyd Robertson; Staff Sergeant Jim Rorison and Detective Ronda Ruzycki of the Economic Crime Unit, who provided a frank and fascinating look into the world of fraud investigations; Crown Prosecutor Jonathan Hak, who answered a long list of questions; and Constables Colin Foster and Greg Mercer of the Calgary Police Service's Collision Reconstruction Unit, who not only walked me through the would-be accident scene investigation at Ogden Road on a blustery cold day in January, but even managed to solve several plot points for me along the way.

Many thanks to all of those listed above. I strove to present the entire sweep of the investigation, from the initial accident to the Economic Crime Unit's later involvement, as accurately and as honestly as possible. This is a work of fiction, however, and any errors or inaccuracies remain solely my responsibility and should not reflect in any way upon the individuals who helped me during the research for this book.

I was fortunate as well to have several superb early readers who provided insights, advice, and corrections: Kirsten Olson; Jacqueline Ford, who has travelled extensively in the francophone region of West Africa; Kathy Robson, who has lived and worked in Nigeria; and Helen Chatburn-Ojehomon, who is married to a Nigerian citizen and working in Ibadan, north of Lagos. Many thanks to all of them for the feedback! The depictions of Nigerian culture and customs are solely my responsibility, however, and should not in any way be attributed to the views of any of the people listed above. Helen and Kathy in particular gave me excellent advice on the English spoken in Nigeria, but in the end I found the richness of the dialect too difficult to capture on the page. Instead, I added only the slightest touch, to give readers just a hint of the full flavour. Likewise, the image on the cover of this book is of a woman in the Sahel region of West Africa and is not meant to represent Nigeria as a whole, but rather the larger cultural group to which the character Amina belongs.

As well, I would like to acknowledge my debt to Lizzie Williams's entertaining and comprehensive guidebook *Nigeria: Second Edition;* Toyin Falola's *Culture and Customs of Nigeria;* Chidi Nnamdi Igwe's *Taking Back Nigeria from 419;* John Ghazvinian's *Untapped: The Scramble for Africa's Oil;* Philip E. Leis's *Enculturation and Socialization in an Ijaw Village;* Karl Maier's *This House Has Fallen;* and Michael Peel's *A Swamp Full of Dollars: Pipelines and Paramilitaries at Nigeria's Oil Frontier.* For a full list of the sources used in writing *419* please see my website, willferguson.com.

At Penguin Canada, I would like to thank Editorial Director Andrea Magyar, Senior Production Editor Sandra Tooze, Managing

Editor Mary Ann Blair, and proofreader Catherine Dorton. Finally, with a novel whose main protagonist is an unflinching editor [redundancy, no?—*ed.*], it is particularly important to thank my own editor Barbara Pulling and copy editor Karen Alliston, both of whom did a fantastic job with *419*. Any eccentricities of style or quirks of narrative should be ascribed to author intransigence and not to a lack of editorial input.

Noao!

419

About the Book 402

An Interview with Will Ferguson 403

Discussion Questions 409

A Penguin Readers Guide

ABOUT THE BOOK

It starts in a crowded internet café in Nigeria, in any one of a cluster of noisy, ramshackle places where rows of young men peck away at dusty keyboards. These men operate behind a series of false identities, sending out multiple emails pleading to their recipients for help and in return promising a great reward. It's a simple scam that starts small, preying on kindness and guilt and greed, asking first for only a few hundred dollars to save a troubled soul, but quickly escalates, swallowing up savings and destroying lives.

It is known as a "419," named for the section of the Nigerian Criminal Code that covers fraud. It may start in a Nigerian internet café, but it spreads across the world from inbox to inbox, and while most people hit delete without a second thought, there are some unsuspecting recipients who open that email and are taken in by the deception.

419 is a hard-hitting novel that explores not only the tragic impact that one of these scams has on a family in an unnamed Canadian city (though clearly Calgary) but also on the lives of young Nigerians struggling to survive. *419* casts out a handful of character threads that cross and intertwine in unexpected ways, spanning continents and cultures, illustrating the ways in which people can cause damage to one another even though they are oceans apart.

In Canada, a lonely copy editor named Laura is struggling with the aftermath of her father's suicide and the alarming discovery that he has lost everything to a 419.

In Festac Town, the rundown part of Lagos, Winston is a young, Western-educated scammer who prides himself on the finesse of his work. His diligent successes will bring him to the attention of the dangerous gangster Ironsi-Egobia, who is eager to profit from Winston's skill and a man not easy to turn down.

Out on the muddy banks of the Delta, Nnamdi is a young man who has seen his home and his family slowly poisoned by the encroachment of the Western oil industry. Faced with few legal prospects to earn a living, he turns to the less legal and more dangerous world of black-market fuel smuggling. A good person trying to navigate impossible currents, he uses his wits to take advantage of whatever situation presents itself, even when that puts him in jeopardy.

And at the heart of the novel is Anima, a pregnant woman fleeing for her life across the brutal conditions of the Sahel.

Each of these threads starts to entwine, leading to a breathless 03 confrontation and a powerful ending both tragic and hopeful.

Multiple award–winner Will Ferguson applies his keen eye and literary skills to a story of everyday people swept up by circumstances beyond their control, the hardships of life in one of the most dangerous regions of the world, and the crimes of opportunity, of desperation, and of revenge that people commit in order to survive.

AN INTERVIEW WITH WILL FERGUSON

Q: How did you become interested in writing a book involving the 419 scam?

I was researching my previous novel, *Spanish Fly*, a tale of con men and call girls set in the jazz clubs of the 1930s, when I came across a reference to 419 internet fraud. I wasn't interested at first because at that time I was only looking for classic "golden age" cons, and 419 involved email. But there was a footnote that read, "Today's 419 email scam is a modern variation of the 'Spanish prisoner' swindle which dates back to the Elizabethan era."

That caught my attention! So I read up on the "Spanish prisoner" and learned that in the wake of Spain's failed Armada of 1588, many an Englishman drowned, died, disappeared. And soon after, messages began to circulate—not as emails, of course, but written in quill and ink: "Dear Sir, I am the daughter of an imprisoned English nobleman and I need your help..." When I realized that the emails cluttering my inbox could be traced back five hundred years, I knew I was on to something much deeper in human nature than mere spam. ■

Q: In an interview with *The Globe and Mail*, you mentioned that the book started out as a more traditional narrative focusing on Laura's storyline and the Western perspective of the problem. What brought about the rather significant changes in perspective and structure?

Everything changed when I crossed over to the other side of the window/mirror. In researching the 419 con, I learned more about Nigeria, and the more I learned, the more I realized that the real story was over there. Nigeria is a vast, tragic, heroic, daunting story of its own—and I set out to bring in characters from each of the main regions: the northern Sahel, Lagos in the Yoruba west, and the Niger Delta region in the east (part of what was once known as Biafra). After that, the novel really came alive. It was electric. ■

Q: In addition to your fiction work, you've written a number of well-received memoirs of your experiences travelling the world, but I understand that travelling to Nigeria for research purposes was out of the question. How did you achieve such a strong sense of verisimilitude writing about a place you've never been?

Fiction requires a lot more research than travel writing, I can tell you! The outer Delta is off limits to all but the most foolhardy flak-jacketed investigative journalists, and the Sahel region around Kaduna is riven with religious violence (the Mammy Market that Nnamdi and Joe stop at on the way north was later bombed by extremists), so I was forced to rely on deep readings and the kindness of Nigerian-savvy proofreaders. That said, it is a work of fiction. It's not meant to be a guidebook or travel essay about Nigeria—or Calgary for that matter. ■

Q: What kind of research did you do regarding the technical aspects of how a 419 works and the legal procedures of the various international authorities that investigate them?

A good deal of the emails that Laura's dad receives are cut and pasted directly from actual 419 correspondence with fraud victims. I spoke at length with detectives at the Economic Crimes Unit of the Calgary Police Service, including two who had dealt with exactly this sort of scam. I interviewed Crown prosecutors and went into the field with a police accident-reconstruction team. I asked lots of questions, took lots of notes—not just on the machinations of the crime and its investigation, but on how the detectives, prosecutors, and police officers spoke, their cadence and vocabulary. (Clipped sentences with ironic undertones, in case you're wondering.) The Calgary Police Service was immeasurably helpful in the writing of *419*. I had never written about police procedures before, so this was all new to me. ■

Q: In the real world, these types of internet scams rarely end well for the victim, and while Laura's character might not get a happy ending, it's a resolution that she can live with because she's given Amina a chance for a future. How important was it for you to leave the reader with some sense of hope at the end of this often heart-breaking story?

Laura succeeds (inadvertently) where her father failed. She really does rescue a young woman from a hopeless future. However, it was important to me that Amina succeed on her own terms. If she had gotten off that plane at the end, it would have been very patronizing, I think—the notion that somehow coming to a Western city (with its food courts and shopping malls) is a "victory." Amina wanted to have a market stall with living quarters, she wanted a future for her child, and that's exactly what she got. It's one of the perks of being an author that you can give characters what they long for, what they wish for. The real question for me is: Did Laura buzz Brisebois in at the end? To tell the truth, I'm not sure. I'd like to think she did, but I am haunted by doubt. ■

Q: As readers, we're forced to question the morality behind the actions of characters that have earned our sympathies over the course of the novel. In many ways, we struggle more with the ethical implications of the decisions that Laura, Nnamdi, or Amina make than they do themselves. Was it difficult for you as a writer to put such sympathetic characters into a moral grey area?

No, not really. I think one's true character (in fiction as in life) is revealed more by what we do than what we think we might do—or who we think we are. I'm not a fan of the "elderly character looks back on her life and reflects" school of storytelling. I think life forces decisions upon us, and I'm more interested in how characters respond, what they choose, what they do. I think that's the true measure of any person. ■

Q: In an interview with *The Vancouver Sun*, you mentioned that Amina was inspired by a real Nigerian woman. Can you tell us a little bit about her story and how it came to be part of the novel?

It's funny. Several readers have commented upon the "unresolved mystery" of the character Amina. But I always thought it was fairly clear what she was fleeing and why. If you want to know exactly what was going on, you can look up the case of the real Amina, a young woman named Amina Lawal from the Sahel region of northern Nigeria. ■

Q: Which one of the novel's diverse cast of characters spoke most to you? Did any of them pose more of a challenge to explore than the others?

Laura was hardest to write because I didn't want to take the easy way and make her warm and fuzzy. I didn't want to stack the deck. What she does has real moral implications. That said, I admired her immensely. She is intelligent, methodical, cool to the touch, but with a ribbon of steel running through. A Rapunzel that doesn't need rescuing. (I never thought of Laura as timid in the least. Alienated, distant, lonely—certainly—but not timid. Some readers have said that they did find her timid, so perhaps I didn't convey her sense of resolve as well as I might have.)

Laura's journey is a physical one—out into the world and back again—but it is also a moral one, from a position of "let justice be done though the Heavens fall!" to a more nuanced view: "Let Heaven be done though justice falls." It's the conflict of justice versus love that she has to face.

Laura is the catalyst, but she's not the heart of the story: Amina and Nnamdi are. I fell in love with Amina as I wrote the novel—I admired her strength and determination, especially at the very end. But the character I grew closest to was Nnamdi. He is the only one whose entire life is presented from start to finish. I wanted to give a biography to someone whose life Laura would never edit, and it broke my heart when I sent him into the darkness like that. (I was in a down mood for a week after, as my wife can attest.)

My favourite scene to write was the dinner at Winston's parents', with Laura in attendance, because of all the swirling subtext. Each character has a starkly different—and competing—agenda, and yet, on the surface, it was just a meal and some small talk. ▪

Q: How important is the naming of your characters?

Very important. The main characters in *419* are all named for heroes, factual or otherwise. What appear to be small lives and peripheral existences are in fact imbued with history and heroism—that was the idea. Laura's father tells her she was named after Laura Secord, the heroine of a long and arduous trek on foot (which of course parallels Amina's own story). Amina is never actually named; she takes hers from Queen Amina of warrior fame. It was also an allusion to Amina Lawal (see above). Nnamdi is named for the father of Nigerian independence. Winston's anglophile parents clearly named him in honour of the English statesman. And even Sergeant Brisebois and Laura's father, Henry Curtis, are named after heroic/historic figures. Brisebois for the NWMP officer who was the original namesake of Calgary, and Henry Curtis from the classic Euro-centric caricature of the African adventurer. (I had wanted to make Laura's surname Kurtz, but my editor thought it was too heavy-handed. So Curtis was the compromise—which then allowed me to sneak in a reference to *King Solomon's Mines* instead.) ▪

Q: The imagery of windows and mirrors runs through the novel from the sunglasses of the security guards to Warren's twin daughters to Amina's entering Laura's washroom at the end only to be startled by her own reflection. Why?

It's central to the story, I think—the sense of separate lives, separate worlds, mirroring each other. In particular, the way windows can become mirrors. We think we're looking out at the world when, in fact, we're looking at our own reflections. Nnamdi's father tells him that the reflections in water are looking up at us, thinking we are the illusionary creatures. I think Laura's world is the pale reflection of something richer, sadder, deeper.

The lives in *419* often parallel each other—Winston/Warren; Sgt. Brisebois and Inspector Ribadu; Nnamdi's storytelling father and Laura's; her memories of the Stampede and those of the horse riders of the *durbar*; the Native man from the tar-sands town of Fort McMurray, who gets soaked in gasoline and set on fire, and what happens to Nnamdi; even the board games that Joe and Nnamdi play can be compared with those of Warren and his sister—but the most tangible parallel is between Laura and Amina. When Laura sees Amina in the hallway, Amina looks familiar to her even though they've never met. Earlier, when Nnamdi first meets Amina, he recalls an Igbo belief that we are born with two souls. The idea of a soul trying to find its lost half (not in the romanticized idea of soul mates, but deeper than that) is what binds Laura's and Amina's fates together. So, in Chapter 16, for example, when Laura has a vision of a salamander, she is seeing what Amina sees in the Sahel. Later, back home and suffering from fever, Laura sees flamingos taking flight, a memory that is actually from Amina's childhood. Laura can't have children; Amina is desperate to keep hers alive. And so on. They are two sides of the same soul, separated. ▪

Q: We don't usually see indexes in a novel. Why does *419* have one?

It's a final, parting note from Laura. (You can see her initials, *L.C.*, at the bottom.) I thought, What if Laura were the copy editor and indexer of *419*? What would she include? If you read Chapter 15 and then read Laura's Notes toward an index at the back, you'll see her take on what was important. ▪

Q: The novel has received very strong reviews and won the prestigious 2012 Scotiabank Giller Prize. What sort of reaction have you seen from your long-time readers?

A few readers did complain that it wasn't funny, as though I owed them some jokes, which is odd. Writers should be able to write in a wide swath of styles and subject matter. I don't think having a limited range as an author is necessarily a virtue. Even Guns N' Roses wrote ballads, after all. The approach I follow with any given novel comes from what the story demands. My first novel, *Happiness™*, was based on the notion of a self-help book that actually works and destroys the world. It was over-the-top satire right from the start, and that dictated the tone. With *419*, once I realized just how disturbing the world of internet cons is, I couldn't very well write a wacky novel about it. Overall though, the response has been good. And I truly appreciate the fact that book reviewers and the Giller jury took the novel on its own merits, without bias or preconceptions. ▪

Q: What are you working on next?

A book about Rwanda, a travel memoir. With major projects, I like to switch between fiction and travel: *Happiness™* (fiction), *Beauty Tips from Moose Jaw* (travel), *Spanish Fly* (fiction), *Beyond Belfast* (travel), *419* (fiction). Travel and fiction use different parts of your brain, so it's good to alternate—to avoid a muscle cramp of the mind. ▪

DISCUSSION QUESTIONS

1. Instead of a standard linear plot structure, *419* skips back and forth in time and location, and follows a diverse cast of characters from very different cultural backgrounds. How does this structure create dramatic tension and propel the story forward? And how does it relate to Laura's work as a copy editor, which involves trying to impose a chronological timeline on overlapping events?

2. Many of the main characters in the novel willingly take part in some form of illegal activity and feel somewhat justified in doing so. Do you believe that any of the characters have good reasons for their actions? Did any characters cross a moral

line that changed your sympathy for them? And while all the characters felt somewhat justified in their actions, do you feel, at the end of the novel, that any of them got what they deserved?

3. Laura edits other people's lives. What is the significance of this, symbolically as well as practically, in the plot line?

4. We like to believe we inhabit a borderless, interconnected world. Laura lives online, works online, yet she is isolated and alone. Her experience of other cultures comes primarily in a food court. On balance, do you feel that technology brings people together or alienates them?

5. Which character's storyline did you find most interesting? What are your thoughts about that character's fate at the end of the book?

6. Nnamdi's journey from the oil-soaked Delta to his horrific death in Lagos is an incredible arc that dominates a considerable part of the novel. Why is his story so central to the book and to the lives of the other characters?

7. While Winston's 419 scam sets the whole story into motion, the author stops short of making him the villain in the story. What were your initial feelings toward the character, and did you develop any sympathy for him when Ironsi-Egobia and Laura closed in on him? How does the scene where Laura visits Winston's parents affect your sympathy for him?

8. What do you feel about Laura's quest for revenge against Winston in the latter half of the book? Do you believe that she is justified in doing so? Is it morally acceptable for her to use lies and fraud because she feels she's a victim? Do you think that she ultimately acquits herself by the way she helps Amina find a new life?

9. Discuss the ways in which the destructive nature of the oil industry and Western cultural influence in Africa affect the hearts and minds of characters such as Winston and Nnamdi. To what extent do you think Western culture should be blamed for certain tragic conditions in Africa?

10. The novel offers a look at three families in three very different parts of the world—the Curtis family in Calgary,

Winston's family in Lagos, and Nnamdi's family in the Delta. In light of the widely distant locations, what traits do these disparate families have in common, and what makes them different?

To access Penguin Group (Canada) Readers Guides online, visit the Penguin Group (Canada) website at **www.penguin.ca**.